THE
PERFECT
GIRLFRIEND

THE
PERFECT
GIRLFRIEND

KAREN HAMILTON

GRAYDON
HOUSE

GRAYDON HOUSE

ISBN-13: 978-1-525-83173-7
ISBN-13: 978-1-525-83150-8 (Library Exclusive Edition)

The Perfect Girlfriend

Copyright © 2018 by Karen Hamilton

This edition published by arrangement with Harlequin Books S.A.

® and TM are trademarks of Harlequin Enterprises Limited or its corporate affiliates. Trademarks indicated with ® are registered in the United States Patent and Trademark Office, the Canadian Intellectual Property Office and in other countries.

BookClubbish.com
GraydonHouseBooks.com

Printed in U.S.A.

For A, A, O and E.

THE

PERFECT

GIRLFRIEND

PROLOGUE

July 2000

Looking down, there are two pairs of feet dangling. My shoes are daisy-edged, white-and-yellow sandals. His are a muddy brown with Velcro straps and a navy tractor on each side. His socks don't match; I can never find two the same. One is crimson and the other one is black. And they're too tight—a ridged pattern has already formed a ring of little marks on his calves, just above the elastic. He kicks the edge of the wall. Thud, thud. Thud, thud. The noise bounces off the four walls. Below, pond skaters skim the stagnant, murky water which I know conceals a tiled dolphin in shades of silver and blue, the twin of the one visible on the exposed ground of the shallow end. Strands of fine slime brush the slope just above the water's edge.

The sun burns; red spreads across his cheeks, smudging the tip of his nose. He should be wearing a hat. Everyone knows that young children should wear hats or a high-factor sunscreen, but I couldn't find either this morning when the time came to be "Outside!" in a hurry. We have enough food for a picnic, though; I had prepared it earlier this morning. The white loaf I'd unevenly sliced was a little stale, so I'd layered on extra cream cheese to compensate. We also have ready-salted crisps, so when I smooth out the carrier bag to use as a tablecloth on the concrete tiles, I pull the triangles of bread apart and place some crisps inside before folding them back neatly.

It is the wrong thing to do.

He bursts into tears. "I don't want crisps in my sandwich!"

"Well, you should've said."

His screams vibrate inside my ears. My stomach churns. I pull him from under his arms, away from the edge. I hastily pick out the crisps and drop them back into the foil packet. But that is wrong too— because barely visible residues of pale cheese remain glued. I sit cross-legged opposite him.

"Have some grapes!"

He stops and stares. Half-formed tears pool in the corners of his swollen eyes.

Our mother doesn't like him eating grapes if they aren't halved or quartered, in case he chokes, but I hadn't thought to pack a knife. I could bite them in half but I don't like tasting anything sweet before my sandwich. Besides, our mother doesn't know a lot of what he gets up to and, seriously, eating a few grapes is way, way down the list of potential dangers I've saved him from.

"Have some," I repeat, my voice calmer than I feel. "They're the purple ones. Your favourite." I grip with my forefinger and thumb, easing grapes off their stems, and hand them to him.

He clutches them in both hands and feeds himself one at a time, biting hard. Juice runs down his chin.

Relief. The older he gets, the harder he is to placate. He is quick to assert himself and demand whatever he desires.

I take a bite of my sandwich, crunching the crisps into the dough. A breeze, so gentle—almost as though it knows it is unwelcome on such a glorious day—brushes my arms and legs, then dissipates. Stillness.

"More!"

"Please."

He frowns.

As I pull off more grapes, I wonder what my next-door neighbour is doing. She is eleven, nearly a whole year older than me. Eating ice cream? Burying her feet beneath soft sand? I was invited to go along with her family to the beach today, but I have a responsibility in the form of a four-year-old, so the answer was no.

I inhale the strong smell of lavender. Nearby, bees hum. In the not-too-far distance, a lawnmower bursts into life. I swing round in case it is the head gardener, the one who always smiles at me and says I have a pretty face. Curving a hand above my eyes, I squint. I can just about make out a shadowy man in overalls, but his face is concealed by a denim bucket hat.

"I'm thirsty!"

"There's no water, you'll have to have some of this."

I snap open a can of lemonade. He is not allowed fizzy drinks or too much sugar. There are so many rules for him that sometimes I don't know whether to laugh or cry—to be glad that she cares, or just plain annoyed. I often feel like this—like I don't know how I'm supposed to feel in certain situations.

He makes a face at the lemonade bubbles fizzing inside his mouth. He must be really thirsty as he hasn't made any fuss. He looks kind of cute with his scrunched-up face and, for a few seconds, I feel warm towards him. But then he drops the can. It clatters on its side, spraying cartwheeling liquid as it rolls down over the edge. It hits the water with a splash so slight, I barely hear it. We both lean forward and peer down.

"The frogs or the fish will drink it," I say brightly.

I hold out my arms to pull him close.

His arms are strong, his push violent. "No! I want it back."

I can't bear the thought of it. I can't stand the thought of his screams; they pierce me and make me want to block my ears and scream myself.

"Go and find a long stick, then," I quickly say.

He stands up and runs off eagerly past the lavender towards the base of the oaks.

The last thing I call out is, "You'll need an extra-long one!"

I dangle my feet over the edge again and lie back down, closing my eyes, revelling in the seconds of blessed peace. I can feel warm concrete tiling against my thighs, through my cotton skirt, whilst the upper half of my body lies on the grass. It tickles my neck. I hear the lawnmower moving further away. Laziness takes hold and I inhale a deep breath of summer air before I pretend I can feel sand—not concrete and grass—beneath me.

Reality creeps in and out. I think I hear a splash like a swooping seagull which has spotted an unsuspecting fish.

Then nothing.

I jolt up, dizzy and disorientated. I look around, down.

I run, I climb, I reach, I grip, I pull.

But it is futile because Will is not there. He is not there because he is deathly still. Somewhere, deep inside, a piece of me detaches before disconnecting completely.

Ever since, my mind excels at taking me to safe places, whenever I need it most.

CHAPTER ONE

Present Day

I apply fuchsia lipstick to complete my transformation. All the best ideas are so brilliantly obvious, once you've thought of them. My reflection in the water-splashed mirror is of someone with thick make-up and dark brown hair, but my own eyes. The polyester necktie scratches my skin and, although it feels alien to wear the uniform, the starchy trouser suit with eighties-style shoulder pads allows me to morph into an anonymous airline employee. My expression is neutral and professional; calm and controlled. A new year, a new me.

Amy, her reflection beside mine, wrinkles her nose. "The stench of these toilets reminds me of school."

I wrinkle mine back. "The cheap loo roll and miserable sound of dripping water doesn't help."

We both pause for a second or two, listening.

She glances at her watch. "We'd better go, we don't want to make a bad impression."

I follow her out. Her auburn hair is woven into a bun so neat, it doesn't look real. Her perfume is floral and understated.

Mine is too strong, and the sickly smell has been irritating my nostrils all morning. As we merge with the other eighteen trainees filing back into the classroom, Brian, one of our instructors, raises his hand, palm outwards.

"Ahem."

Silence falls. I wonder if anyone else feels like me, suffocating the desire to scream because—seriously—how hard can the work be? I intend to show up, take off, chuck out a tray of food, whip it back, job done. I expect passengers to be capable of entertaining themselves with the in-flight entertainment system once fed and watered. After landing, I imagine I'll have plenty of time to chill by a hotel pool or explore local markets.

I realize that Brian is still speaking. I force myself to listen.

"There's no need to sit down as we'll be heading into the mock-up area for an examination of the training equipment."

We traipse out and gather in the corridor, before being herded along by Brian's partner in crime, Dawn. We follow her downstairs and through the main reception area. Dawn jabs a code into a keypad and we enter a small room. The walls are lined with pegs, hanging off which are mounds of dirty-looking overalls.

"Listen, please, everyone. We'd like you to wear an overall over your uniform. Place your shoes on the racks at the bottom and put on the white feet-protectors."

I freeze. Everyone but me starts lifting overalls off the pegs and checking them for size. God, I can't do this. They are filthy. They look as though they haven't been washed since...ever.

"Juliette? Is there a problem?" Brian's expression is of exaggerated concern.

"No. No problem." I smile.

He turns away. "Now, ladies, for those wearing skirts, make sure your legs are properly covered. Velcro on some of the equipment wreaks havoc with your tights."

Crap. I'm going to have to do it. I slide my arms in before doing up the buttons. I don't know why I bothered to get my suit dry-cleaned. I look ridiculous in the baggy jumpsuit, complete with elasticated material around my ankles. All that's missing is a face mask and I'd look like I'm about to investigate a crime scene. Even Amy looks less immaculate than usual. "This is going to be fun," I whisper under my breath to her.

She beams. "I can't wait to try out the practical drills. I've been dreaming of this since I was small."

"Really?"

Why would anyone dream of becoming a waitress, albeit a flying one, from childhood? When I was young I had plans.

Big ones. Proper ones.

"Any time today, Juliette." Brian is holding open a door.

He is really getting on my nerves and yet I still have another five weeks of his company to endure. I follow him into a giant warehouse containing sections of various aircraft; some at ground level, some on raised platforms with stair access. We catch up with the others walking alongside the building. The front door of a plane bursts open and several overall-clad people fly out and down the slide. A male, uniformed crew member operates the door, barking instructions above a shrill alarm. "Jump! Jump!"

We whisk past until Dawn and Brian stop beside a blown-up, silvery-grey mass, not unlike a kids' bouncy castle. "Now, before we board the slide-raft, I'm going to talk you through the survival equipment. A landing on water will, from now on, be referred to as a 'ditching...'"

Dawn's voice fades as I zone out. I know the statistics. They can call it what they like, but the chances of surviving a plane crash on water are not good.

At five on the dot, we are released through the secure gated area and back into the real world; the airport perimeter road. The roar of low-flying aircraft and rush-hour traffic is briefly disorientating. I inhale cold, crisp air. My breath mists as I exhale. The group divides into those going to the car park and the rest of us, heading for Hatton Cross. I only half-listen to their excited chatter. The group splits again; those catching buses head off first and the rest of us, including Amy, enter the tube station. I walk alongside her as we make for the platform.

"Not on the westbound side today?" she says. "I thought the train to Reading leaves from Heathrow?"

I hesitate. "I'm going to visit a friend. In Richmond."

"You've got more energy than me. I'm so tired, I don't think I could face going out tonight. And I want to go through my notes."

"It's Friday night," I say.

"Yeah, but I want to recap whilst it's all fresh," says Amy.

"Fair enough; I'll know who to sit next to in the exams." I smile.

Amy laughs.

I pretend to join in, then stare out the window; the light inside reflects us into the outside darkness.

Amy gets off at Boston Manor. I wave and watch as she walks towards the exit steps, tall and proud in her uniform.

After changing at Hammersmith, I am the only uniformed person among the crowd of passengers. Alighting at Richmond, I cross the road, pulling my coat around me tightly. My bag cuts into my right shoulder. I aim for the familiarity of the alleyway, my heels clicking and echoing with each decisive step. I avoid a broken bottle and head for the outskirts of the Green. Stopping outside a set-back period mansion block, I lean against the railings and pull off my heels, exchanging them for ballet pumps. I pull up my coat hood and let it drop over my forehead before treading along the path. My key slides into the communal door. I enter, checking for sounds. Silence.

Taking the steps to the third and highest floor, I let myself into apartment 3B. Once inside, I stand still and inhale the welcoming scent of home.

I rely on the glow of the fish tank instead of switching on any lights. Sinking down into the sofa, I remove clothes from my bag. I undress, folding my uniform carefully, then change into black jeans and a jumper. Using my phone as a torch, I pad, barefoot, into the kitchen and open the fridge. It is almost empty, as usual, apart from beer, some chillies and a readymade macaroni cheese for one. I smile.

Heading back to the living room, I risk switching on a side lamp. From my bag, I remove a photo and place it on the mantelpiece. In a perfect world, it would be framed, but I like to keep it close so that I can look at it whenever I like. In the picture, I am grinning happily, alongside Nate, the man I am to marry. I fold my uniform over my left arm and make my way to the bedroom. Next, I place the trousers, blouse and jacket on the bed and bend down, burying my face into his pillow. I inhale deeply before lifting my head and shining light around the room. Nothing has changed since I was last here. Good.

As I roll back the mirrored sliding door to the wardrobe, a reflective flash of my beam catches my eyes. I blink, whilst my sight readjusts. Nate's spare pilot's uniform, his jackets, shirts and trousers, all hang neatly, but not as neatly as I can hang them. I carefully space them out, each roughly three centimetres apart. I leave a gap as I hang my uniform next to his.

The way it should be. I stand back to admire my work. Light catches the gold emblem on his hat. I slide the door closed.

My last stop is always the bathroom. I check the medicine cabinet. He's had a cold recently; the menthol inhaler and cough medicine are new.

Returning to the living room, I help myself to an apple from the fruit bowl. I press my forehead against the living-room window, crunching small bites whilst looking down below. I can't see anyone. Rush hour is over and, presumably, most people are at home, cosy and settled. Unlike me. I am on the outskirts of my life.

Waiting. That's what I do, a lot of waiting. And thinking…

I know so many things about Nate: that he loves skiing and always smells fresh; the scent of citrus soap clings to his skin. I know that he wants to be promoted to captain before he reaches his mid-thirties.

I know his background inside out: the childhood holidays in Marbella, Nice, Verbier and Whistler; tennis, horse-riding and cricket lessons; the lack of approval from his father when Nate chose to pursue his dream of becoming a pilot instead of following in his footsteps as an investment banker.

His younger sister admires him, but she doesn't like me.

From social media photos, I can see that he could do with a haircut; his blond curls almost touch his collar.

But what I know, most of all, is that deep down he still has feelings for me. Nate just suffered a temporary fear of commitment. Although it was crushing at the time, I now understand things a little better. So, when the perfect time comes to disclose that I now work for the airline too—when he appreciates the lengths I've gone to, just to save *us*—everything will fall into place.

Until then, I have to be patient. It's difficult, though. Whenever I see a fresh image of him, I find it hard to eat for days afterwards.

My phone alarm reminds me that it's time to leave. I've had to train myself to do that, because the thing I've realized is that you get away with something once. Then twice. Then, before you know it, you are taking bigger risks. Time passes in a daze and gets cut too fine. I check to see whether Nate's flight from Chicago has landed. It has—five minutes early. I rush to my bag, and fumble. I wrap my apple core inside a tissue and pull out a packet of mini chocolate muffins. Nate's favourite. It's a habit I can't break—adding his preferences to my own food shopping. I open the freezer door, causing white light to illuminate the wall. I shove the packet towards the back, behind the meat that I know he will never defrost and the peas he never bothers with. I'd love to leave them somewhere more obvious, like by the coffee machine, but I can't, so this will have to do. When he finds them, hopefully he will take a moment to think of me. My shopping lists were always full of food he loved. I never forgot anything.

I retrace my steps to the bedroom and yank my uniform off the hangers which swing, then clatter, as they hit the back of the wardrobe. Returning to the living room, I take down the photo before reluctantly replacing it in my bag. I put on my ballet pumps and switch off the side lamp. The multicoloured fish stare at me as they complete their lengths. One, in particular, watches, mouth gaping. It is ugly. Nate named it Rainbow. I have always hated it.

I swallow hard. I don't want to go. This place is like quicksand, it sucks me in.

I pick up my bag and leave, closing the door quietly behind me, before returning to the station to catch the train to my shoebox, postage stamp, doll's house of a flat in Reading. I can't call it home because being there is like hanging out in the departure lounge of life. Waiting, always waiting, until the gate to my proper life reopens.

CHAPTER TWO

I lie in bed and stretch. Thank God it's the weekend. Although the airline is a twenty-four-hour operation, training is structured around a normal working week. Tonight, I plan to attend a children's charity fund-raising event at a luxurious Bournemouth hotel. It's an auction, with a seafood buffet and unreserved seating, and I'm looking forward to it, despite the lack of a formal invitation. It doesn't matter, as I've discovered at similar events; as long as I look and dress the part and don't draw unnecessary attention to myself (of course), people rarely question my presence and, with fund-raisers, surely it stands to reason that the more attendees, the better.

I get up, shower, change and press the button on the coffee machine. I love the sound and smell of beans grinding. If I close my eyes, for a second or two each day, I can pretend I'm at home. It's the little things that keep me going. Bitterness brushes my tongue as I sip my espresso. In between mouthfuls, I glance at my tablet. I scroll. Bella, the organizer of tonight's event, always posts plenty of photos of past events. She is in most of them, grinning, not a highlighted hair out of place, and her jewellery, usually gold or sapphires, looks expensive, yet not ostentatious. Faultless, as always. Bella excels at raising money for good causes, making herself look like a real-life Good Samaritan without having to dirty her hands. Anyone can organize a party and swan around drinking champagne, however if you really, truly meant to do good, you'd drink cheap wine and volunteer for something unpopular. But Bella's main life skill is being fantastic at making herself shine. My phone vibrates. A text.

My flatmate decided to throw a party tonight. If you can't beat them… ☺ Fancy it? I'll invite others off the course too. Amy x

I am torn. The more friends I make within the airline, the better things will be for me. And I do need friends. There is hardly anyone left from my old life—apart from those I keep in touch with on social media and a handful of dropouts from my film extra days—thanks to putting my life on hold for Nate Goldsmith. Being near Bella is like picking at a scab. But…the closer I am to her world, the more of her luck and fortune is bound to rub off. I stare at my phone, undecided, listening to the rain trickling down the gutters outside the window.

A fortnight after Nate's bombshell, he'd stood over me whilst I packed my belongings.

"I've paid six months' rent on a super place in Reading. As a gift. I'll even drive you there and help you sort out everything you need in order to settle."

"Why Reading?"

"I lived there briefly during my training and it's a fantastic place for a new start. Full of life."

"Really?"

He wouldn't let it drop, which, given how tight he could be financially, was a hurtful indication of how keen he was to bin me. At least it had stopped him banging on about me moving back to my delusional mother's. The flat was basic, clean and contained all the essentials to lead a bland, functional life. I had surveyed the living room, in which we both stood rigid, in awkward silence. I think he was waiting for me to thank him.

"Goodbye, Elizabeth."

Elizabeth, indeed, for fuck's sake! What had happened to Lily, babe, darling, sweetheart? He kissed me on the forehead and let himself out, shutting the door quietly behind him. Silence echoed. I gazed out the window, through a blur of raindrops, and watched as his tail lights disappeared, bubbling with fresh rage and humiliation. I loved him and yet I'd been unable to stop him making the biggest mistake of his life. He was mine. As I sat there—mentally deflating on the hard-backed sofa—it was then that my Plan of Action had been born. Elizabeth/Lily was disappearing into her cocoon and waiting to emerge as Juliette—my middle name—to complete a metamorphosis into a social butterfly.

Hmm. So now... Amy? Bella? Bella? Amy? *Eeny, meeny...* I reach down under the coffee table for my handbag, fumble around for my purse and take out a coin. I flip it. Heads Bella, tails Amy. The coin wobbles on the table and settles on tails. Bella has lost out to someone else, on this occasion. I message Amy back: Love to come xxx.

She sends me her address. The only problem now is that it leaves me with an entire day to fill. I don't have to bother with my appearance as much, now that I am only going to a small house party. It's so grey, it's almost dark. I pace the tiny room. Outside, I can see car lights illuminate stabbing rain in their beams. I should learn to drive. Then, I could head over to Richmond right now. I could sit outside Nate's. He wouldn't even know I was there. It would be so comforting to be near him. I shower, pull on some jeans and a black jumper, grab my trainers and coat, then speed-walk to the station.

Rain, it turns out, is a serious godsend. Who'd have thought, after so many soggy summers, that I would find it such a luxury to hide beneath a hood loitering anonymously in shop doorways and alleyways. Mother Nature is on my side. During this miserable late January day, people are distracted, heads down, shoulders hunched, umbrellas up. Cartwheeling water sludges from car tyres. No one takes any notice of me.

Nate's living-room lights are on. He'll most likely be watching the latest box set or film on Netflix. I miss him. Not for the first time, I regret my behaviour and capitulation. I almost have a moment of weakness as the urge to dash over the street and kick down his door threatens to overwhelm me. Yet, I must play by the rules, otherwise he won't appreciate me. Second time around, things will be on my terms.

Amy's flat is above a hair salon. Just as well, because if she had proper neighbours below they'd have called the police by now. Ibiza dance-style music blares out. I press the buzzer, but then realize the door is open, so I let myself in. I walk upstairs and through the door. Amy is laughing, her head thrown back, clutching a bottle of beer. I stand still for a moment. She spots me and walks over, kissing me once on each cheek.

"Come in! So glad you could come. That's my flatmate, Hannah," she points to a woman in the far corner of the room, "and you already know some of the others... Oliver, Gabrielle..."

The rest of Amy's friends' names only briefly register in my mind: *Lucy, Ben, Michelle...* I accept a bottle of beer, even though I can't stand drinking out of bottles. I take sips and make polite chit-chat with Oliver, which is hard work as he is one of the quietest people on our course. I am rescued by Amy, who seems determined to let her hair down tonight. We dance. Amy flirts. The evening is pleasant enough. I have read Amy wrong. I didn't think she'd be of much use to me, but now I intend to keep her close and get to know her better. I throw myself into the moment. I laugh a lot. Genuinely. I haven't had so much fun since…well, I can't remember exactly. But it will have been with Nate. Obviously.

Nearly seven months ago, Nate had appeared in a chapter of my life like a scene from a romantic novel. As I'd taken my gaze away from my computer screen at the hotel reception desk—a work smile fixed firmly in place—I'd struggled not to gasp out loud. The man in front of me looked as though he had absorbed the best bits of life and shrugged off anything unpleasant or sad. Blond curls waved from beneath his hat, and his skin was gently tanned. Behind him, matching uniformed crew followed in his wake, footsteps tip-tapping on the marble floor.

"I believe you have last-minute reservations for us? We've ended up with an unscheduled night-stop after engine trouble forced us to return to Heathrow."

Until that moment, the most exciting event in the eight months I'd worked at the Airport Inn had been a minor celebrity smuggling two women into his room, neither of whom were his wife.

"Are you working this evening?" Nate asked when I handed him his key card—I'd left his room allocation till last.

"I finish at eight," I'd replied, feeling a dormant tingle of anticipation begin to reawaken.

"Fancy showing us the best bars nearby?"

"Of course."

That night, I too became a guest at the hotel. It was inevitable. From the moment our eyes had locked, I'd set out to dazzle him.

Six weeks later, I moved into Nate's flat...

"Juliette?"

"Sorry, Amy, miles away."

"Do you want to crash on the sofa here?"

I scan the room, surprised to see only a few people left. I'd been vaguely aware of people saying goodbye and Oliver offering me a lift but I hadn't been ready to leave. Amy is going to make a good social contact.

I slide out my phone from my bag. "It's fine, thanks. I need to get back."

During the taxi ride, I check out the photos of Bella's event on Twitter. Another success for Beautiful Bella, going by the stream of complimentary comments. Motorway lights fade and highlight her. She looks stunning, in an ice-queen way. Pearls—no doubt real—choke her neck. Her long blonde hair is elegantly swept up. In every image, she is smiling, surrounded by the local great and the good. I trace my forefinger around her outline on the screen, wishing I could erase her as easily as deleting an image.

Back home, I pace.

As I mull things over, I reassure myself that I made the right decision to shun Bella tonight. Not that I was going to approach her on this occasion; I was merely going to observe. Practice makes perfect. When I do decide the time is right to confront Bella, it will be planned to the last detail.

Revenge is a dish best served cold, and mine is going to be frozen.

CHAPTER THREE

The remaining five weeks of the course keep me distracted. Although I still keep a close eye on Bella online and visit Nate's flat at least once a week when he's away, I spend a lot of time with Amy. She likes to study together. That isn't really my kind of thing, but it does mean she likes and relies on me. Her flatmate, Hannah, is long-haul crew for a different airline and Amy is the type of person who isn't comfortable with her own company. She is the sixth of seven children.

Finally, after endless jumps down slides, donning smoke hoods and entering smoke-filled chambers to fight pretend fires, resuscitating dolls, handcuffing each other, bandaging colleagues, ridiculous amounts of role play, aircraft visits to the hangar, learning how to lift a suitcase into a car boot without damaging your back and, the worst of it, listening to Brian and Dawn going on and on and on…after all that, our "Wings Day" is here. It feels like good timing as signs of spring are beginning to show: daffodils, thinner coats, slightly longer days, fresh beginnings.

We all shake hands with a manager who is apparently "very important," according to Brian, and thank him as he hands us a cheap-looking gold badge. We pin it on our jackets, above our name badges, and grin. We all grin some more as our photos are taken. Not only am I moving on to the next stage of my POA, it also means no more Brian. Next Tuesday, I am off to Mumbai. Everyone on the course has been rostered a long-haul flight to allow more time for in-flight training. Amy is going to Dallas. In a nearby pub, with too-bright lighting and dark-patterned carpets, no doubt hiding all sorts of stains, we all celebrate with glasses of prosecco.

"Cheers!" says Amy.

We clink glasses.

"Cheers!" I echo.

Amy takes a large sip. "I'm nervous about my first trip, are you?"

"No."

She looks surprised.

I feel secure because I've checked Nate's schedule and he is rostered a Nairobi on Monday. Our work paths do not cross, for now. Although Nate had de-friended me, un-followed me, de-bloody-everythinged-me, he hasn't changed his passwords. In fairness, he isn't aware that I know them. However, he's left me with this as my only option to keep abreast of the situation for the time being. Social media has become my essential tool. Amy knows a bit about "Nick" but not his real identity or occupation, simply that we are on a relationship break. Amy is the perfect confidante: scathing enough about "Nick" to be supportive, but not so much so that I feel compelled to leap to his defence. I had to share something. It's how friendships work: you share secrets.

My phone rings. It's such an unusual occurrence that I
nearly spill my drink. *Auntie Barbara.* Her name illuminates
my screen.

It's a short conversation. I won't be going to Mumbai on
Tuesday after all.
My mother is dead.

My childhood home is situated in the south, just outside the
market town of Dorchester, nestled in a small village. So many
people say to me, "Oh, Dorset, I love Dorset, so beautiful,"
then mention the sea. Sweet Pea Cottage is in the middle of
nowhere and the coast is not in sight. Several farms dot the
immediate area and on the rare occasions I think of my old
home, I picture the oak tree at the heart of the village surrounded by flint-stoned houses and thatched cottages. Public
walkways weave through the nearby hills and are ever-popular
with ramblers and dog walkers.

My father shows up at the funeral, which provides a small
distraction. Whilst The Beatles blast out "In My Life," I study
the old man in the opposite aisle and marry him up with my
younger memories. I'd been ten when he left for the final
time. He had smoked a pipe; I remember the smell more than
I remember him. An ache swells in my throat as an image
of him as a badly disguised Santa thrusts to the forefront of
my thoughts. His wild, curly brown hair wouldn't be tamed
beneath the small, white-bobbled red hat. I swallow hard.

This is only the second funeral I've ever attended, and I'm
not sure I see the point of public mass misery. If someone's
gone, they're gone. Initially, I was surprised at the large con-
gregation, but soon realized that it was for Barbara's sake.
People appear genuinely fond of her. Whilst waiting for proceedings to begin, she whispers snippets of church history to
those in the aisle in front; hints of pride are evident in her

voice, despite her grief. I half-listen, as it is preferable to the aimless, silent waiting.

"...originally thirteenth century, you know. Hundreds of years of gatherings. Imagine! All those people. In 1838 a disapproving parson put a stop to the custom of giving out bread, mince pies and ale on the sixth of January, Old Christmas Day..."

A hush indicates that proceedings are to begin.

"...and so we gather to celebrate the life of Amelia..."

I stand up. Pick up a hymn book. Sit down. My mother would be furious. She is going to come back and haunt Barbara for having her buried in a church. Barbara said that, as Amelia had always got her own way, it was now her turn to make the decisions. Beside me, her shoulders heave. Her blonde, grey-streaked hair is neatly pinned into a bun. She is dressed head-to-toe in black, broken only by a silver chain and cross. I am wearing black too, but only because it is the dominant colour in my wardrobe. I pat her on the arm but quickly remove my hand in case she tries to take hold of it.

The vicar stops talking. It is over.

I follow Barbara to the door and stand alongside her, nodding and giving thanks for all the words of sympathy. Every now and then, I remember to dab my eyes with a tissue—however, the ache in my throat is genuine. I will myself not to give in to the threat of tears because, if I let myself cry, then I don't think I'll be able to hold it together. Broken sentences float around me.

My father shuffles into focus. "Why are you here?" I ask.

"We can talk at Barbara's."

Over egg and cress sandwiches—white, with the crusts cut off—and strong cups of tea, my father and I update our memories of each other. He carries all the classic hallmarks of ageing: a mix of white hair, glasses, wrinkles and a paunch, finished off with an aggressive cough. Pipe smoke clings to his clothes.

"Amelia said that you all but disappeared," I say. "That you didn't bother to keep in touch."

"Well, yes, but it seemed like the right thing to do when I heard…to come here…and see you."

"Bit late. There were phones in the nineties. Even Amelia had one."

"I remarried."

I don't know what to say to that. On birthday cards, his only attempts at contact, he'd always written: *To Dear Lily-flower.*

"Elizabeth Juliette Magnolia," he smiles at his own out-of-date joke.

He always said if it had been up to him, I'd have been an Imogen, but my mother had been insistent. Whilst people in the eighties and nineties had tight perms, shoulder pads and embraced consumerism, my mother decided to remain in the sixties and seventies. Flowers. The Beatles. Parties. Drugs. Drink. Fun, fun, fun. My father was a long-distance lorry driver and my mother's "excuse" was that she didn't feel comfortable being the only adult in the house. She'd conjured up a fear of murderers and burglars forming an orderly queue outside the front door the moment he left for work.

My father taps his watch. "I have to go. Train to catch. Let's not be strangers. I'm even on email now. I'll write it down Maybe you can come and visit sometime?"

"Maybe." Unlikely.

"I do think of her and *him*, you know…"

"Goodbye," I say.

He hesitates. For a dreadful moment I think he is going to try to hug me, but he doesn't.

"Goodbye, Lily-flower."

I turn back to the room full of strangers. Amy had offered

to come, but old habits die hard; I'd never been at ease mix-
ing family and friends.

"I hope you're going to stick around for a few more days,"
says Barbara. "You need to help sort out the house."

She doesn't add that it's the least I can do. Surprisingly,
my mother has left a will. With her skewed logic, she probably thought it would make amends for the past. I'm now the
proud, sole owner of Sweet Pea Cottage.

"I'm going to stay there tonight."

"Alone?"

"Alone."

"Goodbye, Babs. Lovely spread," says a tall, thin man
clutching a walking stick.

"Bye. You look after yourself," says another woman, touch-
ing my aunt's arm briefly before grabbing her coat.

Everyone trickles away. The kitchen is spotless due to
the numerous offers of help. Everyone likes a job when the
alternative is making small talk with people you don't really
know, about a dead person you knew even less.

"Are you quite sure?" asks Barbara as I pack my bag, ready
for the short walk to Sweet Pea Cottage.

I wave a small torch—the one work suggested we buy for
use in the crew bunk area. "Totally. See you in the morning."

My sympathy reserves are dry and I crave solitude. Besides,
I'm in the right kind of mood to face ghosts.

My footsteps echo on the road and then the path. I take out
my old keys, inhale deeply and turn the lock. The wooden
door creaks. It always has, but it's only noticeable now that
the house is silent.

The early years were filled with people. They were just
there; hanging around, laughing. I remember a lot of laughter.
Raucous, drunk, giggly. That's what I remember the most.
And *debates*. My mother got it into her head that what was

wrong with the world was that people no longer expressed themselves.

"Tony Blair does," someone had said.

"Princess Diana did," another voice had chipped in. "And look what her death did. It freed people up to openly express their emotions."

The more alcohol infused their brains with notions, the louder the *debates* became, against an eclectic mix of music. I learned how to make myself invisible. Nothing like a kid to put the dampener on *fun*. It was different for my two-year-old brother, though. When chatting about him with others, the adjectives my mother used were "cute," "funny" or "adorable," whereas I was "quiet," "moody" and "unaffectionate."

During the latter years at home, once the constant stream of visitors had stopped, my mother had usually been asleep by late afternoon. The TV or radio, sometimes simultaneously, were left blaring. I'd turn down the sound and I'd take off her shoes and cover her with a blanket. Once I'd put Will to bed, I'd sit in an armchair, reading or making up stories and plays.

Now a clock ticks. I've always hated the sound, even before "the Incident," as everyone referred to it later. Four-year-old William Florian Jasmin grins at me from the mantelpiece.

He'd have been called Nicholas if my dad had been allowed his way. Six years younger than me, he'd had an inbuilt talent for charming people. All now irrelevant, dead information.

I head for the shiny wooden drinks cabinet. A bottle of gin sits among a random selection of alcohol. Surprisingly, it is nearly full. I open the fridge, not quite sure what to expect. Among the ready meals, some onions and three wizened apples, are six cans of tonic. No lemons or limes. Inside the freezer compartment, there are several trays of ice. Clutching my mother's favourite drink, I go upstairs. The clink of an ice cube makes me jump as I push open her bedroom door, inhaling cold and damp.

I step in. Floorboards creak in familiar places. I pull open a wardrobe door and am hit by my mother's signature perfume. Opium. I hate perfumes that scream of camouflage, to hide odours like drink and neglect. I shiver at the memory and look behind, half-expecting to see Amelia carrying her drinks up the stairs on a doily-lined tray in an attempt to make addiction respectable. I can smell smoke even though no one has smoked in this house for years.

Turning back to the job in hand, I lift hangers off the rail holding mainly dresses. I stare at a rose-patterned one before holding it against me. I look in the mirror; it doesn't suit me. This was her favourite one. She wore it every summer, back in the days before the drink sucked her in completely. In the mornings, before her lunchtime wine, she'd sometimes take me and Will to the nearby woods, pointing out flower names along the way. I remember cowslip, bluebells and foxgloves.

There was a green-fingered woman who had lived along the way and Amelia adored her garden, especially in spring. The woman had died not long after the Incident. The new owners of her bungalow were keen to remodel the place, and years of building work destroyed all the beauty. But by then, Amelia wouldn't have noticed or cared.

I pull open the built-in wardrobe drawers, each wooden front prettily engraved with flowers. Underwear. Tights. Musty jumpers. A gardening book. Inside the front cover are two pressed daisies. I drain my glass before heading downstairs for some bin bags and a refill.

I yank open the last drawer. It's lighter than I expect, so it shoots out, causing me to fall back. It's empty, apart from a yellowing envelope Sellotaped to the back. I rip it open. That's when it all hurtles back; suppressed memories swirl through my mind like water down a chute. And it hits me.

I run to the bathroom and throw up. Turning on the cold

tap, I splash drops on to my face, avoiding my reflection in the mirror. I need to leave.

I go outside and call a taxi to take me to the station. I wait at the end of the path by the wooden gate. As the cab approaches, its beams highlight the overgrown hedges and the suffocating ivy that have always threatened to swallow the cottage. I must stay strong and not allow myself to be clawed back by the past. I quietly repeat my mantras under my breath, hidden in the darkness of the back seat, whilst the driver listens to a football match on the radio.

Stick to the plan, stick to the plan.

Fail to plan, plan to fail.

As long as I don't veer off course, nothing can ever harm me again.

CHAPTER FOUR

I disembark from the coach at Heathrow. The automatic doors to the Report Centre part. Flashes of green and blue—our corporate colours—rush by. In the canteen, I spot a vacant corner table as I order a double espresso. Above, monitors constantly update the tantalizing list of destinations. Rome. Nairobi. Athens. My eyes rest on Los Angeles: my first destination as an operating crew member. I want distance from Sweet Pea Cottage, Dorset and the past. Thoughts are swamping my mind.

LAX crew report to room nine flashes up on the screens.

I stand up, gather my belongings and head for the pre-flight briefing room. I am allocated a working position at the back of the plane.

The flight itself would be a lot easier if there weren't so many passengers. Entering the economy cabin isn't dissimilar to my idea of walking on to a stage because hundreds of eyes watch me and I sense their silent anticipation. I release the brake on the trolley and push it in front of me. Bottles rattle. When I stop at my allocated aisle—row thirty-six—I can almost hear passengers mentally recalculating the order in which they will be served, and it injects me with a surge of power.

I smile. "Lasagne or chicken curry? Red or white wine?"

A well-known chef is in first class and is apparently sharing cooking tips with the galley crew and other passengers. I am half-tempted to go and join them; perhaps he can pass on something new which will impress Nate. However, I get caught up preparing for the afternoon tea service. And before I get a chance, we are commencing our descent.

After landing, people make plans on the crew bus.

"Anyone fancy a tour of the stars' houses?" asks someone.

I can't think of anything worse than paying to catch glimpses of unattainable lifestyles. I choose to join a group of five who suggest brunch somewhere by the coast tomorrow. We are eight hours behind the UK, so even I will want more than a coffee by then. I didn't mention that it was my very first flight, just that I was fairly new and that I'd never been to LA before. I'd heard rumours about "pranks"—I detest the very word and the images it conjures up—such as informing a new recruit that it was their responsibility to carry a bag of ice off the aircraft for a room party or that they had to carry the captain's suitcase to his room.

Venice Beach.

Now I'm here, in a place so familiar that I feel as though I've walked on to a film set, I want to pinch myself. I can't believe that I am here, living Nate's lifestyle. To think…all those times I was at our home, waiting for him, whilst he was cavorting around the world, having a ball. What a mug I was. I gaze at the vast beach. Beneath the tall, skinny palm trees people unselfconsciously work out at the outdoor gyms.

A lifeguard hut catches my eye. I'd watched *Baywatch* a couple of times at Babs' house and I'd been enthralled.

I stroll along the Boardwalk with my temporary new best friends—my colleagues—browsing the market stalls crammed with sunglasses, T-shirts, crystals, souvenirs, whilst dodging beautiful, thin people jogging, roller-blading and skate-boarding. An artist wants to draw my portrait, but I refuse with a smile. I feel almost relaxed.

We decide on a restaurant with outside seating for brunch. I order an egg-white omelette and a sparkling water.

"Don't fancy a Buck's Fizz, then?" asks Alan, the cabin service manager. "You can drink, as long as you stop at least twelve hours before duty."

"I don't drink much," I say. "I'm not really that fussed." Everyone bursts out laughing.

"What?" I say. "It's true." I look round the table of sage faces.

"You won't be saying you don't drink a lot for much longer," says Alan, taking two gulps from his flute glass. "I give you six months. Tops."

They can laugh and make assumptions all they like. I zone out.

As I walk 35,000 feet above the Atlantic operating the flight home, the only thing that keeps me going through the endless demands is the knowledge that this is all a means to an end. I have an uncomfortable moment when I am summoned by Alan via interphone to speak to a French passenger in first class who has some queries.

"Can't he speak English?" I say.

"*She*. Not very well. That's why we need you."

I walk up the aisle as slowly as possible, willing someone to faint and slump over the aisle or ask me lots of complicated questions. The problem is that I exaggerated my ability in French on the application form. I'm barely GCSE standard.

However, I took a gamble and only scraped through the mercifully short oral by cramming with a *Teach Yourself* audiobook a few weeks beforehand and by pretending I had a bad cold on the day. It was such a relief to walk out of the exam room that I forgot to think long-term. I saw it as another hurdle cleared, not as a potential future problem.

I smile as I'm introduced to Madame Chauvin, an elderly lady, who smiles up at me from her seat expectantly and launches into a long speech.

"I can handle this," I say to Alan, who is hovering obsequiously nearby.

He shrugs and disappears through into the galley.

I learned one sentence off by heart in French, which I repeat. *"Je ne parle pas très bien…* I don't speak French very well. Could you speak more slowly, please?"

She frowns, then smiles again and slows down her speech.

I crouch down near her seat, so that hopefully no one else can hear. I catch the words *bagages* and *Paris*. I think.

Still grinning, I say, *"Pas de problème,"* in a voice barely above a whisper and offer her a *café au lait*.

She opens her mouth, but I pat her on the arm and say, "You're welcome," in French, stand up and leave. Before I escape back to economy, I ask the galley crew to make her a coffee with three biscuits, preferably chocolate.

Alan, who is leaning against a counter, tapping his iPad, stops and peers through his glasses at me.

"What did Madame Chauvin want?"

"She was concerned about her baggage making a connecting flight to Paris."

"Oh. Is that all?"

"Well, she also misses her grandchildren and is looking forward to seeing them. She's been away for a long time visiting other relatives. I'd better get back, I haven't completed my bar paperwork yet."

I walk swiftly through business class, then premium class until I reach the safety of the rear cabin. The sea of economy faces is a welcome relief, but I don't properly relax until we land. Every time the interphone rings, my heart leaps in case "The French Speaker" is summoned again.

After landing, I return home briefly to dump my bags, shower and change before I catch the train to Dorchester. I send Babs a message, asking her to collect me, then close my eyes for a little doze on the train. She is waiting for me at the station in her red Mini.

"I think I'm going to sell the cottage," I say to her as we drive past it. "I'll have to hope that someone loves the whole *Hansel and Gretel*, fairies, flowers and toadstools in the merry forest–style theme, though."

"I agree, my love."

I'd expected a list of objections, all stacked up like planes awaiting air traffic control. My mother had been given the house by my grandparents, both of whom had died before I'd reached my first birthday. Barbara was married to Ernie at the time and they were happy in a modern, detached house where "everything worked."

"I'd been on at her for years to sell, but she vehemently refused."

"The cottage was for a family, and as for the grounds…"

"…a jungle, from what I've seen through the window."

Amelia liked to buy mixed packets of flower seeds, tip them all together in a huge bowl, then stand in the middle of the garden and throw handfuls into the sky and watch in joyful anticipation as they rained down haphazardly. Of course, some grew; bursts of colour among the random weeds and grass, until they were strangled or gave up the fight after long periods of warm weather with no water.

"She was never going to heal here, alone, surrounded by memories," Babs says softly, almost to herself.

"She had me," I say.

I don't mention the succession of unsuitable men after Dad left.

"I did keep an eye on you," says Babs quickly. "I made you soup and apple crumble. And you knew that my home was an open house when it came to you."

Occasionally words fail me. Soup and bloody apple crumble. Birthday cards from Father.

My family are like the Waltons. Amelia resigned from maternal responsibility when I was awarded a drama scholarship at a boarding school, an institution that prided itself on its *values*. The Latin for light and truth—*lux et veritas*—was carved into a wooden panel in the dining area. When not in school uniform, my unfashionable clothes and childish Disney pyjamas ensured I was even further set apart from the queen bee and her friends, with their matching silk pyjama sets and designer sweaters, trousers and shoes.

We reach Barbara's house. She parks outside her garage, which she hasn't used since Ernie's sudden death from a heart attack seven years ago. He loved hiding away in there, listening to Radio Four and carving wooden chests that he liked to sell at car boot sales. Babs turns the key in the lock of her white PVC front door and I follow her in, taking my bags up to the spare room.

"Will you help me clear the cottage out?" I say when I return downstairs. "I want to get some estate agents round. Maybe once it's sold, it will start to feel possible to lay some of the past to rest."

"Yes, of course, Lily love."

"I call myself Juliette now."

There's no harm in her knowing.

"Oh. OK. That's fine, as long as you don't expect me to remember all the time."

"Let's have a coffee, then walk over," I say. "I want to get it over with."

The chill of winter is weakening now that the end of March is imminent. Cherry blossom coats the branches of the village trees and clusters of crocuses push their way through patches of grass. Amelia's favourite time of year. Not for me, though, because it is a blatant reminder that time is moving on. Without Nate. We got together in July last year and it is my intention to get us back on track before that anniversary. I quicken my step, mustering up a fresh sense of determination, and shove open the gate to Sweet Pea Cottage.

The first thing I do is go upstairs to my mother's room and retrieve the photo I dropped the other night; the picture of her precious Will, myself and my then best friend, Kim, who used to live next door. I force myself to stare at it for a few seconds, then rip it into tiny shreds. It was one of the last ever photos taken of him—I can tell, because the cuddly blue elephant he is clutching was only given to him by Babs the week before he died, which is why Amelia must've hidden it from sight. I don't want reminders. Kim's family whisked her away shortly after the Incident, leaving me behind with the rest of the local children at our small school, who either didn't know what to say to me or simply treated me as though I was tainted.

I stand still.

Silence.

I close my eyes.

I can almost feel the sun on my skin, just like *that* day. There was barely any breeze. I rarely do this. I rarely go there, and there is no need to now, but an overwhelming desire to mentally self-mutilate dares me to push myself. Just one more time. My breathing quickens at the memory of feeling a resentful carelessness. And laziness. Until I had jolted and sat up. Feeling sick, I'd felt a barely perceptible dribble at the side of my mouth. I'd wiped it away as silence cut through the incessant noise of the bees.

Either it ended or began then; I'm never sure which.

I shiver now, open my eyes, then run downstairs and rummage around in the kitchen. I rip several bin bags off a roll and hand some to Babs.

"Here. If you want anything, keep it. Otherwise it'll go to charity or get binned."

It takes two days. I end up having to stay at Barbara's, but the job is done.

Before I leave Dorchester, I have some spare keys cut. I drop them off with several estate agents before catching a train back to the shoebox.

My life is slowly coming back together. Once the house sale goes through, I will have money. Things may have been more tortoise than hare lately, but everyone knows who wins in the end.

For the first time since I moved in, I sleep the entire night.

On my penultimate day off from work, I get up early and go over to Nate's. He's at home, unfortunately, but I need my fix. I walk past the theatre and a bank, then I cross the road. I stare at his building, which also houses five other flats. It is set back from the main area of the Green, down a small lane. Well-maintained communal gardens, both front and back, surround the property. I walk past several times, completing circuitous laps of the wide open space. I hang out until Nate goes for his usual jog around nine, before rewarding himself with a coffee from his favourite café. The weather is on my side again. Although the dark clouds look fit to burst, a drop has yet to fall, but it means I can justifiably keep my rain-coat hood up.

From my viewpoint, near the café entrance, I can see through the glass that Nate has ordered a croissant. Unusual. A surge of hope; comfort eating can be a sign of loneliness. I take out my phone and stare at the screen. Nate takes his time over his coffee drinking and takes full advantage of the free papers. As I glance up from my phone, fear floods through me. Nate is walking straight towards the exit. Head lowered, I walk away, then step into the nearest shop door-way, holding my breath. He walks past. My heartbeat is vio-lent. Deep breaths.

I walk in the opposite direction, towards the river, and call Amy. I need a distraction.

"Do you fancy meeting up for some tapas in Richmond to-night?" I say. "I know a good place that's cheap and cheerful."

There is no danger of bumping into Nate, as he is off to Boston.

Amy agrees. "Come to mine for a drink first," she says.

The tapas restaurant was a favourite of ours. Alejandro, the gossipy manager, will feed back to Nate how happy I ap-pear if I mention—once or twice—how much more relaxed I am with some fabricated new boyfriend. Nate *should* feel some sliver of jealousy. It's human nature to want what you can't have, I know that only too well, and I bet Nate checks my Facebook page from time to time, through curiosity, de-spite the impression he likes to give that he no longer cares. It will do him good to see me out with a new friend. Even if he doesn't, maybe *someone* will see something and men-tion me in a positive light. I've had to set up two Facebook accounts—Elizabeth and Juliette—and take great care which pictures I post on each page, as it would give the game away if I'm in Melbourne one day, Singapore the next.

I return to the train station, glancing up at its distinctive square clock—it's not even midday yet—and go home for the afternoon. I may as well use my time productively before I head off to Amy's, so I take out my laptop and get to work. After chasing some estate agents, I check on what Bella is up to. She is supporting yet another charity. An anti-bullying one this time. Anger sweeps through me. She has no right, none at all.

In-bloody-hale, ex-bloody-hale. In. Out. In. Out.

Patience is a virtue.

Stick to the plan.

I occupy my mind by searching for a driving instructor, and I finally book some lessons.

I catch the bus to Heathrow for a change of scene, then another one to Brentford, even though it makes my journey longer. It doesn't matter, as I still have plenty of time, despite my busy day. Each trip we do generates between two and five rest days off, depending on the destination—"Time at Base" days, generally known as TAB days. The bus stops and starts, snaking through Hounslow, then back on to the A4, passing rows of houses set back from the main road. Even above the noise of the bus engine, I am aware of the constant stream of whining aircraft on their final descent. Glancing up through the window, on each approaching plane I can see—despite the daylight—the flashing lights of the anti-collision beacons, and the landing gear; thick, black tyres poking beneath the metallic underbellies.

I alight at Brentford High Street, outside the County Court, and from there it is a forty-minute walk to Amy's. I pass tall, shiny glass buildings and the depressing grey pillars supporting the bridges of the M4 above. The final leg of my journey takes me up a wide, residential road.

I am sweating by the time I press Amy's buzzer.

She opens the door in a peach towelling robe. "Sorry! Running a bit late. Help yourself to a drink from the fridge," she calls over her shoulder as she disappears into her bedroom. "I won't be long."

I don't bother. Instead, I wait on the sofa. She takes ages. Bored, I pull open a drawer in the coffee table. It's mainly full of junk. I can't help myself tidying it, grouping random pens and picking out a disintegrating packet of sticky cough sweets, which need to go in the bin. There is a Homer Simpson key ring, a burst of sky blue and yellow, holding two keys. Spare keys? I pick them up and slide them into my bag—you never know when things will come in useful.

"You remember Jack from my party, don't you?" Amy says when we're finally en route. She doesn't wait for a reply before continuing. "I hope you don't mind? He was at a loose end tonight, so I said he could join us."

I smile. "How lovely. The more the merrier." Of course I fucking mind.

As soon as I enter the restaurant, my mood drops further. There is no sign of a welcoming Alejandro and I sense his absence, made more obvious by the lack of a decaying cactus on a high-up window sill and the missing paper tablecloths, decorated with badly illustrated sombreros. Instead, the place looks…sleek. I just know that he's sold out, moved on. I feel a tiny stab of betrayal. I was a loyal customer.

A waitress shows us to a table set for four. I can see the back of a man's head; he swings round and grins.

"Hi, Jack," I say with a big smile. "Who's the empty seat for?" I casually slip in as I take a seat opposite Amy.

"My pal, Chris," says Jack with a grin.

A tingle of unease seeps through my chest when things are out of kilter. I don't want to double-date or hang out with other men—there's no point. I have Nate. Clenching my fists beneath the table, I force myself to pick up the menu and study it.

Just as I am about to suggest that we don't bother eating and head for a bar instead, Chris arrives. He is larger than life in every way: tall, loud, with a beer belly. Although I grin and appear welcoming, the next few hours are an endurance. I feel trapped. I hate the fact that I am here, going through the motions in the wrong life, with the wrong people. I haven't endured the nightmare roller-coaster ride of my early twenties to now experience such a brutal stab of hollowness. My beliefs entitle me to a cosmic reward like…contentment or stability. I belong at home, with Nate. Every moment that we are apart is a waste of time, because the outcome is obvious—we *will* be together. Being with Nate was as though I'd begun a homeward-bound train journey, only to be booted off halfway through, on a winter's night, and instructed to reach my destination on a series of replacement buses.

I want it all: Nate, his family's welcoming acceptance, the comfortable lifestyle and kids who grow up to be a footballer— Will loved kicking his football—and an actress. I'd look after my children myself; I wouldn't trust anyone else to watch them properly. I want to be the sort of person who other people might glance at—in a restaurant, say, or even just taking the kids to the park—who people might aspire to be. I want them to imagine that I am the sort of person who is "together" and to picture my orderly home, with children's pictures stuck to the designer fridge with magnets, whilst my husband opens a bottle of chilled, expensive wine as I stir a risotto.

Approaching midnight, they are all pissed and laughing at things that aren't funny. If Jack shows me one more You-Tube clip of a man flying off a motorbike into a conveniently located haystack, I will scream. And I don't think I will be able to stop.

We are now trapped in a long queue at the deserted taxi

rank. The smell of kebabs from a nearby takeaway is over-powering. I can't bear it a second longer. Childish defiance takes over.

"I have an idea," I say. "A friend of mine lives nearby, he's away, but he lets me use his place from time to time. He likes me to feed his fish and keep an eye on things. Let's go there for a nightcap."

"Are you sure?" says Amy. "What about—"

"Come on! I can't bear this queue a second longer. We can have a drink in the warm, and I'll call a minicab." Amy still hesitates.

"Follow me," I say and head off down the alley towards the Green. "You'll need to be quiet as we walk upstairs, some of his neighbours work shifts. Once we're in the flat, it's fine."

I feel smug as I let everyone in, like I'm taking even more control of the reins. My eyes dart around the living area. It is neat. No work manuals, no post, nothing too personal. Nate and I are both tidy. I don't believe that opposites attract; I'm sure it's a myth. I pull the blinds down and insist that every-one has a liqueur coffee. Nate won't notice if the amount in the bottle goes down, he hates the stuff. Jack is sitting close to Amy on the sofa. There is a space next to Chris who is sitting on the other one, in Nate's spot. It serves him right that another man—albeit an unsuitable one—is in his place.

The fish are doing laps. If fish could talk… For the first time ever, I feed them, sprinkling a layer of vile-smelling confetti shapes over the surface. Rainbow's mouth opens and closes as he glares at me.

"I'll be back in a minute," I say. "Just nipping to the bath-room, then I'll call us a cab for later."

They ignore me; roaring at yet another YouTube video on Jack's phone.

In Nate's spare room, I check his desk. Mostly bare, as usual, apart from a pot containing an assortment of hotel pens.

He tends to take his admin away with him, but I can't resist checking his drawers. With my phone clamped between my ear and shoulder I dial a taxi firm.

It rings.

A male voice answers. "Hello?"

My eyes fix on an expensive cream envelope. An invitation? To what? From whom? I carefully slide out a card, even though it's already been slashed open with Nate's paperknife.

"Hello? Bob's cars?"

I force myself to speak. "Oh, hello, yes… I'd like to book a taxi please…"

Hanging up, I sink down on to the bed, reading the words as they blur in front of me.

CHAPTER FIVE

Whenever I choose to encounter Bella, whether online, from a distance or in photos, I always mentally prepare beforehand. I form an imaginary protective barrier around myself. To anyone else, what I'm looking at would seem like nothing— but to me, it is another setback. Another painful reminder of how *she* leads the type of life that I desire.

It's an invitation to Bella's home to celebrate a friend's thirtieth birthday. And it's not the fact that her friend is a fairly well-known celebrity—I couldn't care less—it's the brazen *exclusivity* that needles. I would love to be invited and to mix in the same social circles as Nate. I knew Bella too, once.

"Juliette?"

Amy is standing at the door, frowning, clearly puzzled despite the glazed look in her eyes.

"Sorry, I got distracted. I messaged my friend to tell him we were here and he asked me to check something for him."

I put the card in the drawer, switch off the light and follow her back into the living room. "More liqueur coffees?" I say with a hostess smile. "The minicab controller said it's really busy. The taxi will be about an hour."

It's a struggle to remain present. I smile and nod and try to join in, as best I can. But I want to whoop out loud with relief when the cab calls after forty-five minutes to say it's downstairs. "I've ordered two," I lie. "I'll get the next one back to mine. I want to stay and tidy up a bit more, anyway," I add when Amy opens her mouth, as though to protest.

It's true that I do need to check that I've replaced everything correctly. I can't leave any signs; Nate is fastidious. I check that his Boston flight is well and truly en route before feeling secure enough about my decision to stay for the night. I don't see why I shouldn't. I return to the spare room and once again pull out the stiff invitation card.

I'd be delighted if you could join us in celebrating…

Amelia's decision to apply for a boarding school scholarship, rather than letting me continue at the nearest secondary school, neatly coincided with my teenage hormones starting to kick in. She helped me prepare for it, even though I found it straightforward enough to discuss contrasting monologues and perform a series of improvisations. Student head of year, Bella, was assigned to look after me by the House Mother and show me the school ropes. Which, in fairness, she did. At first. Bella was elegant, intelligent, witty, slim and beautiful. Under Bella's wing, I was protected from those who looked down at my too-tight, dull clothes, unable to conceal my puppy fat.

Most of the "inner circle" were weekly boarders. Bella's family lived in an exclusive area in Bournemouth. I was vague about how close my home was. "Out in the countryside," I used to reply, if asked, when in fact it was a thirty-two-minute drive away—I'd timed the taxi driver who'd driven me on my first day. The weekends dragged. I used to keep my head down in the library and escape by flicking through the permitted magazines—*Vogue* and *Tatler*—picturing my future invitations to parties where I too would be in the photos on the back pages.

In drama, Bella's parts were always the equivalent of Mary in a primary school nativity play, and the roles of her closest friends—Stephanie and Lucy—were comparable in status to the wise men. Mine were the bit parts—like a shepherd or a donkey—despite my scholarship, even though I was allocated extra behind-the-scene roles such as script writing and directing. I tried not to mind, but it hurt because I wanted my rightful turn to shine, to have everyone applaud, and to elevate my popularity status.

"It's because her family are loaded. They donate generously to the school. No one else ever gets a turn," Claire, a quiet, fellow scholarship girl who excelled at most sports, whispered to me once when Bella got another coveted role.

I had quite liked Claire, but I couldn't befriend her because I'd sensed that Bella—although she'd outwardly made an exception for me—generally didn't approve of scholarship students getting a "free pass" whilst most of the inner circle had parents who'd worked hard to achieve their wealth. The thought of Bella ever seeing where I came from filled me with shame. At night, I'd pour out my feelings of inadequacy, writing my diary by torchlight whilst remaining cautious with the precise details.

Things hurt more if they are properly acknowledged.

I yawn; it's 3:00 a.m. Outside, a full moon hovers.

I go to the bathroom, remove my make-up with soap and tepid water and brush my teeth with Nate's electric toothbrush (he has a battery-operated one he packs for work).

I climb in on his side of the bed and give in to sleep.

When I wake up, I experience precious fleeting seconds during which I believe that everything is as it was. I am in our bed, happy and content whilst Nate makes breakfast or is out for his jog. But, as always, crushing reality hits and the floating, intangible happiness bursts.

I look at my phone; it is midday. I make a coffee and check inside the freezer. The muffins remain untouched, so I pull them a little further forward.

My phone rings. An estate agent.

"Fantastic news, Miss Price," says the young male voice. "We've already had an offer for almost the asking price. No chain, they're in rented accommodation."

This will shortly provide me with more cash than I have ever had access to in my life. Amelia's guilt money. This means I can choose where I live; I no longer have to remain exiled in Reading. I look up properties in Richmond, but they are extortionate. All I can realistically afford is a small flat. I bookmark several potential ones.

I switch to Facebook. Amy is quiet. A half-Italian friend from my long-ago film extra days, Michele Bianchi, has landed a small role in a TV drama as a vet's assistant. I type *Congratulations!* No one ever called him by his first name alone—he was always known as Michele Bianchi. We used to have lunch together, watching the proper actors at work. If I had put my mind to it, I'd have liked to train as an actress. I liked the thought of leading a dual life; one as myself, one as a fictional character. But, having left school at the earliest opportunity, I ended up drifting from one job to another: florist, silver service waitress, admin assistant, sales rep, to recall a few. Ditto with my living arrangements. I'd rented a series of rooms, but I always returned to Dorset after a few months because I hated living with strangers. Come to think of it, my life has followed a similar pattern with men and friendships too. Whenever I get to know people, they generally disappoint me. But I have faith in Nate. With him, it feels *right*. There's no other way to describe it.

I scroll through his Facebook page; he has been to the gym in Boston.

Bella has tweeted that she is going to try out a hot yoga class this morning.

I poke around, as usual. It never does any harm, and even when I lived here there were always things that were useful to copy or keep hold of. Because you never know in life, you just never know. There's nothing that stands out as new or unusual, so I wash and dry my cup, replacing it on the mug tree, then triple-check that everything is in order. I stare at the fridge door; there are patches of smoothness among the few photos and leaflets. It used to be crammed with brightness. Nate bought me fridge magnets or mugs from each new country he visited. Proper tourist souvenirs because he knew I loved things like that—to me they aren't tacky. He said he did it so that I would 'know I think of you whilst I'm away'. I've kept them all packed; I won't use them again until I can put them back here in their original home.

I take one last look around my former and future home, then force myself to leave, taking the train back to the shoe-box. Once there, I dial the number of Bella's hairdresser to make an appointment. Bella still lives in Bournemouth, near her family home, and it's not that far away. I settle down on the sofa and study for my driving theory test. Nate is not going to recognize the confident, independent future wife he let slip through his fingers.

He won't stand a chance.

I rise early for a short return trip to Frankfurt.

Once back, I change in the airport toilets, hand my uniform into the dry-cleaners, and catch a coach to Bournemouth.

"What can I do for you today?" asks Bella's favourite stylist, the smiley Natasha.

I pause. I was going to go blonde, like Bella, but come to think of it, Amy is so confident with her auburn hair. She portrays the right mix of confidence, yet is still disciplined enough when required. Maybe I could learn something by imitating her.

"I'd like to experiment," I say. "I'm thinking of doing something a bit more drastic..."

Over coffee, I point to the colour chart and select the shade closest to Amy's, then relax and flick through a magazine. Whilst Natasha styles and cuts my hair—"Just a trim," I insist (I don't want *exactly* the same style as Amy)—I chat away about some of the more difficult passengers I encounter, trying to get her to open up about her trickier clients. I'm sure Bella must be one. I simply can't picture her treating anyone with respect. Natasha, however, doesn't bite. I leave a big tip to ensure that she is chattier next time. I stroll to the station with the coastal wind blowing my hair, surprising me each time I catch sight of auburn strands.

As I approach the platform, my eyes catch sight of a name on the departures list. It is the name of the village where my boarding school was located. There is no reason for me to travel there but I feel an impulse to return, even though the school is now a care home. Before I can talk myself out of it, I buy a ticket and board the next train. However, I've made an error by not checking the timings as it takes over an hour to be transported into deepest Dorset. It is a half-mile walk from the station to the driveway entrance. A shiny gold sign reveals its new name, beneath which it states that: *We care.* I hope that they *care* more about old people than they did about teenagers. I continue past, wandering along the narrow village pavement—a long-ago, familiar route.

The village newsagent remains. During afternoon break,

between 4:00 and 4:25, we were allowed to brave the three-minute walk and stock up on junk food. I push open the door. I can't remember the staff, so I've no idea if the man behind the old-fashioned till used to serve me, but I suspect he did.

"I see the school has changed hands?" I say, pretending to browse the magazine shelf.

He nods.

"I used to come in here as a teenager."

"Did you? There were so many of you."

He doesn't mention the village boys who used to stand on the street opposite, laughing at us. We were always instructed to ignore them, but I didn't blame them. Any breach of uniform regulations was an immediate fortnight's curfew, so if we weren't in summer straw boaters, we were in winter cloaks—not coats, like normal students—marking us out as figures of fun, as though we were teenagers from a strict religious cult or another era.

I select two bridal magazines. Whilst handing over payment, I spot brown paper bags. I used to fill mine with as many treats as possible; a blatant attempt to bribe others into spending time with me. We exchange goodbyes and I leave in the direction of the care home. I have no idea what to expect, but now that I am here, it can't do any harm.

As I approach the Victorian building, I can immediately see that the reception area is in the same location, although the main entrance is wider. Double doors open outwards instead of the old wooden white door that creaked. A metal wheelchair ramp rests at the side. Leaves spin, trapped in mini whirlpools. The cars are new; gone is the headmistress' old Rover and the drama teacher's VW Polo. From where I'm standing, I used to be able to see a black door to my left. Instead, in its place is a brick wall. During morning break, the old black door would open and the prefects would hand out any parcels or post from home: birthday cards, valentines, or postcards and letters from older relatives, especially those who hadn't yet embraced email.

I take a deep breath now and step inside my old school. The space is totally different, but the institutional smell remains. It is a shock, I expect to see *her* or to hear her distinctive footsteps. Rooted to the spot, I remember something—Bella telling me that I couldn't sit next to her at the dinner table one evening because she'd saved the space for Stephanie. It took humiliating minutes to find a spare seat in the crowded dining hall. I add it to my mental list of slights.

I concentrate on the present-day surroundings. Stained-glass windows remain embedded in the high walls, and the original large open fireplace is still in situ. But nailed to the wall above is a shiny wooden plaque. My eyes skim the Latin, resting on the English translation: *Fortune favours the bold.* Whilst trying to figure out the motto's relevance in an old people's home, my thoughts are interrupted.

"Can I help you?" A female voice.

I swing round and smile at a receptionist who is dressed in a fussy, peacock-blue blouse. Her reading glasses are attached to a string around her neck. She looks like she *cares*.

"I'm sorry," I say. "I used to come to school here. It's strange being back."

"When was that, then?"

"I left about ten years ago. I wonder…can I take a look around?"

"I don't think so, I'm afraid. Not without prior arrangement. And if you don't have any relatives, then I'm sorry, but no."

"What about the grounds, then? Does the stream still run along the bottom?"

"Yes, it does, but I'll have to check if you can go there," she says, picking up the desk phone. "But I don't see why not."

The stream is shallow. In my memories, it was deeper. Although the grassy banks are naturally overgrown, it is still accessible via the old pathway. I wonder if anyone comes here now. It's not as if the residents need to sneak down for a sly cigarette or anything else clandestine.

This used to be my hiding place. I would take off my shoes and paddle in my bare feet.

They thought I'd instinctively shy away from water after Will. But instead, I found it comforting.

Weeping willows still sweep the water's edge as a chilly breeze ripples the surface. I sit down on the uneven stones, then I turn back and glance at the main building.

I last sat here on the night of our school leavers summer ball.

Ten years ago.

Fifth- and sixth-formers from other schools—boys too— were invited, coached in from around the county. Rumours swiftly spread that the fruit punch was spiked by sixth-formers who'd shared their alcohol allowance. I sipped mine, even though it tasted like cough medicine, but in the back of my mind I didn't want to end up behaving stupidly, like my mother, all giggly and crass. I wore a red dress bought with some money Babs had sent me. But, although I looked different on the outside, inside I was still me. I grew bored of feeling insignificant, sitting on a hall chair at the side, next to Claire, so I slunk away from the main building when the supervising teachers weren't paying attention and walked across the sloping lawn and down to the hidden spot. My throat burned a little and I felt hot. I took off my heels and dipped my feet in the water. The darker grey of approaching night thickened as the temperature dropped slightly. I felt almost happy; soon I'd be free of the place I loathed. A soft breeze brushed my limbs and I felt anonymous, safe and cocooned. I sat down near the edge of the stream, hugging my arms around my knees.

As the light faded further, I had intended to slip back to

my dorm and make myself small beneath my duvet, but sliding pebbles and footsteps alerted me to someone else. I stood
up quickly, ready to defend myself, but to my astonishment I
could just about make out that it was a sixth-form boy, one of
the well-known "cool" ones who'd been part of the group of
boys who'd clustered around Bella, Stephanie and their gang.

Alone.

I briefly wondered if he'd followed me, but his eyes wore a
faraway look and he appeared puzzled at seeing someone else.
He'd removed his black tie and two of his shirt buttons were
undone. He clutched a glass with his right hand. I sat back
down and he joined me, placing his drink on the ground and
twisting it in the soil slightly to create a flat-enough surface.

"Hi," he said, as he lit a cigarette, the flame of a match
lighting up his face as he did so. He pulled off his shoes and
socks with his free hand and wriggled his toes in the water.

"It's cold!"

I laughed.

The amber tip of his cigarette glowed. He offered it to me.

I didn't want to say no, so I took it but only inhaled as
gently as I could. I felt my head go light. I struggled for something to say, something that would make him laugh or want
to stay here, with me, for slight hope had begun to take hold.
Maybe, this evening would turn into something that could
change everything.

"Have you been to many balls or parties?" I blurted out,
inwardly cursing the clumsy, naive-sounding words.

"Three, this season."

I couldn't think how to answer, even though he made me
feel like I was worth talking to; that I wasn't ugly. Or too
overweight. My stomach felt hollow. I wished I had brought
my drink down here with me.

"Can I have a sip?" I asked, pointing at his half-full glass.

"Of course." He lifted it up and held the edge of the glass against my lips.

I took a small sip, then another, bigger one. It tasted better than it had earlier. I shook my head when he offered me another sip. "What about you?"

"I've had enough. Why are you out here alone?"

I hesitated. "I felt like taking a break. Being with the same people day in, day out, it gets a bit much."

He laughed. "Tell me about it. At least your school is large enough to hide in places like these. And there are loads more pupils than at mine."

He crushed out his cigarette on the ground and I was surprised at how much light such a little glow had offered as I became acutely aware of the swiftness of the accelerating darkness. Neither of us spoke. I could hear the slight trickle of the water and, much further away, the thud of blaring music but I couldn't quite make out the track. It struck me how surreal the moment was, like being temporarily removed from my real life.

I don't know who leaned forward first, but our lips touched and we kissed. He tasted of alcohol and cigarettes.

"You smell really nice," he said as we broke away.

It must have been hairspray because I couldn't afford perfume and I hadn't risked stealing any of Bella's. I leaned forward and took a tiny sip from his glass before replacing it. We kissed again. And then lay down. I felt the soil, stones and moss beneath my back and only momentarily cared about my dress. But then he kissed me harder and I forgot about everything. Nothing else mattered. Time began here. I remember thinking that this was *it*. He was my ticket to my real life and it was from today onwards that my life would begin afresh. Everything would be all right again.

I gave in to my feelings. I felt protected. It felt right.

When it was over, the whole moment seemed to dim, like a disintegrating shadow in a dream.

"Have you got any cigarettes?" he asked. "That was my last one."

"No," I replied, but I desperately wished that I had.

Before we could say much to each other, I heard him pull up his trousers and do up his belt. He put on his shoes. I struggled to gather myself together, my legs felt weak.

"You coming back?" he said.

"Yeah. In a bit." It sounded cooler than *Please, don't go.*

"OK. See you."

I stood up and tried to hug him. He gave me a quick squeeze and a peck on the lips. I wanted to tell him that I loved him, but I sensed it would be too soon. So, I let him go. I heard his footsteps negotiating the slope. Away from me. I felt around for his drink, but the glass had tipped over and was empty. I tried to make sense of everything, wondering whether I was an adult now, even though I was still fifteen, every now and then gently placing my fingers on my lips where he'd planted his final kiss. I focused on the thud of the music, finally able to make out a track—Will Smith's "Switch."

When cold and discomfort had taken hold, I slunk back to the dorm area and cleaned myself up. Blood, semen, mud. I forced myself to rejoin the party. He was back in there too, and I naively assumed he'd approach me, that he'd announce we were boyfriend and girlfriend, and that I'd instantly be elevated in social popularity, even if only temporarily. But he appeared to be sharing a joke with Bella. She laughed in response to something he'd said. Shortly after, he had his arm around Stephanie.

For the short remainder of the evening I watched from the side, forced to half-listen to Claire, taking pretend trips to the toilet, hoping that he would come over. I hated myself for not having the guts to go over and join in, just like I had every right to. I blamed Bella for my lack of confidence. I still blame Bella for that. Had she been a nicer person, a friend, I'd have naturally fitted into their social gathering. But I was scared of her. Scared that she'd make me look stupid in front of him.

Twice, I thought he looked over. But each time it was too fleeting for me to catch his eye. I looked at my watch, again and again; torturing myself, because at 11:45, the coaches were due to leave. By 11:00, I was starting to feel desperate. I downgraded my hopes to a brief promise that he'd call or email. By 11:15, I'd persuaded myself that he was embarrassed. But there were no furtive glances, no sense that anything had happened at all. His eyes never caught mine. I began to suspect that I'd imagined it—but I couldn't have—and anger and hatred lodged inside me, along with bitter determination.

I vowed to myself that no one would ever treat me like that again. Never again would I allow myself to be discarded.

Yet I wasn't quite ready to give up all hope. For the remaining few weeks of that term, I'd check my mail each time I went to the library. Or wait in view of the black door for a romantic card or small gift—something, anything—during every break. Each time the phone near the common room rang in the evening, I'd wish that it was for me. Because, intermingled with all the longing and hope, it would also have made a difference; made another horrible result of the evening more bearable. Even nowadays, I flinch when I'm caught off guard and hear certain words, the ones I was called when my mistake became common knowledge.

I stand up, feeling a renewed sense of optimism and belief in myself. It was good to come back here, to remind myself of my decade-long promise, which is that I deserve to be treated with respect by others.

Especially men.

Back on the train I naturally have plenty of time to think things through:

Nate had no right to dump me in Reading as though I was worthless.

He definitely led me to believe that we had a future, that he loved me as much as I loved him.

I should've got pregnant. I allowed myself the luxury of a honeymoon period, and it has cost me dear, but I'm not giving up.

I'll win him back and go to great, careful lengths to ensure that our lives are soon interlocked by unbreakable bonds.

I've read in so many self-help books that nothing in the past can be undone, that only the future holds hope for change. So, in between my forthcoming trips to Bahrain, Washington, Lusaka and Barbados, I need to fill my time with purely positive steps, such as squeezing in hours of driving lessons at any opportunity. And flat-hunting. I generally feel much better when I have a proper focus.

I flick through the magazines I bought in the village shop. One of the models looks similar to Bella. I will cut her picture out at home and add it to my pinboard collection, which is a work of art, a maze of hundreds of pictures of Bella and Nate: faces, arms, legs, outfits, bodies.

For better, for worse. For richer, for poorer. In sickness and in health. Until death do us part.

Instead of my mantras, I repeat these words over in my head, fantasizing about my future with Nate to keep me occupied on the journey back to my temporary life.

CHAPTER SIX

My flight to Barbados is delayed after boarding. Two hours, so far. Initially I'm patient with the complaints, but before long I struggle to contain my frustration. There's a problem with one of the cargo doors. Engineers are trying to fix it. End of. I—*politely*—explain that there'd be no point in taking off regardless, allowing passengers' precious bags to fall out mid-air and rain down on to London. Dealing with hotel guests was easier. They weren't trapped in their rooms, stuck in the hotel with nothing to do but demand my endless attention.

"Excuse me?"

I swing round, ready to bat away a request, but realize that the voice belongs to a girl, no older than nine or ten. The adjacent seat is empty.

I crouch down to her level. "Yes?"

"Is the plane going to be OK? I'm travelling by myself."

"Yes, it's going to be fine. There's a minor problem with a door that's jammed, which is easily fixed. Why are you on your own?"

"I'm going to visit my mum. I live with my gran, because my mum has a new boyfriend. But now she says I can go and have a holiday with her."

A familiar wave of rage hits me so savagely, I nearly lose my balance. I steady myself on an armrest and stand up.

"I tell you what, I'm not allowed to take you into the cockpit during the flight, but after landing, whilst everyone is disembarking, I'll take you up there, if you like?" She nods.

"And during the flight, if you feel afraid, you come and talk to me." I point to my name badge. "Ask for Juliette."

"OK." She turns and looks out the window. "Thank you."

I seek out the crew member responsible for looking after the girl's welfare and inform her I'll take over.

Finally, we push back from the stand. A large group of holidaymakers near the front start clapping. I nearly join in.

Barbados.

Hot. Sunny. Sandy. Relaxed.

According to the hotel reception staff, this time of year—late April—is a great time to visit. There are nine hours of sunshine a day, and the hurricane season is still safely far off. I join everyone by the pool on the first morning and lie on a sunlounger, sipping a weak margarita. A rare sense of calm descends upon me. I close my eyes and allow the warmth to seep into my bones.

Nate is in Shanghai. Wondering what he's up to, I sit up, take out my phone and head for a shady spot beneath a nearby tree.

I scroll.

I keep expecting Nate to change his passwords. I'll be pissed off when he does. But, as yet, I am free to keep tabs on him to my heart's content. I don't feel bad. All's fair in love and war. Besides, he hadn't been thinking about my feelings when he asked me to move out.

★ ★ ★

I'd cooked him a special curry that night and it was then—seven months ago—that I started to have moments where I felt as though I was physically falling. At one point, I remember gripping the edge of the kitchen counter, as though it would save me. The strength of my buried feelings rushed to the forefront of my consciousness and threatened to overwhelm me. One thing shone through the jumble in my mind: I had made a misjudgement. I had thought that our future was a foregone conclusion, that we were merely stepping the stones in the correct order—live-in lovers, proposal, engagement, wedding and so forth.

I'd been in the kitchen when I heard the front door shut. I rushed to greet him, but he didn't reciprocate my hug.

"It's not that I don't have feelings for you, it's that I don't think I can give you what you need from a relationship right now. I need some space," he said, after announcing that we were over.

I locked eyes with him. "You're going to have to do a lot better than 'it's not you, it's me...'"

"Well, let's face it—even *you* must agree that it was all rather rushed. You... I...should've taken things at a slower pace."

I tried to breathe. To think. I could feel the evening I had planned slipping away to nothingness, and my brain hadn't quite grasped it yet. I needed to pull it back together, make it all right. Behind him, I surveyed the open-plan dining area. All the feminine touches were mine. The shelves were filled with tasteful ornaments and vases. Pictures, drinks coasters, cutlery, crockery, wine glasses, a fruit bowl. *Things.* The scatter cushions in the living room. And a rug, rich with autumn colours. *I'd* turned this place into a home.

I turned my back on him and carefully put down the wooden spoon with which I'd been stirring—I'd spent all afternoon following the recipe to the *letter*, for God's sake—

and untied my apron in order to reveal my new, short, clingy dress. Outwardly calm, inside gut-churningly sick, I turned to face him.

"You're tired and jet-lagged. Exhausted even, poor you. Zigzagging between east and west isn't healthy. I'll pour you a drink whilst we talk and work things out together." Even I was surprised at my generosity of spirit, given the circumstances.

"I meant what I said." Nate raised his voice several notches and made no attempt to accept the bottle of perfectly chilled beer I was trying to hand him. "Lily, Elizabeth…it's not working. For me. This is all too intense. I want, no, I really need… space." He raked his hands through his hair, his eyes staring intently as though he genuinely thought I was going to acquiesce.

"Is it another woman?"

"No. No, there's no one else. I promise you that."

I turned away again, not trusting myself to speak, and poured the beer into his curry. The sound of the waterfall was so momentarily satisfying. I added several more chopped chillies, including two whole Scotch bonnets. I stirred furiously.

My thoughts galloped.

I could refuse to move out. No way—no way!—was I going back to my mother's. Richmond had become my home.

Ribbons of anxiety knotted together, kneading my insides and evoking the familiar feeling of injustice. It wasn't fair, I'd been the perfect girlfriend. He couldn't do this to me. My dreams were slipping out of reach and I wanted to claw them back. However, in the midst of all this was a moment of stark clarity. If this did have something to do with another woman, if Nate was lying, then she'd better be afraid, very afraid.

Because I knew that if I found out that someone else was the cause of my broken dreams, I'd have no qualms about breaking theirs.

★ ★ ★

Anger is no use at present, not whilst I'm here, in paradise.

The sun drops. Billy Ocean's "Caribbean Queen" blares from the loudspeakers attached to the side of the thatched bar hut. Cocktails are mixed, drinks are flowing. I inhale the smell of the sea and suncream.

Laughter. Happiness. Fun.

This is what I wanted to do with Nate.

Travel.

I need a moment alone, so I return to the sunlounger, put my phone in my bag and remove my sunglasses. I dive into the warm pool, then I float like a starfish. Water muffles sound. I love the sense of isolation and numbness, the sense of being alone and cut off from a distorted world.

One of the few good things to come out of my years at boarding school was that I was forced to learn to swim.

Three weeks after Nate and I split up, I bumped into a couple we'd chatted to in the pub once or twice.

They appeared surprised when I broke the news of Nate's decision.

"But you seemed so happy," said the woman. "You were planning a holiday, weren't you?"

"Yes. To Bali."

I'd spent hours online, choosing the perfect place. Couples massages, romantic walks, secluded beaches. Yoga and meditation. It would have been an ideal opportunity for Nate to explore the "meaning of life" that he now appears to be searching for. His fear-of-commitment wobble would have been done and dusted in a fortnight.

"I'm so sorry," she said. "He must be mad to let you go. We had such a laugh with you two. I thought he adored you."

I shrugged. "I have to respect his feelings. There's nothing else I can do."

But it felt reassuring to know that I wasn't the only one who had been blind.

And I wasn't completely blind, not really, because he didn't act like he'd totally fallen out of love with me. We'd slept together once more before I'd moved out.

I emerge from the pool, feeling refreshed. I comb my hair and settle down to dry off before I go and change for dinner.

I pick up my phone and post several pictures of the pool area on my Juliette Facebook page.

I check Nate's freshly published roster. He and I are due into New York at the same time next month, thankfully on different flights. Nonetheless, I will have to remain on guard.

Bella is quiet at the moment, which makes me wonder what she's up to. She rarely takes a break from self-promotion.

Amy is having a ball in Nairobi; her whole crew have gone on safari for two days.

On the homeward-bound flight the following day, during take-off and the initial climb, I stare out at the brilliant blue above the carpet of clouds. I crave Nate. Not too long now until I can show him how well I have stuck to our bargain and given him space.

Senior crew report to your stations.

The announcement blares over the public address system, shattering my fantasies. It is the emergency alert call to warn the rest of us to be prepared for something out of the ordinary. I'm not in the mood to a) die today, or b) evacuate a load of disobedient, panicked passengers down the evacuation slides. I look out into the cabin. Passengers have sensed something is wrong and have actually removed their headsets. Some are looking expectantly in my direction. My colleague at the opposite door looks at me. Her face is white. The interphone rings, emergency colours flashing on the panel above. It is the in-flight supervisor.

"We have a suspected engine fire on the right-hand side and are returning to Bridgetown. The captain has indicated that this may take up to thirty minutes whilst we dump fuel. Although that engine has been shut down as a precaution, due to another potential complication, we are to prepare passengers for a possible land evacuation. Any questions?" Silence.

"Right, starting from Door One, repeat back your instructions…"

As I slide my interphone back into its slot, Anya, my fellow Door Four colleague, starts crying and shaking in the galley.

"I've only just come back from maternity leave," she sobs. "I don't want to die."

"Well, don't, then. Pull yourself together. You've been trained in what to do. Mentally get a grip, then get out there and do your job. Time will pass more quickly. Be ready to open your door when we land and, if needs be, save yourself. Don't worry about anyone else." A morbid thought suddenly flashes through my mind—I too could get injured—and so I add, "Unless it's me who needs help."

She looks at me, wipes her eyes and trots off to her allocated position in the passenger cabin. We both stand like traffic policemen as the pre-recorded emergency procedure announcement booms over the public address, before launching into our passenger preparation drills and briefings. I force myself to concentrate on my job, so that I don't let myself be sucked into any kind of panic. I know what to do and I have the advantage of sitting near a door. I am pleasantly surprised that, on the whole, people are generally calm and willing to listen for once. We practise adopting the brace position—seat belts tight, passengers bent over, hands over their heads—and everyone points to their nearest exit. All the endless, repetitive drills and practice seem to have come into use. I secure the cabin by putting away bags and loose items. I double-check all the catches on the galley canisters and trolleys.

Cabin crew. Seats for landing.

I strap myself in tight. Anya's lips are moving as though she is praying.

I wish Nate was in the cockpit. He's too selfish to die. The plane rocks from side to side. A wind must have picked up. It reminds me of a local fairground ride that my mother and one of her boyfriends took me to one evening. I loved the exhilaration, the giddiness of the roller coaster and wanted to go back, but we never did.

We break through the clouds. The ground is in sight. The announcement comes from the flight crew: *One thousand feet.*

Navy sea appears in the distance, as do houses with aqua-coloured pools among patchworks of greeny-brown land.

The whining of the engines heightens.

In the cabin, I can see some passengers holding hands.

A child cries.

There is silence from the galley apart from the rattle of the coffee pots in their metal holders.

One hundred feet.

"Brace, brace," I yell, adopting the forward-facing brace position myself, my hands protecting my head, for what it's worth.

"Brace, brace," yells Anya, with a force I didn't think she'd have in her.

The harness is taut against my torso. The ground is coming up to meet us as I catch sight of the runway and we whack on to the tarmac with a deafening roar. The plane begins to reduce speed. The pressure of my harness begins to ease as we slow down a little more. The aircraft makes a sharp turn before coming to an abrupt stop.

We are safe. Drama over.

Until…the shrieking of the evacuation alarms shatters the calm. Red emergency lights flash on all panels.

Smoke. I smell smoke.

I unharness my straps and pull open the heavy door, standing back into a gap so that I am not pushed out in the stampede. A grey slide unfurls for several seconds as it inflates. Hot outside air blasts me; a sharp contrast to the air conditioning.

"Come this way and jump," I shout. "Keep moving."

On autopilot, I push a man who hesitates a fraction too long. He shouts all the way down. In hardly any time at all, the passenger cabin is empty.

There is no sign of fire and I can no longer smell smoke; however, I am not going to hang around any longer. I've done my job. I grab my bags. I know I'm not supposed to, but if we're going to be stuck here for a while, I'm not leaving my stuff to be burned or lost. I'm glad I kept my flat cabin shoes on; I bet that tarmac is scorching. As I slide down, my polyester skirt gives my thighs friction burns.

It takes forty-eight hours to complete endless paperwork, be interviewed, give statements and refuse counselling. Every time I think my role in the non-drama is over, I'm summoned from the pool by someone with a clipboard or a tablet and questioned about something I've already answered.

I cheer myself up by reminding myself that, whilst I am here—working on my tan and spying on my enemy and my beloved—I am earning huge amounts in overtime.

We position back to Heathrow two days later, meaning that we travel as passengers, not operating crew. I watch two of the latest films—a comedy and a horror.

Upon landing, I feel a sense of restlessness. The first May bank holiday is approaching and I will be trapped at home because I have four days of standby duties. This means that I can be given just two hours' notice if they need crew cover due to illness or flight disruptions. Babs has gone away to the Lake District with some tennis friends. I don't want to go back to my claustrophobic place. Nate is back home, so I can't stay there. But... I have Amy's key.

I keep tabs on her rosters so I know that she's still in Kenya and that Hannah has gone to New Zealand for three weeks to visit family. I could go to their flat. If I water a house plant or two, then it won't be so bad. I'd be doing something useful. Mind you, I'm not sure if they have any plants.

Instead of making my way to the bus station, I head for the tube. I'm feeling pleased with myself, intermingled with the constant sickness that comes with jet lag. I drag my suitcase and wheelie bag towards the tube. They bump over the cracks in the pavement.

Alighting at Amy's station, warm sun beats down on me as I walk to hers. Summer is not far away. I feel optimistic that the perfect time is imminent for me to break the news to Nate that I'm once again a presence in his life.

CHAPTER SEVEN

My phone is ringing. At first I don't realize because I recently changed the ringtone so that my heart doesn't jolt in the vain hope that it's Nate every time I hear it. It cuts off to voice-mail. It rings again. I don't recognize the local number. I am in Amy's bed. It is briefly disorientating. Pale sun forces its way around the rectangle of the blind.

I answer. "Hello?"

"Elizabeth?" says a jolly voice.

"Who is this, please?"

It's hard work at the best of times, remembering who people are and what my relationship is to them. I need coffee. I step out of bed, still clutching the phone, and make my way to the kitchen.

"I'm Lorraine," the voice continues. "Your new work team manager. We'd like to invite you in for a chat about your Barbados trip."

"Hi, Lorraine. I use my middle name for work, Juliette.

It's in the system. I've told every department there is, but still my name comes up as Elizabeth. Please can you change it? It's very confusing." I flick the switch on the kettle.

"I'm afraid that's a matter for central admin. I'll give you their email address."

"Don't worry, thanks. I've emailed them at least ten times. As for a chat, that sounds great, but I'm afraid I don't think that I can help any more than I already have. Sorry about that."

I will her to go away. I have so many things to mull over. I need to seriously consider and narrow down the ideal time to approach Nate. There is Amy's friendship to maintain, my social media accounts to keep updated and Babs wants me to visit soon. On top of all that, there are driving lessons and flat-hunting to shoehorn into the schedule. My life is really quite full and exhausting, and I now fully sympathize with the whole work-life balance debates I've heard discussed on radio shows. I pour water on to the coffee granules. I'm not a fan of instant, but needs must.

"Elizabeth? Sorry, I mean Juliette? We must insist that you come in for a meeting at your earliest convenience. Four o'clock today or eleven tomorrow morning? Your time will be paid and it will be worth your while." She lowers her voice. "I don't want to give too much away on the phone, but I promise, you will be delighted."

I doubt it, but the sooner I get work off my back, the sooner I can get back to my real life.

"I'll be in at four today," I hear myself agree.

I take my coffee back to Amy's room and lie on her bed. The outside sounds are unfamiliar. The bin lorry comes on a different day to mine. It's disorientating. I feel exhausted and I shut my eyes. It's not just the job, it's everything. I feel like an actress onstage, waiting until I can finish my scenes. It has crossed my mind, from time to time, to give up, to move on.

★ ★ ★

But I don't know how to. Everything is different when it happens to you. How do I simply forget? Action feels like the only way forward. Besides, I genuinely love Nate. And what I want isn't too awful: a few friends, a job for the time being. Then a proper, grown-up, adult life, finished off with a comfortable old age, preferably not getting abused in an old people's home that smells like school dinners. It's not asking for much.

I'm owed that.

I get up, shower and change. I'll have to leave my suitcase on the luggage racks at the Report Centre before heading off to my mystery meeting, because I can't leave it here. A sudden thought flashes into my mind: maybe they want to put me forward for a special services flight, such as taking the Prime Minister to a peace summit, or a deeply private celebrity to an exclusive island. My mood lifts.

Before I leave, I can't help but tidy out the airing cupboard, folding the towels neatly and putting them in colour order. That's the good thing about flatmates, they'll each think the other did it, even though it's me they should thank. I give in to the temptation to explore the flat, for no other reason than to gain a deeper sense of *Amy* and what makes her tick. She is so at ease in her own skin, so self-assured. I want to be more like that and not wear my heart on my sleeve.

Bedrooms are always the places I find secrets, and Amy's is no exception. Burglars must love the general public's lack of imagination. The third drawer inside her wardrobe contains a small collection of sex toys, skimpy outfits and several wigs, but it's the contents of Amy's bedside drawer that shock me. Antidepressants. Who'd have thought? I feel slightly betrayed by the discovery. Come to think of it, it's not *normal* to be happy all the time. Maybe I should try some? I push six out of the foil, wrap them in a tissue and place the bundle in my bag.

In the living room I put on a CD quietly, and then another. Everything reminds me of Nate. Every lyric could have been written about us and our love, as though the artists have experienced exactly the same amount of pain that I'm enduring. What a mess people make of their lives. So much wasted, pointless time spent apart, when things could all be so different. I select a final song, singing along with the chorus. I swallow two of Amy's pills before I make myself leave. Public transport is becoming tiresome; I resolve to increase my number of driving lessons. I've read that it takes the average person forty-five hours of instruction and twenty-two hours of practice to pass a test. I intend to be a lot quicker than that.

At the Report Centre I am shown past a series of rooms that I've never noticed before, until we reach the end one. Three people sit along a table facing me. Two men and one woman, Lorraine. Are three people good or bad? Images of the non-crash site are blown up on to a large screen. The plane looks like a white insect with grey legs.

"Please, sit down." Lorraine smiles. "Thank you so much for coming. We invited you here today as we want to thank you in person. We have received numerous messages of praise from the passengers you assisted during the recent incident. Please, let us all take a moment whilst I read out a sample of the words that have been used to describe you. *Calm. Professional. Cool. Level-headed. Reassuring. Brave. A credit to your airline. Capable. A heroine.*" She stops.

Everyone stares at me.

"Wow," I say, feeling a sense of rising dread.

"So, as well as a Going Above and Beyond Award, we would also like you to become our safety ambassador. This is a brand-new, vitally important role and one which will require you to be highly visible among the airline community. This is an amazing achievement for someone who has been flying for only a short while. So, well done. You will receive many benefits as a result and..."

I can't bear to listen. I want to put my hands over my ears. What a disaster. Any good PR stories are ceaselessly promoted by the in-house magazine. Grinning pictures of favoured crew, not a hair out of place, adorn the cover. *Shit.* The man on the far right picks up a giant camera with a long lens. I cover my face with my hand.

"Stop! Please. This is all very kind and extremely flatter-ing, but you do all know that I didn't land the plane, don't you? There hasn't been some kind of mix-up? I did my job, which I have been more than adequately trained to do by the company. And as much as I cannot think of anything nicer than being a safety ambassador, I must insist that I am not the woman for the job. There are many crew who are more safety-conscious than me—"

I stop because I'm feeling more detached and spaced out than usual. I wonder if it's anything to do with Amy's pills?

Lorraine smiles. "Stop right there, Juliette. Perhaps we've overwhelmed you. Why don't you go home and sleep on it? I'll call you tomorrow."

Bloody hell. Everything is conspiring to eat up my valu-able time and energy, right at the moment when I need to be putting all my efforts into more important things, such as finalizing my reunion with Nate.

On my way home, I allow myself a little fantasy. It *could* work. When we get back together, he could pose with me, like a celebrity couple in *Hello!* magazine.

Nathan and Elizabeth at their Richmond apartment. Nathan and Elizabeth in first class.

No, I'm not sure...

It feels just a little too soon to blow my cover, and Nate can't fail to recognize me if I am plastered all round the

Report Centre, no matter what my name or hair colour. He wanted *space*. If I reappear in his life too soon, there's a risk he'll smell the proverbial rat. I'll call Lorraine tomorrow and invent a phobia or two. Fear of public speaking, that type of thing. I'll remind her how Anya held the hand of an old lady as they slid down the evacuation chute together. They'll love that.

At home, I work on my POA. I book in for some extra, intensive driving lessons and start arranging some flat viewings.

Before I know it, it is midnight. I force myself to bed. I need energy for the morning, but I can't sleep because I've thought of something I forgot to ask.

I call Lorraine as soon as she is in the office.

"*If* I agree to become a safety ambassador, when will it come into place?"

"We're planning on launching the new role in August or September, I don't have an exact date yet, but you'd probably be rostered a training course by late summer."

"In that case, I'd love to accept your offer, thank you."

Arriving at Bournemouth train station, I walk to Bella's gym. I've made an appointment to see the manager, Stephanie Quentin.

I give my name to a receptionist and am directed to a sofa, where I wait, watching the entrance just in case Bella comes in. Anonymous people push through the turnstiles clutching gym bags, water bottles or tennis racquets.

"Elizabeth?"

I stand up as Stephanie, Bella's second in command, comes into focus walking towards me. Her gait is so familiar.

"Stephanie? What a surprise. I never expected to see you working in a gym. Not that there's anything wrong with it," I quickly add—which is quite magnanimous of me, given some of the insults she's thrown my way.

She smiles but her eyes give away that I've hit a nerve. I *was* surprised when I did further digging into Bella's world and Stephanie's name popped up as the manager of her gym. She was on a clear path to becoming a barrister like her mother.

"Long story," she says. "Do you want to come into the office?" She points to a room visible through the glass walls.

I follow her in and take a seat opposite her desk. There are several pictures of a boy who, at a rough guess, must be around eight years of age. *That* must be her long story.

"Would you like a tea or a coffee?" she says, handing me a questionnaire on a clipboard.

"A black coffee, please. I've already filled in a form online and I've explained that I'm undecided, as yet, whether to join or what type of membership will suit me best."

She pulls an apologetic face. "Yes, but we need you to fill this one in too. I'll be back in a moment, I'll just go and get your coffee." Stephanie leaves.

I breathe in. And out.

Aware that I'm on display through the glass, I glance around discreetly but there is nothing else of any interest. No photos of her school friends—not that it would be likely—but if there were, they'd definitely be of her, Bella, Lucy and Gemma. The main four.

Bella was allowed to take two friends with her on her family's annual winter half-term holiday to her aunt's in Whistler. Stephanie was always chosen, Lucy and Gemma had to alternate. I used to lie and pretend I was going skiing too "in France."

The form blurs in front of me. I can't remember the fake address I originally gave. Not that it really matters, I remind myself, because she no longer has any power.

The first term at school was bearable. I knew—and reluctantly accepted—my place. I so desperately wanted to be

Bella's real friend. I knew deep down that I'd never be allowed into her inner circle but that I'd settle just to be in the outer one.

The girls all came from the same background, they just *knew* the right things to say and do, just *knew* they all had the potential to do well with effortless ease. They skied, they spoke fluent French and they knew how to bake soufflés.

I tried to fit in—to say and do the right things—but the more I got it wrong, the worse it became. I was clumsy and tongue-tied around them. I'd lie in bed at night, pretending to be asleep, whilst listening to conversations about boys, make-up, fashion, music and teachers they liked or disliked, trying to think of ways to join in.

And, when that didn't work, I began to think of other options.

"Here's your coffee," Stephanie says, returning and placing a mug on her desk. "Right, let's get on…"

"How long have you worked here?" I ask, leaning forward and taking a slow sip.

"A few years. If you finish off that form, I'll run through a few things and then I'll get someone to show you around."

"Can't you? It would be nice to catch up."

"Well…"

"You *are* the manager," I say, smiling.

"It will have to be quick, I'm afraid. I have another appointment," she glances up at the clock on the wall, "soon."

"Thank you."

After I've completed and signed the forms, she leads me into the main gym area and I nod politely as she points out the latest equipment, indicates the exercise class studios and mentions personal training and induction sessions. I follow behind as we descend the stairs to view the pool. I could push her. It would take a violent shove, but if I did it properly she'd take quite a fall. I look up at the dark, rounded lens of the security camera.

"Are you in contact with Bella or any of the others?"

"Yes."

Her work heels clatter on the wooden staircase. My trainers are silent.

"How is Bella?"

She stops and looks round, as though trying to gauge my reaction. "Fine."

I shrug. "Just wondered. It was a long time ago."

"She's about to announce her engagement soon."

I grip the handrail. "Who to?"

"A wealth management adviser, Miles."

I've noticed him tagged in pictures at various events. He looks like a drip.

I take my phone out of my bag and glance down at the screen. "Damn. I have to go. I'll orientate myself if I join. Let's keep in touch."

"Yes." She smiles, turning round to walk back upstairs.

"Your mobile number?" I say, pausing outside her office.

"You can always get hold of me through reception," she says. "If you need to."

"How about Facebook?" I search. "Ah, yes, here you are. I've sent you a friend request."

I stand still. She has no choice but to take out her phone and accept me. Her hands shake slightly.

"Wonderful. A real pleasure, Stephanie. Super seeing you." I walk out and don't look back.

The journey home shoots by as I delve into her Facebook page.

Thanks to Stephanie, I am able to gain fresh insight into Bella's inner world. Another door of opportunity has opened itself up to me.

I love the internet; it is my friend.

CHAPTER EIGHT

I knew Nate would be home alone. He'd posted his intention to stay in and watch the latest series about a serial killer. Sure enough, his black Jaguar is parked in its usual spot. I pace up and down. We had a conversation once about what old or historical film roles we'd pick, given the choice. His was Russell Crowe's Maximus Decimus Meridius in *Gladiator*; mine was Gwyneth Paltrow's Helen in *Sliding Doors*.

"I'd definitely be the one who cut her hair short and dumped him," I'd said, basking in the confidence of love. "No way would I put up with not being treated properly."

I once heard someone say that you're always made to eat your own words; I sincerely hope that's not true. I don't want my beliefs twisted round into a self-fulfilling prophecy.

Nate still hasn't drawn the blinds, so I wait, just a little bit longer, hoping to catch even a brief glimpse. I haven't seen him in the flesh for over a week because I spent two days trapped inside the shoebox, on standby, before I got called out for a Kingston with the minimum two hours' notice. As the early grey of the unseasonably dull May evening thickens, my patience is rewarded. His silhouette hesitates and I feel sure that he's looking in my direction. I turn and walk slowly away, although my legs feel weak and the habitual hollowness begins to fill my chest.

Because Nate was born into privilege, it's not entirely his fault that he takes things for granted. He doesn't know what it's like to go without. Everything he wants, he gets. Just like Bella and others like her. Money gives them protection from the inconveniences of life. I try to give Nate the benefit of the doubt, I really try my best. But there are times, like now, when I could pummel him in frustration for wasting our time.

I stop and lean against the cold brick wall.

Inhale.

Exhale.

Patience is a virtue. Stick to the plan.

My shoulders relax.

I walk on.

Back home, I message Amy asking if she'd like to come over to Reading next week when our days off match. Our rosters have clashed recently and I haven't had a chance to see her for weeks. I have a feeling that we could have a fun night out. And possibly, through her, I could follow through with my plans to start widening my friendship net.

She messages back with a "yes."

I book an Asian fusion restaurant by the river Kennet for the following Wednesday.

Before Amy's arrival, I take great care to tidy my place, removing my pinboard, placing it safely away on top of the bedroom wardrobe. I also hide my shopping from my most recent trip: two voodoo dolls, one male and one female. As I fling open my door to welcome her in, she stares.

"Your hair?"

I'd grown so used to it, I'd forgotten. "Do you like it? I know it's a bit similar to yours."

"It's kind of OK...but we do look a bit like Tweedles Dee and Dum."

Shit. I've pissed off my only friend. And in hindsight, auburn could be a beacon rather than a disguise.

"It's a wash-in, rinse-out job. I was experimenting." I take her overnight bag from her and place it by the sofa. "Let's head straight out."

We order champagne, to celebrate our first three months of flying.

"It's like a dream come true," says Amy. "Every time I land somewhere different, every time I walk into a four- or five-star hotel, I just can't believe it's my life."

"We should request a trip. It's the only way we'll probably ever get to work together."

"Yeah, that sounds like a good idea." She pauses. "A strange thing happened whilst I was away," she says.

"I was going to ask you what it was like on safari. I've heard that it can be a bit *I'm a Celebrity* with all the snakes, creepycrawlies and some really weird restaurants that serve exotic wildlife."

"It felt safe enough. There were meat places that served crocodile. But anyway, no, it wasn't whilst I was in Nairobi —I meant, when I got home."

"Oh?"

"Yeah. Well, Hannah's still away but it was like...someone had been in our place. Things looked neater."

I laugh. "That's good, isn't it?"

"Yeah, maybe. But I can't quite put my finger on it. We definitely hadn't been burgled, because a burglar would've..."

"Burgled," I finish off.

We both laugh.

I pick at some squid but it is too chewy. I nibble olives coated in wasabi and ginger instead, dotting the stones neatly around the edge of my plate.

"It was a CD that really got to me. When I switched the player on, it was stuck on repeat. On a really cheesy track."

"It's your own fault for having equipment that's so last decade." I make a face and smile.

She reciprocates my smile. "Yeah, maybe."

"Never mind, these things always have a logical explanation in the end. Trust me, I know. How's Jack?"

"I'm not seeing so much of Jack now. It kind of fizzled out."

"Sorry about that." I hold back a smile. "What happened?"

"He hadn't taken down his online dating profile. It turns out he was keeping his options open. But I'm keeping busy. Some of my old school friends are having a reunion meal next week, which I'm really looking forward to."

"What date? Maybe I could come with you."

She shifts in her seat and mutters something vague about her not being the main organizer.

I take the hint, but I feel piqued.

Amy's eyes glaze over after her second glass of champagne. I'm not surprised. Her concealed pills contained a *do not mix with alcohol* warning. It's strange when you know something about someone else that they don't know that you know. It's like, if they stared into your eyes hard enough, they'd be able to tell.

I wonder about these sorts of things a lot.

"Let's go to a club," I suggest, to wake her up.

As we walk outside to our Uber, arms linked, laughing, I want to say out loud how useful it is to have a friend, but I stop myself. I said that to someone once and she gave me a weird look.

I hope Amy stays as she is and doesn't do anything to mess up our friendship.

★ ★ ★

As soon as Amy leaves the next day, I ring to book an appointment with Bella's hairdresser to change my colour to blonde. Unfortunately, she is on holiday.

I decide to get it done on my next work trip—a Miami—the day after tomorrow.

The flight to Miami takes nearly nine hours. Every cabin is crammed with holidaymakers, either with people joining cruise ships or those heading off to Disney World. I barely sit down, and we run out of juice, wine and children's activity packs.

Three hours in, I phone the captain to request that he contact the airline's medical advisers when a six-months-pregnant woman complains of severe stomach pains. I am summoned up to the cockpit to speak to them myself. I put on headphones and listen. The voice—a doctor in Arizona—asks endless questions and finally advises offering the woman indigestion tablets.

It works; within half an hour, she is pain-free and calms down, no longer assuming that her first child is making its way into the world mid-air.

I too am relieved.

After landing, there are further delays as the airport is crowded. Even the crew channel has two other airlines in front of us. By the time we have cleared immigration and waited for our baggage, my legs ache as I sit down on the crew bus.

In the hotel lobby area, the captain invites us all to a room party in an hour's time. I decide to go. It's still early in Miami and if I stay in my room, I will fall asleep.

I ask a receptionist about nearby hair salons and she makes an appointment for me.

Then I take the elevator to my room, unpack and shower.

★ ★ ★

The door to room 342 is wedged open with a suitcase. Four people are already there, sitting on the edge of the bed or huddled on the small sofa. Jim, the captain, is leaning against the desk, clutching a can of beer.

"Hi. Come in," he says.

"Hi." I join the others on the bed, feeling suddenly awkward.

Everyone else has brought their own carrier bags containing crew purchases: wine, beer or mixers.

"Drink?" says the captain, handing me a beer.

"Thanks," I say, snapping the ring pull.

It is warm and I don't want it, but I don't have to stay long and I may as well fit in whilst I'm here.

An hour later, nearly everyone is crammed into the room. A steward, Rick, working in economy in the adjacent aisle to me, is sitting close to a woman working in business. She is laughing at nearly everything he says and it's irritating me, although initially I can't quite put my finger on why.

Then I realize that it is because she reminds me a bit of myself—the way I used to hang on to Nate's every word. I wonder what he's up to right now and whether he's at a party, similar to this, in Mexico.

I decide to call it a night, even though late afternoon sun is still evident outside.

Next morning, my hair takes nearly three hours to dye blonde, but I am pleased with the results.

I walk back, past the beaches, palm trees and the pinks, lemons and powder blues of the Art Deco area, passing the Park Central Hotel where, according to a brochure in my room, Clark Gable used to hang out.

Back in my nondescript room—all hotel interiors are starting to look similar—I get ready for the return flight: ironing my blouse, polishing my shoes, packing and squeezing hotel shampoo miniatures into my washbag.

The return flight is just as busy as the way out. There isn't one spare seat and the plane is full of passengers fresh off cruise ships, used to high standards and several courses a day—plus snacks—reduced to a tray with a hot breakfast for one, a rock-hard bread roll and a fruit salad.

During the hour-long crew break, it is clear that something happened between Rick and the giggly woman after the room party last night. They don't go up to the bunks but sit in the rest seats below, alongside me. She is trying to engage him in conversation, but it is painfully clear—to me—that he just wants to read the paper.

I know what she's trying to do. I recognize the signals, because it takes one to know one.

She is how I *used* to be. Mandy wants *something* after their night together. She is desperate for hope: a token gesture, however small, even if it's just a false promise to get in touch.

I throw him a dirty look behind her back.

He doesn't react.

I have to drag myself out of bed the next morning for my driving lesson, even though my whole body aches.

Before I started flying, I never gave any thought to how physical the job would be, not to mention all the lifting and carrying of baggage, containers and supplies. I often find bruises on my thighs and arms where I've been bashed by passengers carrying too many bags or been hurt in the galley by items falling off the edge during unexpected turbulence.

Running late, I rush outside and climb into my driving instructor's hatchback before going through the motions of checking the mirrors and adjusting the driver's seat. He's so pedantic about little things like that.

Pleased with my progress, he books me in for my tests—theory first, practical second.

In between studying I spend the rest of my three TAB days off viewing several properties in Richmond. Well, I say properties—in truth, they are tiny flats which are even smaller than the shoebox. But I can't think of anywhere else I'd like to live when I move out of Reading.

Richmond is my home. And besides, when Nate and I are back together, it will be an investment.

I put in an offer on the smallest, yet closest one to Nate's, as my solicitor says I should receive the money from the sale of Sweet Pea Cottage soon.

Whilst getting ready for my work trip, I can't help singing "New York, New York." I double-check: Nate's flight has already taken off. We are heading in the same direction, for once.

The flight is only two-thirds full but I am kept busy with duty-free requests. I walk the length of the aircraft several times over, seeking out the different carts—two located in each galley—for the right stock.

The higher-value items are kept in a smaller container near first class. After spending over twenty minutes examining a bracelet, then a watch, the passenger who requested to view them decides they're not quite right. The meagre commission we earn on the sales is not worth the hassle.

As the top of descent into New York is announced by the flight crew, my heart starts to quicken, which is ridiculous, given that Nate would have landed hours ago.

As the crew bus emerges from a tunnel, the cityscape is exhilarating. I looked up a map in the in-flight magazine and familiarized myself with the easy layout of streets. As the traffic stops and starts I observe through the window. I watch the ant-like crowds hurry past signs advertising one-dollar slices of pizza and all-you-can-eat Chinese buffets. Open-topped red tourist buses, not dissimilar to London ones, mingle with the yellow cabs and the screeching emergency vehicles, sirens blaring. Uniformed doormen stand patiently outside glass apartment entrances. Soon after we pass Bloomingdale's our bus pulls up outside a narrow high-rise hotel sandwiched between two other buildings.

It's such a shame that, although Nate and I are both here, we cannot go out exploring together.

I take care whilst checking in at reception to keep an eye out, and I ask to see a flight crew list. Nate is on floor twenty seven.

In my fifth-floor room, whilst awaiting delivery of my suitcase, I stare out the window at the office block opposite. I tap the hotel Wi-Fi code into my phone. Nate hasn't posted anything about what he intends to do here. The safest bet is that he will go for a jog early tomorrow morning. But until then, I am free.

I take a look at Bella's blog. I feel sick. Even though I was prepared—thanks to Stephanie—even though I knew it was coming, it still gives me heart-sink. And fills me with envy. Bella and Miles have announced their engagement. I check Stephanie's Facebook page. The phrase "Cheshire Cat" comes to mind. Bella's ring is a diamond rock, set in platinum.

Congratulations, Bella and Miles.

Wonderful news.

So happy.

Perfect couple.

Blah bloody blah.

The last comment is written by Nate: *Wishing you every happiness, and welcome to the family, Miles. Hope you know what you're letting yourself in for! Only joking. X.* I was careful, very careful to ensure that Nate and I had nothing to do with his family whilst we were together. It wasn't that difficult, given how often he was out of the country, and I kept him busy during his days off. I couldn't take the risk that Bella would make up lies about me and poison Nate's mind. She adores her older brother and is protective of him. The only way that I can be officially reintroduced to her is as a fait accompli, a legal wife and sister-in-law. I'd love to beat her up the aisle, to have her forced attendance at *my* wedding, sporting a brave face, but meanwhile realizing that she'll have no choice but to be nice to me from now on.

I go for a walk. Block after block I stride, but too many things remind me of weddings: jewellers, department stores, hotels, bridal shops and even a passing white limo.

I am forced to invent endless ways to keep busy. I drink coffee. I wait and bloody wait.

Back in my room, I can't settle to anything or sleep. I channel-hop, but my mind can't concentrate, so I find myself watching half-hour-long promotions. A smiley woman with a silver bouffant demonstrates a swanky vegetable chopper. Special offers flash across the screen multiple times. I stare. Perhaps it will come in useful once I am back at Nate's. He does appreciate my cooking. And I've always hated the way the stink of onions permeates my fingers, long after I've washed my hands over and over.

Jet lag has started to play tricks on my mind.

At 6:00 a.m., I head for the lobby, dressed in running gear. I settle down on a corner sofa and conceal myself behind a copy of the *New York Post*. My eyes fix on an article which I read over and over. Every time the lift bell chimes, my heart thuds. Quite a few crew are up and about already—which is not surprising, given that it's late morning back home.

Perhaps I got it wrong?

Maybe Nate went to the gym. He won't stay in the hotel all day, so I'm prepared to wait this out.

Ten past bloody seven. The lift bell jingles. I just know, can just sense it, before the doors even part, that it's going to be him. My chest pounds. I hold my breath. It is! Nate is in jogging gear, clutching a bottle of water, with his earphones in. He exits through the sliding doors and turns right.

Pulling my hood down low, I follow. Conditions are perfect. The work crowds are busy enough, but not so thick as to be a hindrance.

One block, two blocks.

Past delis advertising coffee, bagels and doughnuts. Car horns toot. Sirens screech in the distance. At each road crossing, I hang back until the pedestrian warning is about to change to the stop signal.

Nate speeds up.

I quicken my pace.

Across the road I spot horse-drawn carriages. Behind the carriage wheels and canopies are open space and greenery.

Central Park.

I get bolder, so much so that I am now merely two paces behind Nate. He stops at the entrance to set the timer on his watch. I hang back, inhaling the smell of horse shit. Keen tourists already line the pavements. A poster pinned to a nearby railing advertises Memorial Day services on the last Monday of May, in a few days' time.

Nate breaks into a jog.

So do I.

Skyscrapers look down on us. He leaves the main road at the first opportunity and sticks to the paths—as do other runners—which is perfect. Shadows from blossom-laden trees form clusters of shaded grass dotted with pale petals. My breath quickens. There is a flaw in this plan—which is that I am not as fit as him. I hope that he is not going for too long a run because I know that the park is massive. I inhale the scent of lilac. We cross over a bridge and into a burst of azaleas.

Amelia would have loved Central Park, she would have talked me through every plant and flower name. Will would have been happy too. We'd have kicked off our shoes and run across the grass.

I am thirsty and hot.

Nate stops suddenly. His T-shirt sticks to his sweaty back.

He bends over, places his hands on his thighs, then takes a long sip of water. I want to run over and snatch it from him. I breathe as quietly as I can. He stands still.

The sun is deceitfully hot for this hour; I naively assumed that it would be as cool as it is back home. Nate heads for a nearby bench. *Shit*, he will be facing me.

I jog on, until I am behind him. I stand, leaning against a tree, and catch my breath properly.

Nate sits still, as though he's scenery-watching, but he's probably just taking a break. He's had his hair cut. I'm not sure it suits him, it's a bit too short.

My head spins and I feel light-headed. The bark is rough and cool against my skin. I am mere metres away from him. With my phone, I snap a couple of photos. Why don't I go to him now? What am I waiting for? It's been over seven months. I've given him his pointless space.

Space. I hate that word.

It peppered nearly every sentence of his towards the end. Perhaps I should forget about my POA and seize the moment. Maybe fate *has* brought us here, together, away from the distractions of home.

Fuck it! I'm going to do it. I'm going to live dangerously. I step forward. No! My mantras start to jumble in my mind.

Stick to the plan.

Amend the plan.

My head pounds as a throbbing, violent headache forms. I need water. I take another step forward.

Inhale.

Exhale.

I don't know why, but I feel compelled to do this, moth-to-flame-like.

I hesitate.

As I take another step forward, I stand on a fallen branch. It is short, but fairly thick, about the size of a baseball bat. I breathe. Nate looks so relaxed. Once upon a time, I could walk up to him and hug him any time I pleased. Now, I am not allowed.

Those are the rules.

I have not been given any choice or say in the matter.

Nate turns to the side and puts his left leg on the bench, before bending at the waist in a stretch. His calf muscles must be playing up, as they do from time to time.

I crouch down as though I'm picking something up, but there is nothing but the stick. I buy time by retying my laces. As I do so, a surge of bitterness and rage races through my mind. This situation is ridiculous; I have rights too. I grip the branch tightly with my right hand and stand up. I hold it against my leg.

Nate is now standing too, his arms raised, fingers inter-locked in another stretch. I step towards him. His arms fall to his sides. I take a deep breath.

He glances at his watch, then jogs away from me. I stand still, releasing my grip on the branch. It hits my ankle as I watch him follow the curve of the path, until he is out of my reach.

CHAPTER NINE

I must be mad. What was I thinking? I didn't follow my own rules.

Stick to the plan.

Fail to plan, plan to fail.

I am frozen to the spot. It was seeing him in unfamiliar territory. My boundaries went askew. Thank God Nate jogged off. I must never let my guard down like that.

Never again.

"Ma'am, are you all right?"

I look up. An old man, dressed in a suit, is looking at me.

I stand up. "Yes, thank you. I'm fine now. I went jogging without water. Stupidly."

"There's a store that way." He points straight ahead. "It's sixty-four degrees already."

I mentally convert. About eighteen degrees Celsius. "Thank you."

I head in his suggested direction and locate a mobile kiosk.

As well as water, I buy a coffee and a savoury pretzel.

"Excuse me, where's the exit?" I ask the cashier.

I am totally disorientated. I sit on the grass and gulp the water.

The pretzel is salty and dry; it sticks in my throat. I dump the horseshoe-shaped remainder of it in a bin on my way out.

As the hotel finally comes into sight, I experience the same sense of relief as I do the moment the aircraft's wheels connect with the runway. I slide my key card into the door lock and sink down on to my bed and mentally berate myself.

I nearly blew it.

It was being so close to the prize. But I need to stick to my schedule, because by July it will be almost ten months since we split up.

Nearly a year.

That way, I've proved to him that I've given him space to find himself—or whatever it is that he's decided he must do. It hurts, the thought of him sleeping with other women, of course it does, but none feature on his Facebook page for any length of time, so I wipe my mind clear of such thoughts and try to see it as a positive thing. He didn't leave me for another specific woman. He will be properly ready to settle down by the time we reunite.

I need to work on fresh mantras, and I must repeat them more often.

When there's any doubt, don't.

Patience is a virtue.

Stick to the plan.

Even though my head is now totally pain-free, I take two strong painkillers and down several glasses of water.

No matter what the reason was, I can't unravel again.

I am tired and wound up.

Crew boarding on to the Heathrow-bound aircraft is delayed, due to the late arrival of the inbound flight. When we're finally given permission to board, we have to navigate our way past cleaners and their Hoovers, which block the aisles, leaving us with barely enough time to do our security checks—and none of the galley preparations.

Mid-flight, two people fall ill and require oxygen, and there are too many noisy children. The demands seem endless, and there are lots of complaints about the in-flight entertainment system not working.

Maybe I won't last too long in the job, after all.

During bunk rest, I dream of Will. He is younger, only about eighteen months old, and wobbly when he walks. William is swimming like a water baby. Amelia hides in the shade of the garden, picking flowers. She is trying to shout instructions to me, but her words come out muffled, as though she is underwater. By the time I understand what she's trying to tell me, by the time I get the *permanence* of the whole situation, it's too late.

I sit up and fumble for my torch. I take small sips of water. There is a boy sitting in premium economy, wearing blue dungarees. They reminded me of his.

I remain unsettled for the remainder of the flight. I don't feel right. Once I'm strapped into my crew seat for the approach to landing, I nearly blurt out the whole Will tale to my colleague. There is nothing to stop me, and it happens all the time. It took me a while to get used to it. So many crew constantly over-share, spilling all kinds of personal snippets of information, as though they believe they will remain a confessional secret, safe in the middle of the open sky.

But I don't, of course. There would be no point.

Instead, I talk about "Nick" and how I knew, from the moment I met him, that no one else would ever compare. Look what happened every time Elizabeth Taylor tried to live without Richard Burton. I've read that their romance was described as the "deadly love that never died." Without each other, life had no real point.

Nate makes me feel complete, despite his faults, which is why I know it's love.

Infatuation would make me blind. True love embraces acceptance.

I spend my first day off alone in the flat. I relax by scrolling through pictures of Bella and Miles' engagement announcement photos. They are having a party next month. I print out the photos I snapped of Nate in New York and add them to my pinboard. They aren't good quality—not really—but I need to keep everything as recent as possible, because our lives need to stay entwined and up to date, even behind the scenes.

I stare at the board; something feels wrong. I stare and I stare until I figure out what it is.

Bella's happy face doesn't belong in my personal space. I grab a pair of scissors and begin hacking, until her head is chopped off or slashed in every single one where she is smiling. The only ones I keep intact are those where she doesn't look quite so pleased with herself.

I exhale. I feel better.

I take out the two voodoo dolls from the shoebox at the top of my wardrobe. The girl has pins in her head and the boy has just one, in his chest. I want to keep Nate's heart hardened, until he falls back in love with me. When I'd spotted them at a market stall on one of my Caribbean trips, the colleague I was with laughed when I bought them. "Creepy dolls for tourists," she'd said. "What on earth do you want them for?"

"A joke," I'd replied.

I hate shopping with people. The problem I find with colleagues is that some just aren't independent, they latch on to me from as early as our pre-flight briefing, trying to find out my plans for down-route and then inviting themselves along.

★ ★ ★

On my second TAB day off, I pass my driving theory test. Now there is only the practical left to go before I will have new freedom. After I visit a couple of car showrooms, I decide I'm going to order a sleek, grey convertible. I think there may be just about enough room in the boot for a small suitcase.

Afterwards, I have a gaping two-day hole to fill until my next trip to Bangkok. I stay away from Nate's, having frightened myself with my own behaviour in New York. I need to refocus and make sure I'm strong enough to be near him and not fuck up.

Amy is on an Australian trip, so is of no use. My Juliette and Elizabeth profiles are up to date on Facebook, with the correct comments and photos for the right personas.

I ring Babs. "Fancy a visit?"

"Of course, my love. Perfect timing, I've made a beef and ale pie."

I pack a small bag and head for the train station.

I didn't mention my arrival time to Babs, so I catch a bus which takes me past Sweet Pea Cottage. The *For Sale* sign says *Under Offer*.

I wait to feel something—some emotion—but no, there is none.

Babs flings open the door the second I ring the bell, wearing an apron decorated with cherries. She has flour on her face. Barbara looks how a mother probably should look.

"Fantastic to see you," she says. "I'll get dinner ready."

Over pie—I pick off the pastry—new potatoes and green beans, Babs fills me in on the village gossip: two divorces, one death and a burglary.

I update her on my driving lessons.

"Wonderful news, you'll be able to visit more often now."

I nod.

Silence.

The dominant sound in the kitchen becomes the clinking of our cutlery, which means that Babs is psyching herself up to tell me bad news or ask me something.

I wait.

"Are you up for a visit tomorrow? To see William?" I get up and fill our water glasses from the tap.

"It's his birthday soon, and…" Babs perseveres.

"No, sorry, I don't want to go."

"Well, I'd appreciate the company. We could also place some flowers by Amelia's plaque."

"Dead people don't care if they have flowers on their grave or not."

"I'm going. I always go."

"He's not there. She's not there." Babs clears her throat.

I think I know what's coming and I don't want to hear it. "What's on telly tonight?" I say, as I stand up and begin to clear the table. "Stick something on and I'll wash up."

I turn on the hot tap and squeeze a large dollop of lemon washing-up liquid into a bowl, staring at the foaming bubbles.

Babs selects a soap opera; I can hear the theme tune emanating from the living room. We used to watch it in the common room at school, crowded on sofas and cushions on the floor, in our pyjamas and dressing gowns.

I join her on the sofa ten minutes later. If I didn't know that it was one she watched regularly, I'd have assumed she'd chosen it on purpose. Because tonight's episode involves a graveside scene in which a character attains "closure."

I leave early the following morning, full of promises to visit again soon.

On the train home my phone rings. My solicitor. The house sale has gone through.

I am rich.

I imagine some junior estate agent being dispatched to the cottage to change the *Under Offer* sign to *Sold*.

Annoyingly, the flat I'd had my eye on in Richmond has been taken off the market, which means that I have to restart my search for another place. But it will keep me busy until I am back at work.

Somewhere above Europe, then Asia, suspended in no-man's land, hurtling towards Bangkok, I am sitting in the galley on an upturned metal container, freezing cold, listening to a colleague, Nancy, go on and on. She's shown me pictures of her cat, her horse, her godchildren, revealed all about an operation she had four years ago, and told me how her ex-husband was into cross-dressing.

"It wasn't *that* that split us up, though…"

"Oh," I say. "Do you want a coffee?"

I stand up, put a filter bag into the coffee machine and switch it on, willing a passenger to wander in and faint or do something that will take a while to sort out.

"Yes, I'll have a coffee. Anyway, like I say, it wasn't the cross-dressing—"

"I'll be back in a couple of minutes, Nancy. It's my turn to complete the security checks."

Normally I can't be bothered, but tonight I prowl around the dark cabin, checking the toilets for suspicious messages and bomb-makers, ensuring passengers aren't ill or up to anything too unusual. It's quiet. There are no couples trying to sneak into the toilet together to join the Mile High Club, not that it bothers me when they do. I just pretend I haven't noticed.

By the time I return to the galley, Nancy has latched on to another crew member, Kevin, who from his glazed expression clearly wishes he hadn't ventured down from the sanctuary of first class.

"…so, it was the fact that he was so selfish. I mean *really* selfish. I'd get back off a trip, exhausted, having served hundreds of people throughout the night, and he wouldn't have lifted a finger at home. No shopping in, no…" I catch his eye and smile.

"I only nipped down for some spare napkins," he says. "I've left the first galley unattended. I'd better pop back."

Kevin used to be an accountant, but the burning desire to travel made him change career in his early forties. He seems fun. He made everyone laugh in briefing with a tale about how he'd missed a crew bus to a remote stand on his previous flight and had ended up getting lost in the labyrinth of corridors beneath the terminal. Kevin winks at me before escaping through the thick galley curtains. Maybe I'll hang out with him. He seems intelligent and entertaining, so far.

A call bell chimes. Hallelujah!

I make my way along the aisle, among the sleeping masses buried beneath blankets, avoiding sticking-out feet and random shoes, until I reach seat 43A, above which the call light is illuminated white.

"Please may I have a cup of tea, dear?" asks an old lady, switching on her reading light.

"Of course."

I scan the darkness for any other lights. This is what my life has come down to: looking for people to serve so I don't have to listen to any more chatter.

In the galley, as I pour boiling water from the hot tap on to the tea bag, Nancy resumes.

"Any plans for Bangkok?"

I consider. What wouldn't Nancy do? Hmm. Not sure. Better play safe and keep it vague.

"Not really, I like to go with the flow and not make definite plans. I never know how I'll be feeling or how I'll sleep."

I pour milk into the tea and grab a few sugar sachets, place them on a tray and return to the cabin.

The moment I'm back, Nancy opens her mouth.

"I'm going to visit The Grand Palace, with the first officer, Katie. We live in the same village and when we realized we were on the same trip, we decided that it was time to venture out for a bit of culture and do something rather than the same old market shopping."

"Good for you."

"You're very welcome to join us."

"Thanks, you're kind, but I'll see."

"Probably wise. Katie's all loved up at the moment. She's at that initial stage where she can't help dropping her new boyfriend's name into every conversation, regardless of the topic. I don't begrudge her, of course I don't. She's been on her own a while, never had much luck with men. But, between you and me, I bet it will be 'Nate this' and 'Nate that' whilst we're at the temple."

"Nate? That's an unusual name." I am surprised at how normal and casual my voice sounds, as inside I feel heartsick.

"Is it unusual? I hadn't really thought. It's probably short for Nathan or something."

"What's his surname?" My heart is beating just a little faster.

"I don't know. Anyway, it's time to go and wake the others, it's our turn for bunk rest now."

I prepare some hot towels and pour several glasses of juice. I place them on a tray. My hands shake a little. I head towards the tail of the plane, once again negotiating limbs and debris, the most dangerous of which are always magazines—I've seen them send people flying. I use a key to unlock the door to the crew bunks, which I shut behind me—it's not uncommon for passengers to make themselves at home if they gain access— and switch the lights on to *dim* as I hold the rail with one hand, clutching my tray in the other whilst negotiating the small staircase.

"Morning, everyone," I say.

Some people shoot up, gather their belongings and head off to the toilets.

Others sit up, visibly exhausted and disorientated, clearly wishing they were at home, in their own beds.

Fifteen minutes later, I am lying on a top bunk, wearing a grey tracksuit and sliding around in a sleeping bag. My seat belt keeps slithering down towards my hips as I toss and turn, like a rag in a washing machine, as we hit turbulence. I feel as though I'm in some parallel, non-existent universe.

One thing is clear in my mind: I will be joining Nancy and Katie on a tour of the Grand Palace, after all.

CHAPTER TEN

After an hour, I give up on my three-hours-and-twenty-minutes break. I can't bear it a moment longer, lying there, trapped. I'm going to go and suss Katie out. I need to see her with my own eyes to make an assessment. I feel light-headed as I reapply my make-up in the toilet. At the beginning of the flight I looked presentable. Now I feel sick to my stomach. I knew Nate wouldn't be celibate, of course. I'm not deluded. But to have a name, to be stuck mid-air with someone who is a potential rival, is a horrendous situation to find myself in.

I make my way to the front of the plane and upstairs to business class. The crew member—an older man—is in the small upper-deck galley preparing the breakfast trays.

"Hi. I'm just going to pop into the flight deck," I say. "Do you want me to ask them if they need anything?"

He checks his watch. "Yeah, go ahead. They're due a call."

I know what times the flight crew are called during the

flight, which is why I came up at this point. I pick up the interphone and key in the numbers for the flight deck. My heart is pounding at the thought of Katie's voice answering the call, but she doesn't. A male voice does. "Hi. Mike speaking."

"Hi, it's Juliette from down the back here. I'm upstairs and just wanted to pop in to ask you something. Do you need anything?"

"Hang on a minute." Muffled voices.

"Yes, two coffees please. One white, one black, no sugars. And if you've got any crew sandwiches left, that would be good too, thanks."

"OK."

I make the coffees. Which one is Katie's? I slide out a tray of sandwiches from the crew trolley. I call again to announce my arrival.

I walk up the aisle and wait outside the cockpit door. The captain opens it and as soon as I enter, he closes it firmly behind me. The white, green and blue instrument lights judder brightly in the dimness of the enclosed area. In the FO's seat there is a man. No Katie. The door to the pilot bunk area is shut; she must be asleep.

"Is someone on their break?" I say.

"Yes."

Damn.

The captain takes the tray from me. I remove the coffees and I place them in the space behind each seat.

"I came to ask if it's possible for me to sit here for landing?" I say. "I'm fairly new and—"

"Sorry, no, this is a training sector. James," he points to the first officer, "is preparing for his command—promotion to captain—so I'm afraid I'll have to say no." James turns round and gives an apologetic wave.

"Oh."

"Hopefully, you'll get another opportunity soon—as, normally, I'd say yes."

"Thank you."

"Thanks for the coffee." He peers through the spy hole whilst James checks the CCTV cameras. "All clear."

He opens the door for me and I step back out, feeling deflated but not defeated.

On our journey to the hotel, I sit behind Katie, listening in to a conversation between her and the other first officer.

Her hair is plaited and pinned up—a personal dislike of mine.

Will used to love my hair in plaits. Well, he liked pulling them.

She looks nondescript.

Their conversation isn't interesting—they mainly discuss cycling. I can't imagine Nate on a bike. He wouldn't look right in a cycling helmet. He just wouldn't.

Like most crew, Katie looks completely different out of uniform when we gather in reception the next morning. It is only Nancy, Katie, another guy—called Ajay—and me.

Katie has long, curly red hair and loads of freckles. She looks friendly, yet capable, the sort of person you'd ask for directions. She appears tomboyish, with her muscly upper arms and her sensible beige trousers, as though she is trying too hard to fit in with the male pilots. However, when she smiles her whole face becomes pretty.

At first, I wasn't sure what Nate would see in her. But I think it's because she looks so wholesome, so "girl next door."

On board the tour bus, I look over at her again. She is gaping out the window, her mouth slightly open. We are stuck in traffic for ages, but I'm unable to engage in any useful conversation with Katie because an enthusiastic tour guide talks non-stop whilst standing at the front of the bus with a microphone. I zone out.

The reason I know Nate loves me is because he told me so.

When I told him I loved him, he replied, "Yeah, me too." He'd have just kept quiet otherwise.

Admittedly, he was reluctant—initially—about me moving in so soon after we'd got together. But I pointed out that, although it was a bit of a whirlwind romance, perhaps it was meant to be.

The place I was renting was being sold. That *was* true, even though the landlord said I could have potentially stayed on for another three months. But there really didn't seem to be any point in me finding someplace else to live. It was a tiny white lie for our mutual benefit.

I had briefly considered joining the airline then, but I wanted to be the perfect girlfriend. To be *there* for Nate, when he returned home from trips. Just the two of us.

The words that lodge in my mind upon setting eyes on the palace are *green* and *gold*. I gaze at the dazzling buildings, layered roofs and manicured gardens.

It is hot. According to the guide, it is nearly rainy season, and I'm wearing long sleeves to respect the dress code of the sacred site.

"So romantic, don't you think?" I say to the others.

They nod, but don't reply as they are all, unfortunately, the type of people who are genuinely interested in buildings. They listen to our guide as we are herded around. Sweat snakes my spine. The thing is, to my mind, you can enjoy things quickly. You don't have to walk around at a snail's pace just to imprint places on your memory. That's what cameras are for.

On and on, we walk and listen. At the Emerald Buddha Temple, we *ooh* and *aah* over a jade Buddha whose gold outfit is apparently changed at the beginning of each new season by the King.

Finally, we are whisked off to a busy local restaurant for lunch. Thank God it has air conditioning. I can't take an afternoon of this. All I want is for Katie to mention Nate, then I will make an excuse and return to the sanctuary of the hotel. I plonk myself on a seat next to her. And copy her order: a Diet Coke and a Pad Thai.

"So, what did you think of the palace?" I say.

"It's so...incredible," says Nancy.

"Amazing," says Katie, taking a sip of her Coke.

Ajay just nods; he is still browsing through a guidebook.

"Like I said earlier, I think there's something really romantic about the place," I say.

Katie doesn't bite. I'm going to have to be less subtle.

Our food arrives, steam rising. I wish I'd ordered something cold, I can't face it. I pick up my chopsticks and grab a small prawn. I nibble. The aroma of lemongrass turns my stomach. It was the dominant smell permeating the kitchen on the terrible night Nate broke up with me.

"So..." I say, turning to Katie. "Nancy says you live in the same village. Whereabouts is that?"

"Just outside Peterborough," she says, naming a place I've never heard of.

"Oh, so quite a drive, then?" I tilt my head to one side and look interested.

"Yeah. But I quite enjoy it. I listen to music or audiobooks. It helps me wind down after a long night."

I haven't seen any evidence of her staying over at Nate's. And as far as I know, he hasn't been up to her place. Nate doesn't like to go far on his days off. Perhaps Nancy got it wrong or was exaggerating. Katie hasn't said "Nate this" or

"Nate that" even once. It could have been a short-lived affair, already blown over.

I pick at some noodles.

Katie yawns, quickly covering her mouth.

"The afternoon sounds really exciting," says Ajay. "The guidebook says we're in for a real treat—"

"Well, it would, wouldn't it?" I can't help saying.

All three look at me.

My mouth is burning as a chilli takes effect, biting my throat and warming my face. "I'm sorry. I think I'm templed out. I'm going to get a cab back to the hotel. Are you all meeting up for drinks and dinner tonight?"

"Stay," says Nancy. "You'll regret it, if you don't."

"Actually, I agree with Juliette," says Katie. "I'll need a doze this afternoon if I'm going to last the evening." I warm to her.

We leave Nancy and Ajay behind, and the guide organizes us a taxi. We offer her a large tip, as she appears upset at our desire to leave the tour early.

The drive back is quicker and our driver is chatty, wanting to talk about English football. Katie seems knowledgeable, so I let her get on with it. Maybe she'll be a bit more revealing after a few drinks tonight, even though I suspect Nate has tired of her quite quickly.

It is noon back home but sundowners time in Bangkok, when I, along with several others from the crew—including Kevin from first class and Katie—gather at a rooftop bar. Nancy is too tired to join us. Lights illuminate the nearby skyscrapers.

I sip a local beer from a tall glass. It cools my throat as the heat and humidity gently suffocate me.

"Shall we head for a club?" suggests someone.

I wait to see what Katie's reaction is.

"Sounds good," she says.

"Great," I join in.

Katie turns to me. "Don't you want to change first?"

I glance down at my black jeans. "Why?"

"It's boiling, even though it's night. Remember how hot it was earlier, traipsing around?"

Katie does a twirl. Red and white dots on her dress spin, and bangles jingle. A butterfly tattoo smudges her right ankle.

A rush of relief; Nate thinks tattoos are tacky. She is probably yet another tool, another plaything, to distract him.

I can't be bothered to change. We hail a tuk-tuk that weaves violently as our driver negotiates dense traffic. I grip the metal side-bar, inhaling petrol fumes. A pink flower garland dangles from the rear-view mirror, rocking in time to the jerky manoeuvres. We arrive at a converted warehouse which gives a good impression of being unhampered by health and safety standards; haphazard electrical wires criss-cross above us and wooden floorboards protrude. An Elvis impersonator massacres "Always On My Mind." The tinny microphone screeches at regular intervals.

"I wish I was back home with my boyfriend," I say to Katie as we jostle for space at the bar.

"Me too," she says. "Although, having said that, my boyfriend is away at the moment. He's a pilot too." My legs wobble.

The barman turns his attention to us. We order beers.

I remember to breathe.

We join the others huddled round a high metal table. We chat about work for as long as I can stand it.

"So, any pictures of your man, then?" I say as nonchalantly as I can manage.

"Loads. I love boring people about Nate."

I almost feel sorry for Katie—almost—but it's not my fault that Nate is vain. And weak when it comes to women who throw themselves at him.

"Here, look…" Katie grins. "We were in Rio and…" Nate's image beams from her phone.

I freeze and listen to every stabbing word of her smug, minute-long monologue before excusing myself. Outside, I repeat my mantras, over and over. I can barely breathe. Music blares from multiple directions. Groups of locals mingle by taxis and motorbikes. Clusters of stalls groan under the weight of fake designer goods, T-shirts, shoes, handbags. Neon signs advertise drinks, massages, sleeping pills. The odour of frying onions emanates from a nearby food cart.

I whip out my phone from my back pocket and log on. Nate's crew are spending their down time on safari in Kruger National Park. He's posted pictures of long, brittle grass broken by spiky trees bearing little foliage under the caption *Anyone spot the lion?!* There he is, cavorting with wildlife, whilst I'm dealing with a fresh betrayal on the other side of the world.

Deep breaths. In-bloody-hale. Ex-bloody-hale.

A whiff of sewage temporarily pulls me back to the reality of my surroundings.

Sleeping pills? The words catch my eye again. Maybe I should get some. I can then spend the remainder of my time here in blissful oblivion. They can be a plaster. A temporary fix.

"How much is a bottle of twenty?" I ask the pharmacist behind the counter.

"Why don't you buy forty?" she says. "Cheaper."

Whatever. In for a penny… I drop them into my bag before briefly browsing the stalls. I spot a small wooden Buddha. I buy him too; he could bring me luck.

I force myself to re-enter the bar. Katie's chair is empty. I follow the signs to the toilets. She is in front of the mirror, tying her hair into a ponytail. I can smell her sickly perfume from the doorway.

Don't stand for it a moment longer, my mind silently screams.

I step forward, avoiding wet patches on the dirty tiles, until I am alongside her. I smile into the mirror. She smiles back, albeit with a slightly puzzled expression.

"I thought that I recognized Nate from the picture you showed. His face is familiar," I say. "It's been bugging me, but I'm sure it's him."

"Oh. Have you flown with him?"

"No."

"Where do you know him from?"

"I don't. Something happened between him and a friend of mine. I don't know what exactly, but whatever it was it shook her up quite badly. She said she could never tell anyone."

"It can't have been Nate then. He's a total gentleman."

"Maybe."

I look down and rummage in my bag as a distraction, but not before I catch a fleeting, yet concerned expression flash across her face. I reach for a mascara. When I look back up, Katie is heading towards the door.

"Join you in a minute," I call out.

If she replies, I don't hear. The door bangs shut behind her. I apply my mascara slowly, irked at her dismissive attitude. I didn't tell her a complete fib; Nate does have a shadowy side. As I turn to leave, I replace my make-up in my bag and it makes a clinking sound as it hits the jar of sleeping pills.

That's when the idea hits me.

Inside a cubicle, I remove the blue pills from my bag. The dosage reads one tablet every twelve hours. Hmm. So what is a good amount? Two? Three? Four? I unscrew the lid and re-move three capsules, sliding them into my jeans pocket. After screwing the top back on, I rummage in my bag for the small envelope which contains my room key card. I ram the card into my purse. Carefully, I pull the capsules apart and tip the powder into the envelope. I flush the husks away and leave the relative quiet of the toilets for the noise and mayhem outside.

CHAPTER ELEVEN

The Elvis impersonator has changed outfits into Tom Jones. Same leather trousers, different blouse. He launches into "Sex Bomb," gyrating and swinging a leather jacket like a lasso.

I order several beers. I take one, hold it down low, whilst tipping the contents of the envelope into the bottle.

"Can I have some glasses, please?" I ask the barman.

He shakes his head questioningly.

"*Glasses*, please. And," I scan the counter, "those too, please." I point to some chilli-coated nuts. "Five packets, please."

He hands me four warm tumblers, fresh from the dishwasher, and then a small black tray.

I make my way back to Katie and the others before pouring a beer into the glass in front of her. I have to; I can hardly shake the bottle.

"Sorry about what I said earlier," I say, handing her the beer. "Peace offering. I have a big mouth sometimes. I'm sure I've made a mistake."

She hesitates, picks up the glass and raises it in a "cheers" gesture.

I rip open the nuts and flatten out the foil packets. "Help yourselves," I say to everyone, but of course meaning Katie.

The potential flaw in my plan could be that the pills taste of something strong. Hopefully the nuts will mask anything untoward. Tom Jones belts out the chorus of "Delilah." Several of our group join in, giggling, Katie included.

I smile and pretend to enjoy myself. I hope she falls off her stool. She looks so alert that I fear I may need even more of a helping hand, so I walk off and order some local rum shots.

"Go on," I shout. "Last one to finish gets the next round." Most people, including Katie—phew—rise to the challenge.

"You're going for it tonight," says someone. "Win the lottery?"

I laugh politely, as though he has genuinely said something funny.

"One, two, three..." the group chorus.

It nearly makes me sick. "God, that's hideous," I shout.

"What is it?" asks Kevin, coming into focus. My eyes are watering.

"Rum. No more for me."

"Lightweight," smiles Kevin.

He has nice, brown eyes which compliment his dark skin and cheeky smile.

I smile back before I look over at Katie. Finally, she is looking a little spaced out. "I might head back soon," I say to Kevin. I point at Katie. "She looks like she could do with a ride back too."

"I'll join you. I wasn't planning a very late night."

I slink up to Katie. "Kevin and I are heading back. Do you fancy coming with us? You look tired."

"Tired?" She looks confused. "No, no, I'm fine. You guys go. I'll head back with some of the others later."

"I think you should come." I turn to Kevin. "Don't you?"

He shrugs. "Up to the lady herself," he says.

I pull him to one side. "She looks a bit the worse for wear."

"Seems OK to me."

Katie slides off her stool, leaning against the table for support. She drops her bag in the process. She struggles to retrieve her belongings: a hairbrush, some mints and a lipstick.

Kevin rushes over. He helps Katie upright.

I throw him an "I told you so" look.

Outside, we hail a taxi. A proper one. A tuk-tuk might jerk her into full consciousness. During the ride, she leans her head against the window, eyes fluttering open, then shutting.

A doorman opens the back door after we pull up outside our hotel.

"Help me get her to her room," I say to Kevin. "She looks like she could do with a good sleep."

"I'm fine," she mutters, but doesn't complain when he puts his arm around her to assist.

"What room are you in?" he asks.

"Um…seventeen…six…two." She yawns and frowns, as though in deep concentration. "One. Seven. Six. Two."

By the time we reach her floor, she is practically sleep-walking. I ease her bag from her shoulder and search for her key. I slot it into the door and Kevin walks her to the bed. I remove her shoes. Kevin and I stand side by side, like concerned parents, looking at her.

"Do you think she's all right?" I say.

"Yeah. Probably just needs to sleep it off."

"Let's put her in the recovery position, just in case."

"You think so?"

"Yes. You'll have to help me."

Kevin grips her torso. I hold her legs and we roll her forwards, placing her arms in the correct position. She snores gently. Very ladylike.

"Let's go," he says.

I dim the lights, sliding her key card into my pocket as we leave. The door clicks shut behind us.

We wait for the lift.

"Fancy a nightcap?" says Kevin.

"Thanks. Sorry, but I'm exhausted."

"Fair enough."

The lift arrives. In another time and place, maybe. This is another one of the problems Nate causes for me. Kevin is nice and, let's face it, why should Nate have all the fun? But, sadly, not only am I a one-man woman, I'm too busy. I have things to do.

His room is on the floor above mine, meaning he exits first. "Good night," we chorus.

The lift doors shut. They part on my floor but I stay put and wait for them to close again. I press floor seventeen. When the doors open, I check that the corridor is deserted. There's no obvious CCTV. I slide Katie's room key from my pocket. The lock indicates green. I am in.

She is no longer snoring, but her breathing is heavy. Her hair has fallen over her face. I gently move it away. I sit down in the armchair and watch her. Does Nate watch her when she's asleep? I used to watch him all the time. He always looked so vulnerable, so peaceful, all traces of worry or anger ironed out. I wanted to claw inside his head. I wanted to know what he was thinking, all the time.

He said that his thoughts were wispy and intangible. Well, that was a lie. He kept his thoughts together enough to plan to get rid of me.

Like I was nothing.

I stand up and take out her phone, even though scrolling through any messages from him will be like picking scabs, but it's code-locked. I search her handbag; there is no sign of her passport. Sliding open the wardrobe, I see that the safe is locked. I check her bag again and find a driving licence in her purse. But even by tapping variations of her birth date into the phone—and the safe—I still can't achieve any results.

I search the bathroom, checking out her products. She uses anti-frizz shampoo. I bet Nate doesn't know *that*, does he? That her hair is naturally brittle. I go through her suitcase, it contains mainly clothes, and then I rifle through her flight bag. Manuals. A thriller. A travel book. I recognize it. It is one I bought for him. *Five Hundred Places to Visit Before You Die.*

He has given or lent her a book from me! How dare he?

I flick through. The man has no imagination, none. His default gifts are chocolates. I bet he forgot her birthday— or something—so decided to give her something of mine. Unless…she helped herself from his bookshelf. I stare at her, all calm and peaceful, not a care in the world, then I take the book to the desk and pick up a pen.

On the last page, I write a belated inscription: *To my darling Nate. Love you always. Look forward to exploring the world with you. E XXX.* At best, Nate probably flicked through the book. He won't have noticed whether or not I'd written anything.

It serves him right.

I replace it. I hope it jolts her into momentary jealousy when she is confronted with evidence of Nate's romantic past, if she stumbles across my words. I rummage through her handbag and record her address and other potentially useful bits and pieces of information in my phone. There is nothing more I can do for now, so I place the key card on her bedside table and leave.

Back in my own room, I browse the internet for ideas. I need greater access to Nate's inner world. I discover an app that can track all his messages and activity. A jilted lover's dream. I bet the person who created it was in a similar situation to me, because necessity is the mother of invention. It is marketed as an anti-theft tool, or for those wanting to keep a close eye on their teenagers or elderly parents. There is a warning that it is strictly forbidden to install the application on a phone that you do not own, but I'll ignore that.

All I need now is access to his phone. It seems that the majority of people who have installed it without the owner's permission did so when their partner was asleep or in the shower. To do that, I would have to break into Nate's flat when he is home, in the middle of the night, or hide in the flat until he takes a shower. Not ideal options.

Katie comes down for crew pick-up, right as rain. She doesn't mention the other night and neither do I—or Kevin—as far as I know. She is probably embarrassed, assuming she can't hold her drink.

The pills are going to be more use to me than I originally realized.

I think about things all the way home, mentally tweaking my POA.

As we touch down at Heathrow, the perfect plan dawns on me.

Nate doesn't take his phone when he goes for a jog. He feels it's the one time he can be cut off from the world. All I need to do is hang around, wait until he goes for a run, let myself in and install it before he's back. Simple.

On my first day off work, I have a two-hour intensive driving lesson, in preparation for my upcoming practical driving test. I concentrate as best I can on mastering all the essentials, but it is frustrating to have no control over the other drivers, who overtake or pull away in front of me at traffic lights.

I catch a train early the next morning so I can be there in time for Nate's likely exit from his building. However, I feel more exposed now that summer is imminent. The light is not my friend. I'm slightly concerned that if he looks out the window, he may clock me. I need a better disguise.

I sit on a bench. Pigeons peck around the bare patches of ground by my feet. I shoo them away.

I wait and I wait, but he doesn't appear. Aircraft roar above every minute.

I want to kick a nearby tree with frustration. I *know* he's home. I bet Katie is there with him. He always went out for his jog when I was with him.

I stride to the high street. And then I loiter by the river, in case I spot him there, but there's no sign of him.

Could he have gone to Peterborough? Unlikely, but then how would I know?

That's the problem. That's why I need access to his phone. Deflated, I head home.

Nate has two more days off, which means I have no choice but to trek over there every bloody morning and wait.

Perseverance always pays off. It never, ever fails.

The next day, Nate goes out for his jog. I watch from behind a nearby tree, pretending to tie my laces. I wish I could give him a cheery wave for being so obliging; he has no idea how much teamwork is going into our reunion.

I look at my phone. I've got about forty minutes, if he sticks to his routine. Weather conditions are favourable; sunny, but not too hot. I jog towards his flat without hesitation, as though I have every right to be heading in that direction. I pull up my hood as I approach the communal doors and put on my sunglasses. I don't know his neighbours *that* well, but there's rarely any point in taking unnecessary risks. I run lightly upstairs and let myself in, as silently as I can.

I stand and wait.

No sounds.

I creep towards the bedroom and bathroom. Both un-occupied. My heart lifts at the absence of Katie or any fe-male equivalent. I head for the kitchen. Nate's phone lies on the table, beside a mug which has *I ♥ NY* printed on it. He bought me a matching one. I lift it to my mouth. It's not warm, but it's not cold either, so I know this is the mug which Nate has drunk from this morning. It feels intimate and re-warding. But, I mustn't get distracted. I tap in Nate's code.

Incorrect code.

No fucking way!

I tap it again. It works. Phew. I must concentrate and pay attention. The app starts to download. Halfway through, it stops. Just like my heart almost does. The whole screen freezes. I turn off his phone by pressing down the on/off switch for several seconds, then wait whilst it reboots. On my second attempt, it downloads completely. I scroll through and hide the icon, then return the phone to its original spot. I'll have to set up a specially created account to keep track of the data, but I need to do this at home. I've been given a free forty-eight-hour trial period to see if it works.

I have a quick glance out the window. No sign of a re-turning Nate.

I can't help it. I do a quick scan of the flat.

His rectangular flight bag with the gold catches is lying open. I flick through. Paperwork, manuals, flight plans, maps. Boring. His suitcase is closed. I lift it up; it is empty. His wal-let lies on the side. I open it. Receipts. Restaurant, hotel and bar bills. I scan them. White wine, hmm. A Sea Breeze. A Cosmopolitan. Female drinks. All at a swanky bar in Cape Town, Bar on the Rocks. Perhaps Katie does have something to worry about, after all. I catch sight of his passport and air-line ID resting on the bedside table among a pile of foreign coins. I flick through the fine passport pages. I've done this lots of times; I used to try to drink in every piece of information about him. I slip out my phone and take photos to update my collection. Nate is one of the few people I know who has a decent passport picture.

I open the wardrobe. Nothing female, ditto the bathroom. I check my phone. *Shit*. Thirty-five minutes have passed. I take out a bottle of his favourite red from my rucksack and quickly slide it into the wine rack, because it's his birthday soon. Then I head for the front door, giving the fish a wave as I leave. Rainbow must be bursting with silent indignation.

As I begin my descent at the top of the stairs, I hear the slam of the communal doors below. I wait.

I hear footsteps coming up. Then voices.

"All right, mate?"

"Yes, thank you. Yourself?" *Crap*.

Nate's voice. He is having a cosy little exchange with a neighbour.

"Fine, thank you. My knee has been playing up a bit…"

I've nowhere to hide. Think. I run back up to the third floor and press the lift button. I can hear it cranking to life. It is so old. I hope it doesn't break down. It did once when I lived with Nate. The maintenance man who fixed it mentioned that, even if the residents voted to keep up repairs, it would still probably need replacing before too long. The lights illuminate. Ground floor. Second floor.

The voices stop.

Footsteps.

Shit, shit, shit.

The lift doors open. I step in and jab the letter G. The doors judder to a close. Descending, I hold my breath until it stops. I yank up my hood and put on my glasses. I step one foot out and look around.

Empty.

I head for the main doors, jog down the path and away from the flats, without looking back.

Back home, elation hits.

I did it!

I have full and total access to Nate's world. It's like the best reality show, ever. I analyse to my heart's content, even though it's a bit slower than I expected to access the information.

I can even see his browsing history. He's invited Katie to Bella and Miles' engagement party at a five-star hotel situated on the edge of the New Forest next month, on the last Saturday in June. He didn't make Bella's celebrity friend's thirtieth—he wasn't in a single picture—but of course Bella would have chosen a date to suit her revered brother for her engagement party.

I make a coffee and nurse it, pondering. I stare at my pinboard for inspiration, then go online and type in random words like *revenge* and *cheating partner*. I ignore the ridiculous posts that mention murder, public billboards and garage sales of the cheater's belongings. Nonetheless, the internet proves its loyalty and faithfulness as a true friend by providing multiple solutions. My mind keeps coming back to two words: *honey trap*. Related ideas run through my mind, but I dismiss each one as too risky. And yet, a tangible solution feels within my grasp if I mull things over for long enough.

In some ways, it's like having some kind of "buy one, get one free" equivalent. I will, hopefully, be impacting negatively on Bella's night too if I can execute the right turn of events at her party. Nate is not the kind of person who will disguise his feelings if he's in a bad mood.

I return to the pinboard. The photos are divided into past, present and future. Nate's young self grins at me. He is wearing shorts and a T-shirt and looks happy. Bella had a family

photograph on her bedside table. Even then, he had a knowing look in his eyes, a barely concealed confidence.

My past pictures of Bella are cut out of the school yearbooks
because she featured prominently throughout them, whether
it was to do with drama, cookery, academic achievements
or sport. Although she excelled at horse riding, hockey and
tennis, her real strength was swimming. She was horrified
when she discovered my secret shame, my inability to swim.

"But I thought *everyone* learned when they were young?"
she said in the mocking tone of voice she'd started using more
frequently when addressing me.

I had to arrive for swimming lessons fifteen minutes earlier than everyone else, so that I could have extra tuition,
and during the main lesson I was stuck in the shallow end
like a toddler. One time, when I emerged from the smelly,
damp changing rooms, the pool was deserted—apart from
Bella, who was never afraid of rules because, of course, they
didn't apply to her. I sat on a bench at the side, waiting for
Miss Gibbons, but there was no sign of her as the clock ticked
away the minutes.

Bella saw me. "Come in, I'll watch you," she said, beck-
oning me into the pool.

I wanted to say no, but I never did to Bella. So, slowly, reluctantly, I climbed down the ladder and eased myself into
the water at the shallow end. I shivered. A reel of memories
unravelled, slowly at first. Then faster, until they collided. I
decided to be braver, to edge towards the deep end, egged
on by Bella. Water shot up my nose, stinging the back of my
throat. As I lifted up my head, I was aware of Bella. I caught
a flash of her navy swimsuit before our limbs felt locked together and we both disappeared beneath the water.

I forced myself to open my eyes and, mercifully, the blurred edge of the swimming pool came into sight. I reached up and gripped the edge as hard as I could.

I felt myself being helped out. Miss Gibbons. Sitting on the edge, shivering, I coughed so much that I thought I was going to be sick. I could barely hear Miss Gibbons rant at me and thank Bella.

Although I had no proof, I strongly suspected Bella had read my diary and wanted to scare me. I'd found it facing upwards at the bottom of my desk and I always put it face down. My guilt about Will had been exposed and it felt terrifying to have my own words—*It was my fault*—misinterpreted, as though she'd decided I was some kind of *murderer.*

It had been getting harder and harder to ignore the fact that Bella was a nasty piece of work, that she'd tired of me the way that some people do of a pet. A catty comment here, a snigger there. My drawers messed up in our dorm, my deodorant or toothpaste missing. I tried to pretend that it wasn't happening, to keep a stiff upper lip and hope she and her gang would tire of it. But now I had to face up to the fact that my loyalty had been severely misplaced. And because of that, I don't know who I hated more: her or myself.

That night, I ripped out some pages of my diary and tore them into tiny pieces. Earlier sections detailed my fantasies for the future, my frustrations about my mother, and the difficulties of looking after my annoying little brother. And what happened to Will. The stress, the fear of the worst mistake I had ever made, my own damning words, being read by Bella and any others, burned like acid almost constantly inside my stomach. And that wasn't even the worst thing that she did.

I need to focus and concentrate on the present if Bella is to fully pay for the past. Month by month, small action by small action, I'm getting closer.

Ditto when it comes to my future with Nate. Which is

why it makes total sense that Katie must go. I dismiss idea after idea, until I think of something that *could* work because Nate is going to stay at the New Forest hotel on the eve of Bella's party to catch up with old school mates.

A calmness descends as I update my POA.

Sometimes, now that I have a bit of distance from the situation, I wonder why I persist with Nate. The conclusion I always return to is that, if I hadn't seen below the surface—to the man who can be kind, funny, tender and caring—then, of course, it would have made it harder. But, I love him. I've accepted that I simply can't fight destiny. And, because I am temporarily powerless, a honey trap seems a viable solution to ease Katie on her way out, as it will force her to experience Nate's weakness and vanity first-hand. And simultaneously give Nate a valuable life-lesson on how it feels to be dumped.

CHAPTER TWELVE

On Nate's birthday—the fifteenth of June—after a further eight intensive driving lessons, I pass my driving test. Finally, I am able to go and collect my car. A present for myself, seeing as I can't buy Nate a proper gift. I pull away from a car showroom with the roof down, wearing Sophia Loren-style sunglasses.

Twenty minutes later, I'm already lost; the talking map screen goes blank. I pull into a garage and ask a mechanic how to reset the navigation system properly. Before I pull away, I call Amy.

"Hi, fancy coming for a spin in my new car?"

She hesitates. "Sorry, I can't. My mum is coming to visit and…"

"Maybe later, then?"

"I'm not sure."

I feel a slight sense of unease as I hang up. Amy didn't sound herself, as though someone else was with her. I like Amy, I really do, but sometimes she can be a bit selfish. The sort of person who, if you ask how they are, tells you in too much detail. I call the estate agent and ask if I can view the properties they've lined up for me earlier than arranged. I type *Richmond* into the satnav and set off.

I soon discover that the inconvenient thing about having a car is that you have to park it. I drive around, getting caught up behind buses and bikes, until eventually, I park on the outskirts of Richmond. I send Amy a message reminding her to give me a call if she changes her mind.

She doesn't reply.

As soon as I follow a navy-skirt-suit-wearing estate agent into a contemporary one-bedroomed apartment, I just *know* that this will be the perfect home for me. It feels like mine already. From the bedroom window I can just about see Nate's front door. If I use binoculars, I will be able to watch his comings and goings, which may be a useful thing, even when we are back together.

I will never trust anyone again. Trust is a luxury.

Back home, whilst waiting for the kettle to boil, I ring in an offer for the flat. I get back to work on my plans and re-google *honey trap*. All I have to do is send in a photo of Nate—that's not hard—provide my credit card details and the time and address of Nate's whereabouts. The hardest question to answer is about Nate's type of woman. I'd like to say me. But, in truth, I really don't know. I have brown hair—currently blonde—and am of average height. I did trawl through pictures of Nate's old girlfriends, but the more I think about it, the more I don't think he has a "type." I tell the agency that it needs to be someone discreet and classy, with no visible tattoos.

I didn't question Nate too much about his past when we were together. I didn't need to, I'd kept tabs on him over the years. And besides, a lot of my history was embellished—apart from the area I came from, my school and the fact that I'd never made it as an actress. I wanted an excuse for the succession of job changes.

He once asked me how well I'd known Bella.

I replied, "Everyone knew of Bella, but I didn't have that much to do with her," then changed the subject. I could hardly tell the truth—that I was a loner, drifting unanchored, waiting to put all my eggs in the one basket. His.

I couldn't admit to being virtually friendless either. That's why Amy is so important—every girl needs a best friend, and she'll make me look good.

Nate's bound to approve of my friendship with her. And she'll be living proof that I am not a total social outcast.

The day before *the* party, I call the scheduling department, seeing as I can't be on two continents at once.

"Staff number?"

"959840. I'm calling in sick for my Perth flight tonight."

I can hear the tapping of a keyboard. "Is it a work-related injury? Do you need any support from your manager?"

"No. Thank you. I'll call in when I'm feeling better," I say in a "sick" voice. Smiling, I end the call.

I love the anonymity of my job. Whenever I've faked illness before, in previous jobs, I've had to suffer false concern when, really, colleagues were pissed off that they had to cover my work.

Three hundred guests are expected at the party tomorrow night. A perfect number. It is a James Bond theme. Katie is going in a Chinese blue silk dress, as worn by double agent Miss Taro in *Dr. No.* She'll need to add a dark wig. Nate is going as James Bond. Heaven forbid he'd go as someone interesting, like Jaws. Bella's keeping her costume a secret; like anyone cares. She used to do the same at school, whether it

was a party or a school play. I google *Bond girls* and I suspect
I know who she will dress as, because there is one who is
described as the "most revered." Mine is an elegant, simple
dress similar to one worn by a KGB agent in *The Spy Who
Loved Me*. I can't wear a catsuit; I need to blend in with subtle elegance.

I check Nate's messages. I love my spy app, when it isn't
being temperamental; it's akin to being psychic. As planned,
Nate is still going to stay at the hotel tonight. As am I.

The country hotel is situated in several acres of grounds
and boasts a maze, a lake and a golf course. Ancient oaks line
the long, sweeping drive. As I slow down for speed bumps,
it reminds me of school. I feel slightly sick as the grand, old
house comes into view. Beyond, a break in the clouds becomes
visible as weak evening sun pokes through. The reception is
quiet, probably the calm before the party storm, as presumably most guests will arrive tomorrow. I check in, refuse the
offer of help with my bags and head upstairs, considering it
safer than being trapped in a lift.

The room is dingy and the flowery decor is depressingly
old-fashioned. Delicate, cloying pouches of lavender pot-
pourri, tied with twee mauve ribbon, rest on the pillows.
The overwhelming stench of lavender almost chokes me. I
fling open a window, but it sticks at a few inches wide. I inhale fresh air through the gap, before rummaging through
my handbag to remove my perfume, which I spray generously
around the room. I drop the lavender "sleep aids" through
the crack in the window and watch them disappear as they
are swallowed by a bush. The disturbing memory the smell
evokes is too much to bear.

I phone the honey-trap agency.

"Is the woman vetting my boyfriend at the venue yet?" I

ask. I must sound like a desperate, insecure girlfriend, but I don't care.

"Yes, but please don't worry. Most men are loyal to their partners. We usually find that there's nothing worth worrying about."

"Really?" That's a shame.

I sink down on to the bed.

Nate's phone is silent. No messages, no social media, nothing. Obviously, he is preoccupied.

Inhale. Exhale.

I shouldn't have come here tonight, I should have waited until tomorrow. I am trapped, in this room, whilst downstairs I can only imagine the kind of flirtatious scenario that may be unfolding. I consider my options: I *could* go to the bar, but I don't think it will be busy enough for me to conceal myself adequately. I could also order room service, or try to watch a film. But neither option appeals.

I need to get out.

Dusk is imminent as I walk to the car park. I press my key-fob and slide into the driver's seat. I aim for the exit, with no clear idea of where I'm headed. I make my way along narrow roads, edged with giant redwoods and rhododendrons which are past their full bloom, their leaves sagging. I pass several old cottages with cattle grids at the driveway entrances, before the lane snakes into open heathland with patches of heather and frequent signs warning motorists to *Beware of Ponies* and to *Slow Down*. Clusters of ponies gather near the edge of the road in twos or threes, beneath oak canopies. Initially, I intend to drive for at least an hour or two to keep my mind occupied, but within minutes, I have to switch my headlights on to full beam. Instead of wide-open spaces the darkness shrinks the forest, and I feel isolated—moments away from unseen threats.

I return to the hotel car park. I turn off the engine and sit, in the darkness, staring at the bright lights of the building. A taxi pulls up and a couple emerge from the entrance and descend the stairs. An overweight man in a dinner suit comes out for a cigarette.

I don't move. I don't trust myself.

A woman walks down the hotel steps and into another waiting cab. I sit up straighter. I didn't catch much more than a glimpse of her, but she was curvaceous, with long, blonde, wavy hair, and she was definitely wearing heels. It *has* to be the woman from the agency, because I can't see why else someone would be leaving alone at this time of the evening, all dressed up.

With a renewed sense of purpose, I start up the engine and follow the taxi out of the driveway. It turns right. Ensuring I'm not too close, I keep the vehicle in sight. As suspected, it drives down the gentle slope towards the station. I park in the small car park, beside a four-by-four. Looking up, I can see the driver is reading from an e-reader or tablet, the screen illuminates his face.

I step out of my car, glad that I'm wearing trainers, and walk towards the red-brick entrance. The woman is alone on the platform. I look up at the information board; there is a train to London in seven minutes. She leans against a white pillar, well back from the yellow platform line, tapping her phone. I sit down on a cold metal seat and look around. There is nothing much to look at: a vending machine, a help point and, of course, CCTV. I need to know if she's enjoyed Nate's company tonight. I could phone the agency, but it's late. And even if they answer, I suspect I will be fobbed off with a promise of a "full report soon."

I walk up to her. She startles a little as I approach.

"Excuse me, do you know how long the train journey is to Waterloo?" It's the best I can think of for now.

"It's nearly two hours."

"Oh. That's annoying. I meant to get one earlier."

"Me too." She smiles. "You're lucky. This is the last train tonight."

Her large brown eyes are heavily made up, and she is wearing lipgloss. I can imagine Nate being drawn in by her and I feel the familiar stab of envy uncoil inside.

"Did you go anywhere nice? I was visiting an aunt."

A loud recorded announcement interrupts us: *The train now approaching platform one is the…* White lights appear in the distance, aiming for us.

"Nice to meet you," she says, making it clear that she does not want to be stuck chatting to me all the way to London.

"You too," I say.

The track vibrates as the train gets closer.

On some level, I *get* that it is not this woman's fault if Nate has been beguiled by her. But at this very moment, to me, she represents every *other* woman. Every Katie, every preceding woman and every future one. I try to take a deep breath to calm myself down, but my lungs feel tight and my throat constricted. I can't quite get to the safe place in my head. As the train is about to pull in, I take a step forward. Behind me, the waiting-room door is pushed open. The driver I parked next to appears on the platform near me.

Inside the train, I can see a few heads, reading, watching screens, dozing. I briefly wonder whether to embark and return tomorrow—but that too would be pointless. I've already wasted an entire evening. The woman pushes the button to open the door and steps on to the train. I watch as she selects a window seat. To my side, the man greets an elderly gentleman and takes his small bag, guiding him by the arm towards the exit.

As the train pulls away, I notice my suspected honey-trap woman's puzzled expression as she clocks me, rooted to the platform, staring. I remain standing for several more moments, feeling adrift, until I accept the fact that the best course of action for now is to return to my lonely hotel room and sleep.

The following morning, I lie in bed, staring at the ceiling. My phone rings.

"Juliette? Juliette Price?"

"Speaking."

"It's Stacy. From the agency."

I sit up. "Hi?"

"You said you'd like a verbal report as well as an email?"

"Yes, that's right."

"I'm afraid I have some difficult news. Do you have a friend or someone with a listening ear you can turn to for support?" A prickle of hope and excitement.

"It's fine. Just tell me. Please."

"Well, as you know, our staff do not deliberately entice anyone or—"

"Yes, yes, yes, I know. Just tell me. What did Nate do?"

"He asked for her details. Her phone number specifically. She didn't offer it. He asked for it."

"Anything else?"

"No."

"And in your experience this means?"

"That you need to keep a close eye."

"What was her name?"

"Miranda."

"Is she blonde?"

"Yes, but I wouldn't recommend that you dwell on that as relevant information. Our full report will follow shortly."

"OK. Thank you."

I get out of bed with a fresh sense of purpose.

Leaving the hotel, I drive to a nearby village and sit in a café, working on how best to feed the information back to Katie.

★ ★ ★

Late afternoon, I slide my dress over my head and apply thick make-up and a wig. I recently bought some blue contact lenses in the States, but they are a bugger to put in. I squint and poke my eyes as I persevere; glasses would look like an obvious disguise. I reapply my mascara.

I'm now blue-eyed, with long, wavy, dark-brown hair. I smile to myself in the mirror.

I am ready.

I wait until an hour after the party would have started before walking gracefully down the stairs, head high, and into the ballroom, as though I have every right to be there.

Which I do.

I accept a glass of champagne from a passing waiter and slip through the crowds. My eyes scan. There's no one I recognize yet, but I feel exposed. I find a corner, where I sip my drink. Framed pictures of Bella and Miles' love affair adorn the walls—skiing in Whistler, on board a yacht in Monaco, a gondola in Venice. I take a canapé from a passing waitress because it gives me something to do. I bite into a salmon blini but it's too rich. I feel sick.

My nausea intensifies the moment I spot Bella. She is at the far side of the room. My prediction was right: Honey Ryder from *Dr. No* in a white bikini. She looks like she's stepped off a film set. Bella is, literally, show-stopping.

I turn to an older woman beside me. She is staring at Bella. "Are you a friend of Bella or Miles?" I ask.

"Neither," she says. "My husband works with Miles and…" I smile and nod, but my legs feel shaky. A flash of red hair. Katie. She is heading for the bar, alone. I can't see Nate. But he must be here.

I excuse myself and make my way down the side of the room, away from Bella. A man steps on my toes. I ignore the pain and continue. A band takes up position and, within moments, the dance floor is filled. After two songs, silence falls and the lights dim further. Bella takes centre stage as a light focuses on her from above. I watch. She beckons to some- one. Voodoo Man, from *Live and Let Die* joins her. I recog- nize him: Miles.

My stomach knots as I spot Nate leaning against a wall, clutching a glass of red wine, looking lost in thought. Katie joins him. They don't look happy, but then again, they don't look unhappy either. Katie takes his drink from him and places it on a table. She pulls him on to the dance floor. I watch as they bop away whilst I remain rooted to my spot.

I edge my way on to the dance floor and join a group. Mirrors, lights, darkness. As an upbeat version of "The Man with the Golden Gun" blares, people rush for the safety of the sidelines—apart from Bella, who writhes and twists in a clearly choreographed display. I want to scream as everyone claps and cheers at the end. Why can't they see through her? If this was my event, it would be tasteful and understated. I wouldn't put on a show. I feel faint as Bella points in my di- rection, and I have a horrible vision of her pulling me on to the dance floor and exposing me. A woman from the crowd in front of me joins her. They squeal, hug and air kiss.

I don't even realize I've been holding my breath until I exhale.

The evening does not feel like a success. Bella is having a ball. Ditto Nate and Katie. What a waste of time. I leave, but not before removing my present from my bag and add- ing it to the mountain on a corner table. My unlabelled gift is a book on how to work on an ailing relationship. I'm sick of happy couples.

CHAPTER THIRTEEN

I wait forty-eight hours before I send an anonymous but detailed letter outlining my "suspicions" to Katie from a "well-wisher." I heard those words used in a TV programme once, and they seemed to irritate the recipient.

Feeling a bit euphoric from my meddling, I turn the radio up loud as I make a prawn stir-fry. But, as is so often the case, I cook too much and the sight of enough food for two brings me down again. I miss cooking for Nate, he was always so appreciative of a home-cooked meal after all the plane and hotel food. I turn the music down as I nibble half-heartedly in front of my laptop, scrolling, searching, posting.

In the future, if Nate's family research my background, I want them to see what an upstanding citizen I am. People see what they want to see. In me, they will see the perfect wife for their beloved son and a kind, thoughtful daughter-in-law. I'm far from a one-trick pony. My invented rich and varied CV makes me the perfect candidate for the position. I bake, I sew, I create. I will host every Christmas, New Year, Easter—the whole fucking lot. I want Bella to dread every festive season—like she made me dread each new term—because I will subtly undermine her from behind the scenes and alienate her from her family.

I read an email from my manager. My place on the airline's promotions team will be definite by September, which means that I need to reunite with Nate sooner rather than later. My one major advantage is the element of surprise, and I must not jeopardize that.

I check my spy app. There is silence as regards Katie, so far. Nate has been rostered a Vegas in three weeks. This could be the perfect opportunity to engineer myself on to his flight, because Las Vegas is an unpopular trip: crammed flights and overexcited, heavy-drinking stags and hens. I check the swap notices. *Damn*. No one has requested to exchange that particular destination. I will keep checking over the coming week before adding a request of my own. Ideally, I'd like to leave no online trace that it is anything other than chance scheduling that we operate the same flight.

I have run out of things to do, so I switch on the TV and watch a Wimbledon tennis match. It will give me something to chat to Barbara about as I imagine she's in front of the telly now, Pimm's in one hand, a bowl of strawberries and cream within close reach. It's an annual ritual of hers. But it's difficult to concentrate, as I keep checking for messages from Katie to Nate or vice versa, until the spy app freezes and I can't get it to work. It's annoying, like having my psychic powers turned off. I need to be more cautious as I've read that it can drain Nate's battery, and if that occurs too frequently, he could either try to get it fixed or push for an upgrade.

It works again after a few hours, probably after Nate has rebooted his phone. I force myself to check only once every couple of hours. I discover that he has employed a cleaner to come in twice a week. This, I suspect, is good news; in the event I ever make an error, then the cleaner will be blamed.

The other good thing is that, by the time I leave for my next trip to Delhi a couple of days later, there has been very little contact between Katie and Nate.

As the crew bus bumps along, badly hung window curtains brush my face each time we hit a pothole. I try to tie back the flimsy material with a hairband so I can see outside. This is my first time in Delhi and it's beguiling. Rickshaws, bicycles and cows all fight for personal space on the road, oblivious to the hooting and loud engines of the garishly decorated trucks and buses as they play chicken. Heat, due to the poor air conditioning, intermingles with the pungent smell of fruit and drains, which clashes with the strong scent of the white plastic air fresheners attached to the dashboard.

I'm excited. I've found out from a passenger that there is a locally respected fortune teller who works in our hotel and, seeing as it's my birthday, it will make a good present to myself. Especially as I keep checking for messages from Nate, even though I know it's futile—he would never remember without a prompt—but like so many things, I just can't help myself.

I ask a receptionist about making an appointment whilst we are checking in.

"I will see what I can do, madam," she promises.

Less than an hour later, my room phone rings.

"Madam. This is Reyansh. You would like to see me, I understand?"

I am momentarily thrown. I expected a female.

I find my voice. "Yes, please."

"You're very lucky today. I have a spare hour if you can come downstairs now."

The cynic in me suspects that I've not been particularly lucky, but nonetheless, I am curious and feel drawn to do this, so I agree. In the basement area, among the carpet and jewel-lery shops with displays of yellow gold, sapphires and emeralds, I politely decline various shopkeepers' offers of tea—*chai*—as I'm beckoned by a short, old man towards a curtained-off area at the end of the wide corridor. Behind the curtain, I'm offered a seat, which I accept as Reyansh sits opposite, on the other side of a large wooden desk.

"Please. Can you let me borrow a piece of jewellery or something that means a lot to you?"

I hand over an eternity ring. It is worthless, but I like it because it is a replica of the kind of ring I'd like Nate to give me one day. Reyansh spends time studying it in his palm, then speaks with such great speed that it is hard to keep up with everything.

However, by the time I leave—an hour later—the gist of what he has relayed slowly sinks in. I've been waiting for someone for a long time and the man in question does love me. A part of me doesn't care if it's what he genuinely "saw" or "felt" or not, it gives me a strong sense of renewed hope and optimism. Everyone needs a boost now and then, and I'm no different, so I don't begrudge the 5,000 rupees I paid Reyansh.

Later, I meet up with the rest of my crew in a local vegetarian restaurant and try out a roast cauliflower curry. After the meal, we're invited back to the captain's room for drinks, seeing as the restaurant was dry.

Several beers later, an argument breaks out between two stewards who realize they are dating the same person after sharing photos of their boyfriends. Both huddle in the corner of the suite and make angry calls to the man in question—Sebastian—who is in Dubai with his phone switched off. I imagine he's going to keep it that way for some time once he picks up his venomous voicemails.

The woman sitting next to me makes a face. "Everyone

thinks that their Sebastian, Tim, Dave, Jane, whoever, is *different*," she says.

The sick feeling that almost permanently inhabits my stomach, like a ball of mixed poisons, kneads my insides. I always knew that Nate faced temptation every time that he went to work, but I tried never to let my mind go there.

"There must be some decent ones, though?" I say. "Aren't lots of flight crew married with children?"

She looks at me as though she can't quite make me out. "Don't tell me you joined the airline to marry a pilot!" she says.

I shake my head, implying the very notion had never entered my mind.

"Of course there are success stories. But it's hard, though. Take my advice and make sure you go out with someone with a ground-based job. Mind you, that comes with a different set of problems because they aren't always understanding when you've got to work a third Christmas in a row."

I zone out and focus on the positive news Reyansh revealed earlier.

Around me, plans are made to visit the Taj Mahal the following day. I don't want to go. Not only is it a long journey, but the thought of being faced with a monument which took over twenty years to build as a show of love is more than I can bear. Because that's what I want: Nate to love me that much.

The flight home is full and busy.

During the first meal service, a little girl sitting in an aisle seat chokes. I automatically slap her on the back and, thankfully, a piece of bread dislodges, but the sound of her crying gets to me. Her mother remains in a panic and although I try to reassure her, I need to get away from the scene. I go to the galley to get extra bottles of water and try to block out all the general mayhem and noise from the cabin. I look at my watch hopefully, but there are hours left until landing.

The service eventually ends without further disruptions. I sink down into my crew seat after the galley is finally cleared up and sip a black coffee.

I stare out the window into the vast nothingness and think about how much I've achieved, rather than lost.

My session with Reyansh, if nothing else, has helped me to remind myself to stay focused. And try to keep my belief that all will end well.

We land on a boiling afternoon.

Nate's Lusaka flight is due to land in two hours' time. I check. He is delayed by a further ninety minutes. Even better.

I change out of my uniform in the airport toilets and drive to Richmond. I manage to find a parking space only two streets away. Despite the heat, I slow jog there. My running outfit is my best summer disguise because I can legitimately wear something with a hood—which I can yank up, if need be. I walk up to the communal doors and collide with someone.

It's an older woman I don't recognize.

"Sorry," she says.

"Me too! Must look where I'm going in future," I mutter as I walk on and don't look back.

Hopefully she's just a random visitor to one of Nate's neighbours.

I sit down on his sofa whilst I ponder. Katie and Nate were back in touch yesterday by phone so I'm clueless as to what was discussed. A twenty-three-minute chat the first time, a seventeen-minute one next. Then a text from her to him, confirming that she'll be down to stay at his tomorrow night. This probably means he's wriggled his way out of her suspicions, so she needs another nudge.

I've narrowed down my objects to four choices: a hair-band, a mauve rose-scented candle, an old photo and a pink toothbrush. Which and where? More than a couple could be

suspicious, but they have to be things that could have feasibly
been left by someone, at some point, *and* somewhere Katie
may look.

It proves harder than I thought, but I decide upon placing
the candle above the fireplace—if Nate notices it, hopefully
he will think that his new cleaner found it in a cupboard and
decided to put it to good use. I take a quick glance out the
window; no sign of a returning Nate. I leave the hairband on
the floor, poking out beneath the bed on the opposite side to
Nate's, and then, taking the toothbrush out of the packaging,
I conceal it in the medicine cabinet.

Nate has some random photos stuck to his fridge door and
I return one that I removed ages ago, adding it among the
others. He is in front of a Japanese temple, his arms around
a woman on each side. He looks happy, which is why I stole
the photograph. When we were together, I hated being reminded of his female colleagues. On the back of it, someone
had written: *Good times xx.* It's not Nate's handwriting.

I check the wine rack. He has not touched his birthday wine.

Back at home, I decide to risk adding my own trip-swap
request for the Vegas, offering up my San Diego. It's snapped
up within an hour. Now that I have a confirmed reunion date,
I need to prepare and I start online. But as soon as I begin
my search, I feel a slight niggle. There is always a risk with
certain types of research, and I don't want anything coming
back to haunt me later. So I stop myself. Perhaps I should go
and use a public computer, like in the library, but still…if I
buy what I need online it needs to be delivered, which poses
a different set of problems.

I think whilst I scroll through my social media accounts,
pressing "like" several times on random posts without properly taking anything in, until I hover over a post of my long-
ago film extra friend, Michele Bianchi. He is no longer a

vet's assistant in a TV drama and has now landed a part in the chorus of a well-known West End show. Michele wasn't against breaking the law when it came to recreational drugs or buying electronic goods from dubious sources. He could be useful to me now.

I private message him, asking if he'd like to meet up for a coffee.

He is online and replies within seconds. Perfect timing— I'm bored in between rehearsals. Will be good to hear all your news. Tomorrow? PS: I'm broke, hint hint, so somewhere cheap and cheerful.

I respond with a smiley face, a promise of cake with his coffee (my treat) and a cheery Ciao Bello! X.

It is good to see Michele again. I spot him before he sees me. He is sitting on a stool in the window of the café. I wave through the glass and he grins back with his perfect white teeth. We give each other a brief kiss hello on each cheek, and he envelops me in a big hug.

He is comforting, like a protective brother. It is nice. There was never any hint of a romance between us, he just always felt…safe.

It is so pleasant catching up that I wait until we finish our coffees before I make my request.

"So, there's no such thing as free coffee and cake?" he says, folding his arms. "What would a gorgeous lady like you need with a date-rape drug?"

"Don't call it that. I've told you; it helped my friend through a difficult patch. With sleeping. I'm heartbroken. *Heartbroken.* I thought that Nick and I—" I break off, as though tears are about to threaten.

"Can't you get sleeping pills, like, from a doctor or something? I'm really not sure."

"I'm happy to pay over the odds. It's just this once. I promise. My friend swore by them. And...I'm desperate."

"How do I know you won't do anything stupid?"

"I just want to sleep. This new job, it takes its toll. It really does."

He doesn't make any promises, but we arrange to meet in the same place in two days' time.

That night, whilst Katie is at Nate's, I make three silent calls to his phone from a withheld number, starting at midnight.

The first two calls, Nate answers.

On my third attempt, it goes straight to voicemail.

My next meeting with Michele proves successful—apart from another brief lecture—and over the following days, Katie and Nate appear to hit a rocky patch.

Her messages to him indicate neediness and a lack of trust:

What are you up to? Sounds like you're having fun without me.

No kisses.

His, in turn, are defensive, take longer, are guarded:

I wasn't out that late. I'm just with the guys.

It goes silent between them. Nate is not a man who cares about unfinished business.

The evening before I leave for Vegas, there has been no further contact between them.

I dare to hope that it's over.

Two hours prior to departure I walk into the briefing room and pick up a spare hard copy of the crew briefing sheet; I forgot to download it on to my phone.

"Hi, everyone. We'll go straight into introductions and

working positions," says the in-charge crew member. "Some of you may have flown with me, but for the benefit of everyone, I like to be called Stuart—not David, as it says on the crew list." I chip in that I use my middle name.

"We'll discuss a fire scenario today. Juliette, if you are the first person to discover a fire, what is your immediate action?" We are interrupted by the captain opening the door.

"Morning, all. Barry Fitzgerald's the name. It may get a little rough mid–Atlantic. Remember to be extra vigilant when performing safety checks as the terror threat has been raised from substantial to severe. Any questions?"

I raise my hand. "Can I sit in the flight deck for landing, please?"

He glances at Stuart/David, who looks disinterested; rumour has it that he's cruising to retirement. He nods his permission.

The captain disappears and the briefing continues. It's difficult to concentrate on the safety and medical questions as I'm so electrified, but I force myself to think and respond correctly.

It would be a disaster if I were to be off-loaded from the trip for failing routine questions.

The aircraft pushes back. The exterior world shrinks to the size of the plane's interior. A mini world, trapped and cut off from the outside for the next ten hours and forty-five minutes.

We join the queue for the runway, edging along. I am strapped into my jump seat, staring out the window at the overcast summer's day. As it starts to drizzle, drops dot the windows. The plane swings round to face the runway. Stillness. A roar of engines and a surge of power. My harness is tight against my body. My stomach lifts with the aircraft. We shake and bump as we break through clouds, before levelling out.

I inhale and psych up my air-hostess self.

As I prepare the trolleys, I run through the plan in my head. This is it. This is the day my life begins again. I push through the galley curtains.

"Would you like red or white wine with your meal?" I smile.

We run out of chicken casserole within the first six rows. Several people claim to be vegetarian—arms folded, lips pursed—when they discover there is only lasagne left.

I can't face going into my "it's possible to pre-order a vegetarian meal" line. The complaints continue.

"Why is there never enough choice?"

"This happened on my last flight and the one before."

"It never happens on other airlines."

I try to explain about space constraints but realize I am wasting my breath. I crouch down beside a particularly grumpy couple—the type who probably paid the cheapest fare and will spend their entire holiday grumbling—and whisper conspiratorially. "Don't sit in the middle on your return sector. The service starts from the four corners of economy, front to back, so those in the middle rarely get a choice."

They both beam. "Thank you," they whisper back.

The man accepts the lasagne without further complaint. The woman won't give in that easily and takes the tray on the condition I find her an extra bread roll and some "decent wine from first class." I pour a small bottle of economy red, which she turned her nose up at earlier, into a business-class glass and present it to her. She takes a sip and nods approvingly.

I sink down into a hard crew seat when the service finally ends and pick at a lobster salad I took from the first-class galley, but I find it hard to swallow.

During afternoon tea service, I feel weak and dreamlike. I'm so close. I cannot mess this up. All that separates me and Nate is a mere steel cockpit door.

I jump as his voice fills the cabins. *Ladies and gentlemen, this is your first officer, Nathan Goldsmith. We have approximately half an hour until we land in sunny Las Vegas, which is a sweltering thirty-eight degrees Celsius. Despite this, it may still feel a little bumpy on landing, as there are strong winds.*

I stand still, trying to distance myself from the chaos of the galley, and close my eyes, savouring the memory of his arms around me and his smile. But an unwanted memory sneaks in—his anger when I initially refused to move out. And the time when I hid his passport so that he couldn't go to work because I just needed him to *talk* to me.

But that was then, and this is now.

I was a different person back then, driven demented by rejection. I've now obeyed his wishes and given him space. He has to—surely—make allowances for that. There were lots of happy times. He loved my sense of humour.

The standard pre-landing announcements begin. I secure the cabin and remind people over and over to fasten their seat belts. The plane begins to rock and sway as we dip beneath the clouds. *Cabin crew, seats for landing.*

It's time.

The crew member taking over responsibility for manning my door appears. I thank him and make my way forwards, then climb the stairs. The aircraft makes a sudden drop. I clutch the handrail. The engines are whining. On the upper deck, I walk slowly down the aisle past all the business–class passengers, as nervous as a bride. I almost scream as an old lady grabs my arm as I pass her seat.

"Excuse me," she says, letting go. "Do you know if this turbulence will get any worse? I'm not a good flyer."

"It's all going to be fine," I say, walking on, whilst tugging at some loose strands of hair to partially hide my face.

I stand outside the cockpit door and wave at the camera. The green light illuminates. I push open the door and dart

in, shutting it firmly behind me. I slide into the seat behind
Nate. He is too busy to acknowledge me, we are almost on
final approach. The captain points to some headphones. I put
them on. I listen to air traffic control as I study Nate's neck.
I can see the hairs on his exposed skin.

Outside, the Vegas skyline rises up to greet us. An alarm
sounds above the constant stream of words from the ATC
tower. The automated voice counts us down.

One thousand feet. Five hundred.

The rocking and swaying are less noticeable in the cockpit.

One hundred feet. Fifty, forty, thirty, twenty, ten.

We touch down.

My chest swells with pride in Nate.

As we decrease speed, I remove my headphones whilst the
roar of the engines subsides. I observe Barry and Nate complete their routines and checklists.

As we turn off the runway, Nate turns round, a smile on
his face.

I smile back.

He freezes, as though he's seen a dead person, then turns
to face the controls again.

The terminal comes into sight. *Welcome to McCarran International Airport.*

CHAPTER FOURTEEN

I recently came across a quote: *People will forget what you said, people will forget what you did, but people will never forget how you made them feel.* I want Nate to *feel* unthreatened as he digests the situation, so I decide to retreat.

"Thank you," I say and leave, quietly shutting the door behind me.

After the sanctuary of the cockpit, the cabin is hectic. Manoeuvring my way through the mass of bodies pulling bags from overhead bins and bending over whilst gathering their belongings, I squeeze downstairs.

"Excuse me. Excuse me, please," I repeat, making my way through the debris: headsets, discarded earplugs, eyeshades and newspapers.

I am numb. I thought I'd feel terrified, elated, overjoyed, some strong emotion. Instead, my feelings are frozen; my senses dulled. Noise is muted, apart from the loud voice inside my head.

Focus. You cannot fail.

On automatic pilot I pack my flight apron and flat shoes into my bag. Standing on the edge of a seat, I check the hat racks are empty and scan the seats for the bright-orange infant seat belts. I gather two and return them to the sliding stowage behind the last row.

Keeping my eyes ahead, I disembark with my economy-crew colleagues. We pass slot machines situated below a bombardment of advertisements—hotels, car hire, clubs, bars, restaurants, weddings—before reaching crew immigration. The passenger queues are long and bulging. A weary-looking yet resigned mismatch of people shuffles forwards, dressed in everything from summer dresses, three-quarter-length leggings, baseball caps and T-shirts to those who are more cautiously dressed in trousers, with jackets or jumpers folded over their arms.

The crew suitcases have been off-loaded and are by the side of the baggage carousel, lined up neatly in a row. I select mine and continue through Customs, not looking any of the officials in the eye, as though I have nothing to hide, until the automatic doors part. Pulling my bags behind me, I emerge into the arrivals lounge. Among the balloons, flowers, signs and other paraphernalia dotting the awaiting crowd, I seek out the exit signs.

I escape.

Late afternoon heat hits me, but it is strangely sobering and my head clears.

Deep breaths. Faint dread forms a hollow in my stomach.

As I approach the crew bus, I keep my eyes down. I wait my turn, whilst the driver heaves the bags into the trailer attached to the rear. I can see that the three flight-crew bags are already loaded. I stand, rooted to the spot, trying to work out the best time to board.

Generally, the first officers tend to gather near the front

rows, as it is a courtesy to leave the first seat free for the captain. In all likelihood, I can't avoid walking past him. I wait until the last few crew trickle out of the airport building before I step on to the bus.

I catch Nate's eye immediately. I smile and say, "Hi," as though we saw each other only recently, and continue walking towards the back without waiting to see if he returns my greeting. I sink down next to Alex, one of the guys I've been working with in economy. He is wearing reading glasses and is busy looking down at his phone, but I engage him in conversation, regardless. I need a social prop.

"What are your plans?"

Alex looks up, peers through his glasses and shrugs. "Not sure yet. Gym. Pool. Meet up in the bar. The usual."

"It's my first time here. Any suggestions?"

He smiles. "Loads. If you meet up for drinks later, I'll take you to this incredible club afterwards. We can see if any of the others are up for it, because we'll need to book tickets. Or you could take in a show, but they can be really expensive."

"Thanks."

He looks back down at his phone.

I take mine out too, but not before sneaking a quick glance at Nate. He is looking ahead and is not in conversation with anyone.

The journey is brief—too brief—and I swallow hard as I step down off the bus. But I keep focused and retrieve my wheelie bag as the porters hurriedly load the suitcases on to the trolleys, in an obvious attempt to keep the porte cochère clear. I hang back, remaining on the outskirts of reception and pretending to deal with a phone message, as the flight crew and the supervisor sign for their rooms. Tourists wearing holiday uniforms of T-shirts decorated with random slogans navigate the lobby area alongside more formally dressed business people and uniformed hotel staff. I feel as though Nate's eyes are upon me, but I don't think it's a good idea to check.

Alex walks over to give me his room number and a few others gather round whilst we make plans to meet in the bar at six local time tomorrow.

"I'll need to book tickets for the club in advance. I've just looked it up and the DJ is marketed as *'the next big thing'*"—he mimes quote marks in the air—"so it will be a really popular night."

"I'll buy two tickets," I say. "A friend of mine is operating the flight due in tomorrow."

That way, I'll have a spare one for Nate if I can persuade him to come along. As I step forward to receive my room key, I take a quick look around. My stomach sinks in disappointment— I am the last crew member left in the reception area. Nate has scarpered.

"Please can I take out two hundred dollars on my crew account?" I ask the receptionist.

I was so busy preparing for the trip that I forgot about the mundane practical things, like exchanging money at a decent rate.

"Of course."

She counts it out for me and places it inside an envelope, handing it over with a friendly smile.

I head for the lifts and press the *up* arrow, still half-expecting Nate to appear.

Seconds after entering my room, there is a sharp rap at the door. I fling it open. A porter.

"Suitcase for Ms. Price," he says, walking past me. With one hand, he lifts and unfolds the portable luggage stand, then places my suitcase on top.

I slide my purse out of my bag and hand over a couple of dollar bills. "Thanks."

"You're welcome. Have a great stay."

I walk over to the window, pull apart the net curtains and lean my forehead against the glass. This hotel is set back from the strip and my room is situated at the rear. Below is a mass of buildings, streets, signs—a normal-looking city. I stifle a yawn, even though I feel too wired to give in to proper tiredness. Instead, I feel detached and dream-like. I turn round and set about half-heartedly unpacking.

My suitcase is unusually full. Normally, I travel out with an empty one and return with it crammed. I take care hanging up my outfits, especially my dresses. I hold one particular one up against me and stare at myself in the mirror, hoping that I still love it and that it doesn't look different here. I smile. It's still perfect. It has a silk lining covered in plain lace and is cornflower blue, slightly above the knee. It cost more than I have ever spent on one outfit. I love it. The scooped neckline is low, so I can accessorize with a simple necklace.

I decide on a shower to properly shake myself into alertness. Once I feel refreshed, I will consider the best way to approach Nate. He will probably stay up until later this evening, seeing as he is a stickler for "keeping to local time." From conversations with other crew, I know that many people feel the same. Personally, I don't see the point. I don't mind being up in the night or early morning, I can always find ways to occupy myself.

I step into the bath, pull the opaque curtain across and fiddle with the shower controls. It's a recently acquired life skill, figuring out how to get the temperature right in hotels around the world as they vary from scorching to freezing. As I shampoo my hair to remove the sticky hairspray and the stench of the aircraft galley, I try to reframe Nate's earlier non-reaction into a more positive one. The loud, old-fashioned ring of the hotel bathroom phone jolts me out of my thoughts. I reach out through the gap between the wall and the shower curtain and pull the receiver off the wall, holding my arm and head away from the spray of water. Shampoo stings my eyes as I squeeze them shut. "Hello?" Silence.

"Hello?"

I feel for the controls with my free hand, switch off the cascade of water and pat along the wall until I can feel a metal rail. Once I reach the softness of a towel, I yank it down. I dab my eyes.

"Elizabeth? Lily?"

A surge of joy. "Nate?"

"What is going on? You nearly gave me a heart attack!" I smile. He does not sound cross.

"Sorry. I didn't mean to. I'd already asked the captain in briefing if I could come in for landing. I only realized you were operating when I heard your voice on the passenger PA." I shiver. "Hang on a minute; I need to get out of the shower." I clamber out and sit on the edge, awkwardly half-wrapping my towel around me, whilst still clutching the old-style receiver. The stinging in my eyes subsides. "I took your advice when we split up and decided to start afresh. Try something new. But, guess what?"

"What?"

"Other airlines—three of them—rejected me!"

"Seriously?"

"Seriously. The last one said I was too enthusiastic. How can a flight attendant be too enthusiastic?" He laughs.

Sheer relief floods my body as fresh hope resurfaces. I continue, "But, joking aside, you have been on my mind. I wanted to let you know, but at the same time, I wanted to give you space. I didn't want you to feel duty-bound to meet for coffee in the canteen or anything, just because we're now colleagues."

"Okaaay." He sounds as though he is processing his emotions through a filter. "How long have you been with us?"

I smile. My answer is proof that I am totally capable of giving him his precious *space*.

"Seven months."

"Oh…" A pause. "Are you going down to the bar?"

"No, not tonight. Maybe tomorrow. Sorry, again, if I gave you a shock, but hopefully we can catch up at some point. I've got to go now, my boyfriend is going to Skype me soon."

"Oh. Yes. Of course. I won't keep you."

As soon as I replace the receiver, I punch the air. I bet he wasn't expecting that. No—he probably imagined I'd be outside his door on my knees, beseechingly pleading for a scrap of attention. I climb back into the shower and rinse off the shampoo.

Seventy-two hours; that's all I have.

Afterwards, I wrap myself in a hotel gown. It's a bit on the starchy rather than the fluffy side, but it does the job. I turn down the air conditioning and take a seat in front of the desk. I open the hotel information folder and take out two sheets of writing paper from the back. I doodle.

Elizabeth Goldsmith, Juliette Goldsmith, Elizabeth Juliette Goldsmith, Mrs. E. J. Goldsmith.

Miss Price, Miss Elizabeth Juliette Price.

By the time I decide to call the spa and book several treatments—including a pedicure and manicure—for tomorrow afternoon, my hair is almost dry. I finish it off with a final blast of the hairdryer before I allow myself the luxury of bed.

As I drift off, I can feel welcome oblivion pulling me under, and I relax into it.

A noise intrudes on my happiness. It is Amelia. Her sentences don't make sense but I can make out the odd word, such as "responsibility." Like cloud-hopping, I emerge into another scene. Will and I are in the old, local village park with its one small slide, two red baby swings and a climbing frame in desperate need of a fresh coat of paint in a bright primary colour, like sunshine yellow. I am pushing him in a swing and he alternates between fear and demanding to go *higher!*

Beyond, looking above the park perimeter fence, I can see the hills which circle the outskirts of the village. I know that slightly further away lies the coast. A scream pulls me back into the park. Will has fallen out. I don't know how; but something distracted me. Both his knees are grazed. Amelia will be furious.

Bella rushes into the park wearing a nurse's uniform, brandishing a box of plasters. A surge of injustice rages. She tells me I should have saved him. Behind her, I become aware of a river. I push her in and watch as a group of puzzled swans surround her floating body.

I jolt awake. The room is dark. I reach for the light of my phone as William, Amelia and Bella fade back into non-existence. I check the time. Four thirty.

Four thirty where? What time zone? What country?

I shut my eyes. The park felt real. I turn on the side light and reach for a bottle of water. I drink, great big gulps. Drops drip down my pyjama top. My limbs are heavy, but I force myself out of bed, resisting the urge to sink back to the park in my dreams where problems—real ones—didn't yet exist.

I order room service—an omelette with a cafetière of strong coffee—before deciding to go for a swim.

The pool is quiet, apart from an older couple completing slow lengths. I dive in, feeling the sting of chemicals shoot up my nose as I move my arms and pull my body along. I come up for air then drop beneath the surface again. I push myself physically harder than I have in a long time, until I pull myself up on to the side. I leave my feet dangling in the water and I shut my eyes, shivering a little as I mentally rehearse the days ahead.

It's crucial I play it right.

Back in my room, I force myself to rest—I will need all my energy—by lying on the bed, the TV on in the background.

I drift in and out to the sound of police cars, laughing and adverts. The words and sounds mix up in my consciousness, jumbling reality and fiction.

When my alarm goes off, I sit up, feeling sick and disorientated.

Even after a shower, I still don't feel very alert, but I force myself to lift open the lid of my laptop and get to work, updating my plans and double-checking that I haven't forgotten anything. I don't want to tempt fate, but there's no getting away from the fact that some things need preparation, not everything can be spontaneous and organic.

Satisfied I can do no more, I cocoon myself in the spa. I accept an offer of herbal tea, and the warmth of ginger and cinnamon soothes me. After my nail treatments and facial, I sit in the hair salon, trying not to fidget, as my make-up is applied and my hair blow-dried. I ask the stylist to wave it at the ends, the way that Nate likes it.

Pushing the key card into the lock and entering my room, my heart rate quickens in hopeful anticipation when I notice the red message light flashing on the desk phone. I pick it up and press "seven"—as instructed by the automated voice— to retrieve the message, my excitement dipping when it's not Nate's voice.

It's Alex. "Hi, just to let you know we're meeting a bit later than arranged. It will be more like seven o'clock." That leaves me with an extra hour to fill.

I dress. Not in my new favourite one but a simple, black shift. It is also above the knee, but loose fitting. It is the kind of dress that can be dressed up or down, sleek or casual. I place a silver, heart-shaped pendant over my head, which rests in the middle of my chest. I slide my feet into a pair of pale mauve, open-backed heels. I stand back and look in the mirror. The stylists did a good job. I shrug my arms into a plain black cardigan, then pick up the phone.

"Can I have the room number for Nathan Goldsmith, please?"

"Let me just check the crew list," says the male voice. "Do you want me to connect you?"

"No, thanks. Just the room number, please."

"Seven eighty-two."

I replace the receiver and give my reflection a final going over, before I pick up my clutch bag and leave the room.

The door clicks shut behind me as I walk silently along the carpeted corridor. The lift bell chimes as the doors shudder open. I step in and press floor seven. My mouth feels dry as I resist the urge to turn back round.

I stop outside room 782 and listen. I can hear canned laughter on the TV.

Taking a deep breath, I knock.

CHAPTER FIFTEEN

I hear the sound of an object being placed on to a hard surface. The door opens and Nate, wearing jeans and a navy T-shirt, stares.

"Hi."

"Hi. Can I come in for a moment?"

He stands back to make way. "Yes. Yes, of course."

"Everyone at work knows me as Juliette," I say, strolling past. "I use my middle name."

"Juliette?" He pauses, as though mulling it over.

I turn the desk chair round to face the room and sit down. The bed feels too familiar, too intimate. I need him to feel secure; to feel one hundred per cent certain that he can trust me now that I've proved my feelings for him have evaporated.

"Alex, the guy I'm working with, just rang to say that they're meeting a bit later, so I had time to kill. I thought it would be good if we caught up—properly—seeing as we've ended up in this situation."

"Great idea," he says, sinking down on to the bed opposite me. "Drink? I have some wine."

"OK, thanks."

I watch as he takes out two miniature bottles of red. I turn round and reach for the tumblers on the tray beside the kettle. I remove the plastic covers and turn them the correct way round. Nate pours. His hand shakes a little as he does so.

"Cheers!" we chorus and raise our glasses in unison, as he sits back down opposite me.

I take a sip. My mind goes blank.

"I didn't expect to find you in Vegas."

I laugh. "I know. This all feels a bit surreal. What have you been up to?"

"The usual. Away. Home. Away again."

I smile. "You were right about Reading, by the way. My neighbours are great, we go out a lot. Actually, it was thanks to you that I met my new man, he only lives two doors down. I couldn't get the Wi-Fi sorted and he offered to help. It's early days, though—" I stop. "Sorry, I'm gabbling. I'm nervous." I take a sip of wine; it tastes bitter.

"No, not at all. I'm glad you're happy. It's good."

"Thanks." I look down at my watch. "I'll head down to the bar soon. Alex knows this great club for later."

"Any other plans whilst you're here?"

"Well, seeing as I've never been, there's loads for me to do. Today was a write-off, I was so tired. I understand now what it was like for you. Especially when you came home from a trip and I was *there*. No wonder you shipped me off to Reading— you probably needed some peace and quiet."

He shifts uncomfortably on the bed. "It wasn't quite like that."

I smile. "I'm only joking. Anyway, now we've caught up, you can buy me a coffee if we ever bump into each other."

"Definitely."

"I'm sorry," I say. "For everything. It *was* too much too soon. You were right. It just felt so good between us and I lost all reason."

"It was good," he admits. "Mostly."

It's not as though he can say anything else. You can't argue with the truth. And it was *me* who fucked up. I pressed too hard on the relationship accelerator without realizing the need to ease off every now and then. I really, truly get that now.

"You were right to take a step back. Thanks for the drink." I put down my glass. It is still nearly full but I can't face any more. "I'll head off and meet the others. Have you guys got plans?"

"Barry has relatives here, so no, and the other FO is getting up early tomorrow to do a tour of the Grand Canyon."

"Join us if you feel like it," I say.

"I was thinking of wandering down to the bar later."

"Maybe see you later, then," I say, standing up. "If not, then I'll see you at pick-up."

"Actually," he says, "I may as well come down with you now but I need to change quickly. Especially if we're going out after. You're all dressed up."

I shrug. "Not really. It's hard to know what to wear. It's so hot outside, yet freezing inside when the air conditioning is ramped up."

"Your hair is different," he says. "It suits you."

My heart rate quickens. The old Nate is re-emerging now that I seem unattainable. He whips off his T-shirt and pulls a smarter one out of his suitcase. I pretend not to watch but I can see his reflection in the mirror.

We walk side by side along the corridor. I could easily slide my hand into his or put my arm around him, but I look ahead. When the lift arrives, it's almost full, so we are forced apart as we squeeze in among several Dutch tourists and a family with three young boys. We hold back and step out into the lobby, then across to the bar.

As we enter, I am momentarily stunned by the light and noise. There is no escaping the slot machines. I narrow my eyes and spot Alex with a few of the others, which isn't always easy, given that even the men can look different out of uniform. I locate an empty seat next to him and order a sparkling water from a waitress.

I turn my attention to Alex. I am aware that Nate is talking to the upper-deck crew member, Joanna. Alex and I are sucked into a general group conversation which centres on the unpopular overhaul of the on-board service routine, which has been created by office workers who have never had the pleasure of serving the general public in a confined area. I pretend to join in by nodding and agreeing on certain points, but I'm trying to eavesdrop on Nate.

"What about this club, then?" I say to Alex. "I'm bored of talking shop."

"Fancy something to eat first? There's a Vietnamese place which serves fantastic noodles in the same hotel as the club."

"Perfect. By the way, there's a spare ticket going begging. My friend didn't come in the end, she was late for work and got sent to Hong Kong instead."

I go to the Ladies whilst Alex sorts out the logistics with the rest of the group. I don't want to inadvertently let Nate catch any subconscious signals of how desperate I am that he joins us—and hopefully Alex will offer him my "spare" ticket, so that I don't have to. When I return, the entire group is heading for the lobby and Alex is organizing cabs with the doormen. We pass through the revolving doors and I hang back as four people climb into the first one, leaving me, Alex, Nate and Joanna. A second taxi pulls up.

"Do you mind if I take the front?" says Joanna. "I get horribly car sick."

We all agree. Nate walks behind the taxi, opens the rear passenger door behind the driver and gets in. I slide into the middle, Alex is on my left. I am sandwiched between the two of them and I can feel Nate's thigh against mine.

I can barely breathe.

We pull on to the strip and my senses are hit further by the sheer volume of traffic, neon lights and signs. As we drive past the lit-up Bellagio Fountains, I'm dying to hold Nate's hand. He might not even object; he is looking out the window and his whole posture and expression is relaxed. Instead, I turn to Alex as our driver overtakes an enormous black pick-up truck, which hoots in retaliation.

"Seems there is a price to pay for fun," I say, pointing at the billboards advertising personal injury lawyers and bail bonds, ignoring the slight sense of unease curling through my thoughts as I picture the pills concealed within a vitamin bottle, courtesy of Michele Bianchi.

"Yeah, I can imagine."

We pull up outside another hotel, which looks much the same as ours. The rest of our group have already piled out of their taxi and are waiting at the bottom of the steps. Nate, myself, Alex and Joanna fumble around in our bags for dollar bills, but Alex pays our driver.

"Get me a drink later," he says, batting away offers of cash.

I sit next to Alex when we are shown to our table and ask him for advice on dishes. Nate sits opposite. We order beers whilst everyone listens to the waiter running through the specials. As a group, we select summer rolls to start and I choose tofu coconut curry. I hear Nate opt for a spicy noodle soup. Alex launches into a tale about the last time he was at this club. One of the girls on his crew got so drunk, she went round begging strangers to marry her and had to be taken home by the supervisor, after security threatened to throw the whole group out.

This sets off a lively conversation of similar tales, each one getting worse. No one admits to being the main culprit in any of these stories, the common thread being that they are mostly fuelled by alcohol, jet lag or the need to let their hair down away from the constraints of home.

The thing I've realized about this job is that, although most crew secretly love it—for many it was a childhood dream—and they are attached to the transient nature, there is an underlying loneliness. I was surprised to learn that whilst suicide is not common, it isn't unheard of either. And it usually occurs down-route, where problems can appear magnified when crew are away from friends and family. I look around the table—everyone looks relaxed, they are laughing, drinking, eating, chatting. To observers, we could look like a bunch of holidaying mates. But apart from Nate, of course, I don't *know* any of these people. I only met them thirty-six hours ago and I may never see some—if any—of them again. Secrets spilled, experiences shared, most of these tenuous connections will cease to exist once the wheels touch down at Heathrow.

There is a general impression which emanates through stern emails and newsletters from "the office" that crew "have it easy." Rio one week; Sydney the next. On the surface, it appears idyllic. But although it probably seems simple enough to move crew around the world like chess pieces, every trip I hear different tales of woe. Crew have the same issues as everyone else, and thrown into the mix is the underlying threat of increasing terrorism. I've also discovered that infertility is a common female problem. And there's an urban myth that pilots mostly father girls.

I look over at Nate.

He catches my eye and smiles. It reaches his eyes; they crease at the corners.

I put down my fork. I can't swallow another bite. I remove

my phone from my bag, check it and smile at a pretend message. "Excuse me," I say to the table and go outside.

Despite the outside heat, I need respite from my own emotions. I take a few minutes to try to collate my thoughts and feelings before returning.

The club is out of this world. Almost literally. I can't think of any other way to describe it. It's as though everything else ceases to exist outside of this moment. The up-and-coming DJ is barely visible—a dark, headphone-wearing shadow, raised above the crowds as though he is elevated to godlike status. His worshippers raise their hands and dance among the LED lights. Music pulsates throughout my body.

"I'll get you a drink," I shout in Alex's ear. "What would you like?"

"Vodka shot, please," he shouts back.

We crowd around the bar area, surrounded by gyrating podium dancers. Their costumes twirl and twist, shimmers of gold, silver and black. I buy a round of vodka shots and as we all count down until we knock them back simultaneously, Alan's words from my first trip to Los Angeles—about how it wouldn't take me long to get used to alcohol—flash through my mind. Alcohol is another not uncommon crew issue.

A story shared at the table earlier creeps back into my mind—about a guy who'd been caught and dismissed for not handing over the charity money collected in at the end of each flight. He was charged with theft—he'd amassed thousands, also through duty-free fraud—and initially rumours spread that he was a big drinker. But during his court case it emerged that his son was being badly bullied at school for being mildly autistic and he desperately wanted to get him into a private school. Even though I'd never met the guy, I felt sorry for him. At least he was trying to help his son. I doubt he came out to places like this. I bet he stayed in his room and Delsey dined—brought cheap food from home and ate it in his room.

"Let's dance." Alex grabs my hand, and we merge into the crowds on the main dance floor.

I am aware of the others near us—Nate included—but for the first time in a very, very long time I am so exhilarated, so distracted, that I don't constantly monitor my behaviour and thoughts for the sole benefit of creating a good impression for Nate.

When I glance at the time, I am shocked to see that it is past one in the morning, meaning it's after nine at home. I slip away, out on to the balcony. The heat has subsided, just a touch. I stare at the lit horizon and wonder how many people are having the time of their life and how many others are dealing with heartbreak or disillusionment. I shiver.

Tiredness must be kicking in.

"Amazing, isn't it?" Nate's voice. He appears at my side.

"Have you been here before?" I ask.

"Not here, no. Was that your boyfriend messaging you earlier?"

I fix my eyes on a tall building straight ahead surrounded in pink lights. "Yeah, he misses me." I turn to look at him. "No one special in your life, then?"

"Not really. There was someone recently. She's a pilot too, but it didn't quite work out."

"Sorry to hear that." I grab his hand as a song I recognize blares out through the doors. "I love this song. Let's go back in."

We dance for the entire track. Nate seems relaxed. I am cautiously happy. I wonder if this is one of *those* moments in my life. One of those moments where it's only in hindsight that I'll look back and realize that I had it good. I wish these particular life moments could somehow be highlighted in advance so I'd know. Whenever I spend time reliving my past with Nate, I wish I'd enjoyed myself more and not concerned myself with the mundane—like what I was going to cook that evening or whether his plane would crash and leave me a girlfriend-widow before we'd had a chance to be married. I craved stability so badly that I didn't relax.

I know the answer now, which is that if I can extract a higher degree of security and reassurance from him, our relationship will quickly progress to a much deeper level. All this rationalizing makes me realize that it is the perfect moment to depart.

Like Cinderella, I have to leave him wanting more.

"I'm going to call it a night," I say in his ear. "Say bye to the others. Matt's going to call me shortly."

"I'll come out, get a taxi with you."

"No, I'll be fine, thanks. Stay and have fun," I insist.

This is what I mean. He thinks he doesn't want me, but he's proving that he does. It's all up to me to help him come to terms with his feelings so this whole mixed-messages thing stops. Turning him down is one of the hardest things I've ever done, but I have no choice.

This time, I'm in it for the long haul.

CHAPTER SIXTEEN

I only sleep for a couple of hours, I'm too agitated. I lie on my bed reliving every moment from the evening. I mull over every gesture, every sentence, every word. Each time, I arrive at the same conclusion: Nate is pliable, ripe to be re-moulded back into the man I knew.

Nate has posted several pictures of the view from the club's balcony last night, twenty minutes after I'd left. My room internet connection is really slow; it's frustrating, especially as I can't access my spy app. Although the general group plans are to meet in the bar again tonight, I need to see Nate before then. Alone. In the absence of not being able to find out anything concrete, the gym is realistically my best option. It's way too hot to go jogging.

Mid-morning, I head for the gym. There is a small café in the corner, which means I can sit and watch without having to pretend to exercise for hours. Two coffees later, I'm still rooted to my seat. I've read a local paper and got bored of checking to see if my spy app works, which it doesn't. I pick up the in-house phone and dial Nate's room number, intending to hang up if he answers. At least it will wake him up. It rings. And rings. *Damn*. He has gone out.

I wait another ten minutes, in case he is on his way. I wonder if he is in such a deep sleep that he didn't even hear the phone. Or—my heart sinks at the very thought—maybe he never went back to his own room. He could now, this very moment, be in someone else's bed. Joanna's? I stand up, perhaps rather too abruptly, as the man drinking a smoothie at the next table gives me a strange look.

Back in my room, I check his Facebook. Nothing. My spy app is still refusing to cooperate. There is a chance that Nate may have gone for a swim. It's not his favourite pastime. But perhaps, with a hangover, he will consider it better than no exercise at all.

I put on my costume, replace my gym clothes with a dress, grab a bag and head for the basement floor.

Through the glass, I peer into the pool area. There are several people completing lengths and a couple of kids in the shallow end, but no one who could feasibly be Nate. Just as I turn away, I catch sight of him. He is wearing black swimming trunks and is heading for the Jacuzzi at the far end.

I nip into the changing room and undress as quickly as possible, shoving my belongings into a locker and turning the key. As I step out into the poolside area, the smell of chlorine and floor cleaning chemicals hits me. I stand, dithering, when I realize that the Jacuzzi is empty. Nate is not in the pool either. Bloody hell, I must have been mistaken. I stand, momentarily unsure what to do, when I spot two doors: *Sauna* and *Steam Room*.

I pad over and pull open the first door.

Empty.

I shut it and try the second. An over-strong menthol smell emits as I enter.

Amidst the steam, Nate is sitting on a wooden bench, leaning over, his head in his hands. He doesn't look up.

Placing my towel on an opposite bench, I sit down quietly, feeling the heat against my legs as it moves up through my body. I inhale. I lean back and close my eyes, grateful for the extra few seconds to compose myself. The door opens. I fling open my eyes, ready to go after Nate, but a woman enters. Nate sits up properly. I can tell his eyes are adjusting to the shade and mist, then they widen as he spots me.

"Lily?"

"God, Nate. You gave me a fright!" The woman glares at me. I mouth, "Sorry."

I smile at Nate and he grins back. I make a "shall we leave?" gesture, by nodding in the direction of the door. He stands up and I follow him out into the relative cool.

I place my towel on a nearby hook and take a swift shower, turning the temperature to lukewarm to cool down. Nate waits patiently for his turn. Whilst he showers, I climb into the Jacuzzi, which is thankfully free from anyone else. I lie back and close my eyes, as though I'm so chilled out that it makes no difference to me whatsoever whether or not he joins me.

He does. He sits next to me. Not too close, but not too far away either.

"I thought you were more of a gym person?" I say.

"I am. I woke up with such a bad headache—the worst I've had for ages—and I couldn't face it. I thought this," he points around, "might help."

"And has it?"

"A bit."

"You need some hair of the dog. It's the only thing for really bad hangovers. Come to the Venetian with me a bit later. I'm going to explore."

"I'm not sure. I think I should take it easy today, seeing as we're operating tomorrow."

"Don't be boring." I nudge him with my elbow. "Come on. You can sit in your room anywhere in the world. If you don't come, I'll have to ask Alex or one of the others, but it would be more fun with you. Have you ever been before?" He shakes his head.

"Well, that's it. I've decided for you. I'll come to your room about five. I've had enough in here, I'm off to the spa." I stand up. "See you later."

"All right."

I climb up the steps, clutching the mini ladder. "Make sure you wear something smart," I say over my shoulder.

With my towel over my arm—it's too wet to wrap around me—I navigate around the edge of the pool and push open the heavy door to the female changing rooms without looking back. I shower—again—applying a thin layer of body lotion. It's a favourite brand of Nate's and he always commented when I wore it.

I make my way to the spa reception and sit in a comfortable armchair in the calm, cool waiting area sipping a herbal tea. I feel as though I could drop off and sleep for hours. My name is called out. The same stylist as yesterday washes and blow-dries my hair, which is useful as it means I don't have to explain how I like it done all over again. I ask the beautician who applies my make-up for a more dramatic look around my eyes, much darker colours and an eyelash-lengthening mascara. When she's finished, I stare into the mirror. I look like someone else. Someone happy, confident and in control.

I look like the sort of person who could be Nate's other half. Yin and yang.

I am so thrilled that, as I sign for the treatments to be charged to my room, I hand over a large tip.

I'm back in my room by four, which leaves me exactly an hour. I double-check that the limo I've ordered is still due to arrive at five fifteen, and I send Alex a message to say I won't make it to the bar tonight.

I undress. Opening my suitcase, I choose a new, matching black underwear combination, which I put on before taking my blue dress out of the wardrobe. I rip the protective plastic cover and gently ease it off the hanger before I slide it over my head. The zip is a bit of a struggle, but I manage.

I open my jewellery case and select a simple pair of silver earrings, given to me by Babs last Christmas. On to my wrist I slide a plain silver bangle. I borrowed it from Amy ages ago, but she has never asked for it back. I dab perfume behind my ears, then spray some into the air before walking through. Finally, I try on two pairs of shoes, one pair with higher heels than the other. After much deliberation, I select the slightly lower pair. They are black sling-backs and are elegant enough but without giving away how hard I've tried.

After a final once-over in front of the mirror, I take a deep breath.

This is it.

I pick up my bag, a plain black one containing my passport, a credit card, some cash and a lipstick, plus a few other items that may come in useful, and I make my way to the lifts. As I wait, watching the red lights illuminate and disappear at each floor level, I feel a calmness descend upon me. The lift chimes. I step in.

Nate isn't ready. He opens the door in a hotel robe and his hair is wet.

"Sorry. I fell asleep."

"Shall I choose you something to wear?" I say, instantly regretting my words the moment they come out of my mouth.

"No, it's fine. I won't be long." He disappears into the bathroom and shuts the door.

I sit on the edge of the bed and put my hands under my

thighs to stop myself from nosing through his belongings, which is just as well because Nate takes mere minutes. He emerges, wearing the powder-blue shirt that he wears when he has to position—travel as a passenger—for work.

I watch as Nate bends down, pulling open a drawer and taking out a pair of black socks. I don't see the point of unpacking totally when I'm away. It's not as if it's a week-long holiday, and it only has to be repacked—sometimes as little as twenty-four hours later—plus there's a higher chance of forgetting things. He sits down next to me; I can feel the weight of him as the mattress sags a little. As soon as he has pulled on his socks he stands up, crouches down in front of the desk mirror, runs his hand through his hair, slides his wallet into his back pocket, then turns round to face me.

"How do I look?"

"Good," I say, looking down at my watch. "I've booked a car." I stand up.

He stares at me, as if properly seeing me for the first time.

"Wow. You look...incredible."

"Thanks." I point to his passport on the desk. "Don't forget your ID, otherwise you could end up with a teetotal night." I turn towards the door.

"Doesn't he mind? You know. Um. I don't remember your boyfriend's name..."

I stop and turn round to face him. "Matt. I haven't mentioned yet that I'm going out for an hour or two with you. What's there to say, really? It's early days, we've only been seeing each other a short while. I'm sure he'll be cool with it."

"As long as you're sure?"

I shrug. "He's a great guy. In fact, you and he would get on. There's nothing to worry about."

Inside the lift, I hope that we don't bump into anyone. I don't want any last-minute, unwanted hangers-on. I distract myself by pretending to check my phone. As we walk towards the hotel exit, I act on impulse, but it feels like the right thing to do. I link my arm into Nate's and continue walking as though it's the most natural thing in the world. He doesn't object—in fact, he turns to me and smiles.

A doorman opens the door for us and bids us a "great evening."

"We will," I respond, as we walk downstairs towards a waiting black limo.

"What's this?" Nate turns to look at me.

"It didn't cost much more than a taxi, so I thought we might as well arrive at the Venetian in style. They had a deal on. If we like, the driver can take us sightseeing afterwards. I don't know about you, but I quite fancy seeing more of Vegas."

"Hi, my name is Jackson," the uniformed chauffeur greets us as he opens the door.

"Thank you," I say, stepping in first.

As requested, there is a bottle of champagne and two glasses ready for us on the side. I pour, handing one to Nate, then pouring one for myself.

"I don't believe that the champagne was included too," he says, taking a sip.

I laugh. "Of course not. But I couldn't resist when they suggested it as an optional extra. You'll have to drink it quickly, though, the Venetian isn't too far away. Cheers!"

I lean back into the seat and Nate does the same, as Jackson turns round and suggests we "buckle up."

As we pull away from the bog-standard crew hotel, into the noise and sights of the approaching evening, I accidentally slide towards Nate. I move away. A sliver of barely containable excitement weaves its way inside my chest as we drive towards our destination: the one I carefully selected. It is listed among one of the top ten most romantic hotels in Vegas. Nate is in for the night of his life.

CHAPTER SEVENTEEN

After strolling through the Piazza San Marco arm in arm, Nate and I are seated opposite each other in a restaurant and are now eating marinated prawns at the edge of a canal. A gondola glides past. I pick up my glass of white wine and take a sip. Above the faint smell of chlorine, I catch a whiff of garlic as a waiter delivers the entrée to the table behind us. I am tentatively happy. I feel like I'm moments away from finally living the life I deserve.

The conversation between us flows naturally. He too is happy. He admitted as much when he confessed a few moments ago that he was glad I'd talked him into this outing.

Our starters are cleared and the ice inside the bucket crunches as our waiter removes the bottle to top up our wine glasses.

"I dread to think what the bill will be like," says Nate.

"Don't. The whole evening is on me. As a thank you."

"A thank you?"

"Yes. You were very decent when we split up, paying the

rent and making sure I'd be all right. I'm sorry again that I took it so badly. I was in a confused place back then. Now that my life is on track, I can look back and see how I could have handled things differently."

"Well. Likewise. Water under the bridge." We both laugh, given our surroundings.

"What did you think of the club last night?"

"Incredible," he says. "Whenever I've come to Vegas before, I've tended to explore in the day. Tours of the Grand Canyon, that type of thing. I've been to a few well-known restaurants and local sights, but this trip has actually been fun." We both go quiet.

I think about how we are here, for now, cut off from the world until reality will try to wrench us apart again. Which is why tonight is so important. How the night plays out will have a big impact on my future.

No, *our* future.

"I don't know how we'll beat last night, I felt on such a high. I did look at some tickets for shows this evening, but anything that sounded good was sold out or extortionate," I say.

"It's nice enough here. Aren't they supposed to have street entertainers? And I saw a documentary once about Michael Jackson. He came shopping here and the shops were like Aladdin's cave."

I burst out laughing. "Shopping? You?"

He laughs too. "Yeah. I guess not."

"I think we should go up to one of the bars after this and look out at a proper view of Venice as a taster. I'd love to visit the real one."

I reach over and top up our wine glasses.

A lot for Nate, a little for me.

I distract him by pointing out a precarious-looking gondolier who looks a little unstable as he approaches a white bridge, whilst above us the skylights darken, hinting at the approaching night outside.

★ ★ ★

In the bar, I insist on Kir Royales with extra cassis, even though Nate mutters half-heartedly about "operating tomorrow." We are seated in the centre of the room, so we don't have much of a view, but the room itself is worth taking in with its high ceilings and opulent decor in shades of black, gold and silver. Behind the main bar, with its backdrop of dark, mirrored shelves supporting hundreds of wine glasses, flutes and brightly coloured bottles, sleek bar staff mix drinks, expertly negotiating the space behind the counter.

"We'll just have the one cocktail," I say with a reassuring smile. "When in Rome. Or Venice or Vegas. And we're not even working until late, so let's just relax."

When Nate stands up to seek out the Gents, I take a quick look around. The bar is fairly dark and no one is taking any notice of me. I reach down for my bag, take out a pill, hold my glass beneath the table and drop it into my glass. Using a cocktail stirrer I mix it. I reach over for Nate's Kir Royale and swap our drinks around. As he returns, approaching our table, I take a deep breath.

"I've got a confession," I say, taking a sip, not quite meeting his eyes.

"Go on," he says.

I look up. Since my experience with Katie I've done more research into drugs, and the poison is in the dose. It can take up to half an hour for Rohypnol to kick in, but I now have to monitor his alcohol intake, otherwise this can all go horribly wrong. I feel as responsible as an anaesthetist.

"Jackson's coming back shortly. I asked him to take us on a tour. I thought it would be fun to sightsee in comfort. I'm having such a good time, I don't want this evening to end. I've got a four-day Riyadh after this, which means no gym, no pool, probably no socializing—apart from in a curtained-off family area in a coffee shop, from what I've heard—*and* apparently I'll be stuck in my room with only the BBC World Service for company."

"It's not too bad there; they have other channels." He grins. "But you're right about this evening, and I'm having a great time too," he says. "Let's go for it."

I take his response as a sign that he's up for anything as I watch him sip his drink. I don't finish mine, as I need to stay in complete control.

"Can we take the longest possible route, please?" I say to Jackson as we leave the gold and the brightness of the Venetian behind us.

"Sure."

Our champagne bottle has been refreshed; a new one is in its place. Nate doesn't seem to notice. The surreality of it all is mesmerizing; even I feel a heightened sense of excitement and anticipation. I sit closer to him and point out a tall tower.

"The Stratosphere Tower," he says.

Our thighs touch.

Nate turns to look at me.

I put down my glass, ease his from his hand and place it in the side holder, then I lean towards him.

We kiss.

It is like the first time, only better and even more dream-like, because I've wanted this for so long that every single second I've been in pain now seems blotted out. The overwhelming smell of his aftershave is intoxicating and I feel giddy.

The limo stops. I pull away from him. I need to get my words right, but all the things I need to say are jumbled up in my mind. I look outside. Relief swamps me. We're only at some traffic lights, so we're not *there* yet. The car moves forward. I am disorientated, I've no idea how long we have left until we arrive at our first destination. I hope I didn't accidentally drug myself. I think back. No, I definitely swapped our drinks around.

Facing Nate, I say, "I've had an idea. It's a bit mad, but hear me out."

"You've arranged a bungee jump off a skyscraper."

"Not quite."

His breathing is heavy, his face is flushed. His eyes are bright. I've only ever seen Nate properly drunk a few times and it's usually been after nights out with his uni mates. He stares at me as though ready to listen. He doesn't quite look himself, he's smiling but seems a bit vacant. Nicely compliant. I could tell him anything right now, or do anything at all, and I suspect he'd be none the wiser.

"Part of this tour is of the Little White Chapel. It's got a drive-through 'Tunnel of Love.' Let's go all out for the total Vegas experience."

"Get married?"

"Well, yeah. People must get carried away all the time so they must have *some* sort of cooling-off period or..." I struggle to think of the right word. "Safeguards," I blurt out. "What happens in Vegas, stays in Vegas. Don't a lot of your colleagues say that? You told me that once."

"It's just a saying." He goes quiet.

I give what I hope is an understanding smile before I lean over and speak to Jackson via the intercom. "Can we have some music, please?"

"Sure. What kind?"

"You choose. Something uplifting. And loud."

He obliges, not only with the music but by dazzling us with disco lights.

We both burst out laughing and clink glasses again.

"Probably best to cool it," I say as he takes a sip. "We've drunk quite a lot this evening."

Nate grins, as though nothing in his life will ever trouble

him again. The night-time traffic is slow as we creep along. Nate's grin becomes soppier. He tries to kiss me, but his mouth lands on my cheek. He then asks Jackson for "something different." I assume it's going to be something romantic, but he suggests Guns N' Roses. As he mimes along to "Paradise City"—thank God, without any air guitar actions— I do my best to hide my agitation. I know he's not himself, and that's kind of the point, but he's not taking this seriously enough.

We stop. Jackson opens the door. I step out, as though I'm going to have a word with him. Nate follows me out.

We all stand at the bottom of several steps leading up to a stone building.

"Thanks for your help," I say to Jackson. "Hopefully, we won't be too long."

"Take your time," he says.

"What is this place?" Nate looks at Jackson.

Jackson looks worryingly puzzled. "The marriage licence bureau."

"You'll need your passport," I say to Nate, leaning over to slide it from his back pocket as I try to distract him.

"Why?"

"We need ID to make the arrangements. Jackson's got everything else sorted, don't worry."

I lock my right arm through his left and start walking him up the stairs. He feels heavy and is walking slowly and deliberately, as though every step requires the utmost concentration. "Will there be music inside?" he asks.

Shit. He's supposed to be calm and happy, not totally out of it.

"Later, maybe." I try to think of the name of at least one of the band members of Guns N' Roses to pretend that they got married here, but they all elude me. "This is all very rock 'n' roll, though, music or no music." Inwardly, I cringe at my words, but I can't think of anything else to say. "Come on." I link his arm tighter and almost drag him up the final few stairs.

At the top, Nate hesitates so I lean forward and kiss him. A younger couple emerge from the entrance doors. As they walk past us, the man raises his hand and high-fives Nate.

"Good luck," I say to them. "See?" I turn to Nate. "This is a great thing we're doing."

Holding his hand, we step into a well-lit building. But it's probably good, as Nate blinks several times and looks normal. My eyes seek out the sign for the *Express Lane*. There is a couple ahead of us. I want to scream at them to move out of the way. Instead, I keep hold of Nate and distract him by reminding him of the time we queued for ages to get into the London Aquarium, only for the fire alarm to go off as we reached the tills.

Inside, I silently pray that there is no reference made to the online form I've filled out in advance. When we are summoned forward, I take a deep breath. Thank God.

"Good evening," I say, handing over my reference number, paperwork and both mine and Nate's passports.

"Thank you," replies the bespectacled woman, tapping on her keyboard.

Nate looks ill at ease, so I squeeze his hand. I try to relax, to look calm, as if it doesn't matter how long or short the process is. But it is worrying, because Nate looks as if he expects to wake up at any moment. And then, frighteningly, he opens his mouth as if to say something, but I smile and shake my head. It's hard to concentrate, but I force myself to act how I imagine someone genuinely in my position would.

I keep smiling throughout.

"Good luck to you both," she says as we walk away.

"Remember what I said," I say to him, heading for the

door, resisting the urge to run. "Tonight is on me. Let's head back to the fantasy world."

Jackson opens the door for us again.

"Thanks," I say as I hand the paperwork over to him.

"Thanks, Jackson. You're a great driver," Nate says as he high-fives Jackson. "Where are we off to next?"

"The chapel," Jackson replies.

I step inside the limo first. As soon as Nate sits down, I hand him his glass and kiss him, before breaking away and sitting beside him.

I raise my glass. "Cheers! Here's to a wild night. It's so exciting. Nothing feels real."

We clink glasses. It's almost a done deal. Not long now.

As we approach the chapel, my heart thuds so loudly I can hear it. Jackson parks alongside a white Cadillac. A Ford Mustang emerges from the chapel driveway. As we step out of the limo and Jackson directs us towards the Cadillac, the couple inside the Mustang wave at us and shout, "Good luck."

I wave back. Nate rises to the occasion and gives a brief wave.

On the back seat of the convertible is a bouquet of red roses and a matching boutonnière.

"What's all this?" Nate says, staring down.

Jackson stands near the driver's side, sliding in a boutonnière which matches Nate's.

I whisper, "It's just part of the package." Nate stands still, looking puzzled.

Out of nowhere, a surge of violence rushes through me. I want to push Nate inside the car; his hesitation is going to ruin things, unless he pulls it together. I'm so close. So, so close. This feels like the final hurdle. "You *owe* me," I'm dying to say to him. Which he does.

"All set?" says Jackson, pulling back the passenger seat for us.

"Yes," I say brightly. "Come on," I say to Nate.

He steps in. I want to cry with relief.

"Do many people switch cars in the middle of the journey?" Nate asks Jackson.

Jackson laughs in the nervous way that people do when they're not sure whether or not someone is joking.

I lean over and slide the boutonnière into Nate's shirt button, then sit back, reach over and put my right hand on his thigh. He doesn't put his hand on mine or do anything that connects us to this moment. Never mind. We have the rest of our lives for small gestures. I rest my roses on my lap, stroking the petals with my free hand. But when I next glance over I'm horrified to see that being exposed to the outdoor heat—combined with alcohol and a mere one pill—seems to have had a soporific effect on Nate. His eyes keep closing.

He needs air conditioning.

I lean over. "Nate! Darling, we're nearly there."

He gives me a soppy grin and opens his eyes, but he stares ahead.

As we approach the Tunnel of Love I almost can't bear the suspense any longer. This night has to be as perfect as possible.

"Isn't this amazing?" I say to Nate. "I feel like I'm on a film set, waiting for *lights, camera, action!*" Nate grins.

Relief floods through me. My whole body feels weak.

"This beats last night," he says.

"I'm going to enjoy every moment," I say. "I'm sure I won't do anything like this ever again."

"Me neither," says Nate.

We reach the entrance. Jackson drives up to the window and a minister approaches us from a side door. His dreadlocks are tied back into a ponytail. He is wearing a welcoming smile.

"All set?"

"Sure am," I hear myself say in a fake accent.

I must be more nervous than I realize. But after what I've

gone through to get here, I'm entitled. Every bride is nervous on her wedding day and I wouldn't be normal if I didn't feel even the slightest bit of anxiety. The minister introduces us to 'the officiant' who is a tall woman, with long, dark curly hair. She looks angelic, not unlike the ones painted into the midnight-blue ceiling above us, with stars and silvery crescents among the angels.

Jackson steps out of the car and stands politely to attention.

The ceremony begins. At approximately fifteen minutes, I've chosen one of the shortest ceremonies possible—but still, a quarter of an hour is a quarter of an hour.

"Welcome, Elizabeth Juliette Magnolia Price and Nathan Edward Goldsmith. Are there any guests joining us from the United Kingdom this evening?"

I shake my head and from deep within, I summon up all my self-belief. I picture myself as an actress playing an important, career-changing role at a theatre-in-the-round production. "We are gathered here today…" I smile and take hold of Nate's hand.

He whispers, "Can't we just go back to the bar?"

I whisper back, squeezing his hand, "We can go back in a minute."

"Do you, Nathan Edward Goldsmith, take Elizabeth Juliette Price to be your lawful, wedded wife?" I hold my breath.

He looks at me.

"I do," I gently coax in a whisper.

"I do," he repeats.

When it's my turn to repeat my vows, my voice doesn't sound like my own. I wish William was my page boy but, of course, he'd be too old now. He could be a witness or could have given me away. I feel a twinge of guilt at not inviting Barbara.

We don't have rings to exchange, which is a shame, but I thought it would be a step too far when it comes to Nate believing that this whole night was an impromptu, mutual agreement. I try not to glance down at my watch because, nice as our minister is, he is, unfortunately, a talker.

"I've been married for seventeen years and the best bit of advice I like to share is that you must never, I repeat, *never* go to sleep on an argument. Start each day with a clean slate." I daren't look at Nate as I start to feel him fidget.

Finally I hear the words, "By the power vested in me by the State of Nevada, I now pronounce you husband and wife."

There is a camera flash. I lean over and kiss Nate on the lips. I hear the words "smile" and "congratulations." We are showered with confetti as we sign our names. I'm vaguely aware of handing over gratuities and saying "thank you," several times.

It's a total, utter, exhilarating, overwhelming dream come true. I can feel my hands shaking.

I'd love to be able to announce it on all my social media pages and wait for the outpouring of congratulations and good wishes. I fantasize that everyone would be happy for us, including Bella, and they'd wish us well.

As we pull away from the Tunnel of Love, Nate holds my hand, just like we're in a proper fairy tale and, for once, I'm playing the starring role.

CHAPTER EIGHTEEN

I insist we go back to my room. I want him on my territory for a change.

We are alone on our wedding night; the night I have been dreaming of for years.

We kiss before the door even shuts properly behind us, as though he has missed me as much as I him. Clumsily, I guide Nate to my bed as we half-kiss, half-embrace whilst he steps backwards. He lies down straight away. But before I can even join him, his eyes shut.

"Nate! Nate!" I shake him roughly by the shoulders.

He *has* to wake up. We have to do this properly, otherwise it just won't work. I shake him again, then pinch him hard on the upper arm, but he remains dead to the world.

He snores gently.

After a couple more attempts, I give up and decide instead to savour my achievement. I phone room service and order champagne, plus a selection of luxury nibbles. Next, I call the concierge to check that our DVD, printed photos and USB have been sent over from the chapel, seeing as I paid for an express service. I love Vegas, it is so wonderfully accommodating. I dim the lights by the bed, pull off Nate's shoes, remove his wallet from his back pocket and cover him up with the duvet as best I can. It is hard work pushing him on to his side, he is bloody heavy.

I wait.

He remains unconscious.

In my bag, several sleeping pills and four of the antidepressants I took from Amy's remain untouched. I didn't need any backup drugs. Nate was as docile as a lamb. I succeeded in getting him to the right level of pliability to make him reckless, but not unmanageable. Until now.

There is a sharp rap at the door. I open it. A waiter pushes in a table on wheels, upon which rests an ice bucket and several silver domes.

"Hi. Do you mind leaving this right here?" I say, blocking him from entering the room any further.

I guess they've seen all sorts, but pride prevents me from letting him think that I'm going to drink and scoff my way through this lot whilst Nate is asleep. The waiter takes his time lifting each dome lid, offering an unnecessary description, then pops the champagne cork.

"Don't pour," I say. "*We* can do it."

He hands me the bill to sign. I help myself to some dollars from Nate's wallet. It's time he contributed. As the waiter opens the door to leave, a porter is standing there with the wedding memento package. I dip into Nate's wallet again.

With our wedding ceremony playing on my laptop in the background, I pour the champagne down the basin and tip the empty bottle upside down in the ice bucket. I break up some of the salmon and caper canapés, scrape oysters from their shells and squish them into a napkin. I retch. All this is a huge waste, I know that. But the more memory gaps that Nate has, the more he will rely on me to fill them in. And if he has any doubts that he was any less than a one hundred per cent willing participant, then all this physical evidence will prove to him that he was as swept along in the moment as I was.

We are both to blame.

I brush my teeth, but leave my make-up on. I attempt to brush Nate's, but it is messy and futile. I pull off his clothes and scatter them on the floor. On the desk, I leave out a large photo of us and our marriage certificate. If we get up early enough tomorrow, we could go ring shopping.

He could also call his family and announce the good news. I'm in, I'm finally in! However, I do feel a twist of nerves at the thought of Bella's reaction, but even if she does have anything negative to say, it will be too little, too late.

I undress and slide into bed, falling into a well-earned sleep next to my husband.

I deliberately left the curtains open. I want the sun to stream in. It doesn't disappoint, marking the first day of our honeymoon. Nate is still asleep.

I slip out of bed. The air conditioning blasts out. I shiver and turn it down. I clean my teeth and return to bed, reliving last night.

Nate stirs. I nearly scream as his eyes open suddenly and he stares at me.

Silence.

"Morning, sleepyhead. It's early afternoon. Coffee?" He continues to stare, but his eyes don't look fully open.

I kiss him. "I'll make one. Just how you like it. I intend to start this new life as I mean to go on."

He sits up and in the mirror opposite I can see he is still staring. He doesn't seem to clock our wedding photo or any of the other clues showing indisputable evidence of our love. I push the filter button on the coffee machine and watch as the liquid bubbles into the glass jug, splashes of black dirtying the sides. I look up and smile at Nate in the mirror. He gives a weak one back. I fill two mugs, add plenty of creamer to Nate's and stroll back to the bed, handing him his. He pushes himself up with his left hand and accepts it with his right. I climb in beside him and take a sip. It is delicious; the perfect strength.

"So, it was quite a night?" he finally speaks in a hoarse voice.

I laugh. "You're so funny, babe. That's the understatement of the year. You really surprised me; I had no idea that your feelings for me were still so strong. My only concern is how I'm going to break the news to Matt. He'll be gutted."

"I feel dreadful. You have my word that I won't cause problems for you. There's no point in hurting someone for nothing. I guess we both overdid the drink?" He smiles.

The bastard actually smiles at me. As though his behaviour is reasonable.

I smile back. "Wouldn't that be a bit deceitful?"

I lean over and leave my mug on the side. I take his cup, stretch over him and leave his on the side too. I run my hand over his chest, then I kiss him. He tastes of stale alcohol, despite my attempts to brush his teeth last night. At first he hesitates, but I persist. I know him. I know him too well, and my knowledge is his weakness.

It is over in minutes, but I don't care. The final hurdle is over. I cuddle into him.

After a few seconds, he moves my arm and pulls himself into an upright seated position. "Lily. This has been great. But—"

"But what?"

"But…" He stares ahead.

I know what he thinks he's going to say. But he can't.

He will need a little time to accept the sudden change in his life. I get that. I developed a little theory recently, which I named my "Olive Stone Theory." Whenever I bite into an olive, I expect a stone. I am prepared. I am not like Nate—or pampered people like him, who expect to bite into their bloody olives, pitted, soft and perfect—I anticipate problems and mentally deal with them in advance.

My husband frowns. He holds up his left hand, then his eyes explore the room, resting on our wedding photo. He leaps up, looking around.

I watch.

"Lily? What on earth?"

"Don't you mean *Mrs. Goldsmith*? This is our honeymoon, darling. Come back to bed. It's call-time in a few hours. We're going back home. Remember? I'm moving back in until we choose a place together."

"Lily. I'm serious. Everything's a blur. Just fragments." He stares at the food remnants. "We ordered food? After a meal out?"

This piece of information seems temporarily more incredulous to Nate than the marriage bit. I think he's still under the influence. He'll have to be careful and behave normally—although his alcohol level will be within the flying limits by the time he is due to report for our flight, and Rohypnol barely lasts twenty-four hours, so he should be safe enough.

"Come and lie back down. You don't look well."

He obeys. Lying down, he groans, then closes his eyes.

"Do you want some painkillers?"

He nods. I take two from my bag. He opens his eyes, lifts his head and I help him swallow by gently tipping water from a plastic bottle into his mouth. His head falls back and he shuts his eyes again. His breathing gets deeper.

I leave him alone for a good hour before I shake him awake.

"Nate! Go and get in the shower. You'll feel better. I'll phone room service and ask them to clear this lot up, as well as bring some brunch. You look as though you could do with something to soak up the alcohol."

On his way to the bathroom, he picks up the wedding photo and stares at it. He then spends longer studying the marriage certificate. It confirms that we definitely got married yesterday on *July the eighteenth.*

I hold my breath.

He turns round to look at me. "Lily. We need to talk."

I dial room service. "Hello. I'd like to order…" I say, pointing at the bathroom.

Nate picks up his phone and, negotiating the debris, he shuts the door behind him. I replace the receiver and put on a dressing gown. I wedge open the room door and push the trolley outside into the corridor. I can hear the shower running. I twist the bathroom door handle. He has locked it!

The thing is, he's going to have to make the best of the situation. There's no point in him fighting this—*us*—any longer. The water stops. Silence. He is on the phone to someone.

He is talking quietly, but his voice is clear.

"No fucking idea, mate. You've got to help me sort this."

A knock at the door. I open it and step back to let the waitress in.

"Where would you like the tray?"

"On the bed, please."

I sign, tip and let her out. Nate is still whispering away.

I knock on the bathroom door. "Breakfast, darling."

"Out in a minute!"

"OK."

I remove my robe and pour myself a coffee from the cafetière and sip, whilst looking out the window. I can feel the outside heat on the glass. As far as I can see, there is activity. I imagine other couples, like the ones in the Ford

Mustang last night. I bet they are happy, normally planning their future. I don't want this to turn into a hollow victory. I knew it was a high-risk strategy, but love can grow. And I genuinely love Nate, which is why I'm perfect. I'll be a good wife, and he will never truly be happy with anyone else. I just need him to *understand* that. I wish he'd given us more of a chance when we got together last year, because he only has himself to blame for all this.

The bathroom door opens. I keep looking out the window as though I too am contemplating the situation. If I act too needy now, he'll dig his heels in. He pours himself a coffee and stands beside me. He is wearing a robe. It irritates me, because it appears as though he fears that by simply wearing a towel around his waist—as is customary for him—he will be exposed. He's acting like we're strangers after a one-night stand.

"Let's start from the beginning. Talk me through what happened last night."

I look him in the eye. "The thing is, babe, last night wasn't the wedding of my dreams either. But...we grabbed the moment. *Carpe diem* and all that. Our buried feelings resurfaced. What's done is done. And...we do love each other."

Silence.

Nate exhales loudly. "Lily. I don't understand how last night happened. I guess we were having fun and it went too far. But you need to realize that I don't love you in *that* way. We split up, not because I didn't like you, but because I'm not ready to settle down with anyone yet. If ever."

"So, last night? All those things you said about how much you missed me and loved me, they were lies?"

"I can't remember everything, Lily. There are blanks in my memory. I feel pretty shit." He sits down on the bed.

I swing round. "Oh? So I've cheated on Matt for no reason? Because it's the sort of thing a woman does without encouragement?"

He raises a hand to his forehead and massages it with his forefinger and thumb. "I don't know how you interpreted it, Lily…"

"I love you. That's what you said last night. We got *married*. How would you like me to interpret that?" I mimic his voice. *"Let's do it. Let's do it for real. Let's get married."*

"Lily—"

"Juliette! I've told you, it's Juliette now. We're not getting off to a very good start if you can't even get my fucking name right."

It's my turn to lock myself in the bathroom. He pounds on the door.

"Lily! Lily."

I turn the taps on full blast and put my hands over my ears. My eye make-up is a little smudged, but I don't look too bad considering the stress I've been under. I study my reflection, looking for changes now that I'm a married woman.

Do I look older? Wiser? Or just *married*?

The knocking on the door stops. I remove my hands from my ears, switch off the taps. He bashes the door repeatedly.

"Leave me alone," I say. "I need space!"

I make him wait a further ten minutes before I venture out. He is sitting on the edge of my bed, his head in his hands. I manoeuvre myself on to the bed behind him and massage his shoulders. He stiffens and sits up straight.

"How's your head?" I ask in a concerned-wife voice.

"Easing off, but you need to listen." He edges away from me. I let my hands drop.

"This is all too fast." He softens his tone a little. "This time yesterday, everything was fine." He sighs. "I've made a few calls and we'll have to get this all sorted back in London, there's not enough time left here. When we land, come to my place. A solicitor friend of mine is going to meet us there and we can figure this situation out."

I move to the edge of the bed and sit as close to him as I can. "What about me? What about what I want?"

"Please, Lily. You really must understand that this is too much, too insane."

"Not to me."

He gives me a look I can't quite interpret, but it's definitely not a positive one.

"We'll work out together what's best. For both of us. Jesus. What a mess. I've heard stories about Vegas, but that's what they are, stories. I never thought..."

"Worse things happen to people than getting married to an ex you didn't realize you still had feelings for."

"I'm sorry," he says.

He's always fucking sorry. It doesn't mean anything to me any more.

The lump in my throat is genuine. I feel fragile but resolute. I reach over to hold him tight and he manages to reciprocate.

We sit, arms wrapped around each other, for a full minute.

He breaks away first. Of course he does.

Our wedding brunch of bagels with smoked salmon and scrambled eggs lies ignored on the bed.

"Let's keep this between ourselves," he says. "We need to get through the flight home and then try to sort things out as best we can."

That's what he thinks.

CHAPTER NINETEEN

I busy myself in Nate's—no, our—kitchen whilst James Harrington, Nate's "lawyer friend" sits in the living room, yacking away to Nate.

I catch snippets. *"Voidable marriage. Intoxication. Dishonesty. Non-consummation."* Well, Nate's screwed on the last option.

I carry through a tray of coffee like the perfect little housewife. Espresso for myself, cappuccino for Nate and a latte for "the lawyer." A trio of muffins—courtesy of me—defrosted in the microwave, sit on a small plate. In the absence of napkins, I have folded squares of kitchen towel into neat triangles. I sit down next to Nate on the sofa, opposite James Harrington.

Two against one.

They thank me for their coffees.

"Right, so, Elizabeth, Nate's explained to me that we can't go for non-consummation, so I suggest we go for a voidable marriage in that you were both intoxicated—"

"I wasn't."

Nate glares at me.

James looks confused. "I thought…"

"I want our marriage to work. Nate may have been a little tipsy, but it was probably exacerbated by jet lag." I look at Nate. "I married you in good faith. You told me you loved me. We have a history together *and* I gave up a decent man on the basis of your charming patter. Matt is devastated. I had to tell him by text! How do you think that made me feel about myself?"

There is silence. Rainbow swims up and down.

It's nicely familiar being here with Nate, and now I've inched through the door—legitimately—I'm not giving up without a proper fight.

"Right. Well, this complicates things." He throws Nate a look, then glances at his watch. "I've got calls to make, so I'll shut myself away in your spare room whilst you two sort this out." I fold my arms and settle back into the sofa.

"Lily…" I frown.

"Juliette, no Lily, it's too confusing, you're Lily to me. Please. Be reasonable. I don't love you in the way you want. You *know* that. You can't want this for yourself either. You deserve better." His beseeching tone grates.

"Well, bad luck, I have enough faith for both of us to make this work."

Nate stands up. "This is a serious problem. I'm sorry that you want more than I can give. Whatever happened the other night—and I only have *your* word for everything—it wasn't real. It was way *too much*."

"Are you calling me a liar?"

"No. But I bet you didn't need much persuading to drag me up that aisle."

"There was no aisle, we were in a Cadillac. You know that. And there was no *dragging* involved. Phone the bloody chapel, ask them how *forced* you were!"

"I'm sorry. I know I'm as much to blame. It's just that this isn't a game! These are our lives."

"Yes. Mine and yours."

We both swing round at a theatrical clearing of the throat. "A word, please, Nate," says James.

Nate follows him back into the room. Nate *would* have a lawyer friend. He has a doctor one, a banker one, a financial adviser one, the list goes on. I'm pissed off. If James only left us alone, in private, I could figure something out.

I wait. I can't hear voices.

Several more minutes pass, then James walks out, with Nate immediately behind.

"Righto, goodbye, Elizabeth. I'll leave you two alone."

"Yes, thanks. I'll call you," says Nate.

James raises his arm in a brief wave and lets himself out.

Silence after the door closes. Nate looks happier, and he can't quite meet my eyes.

"Shall we go somewhere for a coffee so we can talk properly?" he suggests.

"No. I'm fine here, thanks, but I'm exhausted. I didn't sleep in the bunks. I need a rest, then we can talk as much as you like."

"Rest where? Here?"

I shrug, as if to say, "Where else?"

"No. You can't stay here. You have to leave. I'll drive you back to yours and we can talk on the way."

"I can't think straight. After keeping me up socializing with your friend, you cannot deny me a short rest. Surely? You can't have everything your own way."

"Everything my own way? This is insane. This is all… wrong. I keep expecting to wake up and feel nothing but sheer relief that all this never happened. I should've known better. I should've known you'd take things too far. This is

why it can never work between us. You're too all or nothing. You don't know when to stop. You have no off-switch!"

"I'll leave you to calm down," I say in the same tone of
voice he used with me when he wanted me to "be reasonable" about our break-up.

He remains in the living room whilst I wheel my bag and
suitcase into our bedroom. I remove my toiletries and have a
shower in his en suite. Even though I tie my hair up, so as not
to get it wet, I place my shampoo next to his in the shower.
Afterwards, I leave my toothbrush where he keeps his. I unpack, putting my clean stuff back into the drawers, their former home. Nate has filled one of them with random things
that look like unwanted gifts—a box containing cufflinks,
two ties and a sealed pack of department-store boxer shorts.
I remove them and put them in "his" drawers.

I didn't tell Nate that I now have a car, so we drive home
together, side by side—a proper couple—in his black Jag.
Everything feels so right. In fact, it feels so right, I cannot
understand why he continues to fight this. He has feelings
for me, I know he does.

"I'll set my alarm for an hour," I call out. "We can order
in some food."

He can think again if he thinks I'll cook, given his current attitude.

Nate doesn't reply.

I *am* tired, that is the truth. I spent the whole ten-and-
a-half-hour flight buzzing with a mixture of adrenalin and
apprehension.

It is still light. I must have only dropped off for a few minutes. My mouth is dry. I look to my left. No Nate. I slump
back. My limbs ache. I can feel sleep clawing me back into
oblivion. Awareness and reality seep back in. I hear familiar
sounds: morning creaks and the whining of the shower pump.

I've been back home a whole night. I force myself up, put on Nate's gown and wander into the living room.

Outside it is a glorious day. My mind fills with plans. I can make a picnic and we can go and sit by the river. I hear the shower stop. An empty feeling in the pit of my stomach forms as I await Nate's latest reaction.

I go into the kitchen and switch on the coffee machine. I open the fridge and stare inside, but realize I don't want anything. I make two coffees. Nate appears, dressed in his running gear.

"Morning! I've made you a coffee," I smile.

"Thank you."

He accepts it and makes his way to the sofa. I sit next to him. For several seconds, we are silent, both sipping.

"Why didn't you come to bed?"

"Why do you think?" I don't answer.

"I slept in the spare room."

"Oh."

"I'm going for the annulment under the grounds that I was intoxicated."

"I see."

"I'd like you to agree so that we can do it together. I don't want this to get nasty. If we work as a team, it will be relatively straightforward. I'd really like us to stay friends."

"Well, that's a lie. You said that the last time you dumped me. You even deleted me as a Facebook friend. You made no attempt at maintaining a *friendship*."

"For God's sake, neither did you, from what I recall. I said we could keep in touch, that it didn't have to be a total clean break. But you wouldn't have it. It was your way or no way." Only because I had no bloody choice.

I'm not stupid. If he didn't want us to live together, then his feelings weren't in the right place. I had to play the long game. If I'd hung around accepting crumbs of supposed friendship and, in all likelihood, sporadic sex if he stayed single for long enough, then I'd have had zero chance of getting us back on track. Zero. No one respects anyone who puts up with less than they deserve. It's exactly why Bella thought she could treat me the way she did. I had to forsake nearly a year of my life to ensure that he would accept me back in the future. And now the future is here.

"Give us a chance, Nate. Give me a week—here, together—and if you still feel the same, I'll go along with anything you want."

"What's the point? Seriously, what is the point? The situation is what it is, and I'm not going to change my mind." I glare.

"It's for the best."

I can't stand up. I feel weak. This wasn't supposed to happen. I thought that if I lassoed him in, if he spent quality time legally tied to me, he would reach acceptance. And his feelings would return. Which they did. He *was* jealous of "Matt," his pride was dented. But I also know what he's like. The last time I made a fuss when we broke up, it just made him dig his heels in further.

"Lily. I'm sorry. Perhaps a total clean break might be best. What about the other airlines? You can apply again, every year. There's so much ahead of you."

"Have you any idea how patronizing you sound right now? How about *you* go to a different airline?"

Ignoring me, he ploughs on with his straw-clutching. "Or…you might even patch things up with Matt. Blame everything on me."

The doorbell goes.

"It's the cleaner," he says as he stands up.

I take a deep breath, stand up straight and head for the bedroom.

"I do blame everything on you," I say over my shoulder.

"You'll look back and thank me one day," he calls back before he opens the front door.

Before I shut the bedroom door properly, I stare through the crack. After a brief hello to his cleaner, he is already on the phone to James. His smug tone as he says it's "all sorted" makes me feel like I'm some kind of dispensable product.

I lock myself in the bathroom, forcing back the urge to smash the bathroom mirror.

Deep breaths.

After a few minutes' consideration, I realize that it's not all bad. Because in this moment, something twists in my heart and mind.

I despise Nathan Goldsmith.

CHAPTER TWENTY

I am in limbo.

Firstly, trapped in a job that screws up my body clock.

It's fine when I'm going to civilized places with working Wi-Fi, decent gyms and non-extreme weather, but not when I'm awake in the middle of the night, sick with jet lag, being dragged off to yet another continent. However, I don't see why I should resign simply because it makes things more comfortable for Nate. Secondly, I'm stuck with a semi-husband.

It's now been six weeks since our wedding and we're still legally married. Luckily for me, things aren't as straightforward as Nate made out, but between him and James, they are working hard to get shot of me. I get regular mails from James Harrington with phrases like *uncontested, incapable of assent, unsound mind*—not references to me but to Nate, apparently, during our wedding—*agree to non-consummation*. What? He wants me to *lie*? I text Nate, asking if he wants me to lie on a legal document, but he doesn't reply.

It can take up to three weeks to get the marriage annulled in Nevada if we travel back there together, or up to a year in the UK. Obviously, I said I'd prefer the UK. Back and forth the mails go. I feel like a child caught up in divorce custody arrangements.

My life is a repeat cycle of going to work, flying home and ignoring Nate's messages as often as I can get away with it.

I land from Washington on a slightly foggy morning after a forty-minute delay. We had to circle the skies above Heathrow whilst the fog cleared.

This time of year will, for me, always be synonymous with the threat of a new school year. The unmistakable drop in temperature—the tail end of summer merging with autumn coolness—hits my face as my heels clatter on the metal steps of a remote stand at Heathrow, whilst inhaling the strong smell of jet fuel. The entire crew gathers on the tarmac in front of the left engines whilst we wait for our bus.

Ascending planes roar just above us as they rise above the runway. I have two hours until my meeting with my manager to discuss my new role as a safety ambassador. I could have had it tomorrow, but it would have meant a special trip back. Soon, I'll only have to fly part-time, because the role is partly office based. I'm also now working on a brand-new POA. However, because it's in its infancy, there aren't enough jobs yet to all-consume me. The best news is that my purchase of the flat is progressing well, and there is every chance I could be in my new home within weeks.

After swiping through Immigration, paying in my duty-free sales money and escaping unsearched through Customs, I head for the canteen to wait for Amy. She called me yesterday, after weeks of zero contact. She's got a new boyfriend, so is clearly one of those women who thinks she doesn't need friends when she has a man. She'll learn.

"Hi," I say with a smile as she approaches. I kiss her once

on each cheek, feeling genuinely pleased to see her. I'm suffering post-wedding blues.

"Hi," she says. "Are you getting anything to eat?"

I shake my head. As she heads to the counter to order a panini, my heart stops as a blond pilot walks past. But it's not Nate. I knew it couldn't be, because I checked; he's in Antigua. I look around, unsettled. I feel out of sorts. I focus on the red and blue of an Air France plane visible through the floor-to-ceiling windowpanes.

Breathe. Something's not right; although Amy greeted me perfectly normally, she seems tense. Nervous, even. Something's definitely not right.

"So, tell me about this mysterious new man," I say when she sits back down opposite me.

"There's not much to tell. I met him on a Lagos trip." She takes a bite of her panini.

"So, crew then?"

She looks at me. "Yes. A pilot."

"What's his name?"

"Rupert. Rupert Palmer."

"Oh." I swallow. "Is he nice?"

"You tell me."

"I don't know what you mean."

"Yes, you do. You know one of his closest friends. Very well."

Damn Nate and his posse of friends. "I do?"

"You took us to his friend's flat. Imagine my surprise when we went round there the other night and I realized that I'd been there before. With you." I freeze.

"I didn't say anything, if that's what you're worried about," she says, like I'm supposed to be grateful.

When in doubt, say nothing. I look at Amy.

"So, I'm guessing Nate is 'Nick'? Why did you lie?"

"I didn't lie, as such. It's complicated."

"I'm sure it is. So, tell me."

"It's a long story and not really anyone else's business."

"Look, I like Rupert. Really, really like him. And I don't want to keep secrets from him. If there's a good reason why you took us to Nate's that night, then fine. But you were searching for something in his spare room."

I stare at her. Judgemental cow. Just wait until Rupert dumps her and she finds herself in my position.

"You had keys, Juliette."

"I don't any more. We got back together briefly, very recently, if you must know. Nate is a complicated man."

"Oh. Complicated in what way?"

I reach out and take her hand. "Please keep quiet about that night. There's no need for you to say anything at all. Nate and I are over for good and I want to keep it that way. If you're ever there again, please don't mention me." I try to sound as though I'm close to tears.

"OK. Sorry. It's just that it was weird going to a flat where I'd been before, and sensing that I had to be secretive. I asked Nate if his fish needed feeding when he was away and he said no, they are very self-reliant."

"Thank you. I'm so grateful for your support." I smile weakly. But… I don't trust her. A true friend would have texted me from the flat and been on my side, willing to hear my part of the story.

Amy is no friend of mine.

"I have to go," I say. "I have a very important meeting with my manager."

We say our goodbyes and I walk towards the corridor.

I sit outside Lorraine's office. My mind is filled with rage and hatred. Bella. Nate. Amy. The world is full of betrayers, everyone is out for themselves. There's no loyalty. No one cares about me unless I'm filling a temporary void in their lives. Amy is a Judas, like Bella.

I hate sitting outside offices, waiting. It brings back memories of waiting outside the headmistress' office, two days after the party.

★ ★ ★

It was a nightmare.

As if being ignored after the first time I'd had sex wasn't bad enough, I'd gone to a local chemist to get the morning-after pill during late afternoon break. I'd tried to convince myself—at first—that it would all be OK. But as the hours passed, and the thought that a real baby could be growing inside me filled me with such dread, I knew I had to take action. I couldn't take the risk of going to the school matron; I just couldn't face the questions, the interrogation, the shame. But I made a mistake. A really stupid one. I can only think that I was so upset, so hurt, that I really wasn't thinking straight, because I left the box in the bin in our dorm. Of course it was spotted—and, inevitably, by Bella. It didn't take her long to eliminate her "suspects" and narrow it down to me.

I denied it to the headmistress, I denied it to them all. But it didn't work. And then, if I thought it had been bad before, I quickly realized that I'd been wrong. Bad news travels fast. Cruel gossip about someone else, even faster. I tried to blank it all out, to ignore it. The names, the sniggers, the cruel notes put in my desk, the pictures of women who'd been body-shamed in magazines cut out with my face stuck on. I kept reminding myself that I'd lasted this long, managed the loneliness for years, it wasn't for much longer. But it was tough. One day I cracked and screamed at them all to leave me alone.

At the time, I felt proud for standing up for myself. But it was short-lived, as I could not win against someone like Bella. Girls like her get to make decisions about girls like me. Who our friends are or aren't, who will or won't speak to us, and even how teachers view us. And I was getting more and more sick of it. But what was even harder to admit was that, still, no matter what, all Bella would ever have to do was say the word and I would, of course, have been so pathetically grateful. I'd have forgiven Bella anything to be a part of her world. Anything.

In the meantime, my options were limited. I wanted to speak to the House Mother about it, but every time I waited outside her door, I couldn't summon up the courage to knock. I feared she'd take Bella's side or dismiss my worries with her standard phrase in response to most things: "Have a good sleep. I'm sure things will be better in the morning."

Instead, I thought of ideas to prove them wrong and make Bella pay.

"Juliette?" Lorraine is standing at the door to her office. She beckons me in. "Thank you for coming," she says, in between mouthfuls of sandwich. "Sorry, I didn't have time for lunch."

"Please, don't mind me," I say. No one else does.

"I'll run through the training schedule with you." She taps her keyboard with the forefinger of her free hand. "Although..." she hesitates. "There have been a few comments lately on your on-board appraisals. *Impatient. Lacking in enthusiasm.* Have you had anything going on in your personal life that is impacting on your work?" Lorraine puts down her sandwich and looks at me.

"My boyfriend proposed. Then, when things got to a crucial stage, it all went wrong. Cold feet."

"I'm sorry to hear that. Thank you for being honest with me. In that case, I'm prepared to overlook these comments, provided we don't receive any more..."

Lorraine's voice becomes background noise: *trial period... responsibility...confidentiality.*

This new role has come at the right time. Once in a position of trust, I will have greater access to information. And with knowledge comes power.

A fortnight later, Amy and I are back at training school. She is completing an aircraft conversion, because she is transferring to short-haul and domestic routes only. I suspect it has something to do with being on the same fleet as Rupert.

When our break times coincide, we meet in the canteen and chat, but Amy is stilted. She is holding back. I can tell by the way she hesitates before she replies to any of my questions.

On day three, my morning session finishes early. I go to the canteen, even though I'm not hungry. But I'm trapped; the training centre is in the middle of nowhere, adjacent to a dual carriageway. I spot Amy, but she is not alone. Beside her is Rupert. He has his hand on her knee.

I watch them from a distance as I pay for my coffee, then walk towards them.

Amy jumps as I approach. "Hi! Juliette!" She reddens.

"Hi," says Rupert. "I understand it's Juliette now, not Lily?"

I sit down opposite them. "I fancied a change. Loads of crew use different names."

"Yeah, but usually because they're called something un-pronounceable and get sick of being called the wrong name," says Amy.

I ignore her and smile at Rupert. "What are you doing here?"

"Simulator," he says. Routine pilot training. Rupert looks at his phone. "Well, must head back to the grindstone. Nice to see you again…Juliette."

"You too," I smile.

I don't look away as Rupert kisses Amy on the cheek. She watches as he walks out and when she turns back to me, she finds it hard to meet my eyes. Bitch. She's told him too much about me. I don't know why I ever wanted her to be my friend. Her eyes are slightly too wide apart and there is a hint of a sneer to her smile. I wonder how it can be that I misjudged her so badly; that I chose another Bella to befriend.

"What time do you finish tonight?" I ask.

"Five. But we've only got door drills left today, so hope-fully we'll finish early."

"Oh, that's a shame, I don't finish until six. We could've gone for a drink."

"Yeah. That is a shame," she lies, not even bothering to feign regret.

She looks at her watch. I open my bag to take out my phone. It's stuck, wedged into the inner zip where I keep my keys, painkillers and passport. I pull and, as I do so, something falls out and clatters on to the table. A flash of yellow. Homer Simpson yellow. *Shit.* I slam my hand over them, but Amy is staring at me.

"Are those mine?" she says.

"These?" I say, revealing them, palm outstretched. "I don't think so. Although I don't recognize them either."

"They *are* mine. Our spare ones went missing. Hannah thought it was me, and vice versa."

"Well, you can take them and check, if you think so? If not, give them back to me, as I guess they're for something I've forgotten about."

"They are mine."

"OK. If you say so."

"What were they doing in your bag?"

I look her in the eye. "No idea."

"It was you," she says under her breath. "You've been in our flat. When I'm not there."

"Oh, don't be ridiculous," I say. "It's just a set of keys!"

"Yes, you like taking keys, don't you? Going into other people's houses without permission."

"I don't like your tone."

"I could go to the police."

I don't understand why people always think they can "go to the police" for any situation to be magically and swiftly resolved in their favour.

"And say what? That I had keys to my husband's house and that a set of yours—allegedly—were in my bag. We're *friends*, Amy. Friends."

"Husband?"

"Yes. Nate is legally my husband. You've been too busy

thinking about yourself and Rupert—so much so—that you've neglected your friends. So, run along to the police." I stand up. "Make yourself look stupid. Nate asked me to marry him a few months ago, so I did. Now, I'm trying to sort out the mess I made. Marry in haste, repent at great leisure. Like I've said before, Nate's a complicated man. You don't know the half of it."

I don't know who she thinks she is.

I seethe all the way back home. It is an effort to drive safely, because I want to put my foot down and take off. I am hooted at twice and I have to brake suddenly when I forget to slow down whilst approaching a roundabout.

At home, I take out my lists. It's a shame I didn't bulk-buy voodoo dolls when I had the chance, but I could probably order some more online.

I update my plans for all three of my enemies and it keeps me going until the early hours.

I force myself back to the training centre in the morning, because I have one more day of my course left. Amy has two. I vow to avoid her all morning, but my rage resurfaces when she pretends not to see me in the canteen.

I really, really hate being ignored. Does she think I'm going to pull her ponytail? It's pathetic.

I check out the course list in reception. Amy finishes an hour after me today. I head towards the practical training area, praying that the code I watched Brian and Dawn key in endless times still works.

It does! I look around.

I walk in, as though I have every right to be here, passing the short-haul aircraft on my way. I can hear shouts as Amy's group complete their emergency evacuations.

I peek through the access door at the back of a Boeing 777. It is wedged open. The economy seats are deserted apart from scattered belongings. Everyone will be huddled by the main doors. I step in, holding my breath. An emergency evacuation alarm screeches, before being silenced, and I hear the rumble of a main door being pulled open and crew shouting instructions.

I search for Amy's bag; hers is the fifth one I come across. I remove her phone and switch it off.

I walk back through the access door, then hide by an equipment training station among the infant cots, oxygen bottles, life jackets and emergency packs.

I wait.

Twenty minutes later, Amy's group emerge from the mockup, led by two trainers. Amy is near the back. She opens her bag, rummages and stops. I bet she's dying to see how many times wonderful Rupert has messaged her today. She walks back towards the mock-up.

I count to thirty, then walk up to the access door. I look around. I remove the wedge, push it shut and walk away once I hear the lock click. Out of sight of any cameras, I drop Amy's phone on the path between the canteen and reception. I swipe out at security and cross the road to the car park.

Whilst driving, I think about Amy alone in the darkness, if all the aircraft exits have been locked. Whatever time Security find her—when it's noted that she hasn't swiped out—it won't be late enough, as far as I'm concerned. But, hopefully, whilst she's sitting in the ghostly graveyard of economy, trapped inside the shell of a plane with only passenger safety cards to pass the time, she'll also have time to think about the error of her ways.

I manage to get a parking space right outside the shoebox.

I have two missed calls. One from the estate agent, the other from my solicitor.

It's good news; I'm going to be Nate's neighbour by Halloween.

CHAPTER TWENTY-ONE

On the day of one of Bella's many pre-wedding gatherings with her clique—today being the deluxe spa experience—I drive to Bournemouth. I park, re-apply my perfume—a musky, strong one I bought in duty free—and walk down a hill towards the centre, until I reach the right address. I give my name to the receptionist, then sink down into a soft chair in the waiting area. The cream walls are decorated with pictures of yachts, mansions and exotic beaches. The carpets smell new.

"Miss Price?" says a man who appears through a door on my left.

I stand up, smile and we shake hands. I hold his hand a fraction longer than necessary. He is easily recognizable from the photos I've seen of him: normal-enough looking, shorter than Nate, with brown hair. Although, give it a few years and his hair will slip to the side and his stomach will swell. Miles must be a good ten years older than Bella and myself.

He has kind eyes, which crease at the sides when he smiles. His fingernails are well manicured.

"Please, come in and take a seat," he says. "Sorry to keep you waiting."

"That's quite all right," I say. "I can totally imagine that you're in demand."

I flash my left hand as I reach into my bag for a file to ensure he can see my engagement ring. It is a single diamond set in gold—bought in Abu Dhabi, duty free.

I've contacted Miles a few times for "advice" and then—slowly, carefully—reeled him in. I know Bella. I know her attitude towards the male sex: not-so-hidden-below-the-surface disdain. An ice maiden who has cultivated all the essential qualities to make good wife material for certain types of men. Miles does not seem the sort of man to take risks, though. If he thinks I am single, he will be harder to snare. He won't take the chance that he could end up in a bunny-boiling situation.

"So, Miss Price—"

"Please, call me Juliette."

"Of course. And you must call me Miles." He hesitates and smiles.

I smile back. "Miles."

He clears his throat and turns the screen on his desk around, ready to refresh my memory of our discussions by phone and mail.

I lean forward and listen attentively. "Thank you for explaining everything so well."

"As I've said before, some people make out that managing money is complicated, when it isn't. I like to dissolve the mystery for my clients."

"I can see that."

My phone rings. My prearranged fake call. I smile apologetically as I decline it, but then listen to a non-existent voice message.

"I'm going to have to cut our meeting short," I say. "But having now met you, I know you're the perfect man for the job. However, I'd like some time to read through everything you've provided, please."

"Of course."

I pretend to think. "I'm around this time next week. I don't suppose you'd be free again to go through any queries?" He checks his diary.

"Not a problem, Miss Pr—" He stops and smiles. "Juliette." I smile.

I shake his hand again before I depart, hopefully leaving behind the scent of my new perfume for him to remember me by.

I make a start on packing up the shoebox. Two hours later, my place is filled with a mini city of cardboard boxes.

My phone rings. Nate. I press ignore, as is customary for me right now. I'm sick of his supercilious voice as he tries to "reasonably discuss our predicament." He'll want me to sign something, or agree to something that isn't in my favour.

I need a distraction, so I check Facebook. Amy has been signed off for stress. Stress! The very word irritates me. She has posted endless boring rants about her "ordeal" of being trapped in the training centre. She was "shocked" and "distressed." Shocked and distressed indeed. People who escape war zones have stories of shock and distress. I have stories of shock and distress. Amy does not. Rupert has taken her away on holiday to Mauritius, so she is lucky. She has a safety net in the form of Rupert, friends and family, ready to help her when she's in trouble. She should try being me for a day, then she'd know the meaning of *stress*.

Nate rings again. I snatch up my phone.

"What do you want now?" I snap.

It's true that there is a fine line between love and hate, and I have crossed it. I will tether Nate to me out of revenge, not love.

"I need to discuss something important, please."

"Now there's a thing. Sadly, I'm busy."

"That's a shame," says Nate. "Because I get the feeling you're stalling, and it's not going to work."

The mere tone of his voice makes me feel so angry that I don't trust myself to speak. I grip my phone, resisting the desire to throw it against the wall. He's like the proverbial dog with a bone: *gnaw, gnaw, gnaw.*

"Lily? Are you there?"

"I tell you what, Nate. I'll come over to yours when I'm back from my next trip. I've got evidence that will make you see things in a different light."

He audibly sighs. "Can't you do it now?"

"No, I'm afraid I can't. I've got to get ready for an early Jeddah tomorrow."

There is silence.

I imagine him summoning up all his patience.

"Lily. We meant something to each other once. It doesn't have to be like this between us. I'm sorry that I can't agree to everything you'd like me to, but please, try to put yourself in my shoes."

"I'll try," I lie. "And it would be great if you could do the same for me."

His voice is quiet. "I have. And like I've said—many, many times—I'm sorry."

I say goodbye and carry on packing.

The flight to Jeddah is quiet. It's only half full, and there are no bars loaded, so there is no Customs paperwork to complete either. As we approach the airport, I see the vast, white, sweeping tent-like roof of the nearby Hajj Terminal.

Upon landing, the ground staff meet the aircraft and offer female crew the option of borrowing abayas—black, cloak-like garments—to cover ourselves, if we choose. Luckily, I'm more prepared than I was on my first Saudi trip to Riyadh, last month, so I've bought my own and packed my own new headscarf, even though the dress code here is more liberal than in Riyadh. I can feel the stares of the crowds outside Arrivals as we are escorted to a minibus. September heat blasts. The outside temperature is 33°, even though it's nearly midnight.

We drive through a flat, well-lit, modern area. I can almost sense that the desert is not far away, rather than actually see any tangible signs of it. Most buildings, if not white, are shell pink or sand-coloured. The green street signs are written in English beneath the Arabic, so I am able to follow them to the city centre. The traffic is dense for this time of night, and there are seemingly endless white taxis queuing up along the palm-lined streets. Multiple evidence of building work is in sight: scaffolding, bright lights and cranes.

We pull up outside a standard hotel chain, with its name written in gold. As I alight, I can almost feel the coolness of a nearby small fountain as it gently trickles. It adds an exotic holiday feel. Our bags are swiftly unloaded as we are bustled into reception by waiting doormen.

Already, there is more freedom here than I'd been led to believe by Galley FM—as crew gossip is referred to—because a receptionist gathers us round a small sitting area to run through a list of sightseeing options. Whilst we listen, we are offered fresh mango and orange juice.

The following morning, several of us congregate at the end of a long jetty at a private Red Sea beach club, awaiting flipper and snorkel allocation. I stretch, enjoying the heat on my skin, even though it is only ten in the morning.

Once I've been handed my equipment by an instructor and have adjusted the straps, I climb awkwardly down a ladder with my webbed feet and lower myself into the bath-warm turquoise sea. Opening my eyes beneath the surface, it is impossible not to feel blown away at the explosion of colour. Rainbow would be lost in here. Zebrafish weave in and out of coral whilst larger, bright-yellow fish with blue eyes watch me. Transparent, purple neon jellyfish with balloon-shaped bodies float gently in the distance. Smaller, metallic fish travel in regimented schools.

Over a lunch of lamb biryani and fresh lime sodas in the club's restaurant—a cool respite from the midday heat—I miss Nate, despite my anger towards him. Nostalgia seeps into my mind and highlights the loneliness of being in stunning surroundings with no one to share it with. I'd love to send him some pictures I took on the beach this morning.

Late afternoon, back in the welcome coolness of my hotel room, I compose an email to Miles. I ask him if we can meet for lunch next week, instead of meeting in his office. He emails back in minutes, with enthusiastic agreement. I have told Miles that I work for a travel company, despite my inherited wealth, because "I love it." I was vague about the specific details of my job, other than the fact that I need to travel quite extensively.

On the quiet six-and-a-half-hour flight home, I work on some scripts during my break: one for my upcoming visit to Nate, the other for my meeting with Miles.

We land in pouring rain at Heathrow. I love going to bed in the morning when the weather is foul, thinking of "normal" people who are only just heading off to work.

In a recently renovated gastropub, I choose a table in a corner with a sofa. I settle in and smooth down my new dress.

Miles is punctual.

I stand and smile. "Miles! You're a sweetheart for coming out to meet me. I hope you don't mind..." I point to the bottle of prosecco I've ordered.

"Why not? Thank you."

I make space for him on the sofa beside me. He hesitates for a mere second, before sinking down next to me. I ask him a question about pensions and he launches into a far-too-detailed response. I don't have as much money left as I've led him to believe but, at a later stage, I will apologetically inform him that my controlling fiancé has insisted I use a wealth-management friend of his instead.

He orders a steak sandwich and I do the same. It is tough, and difficult to eat elegantly, but I cut the meat up into small chunks and persevere.

"Now, that's business out of the way," I say, once we're finished. "I'd like to know a bit more about the man I've trusted with my future. My fiancé, Nick, doesn't have a head for business. We're a good match in a lot of ways and we know that a marriage between us will work well for our families, who have been friends for generations. We're both doing our duty in a sensible, good-natured way. However, I've made it clear that I will be responsible for the finances."

"Very wise," he says. "What does Nick do?"

"He's also in the travel industry, but he specializes more in the business sector, rather than the leisure industry. Cheers," I say. "Here's to the beginning of our relationship." We clink glasses.

He opens up a little about his personal life. He never intended to become a financial adviser, but rather fell into it.

Not that he minds, he insists.

"Does your wife work in a similar industry?" I ask.

"No. I'm not married. Like you, I have a fiancée."

"How did the two of you meet?"

He hesitates, as though unsure of how to answer.

"Sorry. It's none of my business," I quickly say. "I always gabble when I'm a bit nervous." I do my best to appear embarrassed, then I change the subject. "Do you enjoy golf?"

I already know that he does. I allow him a further fifteen minutes of my undivided time, then look at my watch.

"Oh! I must run. Such a shame. I've really enjoyed our chat."

He stands up when I do. "Likewise."

"I'll be in touch soon," I say. I shake his hand and leave, without looking back.

It isn't enough that he seems ripe for being persuaded to cheat on Bella. I want him to fall in love with me. I want Bella to experience heartbreak and humiliation. By showering Miles with my attention, this will be an inside job. *Keep your friends close, but your enemies closer* type of thing.

Speaking of which, I call Nate to tell him I'm on my way over to his flat with my "evidence."

We sit on Nate's sofa, a cushion-width apart.

When it's over, Nate gets up from the sofa and feeds the fish. Rainbow gulps greedily. I stand up too and eject the DVD from the player, returning it to its case.

"Would you like me to get you a copy?" I say. "Perhaps you and James Harrington could get a few beers and a takeaway and watch it together tonight?" Nate ignores me.

I suppress a smile.

In the DVD, Nate looks perfectly normal. Happy. He is smiling and not slurring his words. We look like any ordinary couple in love as we exchange vows. Even though I've watched it many times over, I'm still amazed.

"Try not to commit adultery," I say. "It will cost you dear in the divorce—which, by the way, we can't even apply for until at least a year after the wedding." I pick up my bag. "Oh, and also, you're going to be seeing a lot more of me. I'm being honoured for my role in an emergency evacuation several months ago and I'm going to be on the cover of the in-house magazine."

I yank the door shut behind me.

I'll save the news about us becoming neighbours for another time.

In between trips to Athens, Singapore and Vancouver, contact between Miles and myself increases.

I spend hours carefully wording my emails and messages, trying to come across as someone who is desperately trying to hide her attraction to him, but who knows it is ultimately going to fail.

Our messages become less guarded, less formal and more intimate. Until it's clear that, the next time we meet, there will be only one main item on the agenda.

The following week, on a dreary October Wednesday lunchtime, I park my car in an unfamiliar car park in Poole. It's not too many miles from Bournemouth, but far enough away to be discreet. I walk along the quay to the hotel restaurant, where Bella's fiancé awaits. Seagulls swoop down on to random bits of food lying near bins. Signs flap and the stench of fish masks the sea. Cold wind stings my cheeks.

Miles is waiting at a corner table. He stands up and kisses me continental-style, then pulls my chair out for me. He is well dressed in a made-to-measure jacket and a salmon shirt, which he carries off well. I sense Bella's hand in his grooming. If I've learned one thing about love, it's that you should never, ever give a man a makeover. It gives them a sense of confidence that is not channelled back to you, and another woman always benefits.

When we are both seated, he picks up the wine menu.

"Shall I order a bottle of Pouilly-Fumé?"

"Perfect," I smile. "I'm a bit nervous."

"Me too."

"Second thoughts?"

"No. You?"

"No. I've not been able to stop thinking about you since we met. I was concerned that I'd misread the signals. Like some fool."

"Ditto. I just knew that I had to take the risk, otherwise I'd die wondering. It seemed as though we had such a connection."

We order. I let him choose for me. I give him a little bit of the control I suspect he lacks from having a high-maintenance fiancée like Bella. Once the wine bottle is empty and the main course is cleared away, I broach the subject.

"I feel that we should address the elephant in the room," I say. "Then, it's out of the way and there's no misunderstanding." He nods.

"So, we don't want to hurt Bella or Nick. Our sense of duty ties us to them. We'll be discreet. This—us—will only stay fresh and amazing because we both know it will never lead anywhere. Agreed?"

He reaches across the table and takes my hand. "I couldn't have put it better myself." He leans forward. "I've taken the liberty of booking us a room here."

My stomach lurches a touch. Miles is nice enough, but he's not Nate. But I have to go through with this. And it's not my fault that I've been forced to break my vow of fidelity. Given the choice, I'd be a one-man woman. But my hand has been forced, and I need to take action.

I smile. "How presumptuous. But I do like a man who takes charge. Shall we skip dessert and coffee?"

Afterwards, Nate calls whilst Miles is lying beside me.
I answer.
"Hello, darling." I pull an apologetic face to Miles.
He mimes, "It's OK," and disappears into the bathroom.
Nate gets straight to the point. "OK, Lily. What do you want? What will it take for you to be reasonable?"

Any reservations I felt earlier disappear. "I'll let you know, *darling*," I say. "I'm busy at the moment."

I stretch and yawn. I'm glad that Nate has finally seen sense. I hoped it would come to this. Because I've thought of a way that he can make everything up to me.

CHAPTER TWENTY-TWO

I arrange to meet Nate outside his place the following day.

"Aren't you full of surprises?" he says as he eases himself into the passenger seat of my car. "When did you learn to drive?"

"Recently."

"Is this a mystery tour or are you in the mood to give me a clue?"

"It's too complicated to explain. You'll have to trust me."

Nate folds his arms like a quarrelsome child and looks out the window.

I follow the signs to the M3 and head south. Every attempt I make at conversation with him is thwarted by a grunt or a shrug of his shoulders, so I switch on Guns N' Roses, starting with the track we played in the limo on the way to our wedding.

We pass the services and continue for another hour and a half, through the New Forest, then towards my old village. I pass the small patch of green where the old red phone box remains in situ. I park on the opposite side of the lane, directly in front of Sweet Pea Cottage. The windows are curtain-less, made all the more obvious by the lack of ivy. It has all been hacked off, leaving the place bare and exposed. The hedges have been trimmed and are much lower than I've ever seen them. Clearly, the new owners have nothing to hide and are probably eager to involve themselves in village life. Good luck to them.

I point to the house. "This is where I used to live."

He gives the place a cursory glance before turning back to face me. "Please don't tell me you've dragged me out for a trip down memory lane. Remove any notion that if I get to know you better, I'm going to change my mind. I only agreed to today because you promised that you'd cooperate if I heard you out."

"I want to show you something. Come with me."

I open my door, get out and give my limbs a stretch. Nate gets out the other side and stands looking in the direction of the cottage. I wonder what he's thinking, and if he's trying to picture me living here. I wrap a scarf around my neck and do up my jacket buttons in a futile attempt at shutting out the bitter breeze.

"Come this way," I say, crossing the road.

Nate follows as I walk along the path that leads past the cottage, to the rear. Crisp brown leaves, small twigs and random litter—a chocolate wrapper and a takeaway leaflet—chase our ankles as the wind picks up. I catch glimpses of the garden through gaps in the wooden fence. Parts of the jungle have been cleared; the centre of the garden looks like it has been attacked by giant moles.

The old property behind Sweet Pea Cottage no longer exists. Once it was sold, the land was split up into three plots and new-builds were erected around a small cul-de-sac. The gardens are exposed; there is no fencing or anything to mark the boundaries. I stop in front of the middle house. There is a hatchback in the driveway, with a yellow *Baby on Board* sign stuck in the back windscreen, but there is no one about.

"I had a brother."

Nate looks at me, then ahead. "What has this house got to do with him?"

"Nothing. It wasn't built then. But this was the site where he had an accident. There used to be a dilapidated old farmhouse, which belonged to a couple. They had dreams of turning the place into holiday cottages, but ran out of money mid-project. They struggled on for a few years but the grounds must've been expensive to maintain, and the pool was never completely finished. It was a concrete shell, but to us—as children—it was a magnet, even though the deep end collected rainwater and it was slimy and dirty, with moss stuck to the sides." I smile at the sudden return of a memory. "We used to make up stories about 'Pond World' involving frogs and dragonflies."

"Did he drown?"

I nod.

"How old was he?"

"It wasn't long after his fourth birthday."

"I'm sorry. What happened?"

I shiver. "It's freezing here. It wasn't like that, the day it happened. It was summer..."

I must have been drawn back to *that time* for longer than I realize, because I'm aware of Nate prompting me.

"And?"

"My mum had these moods. And when one engulfed her, it was my job to take William—named after the flower, sweet william—out. Away. Until it passed. Until she could cope again."

"You couldn't have been that old?"

"Ten."

"Then what happened wasn't your fault." It *was* my fault.

But instead, I say, "He had a smile that made me want to look after him, at times. He could make me happy, even when

I felt annoyed that I had to look after him. William Florian Jasmin." I smile. "But he was spoilt too. My mother over indulged him as blatant over-compensation for her inability to parent properly. He could scream when he wanted his own way—and sometimes, it all got too much."

"Seems that your mum had a thing about flower names." He pauses. "So sad, though. What a tragedy for all of you."

"She told me once that her first memories were of picking flowers with her mother. Apparently, she had a capricious nature too." I shiver.

"Why did you tell me you were an only child?"

"What else was I supposed to say?" I pause. "I've had enough here. I want to leave."

As we walk back to the car, I finish the sorry tale with the short version, the one that I told everyone. "He slipped and fell. It all happened very quickly. There was no time for me to do anything."

Nate reaches over and squeezes my hand as I secure my seat belt. My instinct to bring him here seems to be paying off.

I choose the narrow back lanes to the graveyard, six miles away. I inhale the unmistakable smell of manure as we pass remote farm buildings. For several minutes, we get stuck behind a tractor towing a hay baler, sprinkling random stray strands from the rear each time there is a bump in the road. Each time I try to overtake it, another car frustratingly appears on the opposite side of the road.

Nate reverts to silent mode for the whole journey.

The cemetery is surrounded by a tall stone wall. As I pass through the open, black wrought-iron gates I feel hesitant. Perhaps this was a bad idea, after all, because this is the first time that I've visited since the funeral. I park, but don't make a move until Nate opens his door. The sound of the door unlocking jolts me back into this time and this place.

I can't remember the exact spot. I've spent too many years

blanking memories out. We wander along the paths among the wonky headstones, trees and the mixture of fresh and decaying flowers until, with perseverance, we locate it. It's near the edge of the plot by a row of yews.

William Florian Jasmin 1996–2000. We both stand still in front of the stone engraving, silent.

I love you to the moon and back.

I chose those words.

The wind weaves through the branches above, and leaves brush over my boots. I hear whispering sounds. If I believed in ghosts, I'd say hello to him.

"Why didn't you tell me?"

"We weren't together for long enough."

Neither one of us speaks much as we pull away from the village and follow the main roads back in the direction of London.

Nate looks out the window, as though lost in thought.

"Do you ever think about your schooldays?" I ask.

"In what way?"

"Did you enjoy them?"

"On the whole."

"I didn't enjoy mine."

"Well, you had a lot going on in your life. It's understandable, I guess."

"Did you sneak off for cigarettes? Or smuggle in illicit drink? Have parties?"

He looks at me. "Only the organized events—dances at the end of each term, those sort of things. Then the summer and winter balls, of course. Everyone smoked and drank at some point. Why?"

"Just wondering." I pause. "Going back to the area, it always brings back memories for me. Did you have many girlfriends?"

"Not that many."

I look at him—to see if he's going to add anything—but

he turns his head towards the window and disappears back into his own private thoughts. And I disappear into mine.

I stop at the motorway services for lunch.

We stand in a long queue whilst I stare through the glass counter at the sandwiches, muffins and cakes decorated pumpkin orange or with spiders and witches. I can't face the thought of food, but I choose a packet of crisps to have with my coffee. We have to share a table with an elderly couple, as the place is crammed.

When they finish their coffees and leave, Nate waits until he finishes his ham and mustard sandwich before making an attempt at conversation.

"It must've been awful for you and your family."

"It *was* hard." I pause, struggling for the right words. "Devastating."

He reaches across the table and puts his hand over mine. "Is that why your parents split up?"

"It probably would've happened anyway—my father was away a lot—but maybe their grief played its part. My mother was always fond of her drink, even before." I pause, realizing that it might make me less attractive. "It's not hereditary," I add, even though he can't really say much. "I've read loads on the subject."

I remove my hand from his. His attempt at sympathy is strangely discomforting. I know that Nate has *issues* with his parents. His mum can be a bit cold, and his father is impatient; he'd always told Nate and Bella that "second best was never an option." However, Nate is probably comparing his to mine right now and realizing that he has no valid *issues*.

None whatsoever.

"I'm sorry that all that happened to you. Were you offered help? Counselling? That sort of thing?" I shake my head.

"The thing is, I still don't follow what this has to do with our predicament." His tone softens.

Here we go. His next sentence proves my fear.

"Knowing about your brother..." he pauses before continuing, no doubt summoning up all the tact he can manage, "well, it doesn't change what needs to be done."

"We were good together. Why did you spend time with me in Vegas if you couldn't bear to be near me again?"

"Lily, I *like* you. You're attractive and can be fun. But there's a huge difference between hanging out with someone and making a life-changing commitment. That's why what happened between us feels wrong." He pauses, as though he is carefully choosing how to phrase his next words.

I interrupt. "I know what you're going to say, but *why* won't you give us one more chance?"

He opens his mouth to speak, but I silence him by raising my palm.

"I haven't finished. I've bought a place fairly near yours and I'm moving in soon. All I'm asking is that you give me six weeks. Six weeks of socializing—as friends, if you like. Taking things slowly. Then if, after that, you still feel the same, you have my word that I will let you go for good and you won't even know I'm your neighbour." He doesn't reply.

"Well?"

"You're kidding, right?"

"No."

"Why near me? You could live anywhere. *Anywhere.* What about Nice, Barcelona, Amsterdam, Dublin? So many crew do. You should take advantage of having a job that allows you to do that."

"Why don't *you* live abroad?"

"Because Richmond is where I chose to live. Me. By myself. Nothing to do with anyone else. Of all the places, you did not have to choose my area."

"Six weeks, that's all I've asked for."

"And then what? You'll up sticks just like that?"

"Well, I don't know about that, I could lose a lot of money. We'll see. But I can promise to leave you alone."

"Can I have that in writing?" he says in a tone that doesn't sound as if he's joking.

"If you don't trust me."

Like I'm going to do that.

Nate helps me move into my new flat. Even though I get the feeling it's because he wants to keep an eye on me and my new home—which is a strange role reversal—I take advantage. After all, he was happy enough to help me move to Reading in the first place.

Once I've finished cleaning the shoebox and gone through the inventory with the agency, I hand over my keys with a genuine grin. We load up both our cars and I don't look back as I pull away from the place that I never wanted to live in anyway.

Nate follows me back to mine. It is less than a minute's walk from his flat, diagonally left. Leaving my car directly outside, I put on my hazard lights as Nate unloads my belongings from the small boot and back seat. Even though there are two flights of stairs up to attic-floor level, he works without complaint and is generally all-round helpful.

The job is done in under two hours. Maybe I don't hate him quite as much as I thought.

Despite the small size of the property, I need to buy some furniture. A bed—I currently have a blow-up mattress—a table, some chairs and a sofa. I also need various kitchen utensils. However, the flat is already carpeted in a tasteful, thick cream colour and the kitchen is well equipped, with a washing machine and dishwasher.

We order in sushi and sit on the floor, eating from the cartons with chopsticks. It feels like nothing bad has ever happened between us. It's so natural, just hanging out together, and I feel the most optimistic I have for a very long time.

And yet, there is one issue I feel I need to address. I want to get my version in first.

"Your friend Rupert is seeing someone I trained with. Apparently, she came over to yours with him recently."

"What's her name?"

"Amy."

"Yes, I remember."

"She's a bit unstable. She acted really strangely when I mentioned you. Said she'd found it odd that I hadn't mentioned you before—even though we weren't together, so why would I have?"

He shrugs. "She seemed all right to me."

"Well, she would. Who admits to being a bit of a fantasist? No one I know. Anyway, I hope Rupert finds out what she's like."

"I'm sure Rupert is capable of looking after himself."

I add a small amount of wasabi into the soy sauce and mix, before dipping a piece of salmon and rice into it.

Silence falls between us.

Nate seems a little more tense than I initially noticed, as if he's just going through the motions.

I test him. "Have you told your family you're married?"

He looks at me like I'm mad. "No. It would upset my mum."

"What about if she met me?"

"No."

I let it drop.

When Nate makes noises about leaving, I don't complain or make any future demands. Instead, I thank him, bid him a cheery goodbye and let him go. I know he's biding his time until he can relay his "I'm so sorry, Lily, I gave it my best shot" speech, so I'm going to try a fresh approach.

I know that Nate's father took early retirement from some high-up banking position and has a keen interest in golf, but his mother is a social butterfly, into tennis and swimming, and indulges in multiple hobbies. She is also a board member for an art and culture charity. I google it. They provide photographers who offer their services for free. I dig some more. Nate and Bella's mother—Margaret—appears to dabble in photography herself. She has a small studio near the house they moved to ten years ago in Canford Cliffs, an exclusive part of Poole. She opens it on Monday and Thursday mornings.

I google-earth their house. It is magnificent and clearly has breathtaking views of the bay. I zoom in and see a patio area with a large garden table. I imagine that many family gatherings are held in that space. I can picture Nate sitting there, enjoying the view, whilst sharing stories of his latest travels.

I text Miles.

Can't wait to see you again. X

He gets back in five minutes.

Next Thurs? Same place?

As I'll be in the general area, I may as well multitask, so I'll go and admire Margaret's work too. Seeing as I'm in a particularly organized mood, I order furniture: a bed, a small sofa and several throws and cushions.

I'm going to settle in properly here; put down real roots for the first time ever.

I arise early the next morning and put on my uniform, taking extra care. Today is my first day in my new part-time role. I will be photographed for the in-house magazine and I need to be looking my best. Hopefully, it will be the photo that will remind Nate of my permanent existence, every time he reports for work.

I arrive punctually and seek out the manager in charge of the promotions team, who is an earnest man—also cabin crew—but obviously power hungry. He has listed all his ridiculously high expectations in order of importance and exudes desperation to give up flying by working his way into seemingly bigger and better ground-based roles.

As well as myself—the safety ambassador—there are three other people who have been awarded various accolades that encompass welfare, health and team-bonding.

The day is not fun; it is worse than being at training school. Wearing a hi-vis jacket and safety goggles, the photographer and I are sent airside and bused out to a hanger. I have to navigate wobbly, metal engineering steps to board the plane, and it's a constant effort to keep out of the engineers' way. I am instructed to pose by various potential hazards inside the plane: carpets with peeling-up edges, a no-glass sign by the trash compactor. And I have to grip the handrail of the stairs leading to the upper deck *correctly*.

Back in the Report Centre, we have a team photo taken; side by side, we grin. As far as I can make out, the main benefit of the role is that we have an office space—albeit shared—for our own use. This means a gateway to potentially confidential information about others, because my new password offers greater access to the company systems. As well as regular meetings, it is our responsibility to provide regular, positive updates for the magazine, encouraging our colleagues to be more safety conscious, more self-aware health-wise, and to show greater care and concern for each other.

We are informed, by the keen-bean manager, that the team photo will be on the cover and the worst one—of me—will be used on the third page. It is hideous. I am standing in the cockpit, to the side of the centre pedestal, holding an empty mug, with a concerned expression on my face. I will be alongside a warning issued about taking care when serving drinks to the flight crew. The article will include engineering statistics—something dull about defects and new components, or suchlike.

★ ★ ★

It is such a relief to return to my new home. I kick off my heels, switch on the radio, select a channel that plays non-stop chart hits and temporarily remove my pinboards from their hiding place to hang them inside a kitchen cupboard. It won't do for them to be on show whilst Nate is an occasional visitor. Even though he's not as regular as I'd like him to be, he at least shows willing, I'll give him that.

I also have one other box which will need to remain out of sight; the one which contains my most private possessions. I'll share some of them with Nate when I decide he's in the right frame of mind.

My phone vibrates. Miles.

Can we take a rain check? Work. ☹ Have to visit a client in Tokyo, will be gone for a week.

That's frustrating. He's not bad company, and I enjoyed my time with him. Even though Bella doesn't yet know, it is still satisfying. I'm due to operate to Singapore in three days' time. I check the swap lists. There are two Tokyos available in my work grade, but one person specifically wants to swap with a Stateside trip only. I mail the other one.

Whilst waiting for a reply, I text Miles back.

No way! What a coincidence! I was told today that I might need to go to Tokyo too! There's a new hotel to check out. I'll contact you if it comes off ☺ It must be fate.

An email comes through agreeing to the trip swap at the same time as I receive a keen reply from Miles. Like I said to him—it's fate. I'm looking forward to spending a longer period of time with him; innocently, gently probing to find out Bella's vulnerabilities and fears.

Everything comes to she who waits.

CHAPTER TWENTY-THREE

On the twenty-eighth floor of a skyscraper hotel, renowned for its view of the city's Rainbow Bridge, I wait for Miles. The bar is dimly lit. Little candles flicker on the slate-grey tables, intermingling with the city lights outside the giant floor-to-ceiling windowpanes. Red, white and blue illuminate the bridge below, reflections bobbing in the water. The tinkling of a piano provides a discreet backdrop to the various conversations held by the local, designer-clad clientele, separated by scattered clusters of Westerners.

I am bored.

The rest of my crew went off to a fun-sounding karaoke bar, and there was one woman who seems like a good laugh. If I had the time, I would like to have hung out with her. I need a replacement friend after my falling-out with Amy.

"So, so sorry," Miles says, appearing at my side. "My meeting overran."

There is an awkward moment as he seems unsure about how

to greet me. Even though we're far away from home, Miles appears uncharacteristically hyper-aware that we're in public. We kiss once on each cheek, then he sits down next to me.

"What would you like to drink?" he asks.

I pick up the cocktail menu and read the English names helpfully written alongside the Japanese symbols. I select a Green Destiny: a blend of vodka, cucumber, kiwi and apple juice. Miles decides on a margarita.

"My hotel is quite far away from here," I say. "So I hope you don't mind, but I've taken the liberty of bringing a small overnight bag with me."

He shifts in his seat a little. "I guess it makes sense. Will Nick be in touch, do you think?"

"I doubt it." I put my hand over his. "Don't worry, if Bella calls, I'll make myself scarce. I'll lock myself away in the bathroom and block my ears."

He laughs. "She probably won't call."

"Does she keep busy whilst you're away?"

"Bella is always busy."

I stay silent, waiting for him to elaborate, but he doesn't bite. Miles loosens his tie and relaxes back into his chair.

After our second drink, he invites me to his room. The moment the door closes behind us, we reach for each other.

I revel in each and every moment that I am stealing him from Bella.

Miles has fallen asleep.

The room smells of stale smoke—which is such an alien smell, as smoking is now banned in so many hotels around the world. I force myself to wait a good twenty minutes before taking a nose around. His tablet and phone are password-protected. I try a few times—Bella's birthday and then Miles' date of birth, which I learn by flicking through his passport—but it is of no use. His briefcase is open. I sift through client papers, but they are dull. His wallet contains nothing of great interest apart from a dog-eared photo of *her*.

Her smile has always been the same. Every time I see it, I am reminded of a smiling assassin.

There is also a list in Bella's unmistakable handwriting and even the sight of it makes me feel ill at ease. She loops and swirls her capital letters in an overly ornate fashion. Written down among Bella's requests (or demands)—for example, it is Miles' job to arrange the honeymoon—she has also listed several potential venues for their wedding. Her current favourite is an Italian-style villa in some privately owned gardens near her parents' home, with several hotels named in order of preference.

I pick up my phone and take photos of everything I've discovered, as a reminder, then I sit on the edge of the bed and stare at the wall. I can't switch off. If Bella were here, she'd probably be asleep—not a care in the world, apart from her stupid wedding plans. I wonder what I can do to mess with her precious arrangements. She doesn't deserve to live happily ever after. Karma is clearly a myth, if someone as undeserving as Bella gets her happy-ever-after without a struggle, whilst people like me are left to flounder.

Sometimes I think about what will happen when Bella and I meet again. I go over what she says, what I say. And although the situations vary, it always ends up with me winning. I am the one who finally gets a voice. I've learned to ski, to play tennis, to horse ride. I've visited the places she goes to, I've made sure that I've met most of the people she networks with—if not in person, then on social media. I'm totally ready to integrate into her world, so that *she* wants to be *my* friend, not the other way round.

Miles turns over in his sleep. I should leave something in his suitcase for her to find, a little memento to make her concerned when he travels for work. Something to turn her into a neurotic woman, with less self-assurance and a little more humility. Someone Miles won't respect. It has to be something subtle—so that Miles doesn't suspect my involvement. I spray my perfume into the lining of his suitcase and shut the lid, hoping it permeates the contents. It would be ideal if Bella unpacks for him, although I doubt that she does.

I go into the bathroom. I take a peek inside his leather washbag. There is not much: deodorant, a lip balm, hair gel, some nail clippers. I sit on the edge of the bath and study the Japanese toilet control panel, trying to figure out what the pictures on each button mean. After further pondering, I creep back into the room and open the wardrobe. I feel inside his jacket pockets. Empty. I search my own bag, but there is nothing I can leave without Miles knowing it was me. The perfume will have to suffice.

For now.

But I do take a photo of Miles. I freeze as the flash goes off, but he doesn't stir.

I get into bed and lie near the edge, watching the red illuminated numbers change on the bedside clock.

I fantasize that Nate will change his attitude, which will, in turn, allow my feelings for him to revert to love. We could begin again, do things properly: date, fall in love, make a total fresh start. My thoughts grow, becoming even more elaborate, until I can feel myself drifting off.

An alarm call jolts me into awareness. I lean down and check my phone in my bag; it's 7:00 a.m. Tokyo time.

Miles sits up, stretches and then disappears into the bathroom. When I hear the sound of the shower, I go in and join him. He doesn't object. Nate could learn a thing or two about enthusiasm from him.

Once we're both dressed and ready, we make our way along the corridor to the executive lounge for breakfast.

Miles spends most of the time tapping into his phone.

"What shall we do today?" I say as I spear a piece of melon with my fork.

"What do you mean?"

"Well, I thought maybe the Imperial Palace or..."

"I'm working," he says. "And surely you must be too?"

"Yes, of course I am, but I'm allowed a bit of time off. So, what do you think?"

He looks at me. "I'm not here for sightseeing, and I've been there before with—" He stops.

"It's OK, you can say her name," I say.

"Juliette, I'm sorry but I need to get on in peace. I've a lot to get through today."

"Fine. What about dinner tonight?"

"I can't, I'm afraid. I'm dining with my client."

"I could join you? As a business colleague?"

"It wouldn't be a good idea."

"But I'm going home the day after."

"So, we'll have to get together—back at home—another time. You pick a time and a place and wild horses won't keep me away." He smiles, but it is forced. "I'll get going, then." He looks down at his phone. I stand up, feeling dismissed.

"Sorry, Juliette. There's something I need to deal with straight away."

"Of course. I understand."

He stands up and kisses me on the cheek.

I look back as I leave, but he is not watching me. He has already turned his attention back to his phone.

On the seemingly never-ending, twelve-hour flight home, I seethe.

I lie in a bottom bunk, hiding myself away from everyone else.

By torchlight, I list the ways in which Nate and Miles are similar.

★ ★ ★

As I push open the communal door to my flat, the pile of post, pizza leaflets and charity requests creates a gentle resistance. I bend down to pick them up. My downstairs neighbours must have been away for the night as they usually pile up anything addressed to me neatly on the bottom step. Dragging my belongings upstairs, I can't rest as I have to wait for my bed to be delivered.

It arrives late morning, and the delivery men also help to erect the small double frame. When they leave, I wrestle with a bottle-green duvet cover I recently took from Nate's—not his favourite set—and pull on two matching pillowcases, giving them a good shake before dropping them on to my new bed.

Slowly, the place is beginning to look more like mine now. The blank walls need some new pictures, so I sort through my favourite ones of Nate that I intend to get framed.

The following day is a Thursday, one of the days Nate's mother opens her studio.

It is easy to locate. I park on a nearby tree-lined street and make my way to the glass-door entrance.

She is in there, alone, sitting behind a plain desk. She looks older than her pictures, but she has an elegance and aloofness that I remember from when I caught occasional glimpses of her at school. She sits on a small stool, with her back straight, reading a magazine. Her glasses match her navy top. For a fleeting moment I think that there is not much likeness between her and her daughter—much more so her son—but then she opens her mouth. And even if I had my eyes closed, I would know that they were related.

My heart rate quickens a little.

"Good morning," she says, looking up from her magazine,

which I now notice is an art brochure. "Feel free to ask any questions."

"Thank you," I say with a smile. "I've driven past here a few times and your window always catches my eye. I've been meaning to come in. And today, I thought I'd finally make the time."

I browse. I don't know much about art or photography, but I looked up a few useful tips before I left home. It's good, apparently, to compliment the photographer on the work that went into the image and simply appreciate the scene itself.

I express an interest in one of the more expensive frames— a black-and-white picture of a regatta.

"I love this one. The scattered white triangles of the sails caught my eye. Where was it taken?"

She beams. "In the bay, last year. It's the view from my living-room window."

I suspected as much. "I'm going to buy it as a surprise for my husband."

"I hope he loves it too. Does he sail?" she asks whilst packaging up the picture.

"Not very much. But then again, he's not had time. We've only been married a few months. He was really keen and didn't want to wait, so we married in Vegas."

"How thrilling."

"It was definitely the best day of my life. The only problem is that he doesn't know how to break the news to his family."

She looks up, as though unused to a stranger over-sharing.

I could tell her. I could tell her right now who I am. With one sentence I could force Nate to acknowledge me. I could tell her how brutal her son has been with my heart and show her proof that I am not deluded; that her son married me, then cruelly changed his mind. I could tell her that he'd told me things about her, like how she chose his name because she loved it, even though her husband wanted Nate to be called Julian.

"How difficult for you," Margaret says. "What about your parents?"

"They're no longer around."

"Oh," she says, handing me the parcel. No doubt she is smugly pleased that her own life is divorced from such tacky problems.

"He should just tell them," she adds as I walk away. "Good luck!"

She's right; he should. Outside, I text him.

I think your mother would be delighted to hear our news. I've just met her. She's so lovely. I felt really guilty keeping her in the dark about me being her daughter-in-law.

My phone rings immediately. It's truly amazing how quickly Nate can respond to any messages from me when it's in his interests to do so.

I switch my phone off.

CHAPTER TWENTY-FOUR

I drive to Bella's favourite potential wedding venue, which is only a mile away from the studio.

I pay to enter the gardens and, using the map provided, head straight for the Italian section. There is no one else around. I sit on a bench feeling the cold seeping through my trousers and stare into a large pond edged with shrubs. Beneath the lily pads I see flashes of koi carp swimming near an ornate, carved stone fountain which is the centrepiece. Looking around, I try to imagine the garden in summer, because I can tell that it will burst into colour. Behind a patch of neat grass, rhododendrons line the rear. I switch on my phone and take a few pictures so that I can refresh my memory later.

I have seven missed calls from Nate and one from James. It feels like harassment.

I stand up and walk around the pond, passing by a statue of Bacchus until I reach the stone steps leading up to the villa. Looking up, I can see a balcony; ideal for Bella to pose on. I can already picture the scene as it will unfold: the royal wave, the ooh-ing and aah-ing of the guests as they stand by the clipped yews, taking photos of the bride and posing for selfies among the elegant surroundings.

My phone breaks into the film-like images playing inside my head.

It's Nate. Again. He doesn't bother with hello.

"What do you mean you've met my mother?"

"Calm down. I was with a friend who is interested in photography and we ended up in a studio near Poole. We got chatting to the owner and it turned out she was your mother. I only realized because she mentioned that her son was a pilot, so I married up the surname."

"Please keep my family out of our private fiasco."

"Our *marriage*, Nate. I am your *wife*, not a fiasco."

As I jab "end call" my hand shakes. I turn my phone off again and stride along a winding path, through a heather garden, over a small bridge and past several water features, but all the time my mind is racing with murderous thoughts.

By the time I leave an hour later, I am still not calm. Realistically, I have no choice but to come up with some amendments to my plan of action.

At home that evening, I call Nate. "Come over. I've been thinking things through. We can talk as much as you like."

He arrives within fifteen minutes, pressing my buzzer for longer than necessary.

I open my door and he strides in.

"Drink?" I don't wait for a reply and pour him a red wine, handing him the glass.

He refuses to accept it. "No, thank you."

He pulls out a spiral notepad and pen, as though trying to persuade me that *he really means business*.

"What are you going to do? Write a list of pros and cons?"

"This isn't a joke. I want my life back."

"I haven't *taken* your life."

"I want you to stop all this. This scheme of yours—us hanging out like best friends, you sneaking off to my mother's—it's not going to *change* anything. Please just agree to the annulment, then I won't have to bother you any more. If you play ball, it will all be mostly straightforward and there's a chance we won't have to go to court. Otherwise it all becomes a lot more convoluted. And worse, for both you and me. I will have to prove that I didn't properly consent to the marriage due to intoxication."

A change of tactics is overdue. "OK."

"OK what?"

"OK, I'll cooperate. I love you and if this is what you need to make you happy, then I'll do it."

"Thank you. One day—"

"Please don't say that I'll thank you one day. Because I won't."

He turns to leave. "All right, but please can you start answering James' emails."

I fill in the required forms—admittedly as slowly as I can get away with, because I have no intention of allowing this to go through to the final stages—and the process of ending our marriage begins.

If it is all as straightforward as it seems, Nate will no longer be my husband by the spring. However, having lulled him into a false sense of security, I have to come up with another, final fail-safe plan to keep him. But I'll have to be fairly quick. He has asked me not to contact him unless necessary.

Devastated—I realize I love him as much as ever—I turn my attention to Miles. When we next agree to meet, I arrange to pick him up from around the corner, out of sight from his office.

"I've booked somewhere different as a surprise," I say, as he settles in the passenger seat.

"How far away is it?" he says. "I need to be back by five."

"We'll be back by then. Look," I say, pointing to a gift bag on the floor. "I bought you a present."

He pulls it out. It is a book—*Five Hundred Places to Visit Before You Die*—the same one I gave to Nate. I have composed a poem and concealed it in the Japanese section. I know he won't take it home and will probably hide it away in his office, but I wanted to buy him *something* to let him know I care for him.

"Thank you, Juliette. Very thoughtful."

The bag rustles as he shoves the book back in.

As I pull into the hotel car park, Miles visibly stiffens beside me. "Here?"

"Yes. Being in Tokyo made me realize that we don't have to slum it when we get the chance to meet. Hence the gift choice too. I thought that we could maybe do some more travelling together in future."

"Juliette, it's a wonderful thought but I'm not comfortable here, at this place. It's—" He stops, unwilling to tell me the truth.

It's one of the hotels on Bella's venue wish list.

I do my best to look hurt and disappointed. "I've really been looking forward to seeing you."

"Me too. But not here."

Instead, he directs me to a secluded beachside car park. My life is going downhill whilst Bella's still soars. I need to get my act together.

Restless, the next morning I drive to nearby Kingston and wander around an indoor shopping centre. Shops are full of colour and light, with signs everywhere advertising the festive season. Christmas is only six weeks away. Father Christmases grin, reindeer leap, snowmen stare and elves clutch gifts. A band plays carols by a tree smothered with decorations.

I feel even lower than I did last Christmas. This time last year, although heartbroken, I had hope. Now, without any current, undoubting hope that things will soon definitely improve, I am struggling to cope.

I sit in a coffee shop and drink two espressos in quick succession. Tapping in the Wi-Fi code, I intend to look for suitable Christmas presents for Barbara, so that I can go directly to one shop without having to endure too many of the crowded ones. But I can't help myself getting distracted.

Nate is in Miami, but he and James message each other twice. To them, I am a joke—they call me TOTWGA "The One That Won't Go Away"—and James also refers to me as mendacious. I torture myself by reading more: Nate wants "rid" of me as swiftly and as effortlessly as possible. He wants to "move on" without the "threat" of me hanging over his life like a "black cloud." James even has the nerve to suggest that Nate puts his place on the market, "to do what it takes to keep a distance from her." And also, according to James, the Knower of All Things, Barnes (where he happens to live) is "another good option. It's not as if you are tied to schools or a fixed work commute."

When I run out of negative things that Nate and James have to say about me, I check out Bella's blog, which bores on about her wedding dress fittings and how she and Miles are attending the opening of a new restaurant later this evening. I read a comment on Facebook in response to one of Amy's friends asking about her Christmas plans—she and Rupert are planning to spend it in Paris.

Everyone is happy but me.

I stand up and shrug on my coat, fully intending to go straight home, but I spot a window full of red and black lingerie. It gives me an idea. I go inside.

When I leave with my purchases, I feel uplifted; I finally have a focus.

On my way home, I also stop at a DIY store. Now that I own a property, it's undoubtedly a wise investment to stock up on some basic tools.

I let myself into Nate's after dark. Even though I'd rather do something malicious and vengeful, I stick to what I came to do.

Whilst I'm busy, words flash through my mind.

Mendacious. The One That Won't Go Away.

He is slipping away—and soon, there will be nothing more I can do about it. Legally—for now—he's still mine. I still have a chance, although I'm starting to fear that my change of tactics could backfire unless I try much harder.

I walk back home, taking a longer route than necessary by walking around the Green in the opposite direction.

In the flat, I sit on my new bed and look at all my photos. I shake them out of the albums and tip them all over, so that I am surrounded by memories.

I need a distraction.

Maybe it will be a good idea to pay Miles a visit at the restaurant opening Bella mentioned earlier on her blog. He'll be bored, standing around in her shadow. I'm sure he'll easily be enticed away, delighted for a chance to escape for a while.

Before I can talk myself out of it, I grab my bag and coat, then rush downstairs to my car. I tap in the postcode of the Asian fusion restaurant. I don't message Miles beforehand, I want my spontaneity to be a lovely surprise.

I put my foot down hard on the accelerator once I'm on the motorway and break the speed limit. It feels therapeutic as I mull things over in my mind.

Thank God I have Miles' part-time attention. Without him as a distraction, I'm not sure how I would keep it together quite so well.

CHAPTER TWENTY-FIVE

I peer through the restaurant window. At first, I can't pick Miles or Bella out in the crowd, but I soon spot Bella holding court with a group of women. Miles is slightly further back, talking to a tall man.

I want to walk in and stand in a proprietary fashion at his side, slipping my arm through his or openly flirting with him. Instead, I text him.

I'm in your neck of the woods, fancy slipping away for a while? X

I watch as he takes out his phone, glances down, then puts it back in his pocket. He continues his conversation. I sit down on a freezing bench opposite.

Five minutes later, I text again.

?? X

He reacts in exactly the same way. I call. He takes out his phone and we are immediately disconnected.

A surge of rage rushes through my entire body. I push open the door to the restaurant and walk into the warm aroma of spices mingled with incense. I stop at the side and lean against the wall in Miles' line of vision. He stares for a second before recognition hits, yet he does not smile or come over to greet me.

I seek out the Ladies and phone him. No answer. As I'm about to press his number again, a text comes through.

What are you doing here? Bella's with me!

I text back.

So what!? All you had to do was speak to me like a normal person, there are loads of people here, I could be anyone. At least have the manners to reply to me.

As I send the message, the door opens and in walks Bella.

I drop my phone into my bag and quickly wash my shaking hands, staring down. She enters the middle cubicle. I head for the exit, but stop as I change my mind. I was in here first. I stand in front of the mirror and remove a lipstick from its home inside the inner zip section of my bag. My phone vibrates. *Miles.* Let's see how much he likes being ignored. I bet he's in a right old panic, which serves him right. I take a deep breath to calm my inner agitation.

I jump when the cubicle door opens and Bella emerges. She stands next to me washing her hands. I stare at her in the mirror whilst slowly applying my lipstick. She looks up. Recognition filters through her expression as I inhale the scent of musky vanilla. She still smells expensive.

"Elizabeth? From school?"

My legs feel wobbly. In one of my many fantasy versions of our meeting up again, she apologizes profusely and begs me to be her friend.

Just the tone of her voice reminds me how futile my wishes have been.

"Hello, Bella." My voice sounds calm.

"Hi. What are you doing here?" She pulls a hand towel from the holder.

"The same as you, I imagine."

"Yes, quite. Do you live here?"

"A close friend does."

I replace the top of my lipstick and rub my lips together. Taking a final look at my reflection, I turn towards the door and she follows. A frowning Miles is hovering by a nearby pillar. I stop and turn round to face Bella.

"Bye," I say, as loudly as I can, without it sounding too obvious that my final exchange with Bella is for Miles' benefit, then I continue walking towards the exit, leaving them both behind.

The cold smacks my face. I walk to my car and wait. After three minutes my phone rings.

"I bet you're making this call from the Gents?" I say.

"What the hell just went on?" he says. "What are you doing here?"

"I was in the area. I tried to warn you, but you ignored me."

"That was Bella you were in the toilets with."

"I know. I went to school with her."

"You *know* her? What..." There is a muffled sound, as though someone else has entered the toilets. Sure enough, Miles changes the tone of his voice. "I'm at a party right now. I'll call you soon."

"Come outside now and meet me. I'm in the car park opposite."

"It's not possible at the moment."

"Miles, anything is possible when you try. If you don't come out, I'll come back in. You have five minutes."

I hang up. He calls twice more, which I ignore. Then a text, which I delete without reading.

Miles appears by the passenger door less than two minutes later.

He slides in beside me. "What's going on?" he says. "I can't stay long. What do you mean you went to school with Bella?"

"I recognized her. When she followed me into the Ladies."

"And you didn't know that she was *my* Bella?"

"How would I? We weren't friends. I'm surprised at you being with someone like her. She was a nasty bully at school."

He gives me a strange look. "Bella wouldn't hurt a fly. She only wants to do good."

I laugh. I can't help it. And for some reason, I can't seem to stop.

Miles stares at me. "Do you want me to call someone? A friend?"

"Bella was supposed to be my friend."

"Well, that would make things truly difficult. This changes everything. I had no idea. And of course it goes without saying that—"

"How about we go for a drive? You don't seem like one of those couples who keep tabs on each other. Bella surely won't miss you for half an hour or so."

As I lean over towards him, before my hand even touches his thigh, Miles opens the passenger door, blasting me with cold air and flooding the car with light.

"I need to get back. I'm sorry, this has been a mistake. Bye, Juliette."

I switch on the engine and reverse without checking behind. But as I change gears, Miles leaps out and slams the door. He runs, he actually runs, towards the restaurant.

Away from me.

I sit for ages, turning the ignition keys on and off. They click and un-click. I drive past the restaurant several times, but am unable to catch further sight of either of them.

I give up. But it turns out that the outing wasn't a total waste of time. Because the drive home allows me valuable headspace to figure out the finer details of my next plan.

Two days later, the first thing I do when I wake up is to check on Nate's flight. He is due to land at three thirty; it's on schedule.

After today, he has ten days' leave, during which time he intends to "chill," according to a message sent to James Harrington. They are meeting up in a local pub tonight, where they will no doubt have a merry time discussing how Nate will soon be free of his *mendacious* wife.

I spend the day gathering everything I will need to confront Nate.

Back home in the evening, I kneel on the living-room floor and place all my gathered essentials into a rucksack.

I wait.

I lie on the sofa, with the TV on in the background, but I can't concentrate. I'm aware of dropping off every now and then as consciousness and reality appear and disappear.

My alarm goes off at five. I get dressed, put my rucksack on my back and let myself out. On the Green it is peaceful and eerily quiet. I switch on my torch and see why—it's as though I've stepped through the wardrobe and into the winter wonderland of Narnia. Grass and twigs poke through the snow. The occasional house has illuminated windows and I switch off my torch, feeling exposed—as though I'm being secretly watched by hidden people. Nate's flat is in darkness.

I stand for a few moments inhaling the freezing air. My breath is visible, then gone. Visible, then gone.

I let myself into Nate's building and walk up the stairs. I pause outside his door. There are no sounds. I let myself in.

Removing my gloves, I switch on my torch, disconnect the Wi-Fi and make my way to the bedroom, looking for Nate's phone. It is in its usual spot on his bedside table. He isn't snoring, but the smell of alcohol permeates the room. I pick up his phone and turn it off, placing it inside my coat pocket. I creep into the bathroom and take out the things I will need. I push the door until it is almost closed before I drop my rucksack on to the floor. The thud isn't quite loud enough. I peer through the gap in the door. As suspected, Nate hasn't stirred. I try again, kicking the bathroom door with my full strength.

"Hello?" Nate's voice is husky. "Hello?" he says a bit more clearly.

I lie down on the floor, face down, an outstretched hand clutching an empty packet of paracetamol. The carpet smells of damp so I turn my head to the side and close my eyes as I hear Nate's footsteps. The bathroom floods with light.

"What the? Oh God, Lily, what have you done now?"

I can feel him crouching down next to me as he tries to roll me on to my front. I sit up and I throw a towel over his head. He automatically reaches up to remove it so I lean forward, grab his right wrist, slide on a handcuff and attach the other side to the metal towel rail. Then I quickly step out of his reach.

He pulls the towel off with his free hand and stares at me. His hair is sticking up.

"Lily? What? Let me go! I'm calling the police." He feels his pockets for his phone with his left hand, as though he'd forgotten he was wearing pyjamas.

I switch off my torch and the light. We are in darkness. The bathroom fan continues to whir. Metal clanks as he tugs.

"This isn't funny. How the hell did you get in?"

"Long story." I pause as metal clanks again. "I want you to listen to me, for once—"

He interrupts me. "Can you switch on the light?"

"Please."

"Please."

I turn the main light on. Nate blinks. I sit on the edge of the bath. He lunges forward to try to grab me, but cries out as the handcuff holds him back.

"Let me go!"

"Not until I say what I want you to hear."

He tugs his handcuffed hand again and swears several times. He kicks the bath panel with his bare feet. Nate's flat is old and solid, with thick walls and carpeted floors, so he'll have to be very persistent with the noise if he wants someone to hear. Still, it's probably safer if I calm him down.

"If you don't quit the noise, I'm going to leave you here, trapped. You're in control, believe it or not. Play nicely and you'll be free soon. If not..."

I walk out and leave him for several minutes. He stops banging and shouting. I return, carrying my bag. I switch on the bedroom light and I dump it on his bed. He watches me from the bathroom. I sit on the end of the bed. "Ready to talk?" I say.

"I'm a captive audience."

"There's no need for that attitude. I'm serious."

"I don't doubt that you are."

"I don't want us to split up."

"We already have."

"Exactly. And I want you to give us a final stab at our marriage."

"Jesus, Lily. Untie me. You can't break into my home in the middle of the night and handcuff me, then expect me to agree to stay married to you. Come on! You don't seriously think you're going to get away with this?"

"We can make this process longer or shorter. It's up to you."

"What are you proposing now?"

I unzip my bag and remove two photo albums, then I walk over and hand them to him. "Look at these."

Every photo I've taken of him or us, places we visited, things we did, I've had printed. I want him to remember the good times.

I watch him flick over the pages. "Slow down. Look at them properly."

He does so, with exaggerated slowness. "I had no idea that you'd taken so many," he says. "I don't remember."

That's not the only thing he hasn't remembered. Never mind. He'll realize soon enough. Whilst he's busy, I take out a wedding dress from my bag. I bought it years ago, when I first realized that Nate was the man I was destined to marry. I hold the hanger up high and let the dress unfold. It is a classic style, in white and silver. Crystal beads and pearls adorn the bodice. I step into the bedroom and hang it in the wardrobe, smoothing out the creases.

"What's that for?" he calls out from the bathroom, a slight tremor in his voice.

"I think we should have a blessing," I call back. "Like I've already explained many times, our Vegas wedding wasn't the one of my dreams either, much as you like to imply that it was. I've ordered you a suit, but unfortunately it hasn't arrived yet. And we need to buy rings."

I return to the bathroom. Nate is hitting his head against the palm of his free hand. He stops and looks up at me.

"When I finish these albums, are you going to undo the handcuff?"

I ignore his question and carry on unpacking my belongings. By *my* side of the bed I place some bridal magazines, a tube of hand cream and two books. I sit at the end of the bed and watch Nate through the open door. He glances up, then swiftly returns his gaze to the photos. When he gets to the last one, his eyes fix upon it for several seconds before he looks up at me. There is horror—definitely not love—in his eyes.

The final picture he would have seen is a family photo. Nate and I had a picnic by the Thames, the summer before last, and joining us on our rug, either side of the hamper, is a superimposed picture of a young boy and girl. The images cut from a children's clothing catalogue have similar features to how I envisage our children would look.

Above the picture, I have written a simple title: *Our Future.*

CHAPTER TWENTY-SIX

"Oh my God," he says. He looks back down at the picture.

"That's how our lives should've ended up. You can't go around treating people badly. It's not right. Even your mum agrees."

"You agreed to keep my family out of this."

"I bought you a present from her studio."

I take out the frame containing the photo of the regatta and hold it up, Exhibit A-style, for his viewing pleasure. Then I crouch down and lean it against the wall.

"What did you say to her?"

"I told her the truth, which is that I married the man I love in Vegas, but moments later he got cold feet and reneged on the deal. Not only that, he hasn't told his family. She absolutely thinks that you must."

"Lily. I'm sorry. I truly understand now. I hurt you. You thought that we were going to get married and have children. Un-cuff me. We can talk. Properly. I promise."

Rage ravages my entire body and mind. If there is one thing that I have always hated about Nate, it's the smug way he talks—as though *he* is the perfectly rational and reasonable one and I am some deranged, delusional person. It really, really pisses me off. I struggle to remain calm.

"You don't have a good-enough track record of keeping promises for me to believe you."

"I need the toilet and I'm sure we could both do with a coffee. I promise you, Lily, nothing bad will happen if you let me go."

The thing is, I can't. He's going to send me on my merry way—and that's the best-case scenario. I'm not going to think about the worst-case one.

"I can't let you go right this minute, but please don't worry. I have a plan."

I can tell by the way he tenses the muscles in his face that he is extremely angry, but he does a good job of containing it whilst he no doubt ponders ways to manipulate me. He is going to treat me in the old-fashioned way of treating plane hijackers—appease me and pretend to support my views.

I take out a screwdriver and my iPad. I press "play" on the downloaded video and prop the screen up against the wall whilst I get to work on the bathroom door handle. It takes mere minutes to unscrew the gold handle and remove it. "What are you doing now?" Nate's voice is measured.

"I'm doing something so that you can be un-cuffed."

"What? You're going to lock me in instead? Don't rely on amateur YouTubers to provide you with information. I could end up trapped in here!"

I interrupt. "You won't be. But I do need your cooperation. You're going to have to earn your freedom."

"Lily! This is ridiculous! Outrageous!"

I turn round and smile. "It is. Preposterous! Enraging! Do you want freedom to move around or not?"

He doesn't reply.

"Thought so. Don't interrupt me whilst I'm working. I have to start the video over again now."

He kicks the bath panel. I glare at him.

Switching the lock round to the other side of the door handle isn't as easy as it looks, but after two attempts I manage it. The final part is to jam the mechanism. I shove in a fish pellet. Job done. I try out my handiwork. It works! I can now lock him in.

Nate continues to yank at the towel rail—as though, if he tries hard enough, the metal will break.

The bathroom window looks out to the side, not on to the Green. I secure the window locks and pocket the keys. In the—hopefully—unlikely event he does manage to grab the attention of someone through the frosted glass, it won't be my fault that something has happened to the lock. And as for the handcuffs—they come from a sex shop. I'll let people use their imagination.

I go into the kitchen, then back into the bathroom to leave him some food. Not his favourite things; he doesn't deserve any loving touches right now. Whilst I generously unpack a packet of cheese crackers and several apples, Nate catches me by surprise as he lunges forward with his free arm and manages to grab my leg, yanking me down. I grip the side of the bath, winded, as he grabs my left calf and tries to pull me closer. As I pull my leg up, he grips tighter. I kick with my right leg as hard as I can. He doesn't release his grip, so I kick again. This time he lets go, taking deep, heavy breaths as he slumps back against the rails.

Regathering my thoughts, I take deep breaths too. Keeping as far away from him as I can, I lean over and hand him a cheap tablet I recently purchased. It contains a deeply personal message for him. I have spent hours recording and editing a little film aptly entitled: *The Beginning.*

"There's something I'd like you to watch, please."

"What is it?" he says, looking down at the screen.

"Something very important. It's me. Speaking directly to you. From the heart."

He remains expressionless. It's this type of behaviour that has driven me to these measures—his total non-reaction when I try to express myself. So, I do feel that this idea of mine has the potential to work. I'm not the sort of person who believes that by merely *buying* a diet book I will always eat less and exercise more, but I do believe in being open-minded and looking for fresh solutions.

Let's face it, nothing else has worked so far. And the overriding problem I have is that Nate *thinks* he doesn't love me. Once he realizes that he does, everything should naturally realign. For example, I will no longer need Miles in my life. He can be fully returned, as damaged goods, back to Bella.

"Darling. I've been forced into this. You do understand, don't you?"

He stares at me. "Don't you?"

He nods.

"Press 'play,' then."

He hesitates. "Are you going to watch me? How long is it?"

I perch on the edge of the bath and grip the edge. "Long enough. I will wait until I can be sure that you are listening carefully. This is the only way. I've tried so many times but you just *won't* listen."

He presses "play" and my voice fills the bathroom. It sounds much louder in here than it did back in my flat. Nate lowers the volume but I can still hear. I switch off the bathroom light to create a more cinematic effect. I watch Nate watch me. I know that when I say, *"Hello, Nate,"* I give a little wave. I nearly edited that part out but, upon reflection, it made me look friendlier. I didn't want to begin with a stern telling-off, potentially putting him in an instantly defensive mood.

Right from the moment of planning this, I intended to start off slowly before building up to what he really needs to hear. I spend two minutes and forty-seven seconds explaining my actions. I find myself getting sucked into my own words and agreeing with my own sentiments. A vein twitches at the side of Nate's neck. There is a pause before I start the story.

Once upon a time there was a girl, just fifteen, and she was lonely. Nate jabs "pause."

"Please don't tell me I have to sit through some teenage fairy tale. Give me a fucking break!" He yanks the handcuff. "Just tell me what's on your mind and we can manage without the theatrics. I'm getting seriously pissed off."

I stand up. "Your choice."

As I reach for the tablet he jabs "play" again. He obviously assumes that his Wi-Fi is working and that he'll get an opportune moment to send an SOS message to someone.

Very lonely. She had no friends, but it wasn't her fault. It was the fault of another girl. A mean, spoilt girl who delighted in the misfortune of others. The lonely girl spent hours alone with her own thoughts, dreaming of a different life. A life where something—she wasn't quite sure what, because her ideas at that point were still intangible and undefinable—but, nonetheless, something momentous would happen one day, which would mean that her life would change from that moment on, obviously for the better. Then, one day, something momentous did happen. And it did change her life, but not for the better. And the lesson this girl learned very suddenly was that things can turn out very differently than expected.

Nate sighs theatrically. "How much longer?"

"Getting longer by the minute. Listen properly or I'll rewind."

One day she met her Prince Charming. Not in the type of place she'd imagined, like on an exotic holiday or at a glamorous event in a luxurious hotel. Instead, it was at a low-key ball. And the girl wore a dress; the nicest one she'd ever owned. It was the first time she'd ever felt glamorous. It made her feel like she had a chance to shine.

But the thrill of wearing the dress quickly wore off, because she was ignored. Ignored by the boys who attended. Ignored by the mean girls. Do you want to know what colour her dress was?

There is a deliberate two-minute pause, because this is his chance to remember. This is his chance to redeem himself. Not totally—because, of course, that can never happen—but it would at least be a tiny step in the right direction.

I am forced to break the silence. "Answer the question," I say.

"Yellow? Pink? Purple? How the fuck would I know or care?"

"You should care," I say quietly. "Although it was dark; I'll give you that."

I stare into his eyes and will him to recall everything. To acknowledge what he did.

I've done this before. I used to stare into his eyes from time to time when we were in bed together, wishing I could claw into his soul and get him to remember. I silently tried to infiltrate his mind with the memory. Yet his eyes, like now, never showed even a flicker of recognition. Not once.

His blank expression shows that he has let me down. Again.

The dress was red. She has never worn red since.

His eyes widen and he grips the tablet tighter. I think pennies may be beginning to drop.

The girl slipped away from the party and went to her favourite spot. A place by the river. It was the secret place where the trendy girls would go and have a cigarette, but often it was deserted. She knew she'd be safe, because they were all too busy being social butterflies. Even when darkness approached, she stayed. Because although it wasn't quite a full moon, there was enough grey light to see. It was the first time she'd ever tasted an alcoholic drink and she felt a bit floaty and detached. Then, someone joined her. He didn't know the school so one of the "in" girls must've told him where to go. His sister, probably. He lit a cigarette and the flame briefly made his face glow amber. He was handsome. Even though she'd seen pictures of him, he looked even better in the flesh. He pulled off his shoes and

*socks with his free hand and dipped his toes in the water. He offered
the cigarette to her and she didn't want to say that she had never tried
one before, so she took a small puff in a childish attempt to appear so-
phisticated. It is so strange to think of him smoking now, because he
is so anti; the sort of person who wafts away smoke with their hand
if anyone lights up nearby.*

I realize I am holding my breath as Nate looks up and stares
at me. There is shocked realization in his expression.

Finally.

My voice continues. Nate's gaze drops back to the screen.

*They talked for a bit and although she was nervous, she also felt
like maybe she wasn't fat and ugly. When he'd finished his cigarette,
he ground it into the soil and the light disappeared. The boy kissed
the girl, or maybe they both kissed at the same time. It was her first
ever kiss. She thought it would give her instant re-entry into the inner
circle. The other girls shared stories of parties at weekends; the boys
they'd kissed and more. But then he kissed her harder and everything
progressed so quickly. She didn't want him to stop, because it was
so nice not to feel lonely. And there came a point where she didn't
feel she could say no, and she didn't want to say no. But she didn't
know how—or have the confidence—to slow everything down. She
was still wearing her dress, and that felt a bit confusing—even when
he helped her lift up her dress and his hand slid up her right thigh
and then gently tugged down her knickers—because she'd always assumed that you had to be naked, for some reason. She watched him
take down his trousers and then he lay on top of her. It didn't hurt
much. But it also felt wrong, because it wasn't at all romantic in the
way it appeared in films and books; instead, it felt more like how
they'd been taught about "it" in biology.*

Nate stops the film. "Shit, Lily. Why didn't you say? This
is insane."

I don't answer. He has all the answers in front of him and
I have put hours and hours of effort into taking us back *there*,
to my feelings and thoughts in that moment. I point to the

screen. He stares back down and starts it again. The screen shines brightly in the gloom. I stretch my legs out in front of me. My back is beginning to ache, and even though these are my words—even though I've edited and edited this piece—it's uncomfortable. The mix of emotions is unsettling because, on the one hand, I remember the naive hope I'd felt and, on the other, there is the exact opposite. And the next bit coming up is painful.

The girl gave her heart to the boy, there and then. It was a done deal. Their fate was sealed. He was a part of her, and vice versa. He didn't have any more cigarettes. He asked her if she had one. She didn't, but she desperately wished that she had. She still does—because if she had, then he'd have stayed longer. They'd have talked and everything would've been different. They'd have kept in touch and then he'd have realized that he loved her too. But that is not what happened, is it, Nate?

I have factored in a deliberate pause for "discussion time."

"Well?" I prompt.

"Lily. This is serious shit. OK. I get it. Your shock tactics have worked. You want a proper apology and you'll get one. I am sorry. Really, truly sorry. Un-cuff me and I promise—you have my word, I swear—that we can talk and you can tell me anything or share anything that you'd like to." He sounds close to tears.

"You still don't get it. It's not just a mere apology. I want you to *understand*. I need you to get what you did."

"I do understand. I do get it. We were young. I thought… well, in truth I don't know what I thought, but I clearly wasn't thinking too far into the future." He pauses. "I didn't plan it. You know yourself that it just happened. You were clearly attractive and—"

"Was I, though? How do you know? It was dark."

"I didn't know who you were."

"And that makes everything all right?"

"Well, no, but for God's sake, you're reading too much into something and turning it into something bigger than it is."

"Bigger than it is?" I'm surprised at how icy calm my voice sounds, because inside I am ready to explode. I grip the edge of the bath tighter. "Bigger than it is?" My voice makes us both jump.

Like I've said, that's not what happened, is it? You ran away. You left me there, alone, in the dark. I came to find you but you were way, way too busy to even acknowledge me. You left me there and you didn't give a shit. And it stung. It still stings. Because you don't care. You think that you can use people and discard them when it suits. Like I was nothing. Like I meant nothing. Like we meant nothing. And you're still doing it today. Even after we got married, you thought that you could just run to your friend James to dispose of me. Again.

Nate jabs "stop" and drops the tablet to the floor.

"I can't listen to this any more. Why didn't you say anything when we were together last year?"

I don't want to admit that I'd realized that he hadn't put two and two together. "I thought that the subject was, well, not taboo as such, just awkward. I assumed that your silence meant that you were ashamed of your behaviour and that you would make it up to me by being the best boyfriend, then husband, that you could possibly be."

"Look, Lily, I *get* it."

"No, Nate, you don't. You really, seriously don't. Not everything is about you, but it is time you're taught a lesson. When you walked into the hotel where I was working last year, when we got back together, it was like it was meant to be. Fate. I—no, we—said so at the time. Don't you remember?" He shakes his head.

I *had* told Nate that fate had brought us together, but I kept quiet about the fact that I'd given fate a great, big shove in the right direction.

There was no point in organizing our "chance meeting" whilst Nate was busy and distracted, pursuing his dream career by studying for his pilot's licence. I left him alone. He had time to date unsuitable women. I knew he wouldn't settle down until he was in his late twenties at the very earliest. Men like Nate don't. They like to play the field.

He should have been more cautious with his social media posts. Whilst he was happily bragging—sharing snapshots of his sickening, perfect life—he was feeding me all sorts of vital information.

When flight crew only have a short period of time in London, they are put up in an airport hotel. All I had to do was apply for the job, wait and volunteer for every shift going. The working conditions were crap but it was totally worth it, because although it took eight months, it paid off.

Our worlds collided and we fell in love. Which is why it is so bloody annoying, when I'd got that far, that it all went pear-shaped. It's like going down a long snake moments before reaching *home* in Snakes and Ladders.

I intended to make him adore me.

When he realized who I was, then I knew he'd regret his actions. He'd undo the wrong. Explain that it was all a mistake, that some unavoidable event had prevented him from contacting me. That's why I told the truth about where I went to school, despite the risk of Bella.

"Now, darling," I say to Nate with a smile. "All you have to do, it's very simple, is watch the recording at least three times."

He needs to fully understand and appreciate the aftermath. And hear how I sent him an email to which he never responded. The morning-after pill. The worry of sexually transmitted diseases when I plucked up the courage to visit a clinic in the summer holidays. On my own. And how much he hurt me.

"I've already got the gist of it. But, if I agree to your demands, you'll let me go?"

"Maybe. If you comply totally. But, if you make a huge fuss, or persist in making too much noise, then the whole process will take longer. It's your choice."

"I don't want a maybe. Look, please let's just sort this out. I… It's the middle of the night."

I ignore him, just like he has me so many times. "I'd also appreciate it if you could go through the photos again and take the time to study each one carefully, to remember how happy we were. I will ask you questions to check your thoroughness."

"I've said I'm willing to sort this out."

I smile. "How does it feel, darling, to be ignored?" He goes quiet.

"Not very nice, is it?" I say.

He doesn't answer.

"Is it?"

"No, it's not nice," he is forced to agree. "I'll watch it, I'll watch it all, so you can un-cuff me, please."

I pick up my bag and remove my final item—a framed wedding picture of us—and I place it on the window sill. Hoisting my rucksack over my shoulder, I turn to leave. As I stand at the door, I take out the handcuff keys.

"Remember, Nate. The choice is yours. You can leave here sooner, or later."

I chuck the keys over to him and shut the door behind me, wiping my prints off the handle with an anti-bacterial wipe.

Two minutes later, he is banging on the door. It is thunderingly loud. I hold my breath. He kicks it several times before it goes quiet.

"Nate, if you continue to try kicking down this door, the consequences will be a lot worse. From now on, for every attempt you make, I will add a full hour on to the time that you will spend in there. And, once you're finished with the film, there's a page I've bookmarked for you to read. It's about the serious consequences of sleeping with a girl under the age of consent. Especially when the other person involved is over eighteen. There's no way you'd pass your next criminal record check if I report this to the police. So, unless you've already got ideas for an alternative career, particularly one where they don't mind people who are on the Sex Offenders Register, I suggest you keep quiet and get on with the very simple thing I've asked of you." Silence. That shut him up.

Hopefully, after his initial lacklustre approach, he's going to knuckle down and take things a bit more seriously. I settle down on the sofa with a cushion for a pillow and prepare for a doze. Although I drift in and out, my dreams are disturbing and keep jolting me into full consciousness. When light seeps into the room, I get up as my back has started to ache. I make myself a coffee. I nurse it, allowing the warmth to seep through my fingers and the rising steam to brush my face. I yawn. I go and listen outside Nate's door.

Blessed silence.

I'm due to fly to Rome and back today as an extra crew member, checking to see whether recent safety standards are being adhered to in the galley areas. I was going to call in sick but, thinking about it, I may as well go. I'll be back late this afternoon and it will allow plenty of time for Nate to think. It's quite dull being a jailer, there really isn't that much to it.

I knock on the door. "How's it going?" I call out.

"Almost done," he yells back.

"Liar! The film is nearly two hours long. Remember, you have to watch it three times. Otherwise it's your time you're wasting, because you won't pass the test." He mutters something indecipherable.

I decide against mentioning my outing; there's no point in worrying him. I wipe the handle clean from my fingerprints one more time, as an extra precaution, and I leave his phone—switched off—on the coffee table in the living room.

I walk back home, feeling surprisingly awake. The snowfall wasn't very heavy; only slight, scattered patches of white remain. I put on my uniform, ripping the first pair of tights I slide on, so I have to take out another pair from the wrapping. I must spend a fortune on hosiery. I clip my ID on to my jacket beneath my name badge and pack my flat shoes into my wheelie bag.

Before I drive off, I look up at Nate's. There is no outward sign that there is anything untoward occurring inside.

CHAPTER TWENTY-SEVEN

At work, in the safety ambassador's office, I pretend to prepare everything necessary for me to get through the day whilst I surreptitiously check on Amy's roster, out of curiosity. She has been grounded due to pregnancy! I double-check, but there is no mistake. She has been allocated a position in staff travel. I check out her Facebook page. Nothing. She must be in the early stages.

I have twenty minutes remaining before I need to go airside, so I take the lift to staff travel. Amy is behind a counter, tapping at a screen. As I walk over, she looks up, a ready smile on her face, which quickly drops as I come into her line of vision.

"Hi," I say. "Long time no see. What are you doing here?"

On her left hand she is wearing a slim gold engagement ring with a single diamond. She sees me looking.

"Congratulations. Rupert, I take it?"

She reddens. "Yes."

"When is the happy day?"

"Oh, there's no date yet."

"I meant your due date. I assume that's why you're not flying?"

She shifts uncomfortably in her chair. "It's early days. We haven't told many people yet. How are you?"

"Fine. I'm off to Rome and back in my role as a safety ambassador."

"Have fun!" she says, looking over my shoulder at someone behind my back, clearly grateful that she has an excuse to dismiss me.

As I walk through the terminal, I observe the people around me. Families, holidaymakers, even business people look content as they go about their lives. Neon adverts flash high above, each picture depicting smiley, happy, successful people. My stomach feels knotted and hollow. I really hope the video is tugging at Nate's heart strings; I can't bear feeling like an outsider much longer.

The flight to Rome is delayed by twenty minutes due to high winds. I have a moment's panic as I think of Nate, abandoned and alone, but as we take off, I close my eyes and imagine him mellowing towards me as he absorbs my words.

As we level out above the clouds, I unclip my seat belt. I can't be bothered to watch the crew to ensure that they don't twist or bend as they carry out the short service. I will make my report up. But nonetheless I stand around with my work tablet, acting officiously whilst attempting to look efficient and important.

During our turnaround time, I disembark and wander around Fiumicino Airport. I buy gifts for my men: the male versions of my favourite perfume. As I pass a designer men's store, I can't resist buying Nate and Miles matching ties in pale green, decorated with silver zigzags. I glance up at the departures monitor. *Boarding Gate 10* flashes, alternating between English and Italian. I rush, my bag banging against my thigh as I speed-walk in the direction of the air bridge.

Passenger boarding has commenced. Several people glance down at my duty-free purchases, frowning disapproval—as though I should be banned from such a perk if I'm going to turn up late. I negotiate my way past the flurry of activity by the door. A father battles with a pushchair as the mother gives instructions, a baby girl wriggling in her arms. A smartly dressed woman on the phone offers last-minute contributions to her working day. Others stand patiently, as though accepting the chaos as part of the travel experience, clutching printouts of their boarding cards or holding their phones at the ready.

We are delayed pre take-off due to bad weather in London. I try not to look at my watch too often. But by now, Nate has been home alone for seven and a half hours. I force myself to think positive thoughts because, if I allow my mind to wander, dreaded thoughts of what could go wrong start to make me feel nauseous. My mantras are not helping to distract my mind either. They deny me any comfort. The only sentences that form are *"In sickness and in health"* and *"Until death do us part."* These words conjure up images of Nate, alone and frail in his bathroom. Or falling whilst trying to escape down a conveniently located drainpipe, thereby meeting his end in the garden below, making me a very young widow.

The flight crew make another announcement.

Ladies and gentlemen, good news. We've received confirmation that we should be on our way in a little under fifteen minutes. Once again, we apologize for the delay.

Thank God. Inhale. Exhale.

However, it is not their final apology. Two hours into the flight, they have further bad news.

This is your captain, Rob Jones, speaking again. The high winds were stronger than forecast at Heathrow, which has caused further de-

lays. Aircraft are now landing but there is a backlog and so we will be diverting to Stansted. We apologize for the inconvenience. I am assured that the ground staff are working hard to arrange transportation and rebook onward connections...

His words fade out. *Bugger!* I hope Nate's food supply lasts; he's now been on his own for ten hours. By the time I traipse back from Stansted—assuming there's some kind of transport for the crew, because public transport will be overstretched—it will be about ten o'clock tonight before I can return.

"Excuse me?" A woman clutching a baby on her left hip approaches me. "We have a flight to Dubai two hours after we land and we *have* to make it."

"The ground staff have all the information regarding transfers and will be rebooking you on to the next available flight, so please try not to worry," I say. "This happens a lot, and they're very efficient." I have no clue if the ground staff are efficient or not, but I'm sure they must be.

But other passengers aren't so easy to placate. One man in particular stands in the galley, way too close to me. I can smell beer on his breath as he rambles on about cancelling his loyalty card, never getting anywhere on time, and missing out on his daughter's birthday meal. I spout out my usual platitudes, but he just won't go away.

"So?" he finally stops. "What are you going to do about it?" Good question. What am I going to do?

"Would you like a snack?" I say. I offer him a basket filled with confectionery.

He actually sneers, his face contorting with ugliness. "Sorry, love, I stopped getting excited about packets of Smarties when I was six years old."

I place the basket back on the side. "What about a drink, then?"

Without replying, he reaches past me and opens the door to the bar, as though he has every right to do so, and starts fiddling around with the contents. It's a pet hatred of mine, people assuming that they can help themselves to anything they want in the galley. The number of times I've left my meal or a sandwich on the side to go and deal with some issue or other, only to come back and find someone grazing away at my food, is extraordinary. The pressure—the stress of the day—suddenly bears down on me, and this man, this dreadful, red-faced, shouty man, is one challenge too many. I reach above him, yank out a metal canister with my full strength and let it fall on his head.

He cries out and falls back on to the galley floor, clutching the top of his head with his right hand. He stares at me, seemingly too dazed to start another rant. He's lucky I chose a container with napkins and plastic glasses, I was very tempted to go for the one full of canned drinks.

"I'm sorry," I say, trying to sound as if I mean it.

Grabbing a tea towel, I tip a pile of ice into the centre, wrap it up and hand it to him. He holds it obediently to his head. I want him out of my galley and out of my sight before I give in to my urge to kick him.

The supervisor walks in and surveys the scene. "Are you all right, sir?" she says.

"No," he says, and off he starts again with a fresh rant.

I walk away. For fuck's sake, why can't people mind their own business? Her unnecessary interference means that I'm now going to have to fill in an incident report on top of everything else.

I'm not sure how much more I can stand.

At the top of descent, we secure the cabin and take our seats early, because bad turbulence is forecast by the pilots. They are not wrong. The plane rocks and sways whilst the engines strain with a high-pitched whine. Outside it is black. It always goes quiet when passengers are frightened, and it adds to the overall eerie effect.

We smack down on to the runway and the welcoming roar of the plane losing speed is one of the best sounds I've heard all day. I feel as though I've been away for a week.

Disembarkation takes an hour, because the airport is accepting other diverted flights, so we have to wait for stairs and buses. The crew are all offered taxis back to Heathrow, but the queue is—of course—long. And after the freezing cold wait, we're further hindered by the thoughtless members who brought a small suitcase or a massive bag along with them on a mere day trip.

As a result, the first two taxis drive off with only two crew in each one.

As we pull away, leaving the bright airport lights behind us, a sense of impending dread washes through me. Nate has been left unattended for a whole thirteen hours.

On a whim, I dial his phone—even though it is switched off and on his coffee table.

It is not a good move, because I get one of the biggest shocks of my life. It rings.

No sooner does the taxi drop me at the Heathrow crew car park than I practically run to my car. As I drive past the car park barriers, with rain beating down on the windscreen despite the wipers on double-speed, I find it a struggle to concentrate. I don't want to go back to Nate's—or mine—because I suspect that the police will be waiting. But I have no choice. Not really.

The best I can do in the event of a worst-case scenario is to talk myself out of Nate's lies and mud-slinging. Our past will prove that, whatever situation arose, it was a bizarre domestic argument.

I pull over into a side road before I reach Richmond and

try Nate's phone again. After it rang earlier, it had gone to voicemail. This time, it does not ring and Nate's voice clicks in immediately.

Hi, this is Nate. Please leave me a message.

I hang up. Maybe I imagined it ringing earlier. I try to access Nate's information through my spy app, but it won't let me log in. It's frozen. A chill sweeps through my body as I imagine the app being discovered, on top of everything else I've done. I force myself to take deep breaths whilst I think things through clearly, and focus. I delete my tablet history containing the video showing me how to meddle with the door lock. I try to convince myself that nothing bad has happened. I picture Nate, all calm and apologetic, pathetically grateful to see me.

I park away from my place, at the far end of the street, and switch off the engine. I scan the area for police cars, but there are none visible, unless there is a fleet of unmarked ones. I hoist my handbag on to my shoulder and rearrange my duty-free bags so that the gifts are divided fairly. Miles' stuff can stay in the car for now.

The rain has stopped. As I walk over the Green, my heels sink slightly into the ground every couple of steps. I don't want to look up at Nate's but I have to. My heart rate picks up as I spot the kitchen light on.

Did I leave it on? I'm sure I didn't.

Nate's room is in darkness. Is that good? Bad?

Shit. I wish I'd stayed put and hadn't gone on that stupid trip.

I let myself in; the communal door bangs shut behind me. I stand still. I could go home, have a shower and hide beneath my duvet, then deal with all this in the morning. Perhaps it would do Nate good to have a bit more time on his own. But then I picture him, all alone, and my longing for him overrides my fears. I take off my heels and walk upstairs in my stockinged feet.

Outside his front door, I pause and listen.

Silence.

I slide my key into the lock and slowly open the door. The light from the kitchen throws a little illumination into the darkness, but not enough. I put down my bags quietly on the floor and shut the door behind me. Rainbow is still. Nate's phone is switched off, where I left it on the coffee table. The silence is freaking me out. I walk towards Nate's bedroom. The door is shut. Again, as I left it. There are no signs that he has escaped, but I feel bilious. And cold; I'm aware of myself shivering. Tentatively, I push the door open. It is dark. Switching on the lights, I freeze in horror.

CHAPTER TWENTY-EIGHT

The bathroom door is smashed. A jagged, splintered hole has formed down one side. Yet it doesn't look big enough for a man to squeeze through without sustaining serious injuries.

As my mind processes the implications, my right arm is grabbed, yanked behind my back and I'm pushed to the floor. I scream until a hand is clamped over my mouth. I inhale the smell of Nate. I'm then dragged up by the wrist and am temporarily winded as I'm pushed down again on to the bed. I try to stand up, but he shoves me down by the shoulders.

"It's *your* turn to listen now," he says.

I stand up to run for the door, but he pushes me again.

He looks deranged.

I look around. On the floor, my belongings are neatly stacked up. The wedding photo, my magazine, the handcuffs, my dress, everything. It's insulting, as if he wants to be rid of all trace of me. I stare at him.

He stares back, looking down at my uniform. "You went to work? You bitch! Anything could've happened. If there had been a fire I could have died. When you didn't try to stop me breaking down the door, I assumed you'd gone back to yours for a bit. I never thought—"

"How likely is a fire? Really? You've lived here how long— three, four years?—so by now I imagine it's safe to assume that your neighbours are a pretty responsible bunch. Anyway, I bought you a tie and some aftershave. They're in a bag by the front door. I would go and get them, only I don't feel like getting assaulted again." I rub my painful wrist.

"You need more serious help than I fear, if you think that somehow makes up for incarcerating me." I fold my arms.

Nate continues in what sounds like a rehearsed speech. "I understand now what you mean about me being your first love. That it was your first time and I was a bit of an arse. I was young, arrogant, unintentionally cruel and thoughtless, and I'm sorry." He sits down next to me and takes my hand.

A slight sense of hope begins to form in my mind. I stare at him. Has my idea worked? I now realize the flaw in my plan, and it is that I'll never know. I'll never be able to truly trust him. I am exhausted both through lack of sleep and the stress of the day, and now I have this uncertainty to contend with.

"I've had a lot of time to think today. It must've been dreadful for you after your brother. But I think you've latched on to me in a romantic fantasy-type sense and—"

I interrupt. "How did you get out?"

He looks at me, as though he's shocked that I'm not fascinated by his sympathy speech. "I had *all day* to smash it down."

"What with? I removed everything that could be used as a tool."

"Well, maybe you're not as clever as you think."

"Tell me, it's driving me mad!"

"The middle door panels are thinner than the main section. I focused my strength on one of those, then all I had to do was put my hand through the gap and turn the handle." He holds up his right hand; it is badly scratched.

I don't know what else to say; my heart rate is slowly returning to normal. But I can't seem to make total sense of the situation, or quite where all this is leading.

"So, here's what's going to happen," Nate carries on. "We will continue to get this marriage dissolved as quickly as possible. You will not pull any more stunts—and by that, I also mean staying away from me, my family, my home—and at work, I will request that a KA, a 'Keep Apart,' be put in place for scheduling purposes. I also think that you need to seek help, professional help, to get you through. I'm prepared to help you find someone who comes well recommended, if you'd like me to. As long as you agree to all these things, I won't go to the police. If you see me in the street, cross the road. But if you break any of these conditions, I will seek a restraining order against you."

"Aren't you forgetting that I too can report you for having sex with an underage girl? Any time I choose. You'd be looking at a two-year caution and saying goodbye to your dream job."

He looks at me, but I can't quite figure out what he's thinking or feeling. I feel a slight sense of unease, but I have to protect myself. Now that everything is out in the open, it almost feels like we have an opportunity to reconnect by being honest.

"It would seem that we both have grievances. If we both agree to disagree and to keep out of each other's way, then we can avoid a spectacle. There's nothing to be gained by attempting to drag each other down, when the end result will always be the same—which is, that I am not the man for you.

I've had plenty of time to think about it and I've figured it all out. I knew that you'd be forced to return at some point, so we'd be able to discuss this civilly and reach a mutual understanding, especially after you rang my phone." I don't say anything.

"Lily. Let me go. I don't want this to sound patronizing, I really don't, but it would be the best thing you could ever do for yourself. I know it might not seem like it now, but if I ever meant anything to you at all, which you say that I did, then please try to believe me. However hard it is."

"I'm trying, Nate, I'm really trying, but I just can't see what's in this for me. We are married. Who is going to believe your version of events? Seriously? I'm not some one-night stand who wants more. I already have more."

He storms out of the room and returns with his phone clamped to his ear.

"Don't pretend you're ringing the police," I say.

"I'm not," he snaps, but the slight break in his voice gives away that he is more scared of what I can say to damage him than he cares to admit. "I'm getting James over here to witness what you've done."

Oh God, not James again. I can't bear the thought of him judge, judge, judging away before another dual lecture.

I pick up my own phone. "Fine. I'll report you to the police for an historic crime."

Nate is fast. He wrenches the phone from my hand, switches it off and stuffs it in my bag.

"Get out!" he says. "Just get out now, before I really lose it. I've had enough. You should be thanking me for not getting you arrested or sectioned. I'm giving you a chance. A chance you don't deserve, and any minute I'm going to change my mind!"

Exhaustion swamps me. I don't know how to explain any

better that I will always give him all I've got. He will never regret choosing me; I'll dedicate my life to making him happy. I feel distraught, like I've let us both down. But the words in my head have dried up. I stand up, gather my belongings in a daze, put them into my bag. I'll think of something to resolve this. He can't reasonably ignore our past if I persist.

"My keys, please." Nate holds out his right hand, palm upwards.

I hand them over. It doesn't matter; I have another set.

He opens the front door and stands like a security guard, watching me. "Do you *understand*, Lily? That we have a mutually beneficial agreement?"

"Yes, I *understand*. Goodbye, Nate."

"Goodbye."

As I wait for the lift he says something that sounds like, "Don't come back," before he shuts the door. I kick the side of the lift.

The first thing I do in the morning is message Miles to let him know that I'm free for lunch, but his response is curt, informing me that he's busy working from home. I spy on Bella, but there's nothing that reveals what she's up to today.

I know their address, so I take a drive there. There is only one car in the drive—it belongs to Miles—but that doesn't mean Bella's isn't in the garage. I phone Miles. He answers within one ring, with an abrupt hello.

"I've already explained that I'm snowed under."

"Is Bella at home?"

"No."

"Good. Answer your door. I'm outside." He has no choice.

I walk into a gloomy hall. It is nothing like how I imagined Bella's home would be. Stairs edged with a dark wooden railing curve up to the right, and the side wall is a matching wooden panel. The carpet is a rich burgundy, adding to the overall dark effect. Directly in front of me rests a round table upon which is an olive-coloured vase filled with red roses. The wall pictures are gold-framed and depict violence: battle scenes, hunts, blood and misery.

I hand Miles the duty-free bag.

"Have you been away for work again? Thank you, but I can't accept this. Juliette, this isn't on. This isn't on at all. You *cannot* show up at my home unannounced. It isn't what we agreed."

He hands me back the bag. I shove it inside my handbag. For now.

"I know that, but we need to talk. I'll have a quick coffee and then I'll leave you in peace."

"Bella's not due back until after lunch, but she might be early."

"Message her. Ask her how her day is going, that will put your mind at rest."

I walk straight ahead, along a corridor which opens out into a kitchen. Miles follows, ignoring my suggestion. This space is a lot more how I pictured her home. It is contemporary and light. Stainless steel gleams and the surfaces are bare; very minimalistic. A metal fruit bowl is crammed with bananas, oranges and kiwi fruit. A designer coffee machine rests beneath wall-mounted canvases bearing motivational quotes. I'm surprised; I've always assumed that Bella had enough self-belief without the aid of positive affirmations.

Believe there is good in the world.

Own your talent.

Do the one thing you never thought you could.

I place my bag on the floor, then run my finger along the work surface as Miles fiddles with mugs and coffee capsules. I rest my hand on a plastic file decorated with daisies, beneath a small pile of post. Pushing the mail to one side, I pick the file up and slide out the contents. Inside there is an email print-out from her mother outlining details of their annual family trip to Whistler in February. They are staying at their aunt's holiday chalet, as usual.

It is not the only thing: there is also the proof copy of a wedding invitation sent by a local printer. Miles and Bella have brought forward their wedding to mid-January, during the lead-up to Nate and I becoming unmarried. Miles looks over and he frowns when he realizes what I'm reading. I carry on, regardless. They've decided against the Italian villa and have selected a local five-star hotel instead. I scan the guest list; there are hundreds of invitees.

"Juliette! That's private!"

He strides over and removes the file from me, stuffing the contents back inside, and turns his attention back to the coffee machine.

"Is Bella pregnant?"

"No. Nor would it be any of your business if she was."

"Why have you brought the wedding forward, then?" I look him in the eye.

He reddens.

I sit down on a breakfast bar stool. It is hard and uncomfortable. Miles sits opposite, sliding my coffee slowly over the granite work surface.

"We, I, thought it best that we married sooner, rather than later. Seeing you the other night, realizing that you knew her, it gave me a shock. I've behaved badly and I don't want to lose her."

"What about me?"

"We *agreed*. We agreed right at the very beginning that we would never threaten our relationships."

"Yes, but I don't understand why we should be over just because you say we are?"

"You *know* Bella."

"*Knew* her."

"She's told me that, at school, she wasn't always very nice, but that you frightened her."

I laugh. "Me? Frighten her? Do you know the best part of my schooldays?" Miles shakes his head as I continue. "The bearable part was that, once a week, I got to leave the school for an hour or two. I signed up to do the Duke of Edinburgh Award. It was the one group she never joined. For two hours a week, I was free, whilst trudging around muddy fields in all weathers."

"Well, I'm sure she wasn't as bad as you're making out. All sorts went on at my school."

"If you say so." I put down my coffee cup. This is not working out how I expected. I stand up. "May I use the toilet, please?"

He points to the corridor. "On the right."

I pick up my bag and head out. I open and close the toilet door, then unzip my ankle boots and clutch them in one hand as I dash upstairs. All the doors are open and the second room I peek into is clearly the master bedroom. I lie down on their bed and quickly take out my phone from my pocket.

I take a selfie. Sitting up, I scan the room. Bella's bedside table is cluttered: books, nail polishes, cotton wool and three different types of expensive face creams. I take one of her lipsticks, leave Miles' aftershave among her perfumes and one of his ties draped over a chair. I snap several more photos of the room and another selfie sitting in front of her dressing table. I want to capture images of her world.

I dart back downstairs, pull my boots back on and walk into the kitchen, just as Miles is heading out, as though he was about to come looking for me. We almost collide. I stretch up to kiss him.

He steps back. "We can't do this any more. It's really over, I'm afraid, Juliette. You're a wonderful woman and your fiancé is a very lucky man indeed, but I can't take the risk any longer, sad as it is. In fact, it's fortunate that we didn't end up with a professional working relationship too, as it turned out. It will make keeping away from each other a lot simpler."

"My fiancé and I split up."

"Oh. Oh, I see. I'm sorry to hear that."

I stand in front of him, arms at my sides, and say nothing. Realization that I'm not going to be disposed of that easily seems to register in his expression. He looks afraid of me, and it reaffirms my strong sense of the upper hand. I'm going to use my power to my full advantage. I'm just not quite sure how, yet. I walk past him and stand at a window, looking into the garden. It is the type that estate agents would describe as a mature, well-established garden with ashes and beeches lining the far boundary and neat, well-planned flower beds. In a few years, I bet Bella imagines filling it with swings, a slide and a climbing frame.

"You have a lovely home," I say.

"Thank you."

Although there is silence, I can almost hear his thoughts: he is willing me to leave, to not mess things up for him.

"I'll leave you in peace," I say, not looking at him.

"Thank you," he says, making no attempt to conceal the relief in his voice.

"But," I turn round, "if I ever get in touch with you, for whatever reason, please don't ignore me."

"I don't see why we can't simply be adult about all of this and agree to a civilized farewell with fond memories—"

I interrupt his speech because, thanks to Nate, I know the script. Next he'll be wittering on about me being *reasonable*.

"Goodbye, Miles. For now," I add, just to keep him on his toes.

I turn round, pick up my bag and stride towards the front door.

I'm too agitated to do anything useful, so I park near the sea front and stride along the promenade.

The feelings I have buried since last night—the anger, the rage, the humiliation—burn. Not only has Nate decided, yet again, to treat me as he pleases, but now Miles has turned against me.

The wind bites and the waves roar. The blackness of the sea beckons and I fight the urge to run in and submerge myself beneath the surface, to drown out the pain. But I hate the thought of my body being dumped on the beach with all the other crap. It would be too exposing.

Instead, I walk faster, silently willing some angry person to try to mug or attack me so that I can fight back and vent the volcanic spew swirling inside.

I take deep breaths of sea air. I need to channel my anger constructively.

I phone the hotel where Bella and Miles are to hold their wedding reception and ask about waitressing jobs for large events. They give me the name of a local outside agency, so I locate them and register for work.

Back in my flat, I look at the photos of Bella's room and study all her belongings. I take note of the brands of the numerous bottles of perfumes and creams.

I check on Nate. He is away, visiting an old uni friend in Leeds. Fresh anger hits at the thought of him out and about, enjoying his life with not a care in the world.

I can't sit here any more and do nothing. I rummage around in the kitchen.

★ ★ ★

I run over the Green and let myself in through the communal door. As I stride up the stairs, I remove a can of ant killer from my bag—I've read that it's harmful to fish—and place it on the floor as I slide my key into the lock.

It is stuck. It doesn't work.

Access denied.

I twist and turn the key left and right and continue trying, long after realization dawns that Nate really is determined to keep me out of all areas of his life.

CHAPTER TWENTY-NINE

Four days before Christmas, I receive a very formally worded letter from the office of James Harrington.

Annulment proceedings are underway. Nate and I—now known as "the petitioner" and "the respondent"—are soon to be no more.

I sit on my bed for hours staring at the legal words, making it all sound so straightforward and simple, as though there is no emotion involved in the process. When I've memorized every painful word, I go to the kitchen, take out a lighter and, above the sink, I set the words alight. Burnt crisps flutter, fall and land, black curls against the white ceramic.

In the distance, I hear carol-singers launch into "Silent Night."

Babs accompanies me on my Christmas trip to San Francisco on my free family-and-friends ticket. Taking her sightseeing provides a welcome distraction: Alcatraz, the Golden

Gate Bridge, a cable-car ride, Fisherman's Wharf; we embrace the whole tourist package.

Our Christmas lunch is non-traditional as we gather in a seafood restaurant, along with twenty other strangers— my crew and their fellow "cling-ons." Boyfriends, mothers, friends. I eat mussels in white wine sauce and pick flakes off a crab shell. The restaurant does its best—there are crackers and Christmas music—but all this attempt at *cheer*, all this *fun*, is killing me inside.

When Babs is asleep in my room, on one side of my huge king-size bed, I torture myself by reading all of Nate's cheery messages, back and forth, like tennis balls across the world. He is at home with his wonderful, loving family.

A woman—*Tara*—messages him to wish him "a wonderful Christmas." She looks forward to seeing him soon. As does he, in his reply to her.

Bella, Nate, Miles, I can imagine them all sitting around the table, carving the turkey, sipping mulled wine, opening expensive gifts. Happy, living the lives that they believe they deserve.

I switch on the TV and pick a film, a romantic comedy, just to make myself feel worse.

On the return sector I have no patience, none at all. During boarding, a woman in her thirties, who tells me three times that she is the managing director of some large company I've never heard of, refuses to put her bag away for take-off.

"Can't you do it?"

My jaw clenches. "I'm afraid we're not allowed to lift baggage. And if you don't move it, I'll be back in a few minutes to have it placed in the hold."

Mid-flight my supervisor tells me that the woman has complained about my attitude. I try to look contrite. I'm too wound up to take a break. Instead, I sit in the galley and listen to a colleague, Natalie, who is full of chatter about her kitchen renovations for the forthcoming month. She is part-time and is not due back at work until February.

"The fitters have said that they'll keep the chaos to a minimum."

Some people will believe anything. Actually, I don't mind Natalie, and if she lived a bit closer to me—she commutes from Glasgow, which is too far for regular visits—I'd befriend her. I've realized that it doesn't do me any good when I get too lonely.

After landing, once I've finished the passenger PA welcoming everyone to Heathrow, I feel a small twinge of unexpected optimism. A new year is imminent; always a good time for a fresh beginning.

I open the overhead stowage, above the alleged managing director's seat, and offer to take her bag out for her. Before she can answer, I pull it out and drop it on to her feet.

Her face contorts in pain. "Ouch! Think what you're doing."

"I'm so sorry," I say. "Personally, I always find it's safer to travel light." I walk away.

She can complain all she likes, there's no proof that it wasn't an accident.

Three weeks later, I book myself into a hotel close to where Miles will end up ruining his life by tethering himself to Bella, and request a room overlooking the church.

Early afternoon, as guests arrive in their finery, it is—of course—a perfectly sunny winter's day. I look out the window for Nate. When I spot him, standing next to his mother and a woman, no doubt Tara—a petite woman, with dark hair—a huge lump forms in my throat and I am unable to stop the tears.

He looks like he has stepped out of an advert in his grey tailored suit, with a pink rose in his buttonhole. Nate helps his mother adjust her large, cream hat whilst "Tara" looks on adoringly.

Bella arrives, ten minutes late, in a horse-drawn carriage and, from my viewpoint, looks fairy-tale stunning—a true princess. The bouquet she holds consists of pink and white roses. Her long, lacy white dress shimmers. Flashes of gold catch my eye as she takes her father's arm and walks towards the church entrance. She is experiencing everything I ever wanted, but never properly attained.

I dry my eyes with a tissue; I've got a job to do.

I study the seating plan before we start, and request to work on the far side of the room, away from the main wedding party. I am wearing a dark-brown wig and my blue contact lenses, plus glasses to feel extra secure. I've been instructed to wear my hair up, so it's in a ponytail, but I allow strands to fall down by the side of my face. I do feel fairly safe, because no one will be looking out for me—not when there is beautiful Bella as the belle of the ball.

I am among the invisible waiting staff.

No one will be able to truly remember me if they have to. I've heard it said that eye-witness accounts are often unreliable.

People politely remember their thank yous as I serve them tiny bowls of breadcrumb-coated macaroni and cheese and shot glasses of tomato bisque, followed by filet mignon and new potatoes. I top up wine and water glasses, then circle the table with a bread basket, offering extra rolls.

It's just like being at work, but on firmer ground.

Before dessert, we hand out glasses of champagne for the speeches.

I stand at the back, clutching a bottle of champagne, as Miles goes through the endless thank yous and the sickening dedication he has written for Bella. He is a "lucky" man, she is "one in a million."

I discreetly head to a side room and pour myself a glass of champagne. It's too hard to listen to all that rubbish and falseness. Across the corridor, I see that the kitchen is quiet. Everyone is using this time to either take a break or finish clearing up. I look around the room I'm in. As well as gifts and an overspill of coats, I spot the cake—surprisingly, a very traditional-looking white one, with a simple bride and groom on top. It's huge, though, five tiers, and is resting upon a stand on wheels, so it looks as though it's going to be wheeled in theatrically, making an entrance of its own.

I don't think twice about knocking it over. It thuds on to the carpet. I resist the urge to stick a knife into it or ruin it further by grinding it with my shoe. The bride and groom are buried beneath the sinking mess of icing and vanilla sponge.

Returning to the room, the best man's speech is in full flow, full of the usual anecdotes about mad university pranks. I should have tried to track him down beforehand—I could have added extra spice to his tales. I spy the wedding planner being led away by a grim-faced catering supervisor.

Minutes later, Bella is taken to one side by them both and I watch her hand fly to her mouth, her expression full of obvious disappointment. She's lucky—if it had been easier to get closer to her, it would have been her dress or her face.

By the time I serve the next course, described on the menu as a "three-choice dessert"—lemon cheesecake, Baileys in choc-chip ice cream, and a mini chocolate sponge—followed by coffee, I've had enough. The acidic champagne is reacting to my empty stomach and everything is starting to feel surreal and confusing. I ignore a colleague's request to join in a staff gathering, a mini investigation into the dropping of the cake.

"It was probably just kids mucking around," I say, pretending to be busy with a special request from a guest.

The moment I'm about to quit my temporary job by feigning illness, a DJ begins to set up at the side of the dance floor. I'll wait until the first dance, then I'll make an exit.

I slip away and sneak down another glass of champagne. I

need something to get me through the final part of today, and I'm hardly likely to turn into my mother after two glasses. I can feel the alcohol flowing into my bloodstream and it helps numb my pain and sense of isolation.

Maybe Amelia wasn't quite so dumb.

Back inside, the lights have dimmed as Bella and Miles take to the dance floor for their first dance—David Bowie's "The Wedding Song." My throat aches as the song ends and Nate, his arm on Tara's back gently guiding her, joins the crowd filling up the space around Miles and Bella. Mr. and Mrs. Yorke. It doesn't suit Bella as well as Goldsmith; she doesn't look like a Bella Yorke.

I am finding it hard to breathe, so I pull out a seat from a vacant table and place it by the curtains at the side. Miles' jacket is hanging off the back of a nearby seat. I discreetly put my hands inside and feel around. His wallet. His phone. I remove the wallet and place it inside my own bag. I continue watching.

I remember the night of the school party when I fell in love with Nate. I take deep breaths; I don't want to think about that now. It's not the right moment. But seeing Bella and Nate so happy—coupled with the whole happy family scene—is choking me.

The day Will died, I just wanted a few moments' peace. Yet, since then, I've had anything but.

The splash didn't fully register.

It was the gardener who tried to help me save Will. He never told anyone that, because he tried to protect me. He let me pretend to my mother that I'd seen Will fall in and had reacted immediately. That I'd called out for help but that it had just all been too cruelly quick. Any lie becomes the truth after a while. He never said that I was lazy or negligent, or that I probably dozed off.

Before I even looked down into the pool, I sensed what

had happened. I ran, climbed down. The slope down towards the deep end was horribly slippery. A long stick lay by my feet. And his shoes and odd socks, he always took them off before he went near water. It took vital seconds to find him in the murky water. I gripped, but he slipped from my grasp.

The gardener appeared. He'd seen me rush down, he'd guessed and run too. *He* managed to pull Will out, not me. I watched him attempt to resuscitate the barefoot bundle of sodden clothes. Water seeped from beneath him and slid down the slope, rejoining the murkiness. I screamed as he tried to save my brother. My responsibility. The noise that echoed was far worse than anything that had ever come out of his innocent little mouth.

The rest of that day is shattered fragments of memories, apart from the look in my mother's eyes when she saw me.

At first I thought she was going to hug me, but her arms remained at her sides.

Instead, she fell to the floor and sobbed.

The thing I've discovered about guilt is that some days you can live with it. Other days, it hits—like grief—without warning and it burns, all-consuming and acidic. And the worst of it is that there is nothing you can do.

You can't change a mistake. Ever. Instead, it weaves its way inside you, becomes an embedded part, a bad, rotten, suffocating part.

In all my dreams and nightmares, all I've ever wanted was a time machine to take me back to redress the past. When I met Bella, I thought I had a chance to follow a different path—that I could one day heal and have a stab at a normal life, by riding on her coat-tails. I wanted it so much that it hurt.

When she refused me that chance, fate offered up a second opportunity by handing me Nate. He gave me a focus, the possibility to be something other than what I feared—a scooped-out, hollow version of myself. A robot on the outside.

Inside me exists a sense of dread which has never, ever truly left me. And without a major change—something wonderful to focus on—I fear it never will.

Because, without love and acceptance, all that's left is something dark and hateful.

I stand up and walk towards the dance floor. I stop. I am so close. So close to the life that could be mine that I could reach out and take Nate in my arms. He is dancing with Bella.

I stand on the sidelines, watching. I struggle to breathe.

Focus.

I force myself to walk away. I leave them all to their fairy tale.

Outside, the welcome coolness hits me.

"Are you all right, dear?" asks an elderly man. He is puffing on a cigarette.

"No," I say. "I had an affair with the groom. He told me he loved me, but..." I shrug.

"No?" he says, wide-eyed. "Miles? He's my nephew. No, I'm sure he..."

I shrug again. "Sorry. If I'd known...it's just that he hurt me. Greatly."

I walk away, leaving behind the life denied to me.

On the way back to my hotel I pass a homeless woman in the doorway of a shoe shop. I take out all the cash Miles has and give it to her.

It must be at least two hundred pounds; some small good has come out of something bad. I dump the wallet in a bin.

At dawn, I gather my belongings and check out of the hotel after a sleepless night.

Instead of driving home, I head for Dorset. First, I park in Dorchester town centre. After sending Babs a message alert-

ing her to my imminent visit, I push open the door to a florist's shop. I wait impatiently whilst a young woman makes
up four bouquets, tying each stem with twine. She adds a
teddy-bear balloon, attached to a stick, and places it within a
bunch of white carnations.

When I ring Babs' doorbell, she is ready with her coat already zipped up.

"These are for you," I say, handing over the most expensive flowers, a mix of peach and yellow roses.

She insists on arranging them in a vase before we leave for
the cemetery.

We start with William Florian Jasmin. Babs says a prayer
but I silently tell him I'm sorry.

I should've watched you. I should've been a better big sister.

Next, we visit my mother. I don't know what to say or
do, so instead I describe the flowers I've placed beside her
plaque.

"What was her favourite flower?" I ask Babs, suddenly realizing that I don't know.

"She loved them all," Babs says, shivering.

"Go back to the car," I say, handing her my keys. "Put the
heater on. I won't be long." She doesn't argue.

I watch as she makes her way to the car park. Then I search
for the headstone of the gardener who tried to save Will and
who protected me. There is nothing by his grave, even the
flower holders are empty. I place my final bunch down on the
ground.

Michael John Simpson 1946–2004.

He died of lung cancer whilst I was at boarding school.
Amelia casually mentioned it when I was home once for half-
term. I cried.

"Thank you for trying," I say out loud.

★ ★ ★

I refuse Babs' offer to stay for the night when I drop her home.

I need to get back to my own place and work on my plans, even though my app doesn't work any more. Nate must have upgraded his phone and not transferred everything over. Or it has been deleted, somehow.

He has also changed all his passwords. There must be something I haven't thought of yet. There just has to be.

It comes to me in the early hours with such a jolt of *sheer obviousness* that I sit up: Nate still owes me a honeymoon.

However, I'll have to work within the only boundaries left available, for now. He's travelling to Whistler shortly— I recall the exact dates from the file I saw at Miles' house. I tap notes into my phone as I refine my thoughts and ideas. I need to revise tactics again, because actions always speak louder than words.

One thing is certain, though. The annulment is off. A fresh mantra springs to mind.

If you love someone, set them free.

If they come back, they're yours. If they don't, make them.

CHAPTER THIRTY

I twist my hair into a knot and secure it with clips before re-applying a lipstick I took from Bella's dressing table. I take a deep breath, smile at my reflection, unlock the toilet door and enter the first-class galley. I used my position as a safety ambassador to ensure I was selected for this particular working position, after arguing that I cannot possibly represent all points of view if I never get a chance to work in every cabin. After checking the catering against the menu, I sign to confirm I've done so.

"Bye, have a good one," says one of the always-cheerful catering guys as he heads off to another galley to complete the next round of checks.

I count the duvets, tracksuits and giveaway bags, ensuring that there is one per passenger, and arrange pale pink carnations into the fixed silver vase in the cabin. Preparations complete, I busy myself reading the PIL—passenger information list. Despite the familiar stabbing resurgence of raw, green, bitter, hideous, sickening jealousy flooding me, I remain calm. I remind myself that although these aren't ideal circumstances—no one else would have to contend with another woman so early on in a marriage—everything is all working to plan.

I have a few obstacles left to overcome, which I will work through methodically, step by step. *Cabin crew, prepare doors for departure.*

The supervisor's voice jolts over the public address system. This means that the hold doors are sealed, all paperwork is complete and the final passenger door has been closed. I arm my door, thereby locking the emergency slides into position, and cross-check with the crew member opposite. We push back. Outside my window, the air bridge is retracting. Once again, at this point, the world shrinks to the size of the plane's interior. We are trapped; at the mercy of the pilots, the elements, technology and the collective faith that security and engineering have been thorough.

We taxi towards the runway and join the queue, edging along, one plane at a time. Our turn comes. The plane swings to the right in a semi-circle. A pause before an escalating roar, a surge of power and movement as the wheels roll forward and the aircraft gains speed. We lift into the air. I close my eyes and imagine our flight details disappearing—pop!—like a bubble from the departure monitors in the terminal, now already thousands of feet below.

Gone.

I busy myself with food preparations. My two colleagues, Martin and Nicky—responsible for the cabin service—offer drinks and write down food orders, which I then heat, plate up and garnish. Lemon and parsley for the salmon, fresh mint for the lamb. We hit a patch of turbulence around the time we are serving tea and coffee—a fairly typical occurrence.

Once the service is over and the remnants—glasses, plates and food—have been cleared away, Martin and Nicky pull down the window blinds and I dim the lights.

I stand at the back, at the entrance to the cabin, observing. It is quiet and dark, apart from flickering screens. Several people are sleeping—lumps under their duvets—and there's the odd drinker, clutching a glass of whisky or port. The air conditioning hums above the engines. Someone snores. I inhale the smell of cold food, sweaty feet and wind, intermingled with air-freshener and the scent of "Eau-de-Boeing," as it's known as—the unmistakable smell of a plane's interior. All is calm.

My colleagues go on their break. It is just me, alone.

In charge. In control.

I take a moment.

I can see the side of Tara's head. Her dark hair is long and straight; TV-commercial sleek and shiny. Closing my eyes, I take some deep breaths and run through my plans but ugly words force their way into my thoughts; phrases from official letters sent by the office of James Harrington. These innocuous-looking yet powerful pieces of paper clearly state the beginning of the end. Mere months remain until Nate and I will have no ties left. The piercing reminder of it gives me fresh resolve. I've nothing left to lose.

I step into the cabin; the carpet muffles my footsteps. I aim for the wardrobe at the front of the cabin and open it, as though searching for something. To my left is seat 1A, one of the favourite seats of VIPs and celebrities. Today is no exception: there is a Canadian TV actor occupying the space watching a movie and picking at the remains of his cheese and biscuits. The passenger to my right, an older version of Nate, is reading the *Financial Times*. In the seat directly behind him, Bella and Nate's mother, Margaret, sleeps peacefully. Next year, it will be me in one of these seats, sipping champagne or a G&T. I quietly shut the wardrobe door and turn round. Bella is sitting up, rummaging in her handbag. Miles is reclined, watching a movie, the sound-cancelling headphones smothering his ears. On his side table rests a glass of untouched port. Spiteful glee grips me.

I stand beside him, give a little wave and a smile.

He starts to wave me away politely, as though he's assumed that I'm an attentive stewardess who really cares about his comfort, but his expression changes to confusion. He sits upright and removes his headphones. His eyes drop down to my name badge.

"Miles! Miles Yorke!" I say with a beam.

Bella glances over.

"You don't usually go for port," I say, slightly louder than necessary.

He stares at me but doesn't utter a word.

Bella stares too.

I just can't resist pushing it a touch more. "Let me get you a top-up. I like to look after our *special* customers."

I slide the stem of his port glass through my fingers and, holding the base, I whisk it up. Red liquid splashes on to Miles' trousers.

"Oh, I'm so sorry." I clasp my free hand to my mouth. "Come into the galley and I'll get you something to wipe it off."

I saunter out of the cabin, past Nate's seat. He does not look up. Miles is not far behind. Even though all I do is greet him with a peck on the cheek once we reach the privacy of the galley, he jerks his face away.

"My *wife*—Bella—is on board. What the hell is all this about? You lied. You said you worked for a travel company."

I can't be bothered to point out that airlines play a signifi-cant role in the travel industry.

"You're lucky that I'm giving you the time of day. Your treatment of me wasn't fair. You and Nate have more in com-mon than you know."

He stares. "Nate?"

"Yes. Nate."

"Not Nick? Oh my God." He pauses. "You misled me. Right from the beginning. Why?"

Behind him, Bella appears.

"Miles? Darling, did you get your trousers sorted?"

He swings round at the sound of her voice. "Almost."

I run a napkin under the tap, squeeze it and hand it to him. He rubs his right thigh much more vigorously than necessary.

"I know you, don't I? From school." Bella stares at me. "You're Elizabeth Price. You were at that party. In Bourne-mouth."

Miles continues with the unnecessary stain removal. His trousers are dark grey, you can't even see the port.

"And Stephanie mentioned that you'd visited her at the gym."

"Can I get you a drink?" I say. "If not, you'll have to ex-cuse me as I've got things to do."

"What did you mean about Miles not usually drinking port?"

She turns to Miles. "You're not that frequent a flyer."

I decide to help Miles out. For now. "I'm a client of his."

"You? A client of Miles?" Her disbelieving tone irks.

"Was," says Miles, looking up. "In fact, no, that's not even true. Nothing much materialized after our initial meeting. This is confusing. I thought your name was Juliette?"

"It is. Now."

"Why did you choose Miles' company? It's too much of

a coincidence. You did this at school. Always following me around, copying me, stealing my clothes, my make-up. Sucking up to my friends."

Miles looks like he's going to be sick.

"Miles, darling, did she ask you personal questions when she came to your office? Did you have any suspicions about her at all?"

"No. Why?"

"Because I've got a bad feeling about all of this."

I feel my hands clench. This is not the conversation of my imagination. I expected some sort of burgeoning shame or fear from her. Just *something*. Because surely even she can't expect to come out of this conversation completely smelling of bloody roses. I glance towards a low stowage unit which contains a jemmy. Its official use is in the event of a fire, for levering open panels. It is metal and heavy and has a nasty hook on the end.

"Excuse me?"

All three of us look over to the right-hand side. A passenger, the Canadian actor, is standing there.

I summon up my professional self. "Can I help you?"

"Yes, please. My screen has frozen."

"I'll come and take a look," I say, following him into the cabin. I pretend to take an interest in the situation, pressing a few buttons on the control. "I'll get the system reset for you," I promise.

He smiles. "Thanks. Appreciate it."

On my way to the rear of the cabin, I crouch down by Tara's seat. "Hi," I mime.

She pauses her movie—the latest romantic comedy—and takes off her headphones. "Hi," she says hesitantly.

I can tell she is desperately trying not to make it obvious that she is glancing down at my name badge.

"It's Juliette. Remember? We did that Athens together, the other month. Or was it Cairo? Anyway, how *are* you?"

"Fine, thanks."

She still looks confused. She has every right to; we've never flown together. As she struggles to recall a non-existent memory, I point over at Nate. He looks over.

"Is this the new man?"

She grins. "Yes."

I pull a grim face. "Oh. Good luck. I'd watch out, if I were you."

Nate takes off his headphones and sits up straight, still looking over at me. I've never really given any thought to the term "a thunderous expression" until this moment. I can now see exactly what it means, because his whole face is creased into a giant frown. I stand up before she can respond and aim for the galley. Nate beats me to it. He strides over and grabs my arm.

Bella and Miles, who have clearly been in deep discussion, stop and stare.

"What do you think you are doing?" Nate asks. "Why are you talking to my girlfriend?"

I shrug off his hand. "I'm at work. She looked like she needed a drink."

"You've broken our agreement."

"How? I can't help it if you're a passenger on this flight. Downgrade yourself to economy, if you're that bothered. Seriously. There are loads of spare seats down the back."

"This is not a coincidence, and it's bloody exasperating."

I shrug my shoulders. "Believe what you like. Fate clearly has big plans for us."

"So you know this woman too?" Bella asks Nate.

I answer for him. "Oh, Nate and I know each other extremely well."

Tara picks this moment to join us. Behind her right shoulder is the actor.

"Sorry," I say, before he can speak. "It does take a few minutes for your screen to spring back to life. I'll check again in five minutes."

He looks as though he wants to ask for something else, but then seems to decide against it. He makes his way into a toilet instead. We are all silent until the lock clicks shut. I walk over to the interphone located above the crew seat, call the supervisor and ask him to reset the defective screen. I rejoin the ever-growing group in the galley.

Tara is clinging to Nate's arm.

"I said I had a bad feeling about all of this," Bella says to Miles. "Didn't I?"

He nods, avoiding eye contact with me.

"What's going on?" asks Tara.

"It's just that he likes his girlfriends a lot younger, don't you, Nate?"

Nate raises his hand as though he is going to slap me. Bella grabs his arm and holds it down by his side.

"You'll back me up, won't you, Bella? Don't you remember what you used to say at school?" I mimic her voice. *"Sticks and stones, Elizabeth. Rise above it. Sticks and stones."*

"I thought you didn't know Bella that well at school?" says Nate.

"What I said was 'everyone knew of Bella.'"

Tara tries again. "I still don't get what all this is about?"

"Ask *her*." I point to Bella.

"Oh, we teased her a bit because she slept with some boy at school when she was only fifteen. The rest of us used to pretend we had—to show off or look bigger—but she actually went through with it. That's Elizabeth. Always had to take things a step further."

It's Nate's turn to look ill.

"Teased a bit," I say. "Horrible pictures in my desk. Constant name-calling. Tart. Loser. Trollop. Slut. Lily-No-Mates. And those aren't even the bad ones. You used to brag about your boyfriends and how much *fun* you had. It was partly because of *you* that I thought I was doing something grown-up. Something that would make you respect me. Instead, it was the complete reverse."

"Oh God, don't try to pin that one on me," snaps Bella. "You're your own person, surely? No one forced you to do anything."

"You said to me that the boy would always think of me as worthless. That men didn't marry women who were easy. But you're wrong. He did. It was lifelong love, just like I said all those years ago. Tell them, Nate. Tell them about our wedding."

There is silence. Everyone looks at him. He doesn't speak, he just stares at me, as if believing that, if we all stand here long enough, the surreal encounter will end, and he will wake up in some five-star hotel with nothing too taxing to start his day other than where to go for a jog, or what to eat for breakfast.

"Marriage?" says Bella. "And back then...? Oh. God." She puts her hand over her mouth and shakes her head, as though it's all too much to take in. "Nathan?"

Tara finds her voice too. *"Married?"* Tara adds, "To *her*?" I notice that she has let go of Nate's arm.

"No. Yes. Not exactly. That's why I never mentioned it. It was a Vegas thing. It's being annulled."

"It doesn't alter the fact that it happened," I point out.

The toilet door unlocks. We all fall silent as the actor emerges.

"Your screen should be fine now, sir," I say, struggling to remember his name. "Can I get you a drink?"

He appears to survey the scene in front of him and shakes his head. "No, I'm good, thanks." He disappears.

"So," says Tara. "Let me get this all straight in my head—"

Miles leaps in. "It appears to me as though Nathan and Juliette have a lot of unfinished business to discuss. How about we leave them in private for a while?"

Bella agrees. Of course she does. Now that she realizes that she was bullying me over the actions of her own brother, she can't wait to get away, to piece back the memories with her new-found knowledge. I can imagine her reframing them, still trying to make out that she wasn't that bad. Tara, however, is less keen. She shakes her head when Bella tries to guide her out of the galley. She stays put, flicking her hair a couple of times.

Nate walks over to the bar and helps himself to a miniature bottle of cognac. He doesn't bother with a glass but tips the bottle directly into his mouth. Both Tara and I watch him gulp. He exhales, places the miniature on the side and runs his hands through his hair.

"Is this the ex-girlfriend you told me about?" Tara says to Nate. "The one who wouldn't leave you alone?"

"Not ex-girlfriend, current wife," I correct her.

She stares at me, as though all this is my fault. Nate goes over to her and whispers something in her ear. She throws me a look of disdain before she heads for the nearest toilet. The door clicks shut and the *occupied* light illuminates. Nate and I are alone. I walk over to the right-hand side door and lift the window blind. Over the dark clouds the horizon is lined with distant blue-and-orange light. He grabs me by the shoulders, twists me round and shoves his face close to mine. I can smell the cognac on his breath.

"What the fuck!" he says. "None of this was just about me, was it? You've dragged Bella into it now too. How dare you imply that I like young women. You were culpable too."

"Keep telling yourself that. And let go of me." He does.

I sigh and try again. "Nate, you married me. Your sister made my life hell at school because of you. You owe me. Your sister owes me. I want a happy-ever–after, and you're going to give it to me."

"One mistake. One stupid, thoughtless mistake I made so many years ago." Although he's speaking out loud, it's as though he's speaking to himself. "One reckless moment."

"In fairness, the only mistake you've ever made was in thinking that I'd give up."

He opens the bar trolley and reaches for another minia-ture. I resist the strong urge to slam the door shut, trapping his hand.

I continue. "Acceptance is the key to this situation. I'm not going away. Accept that and everything will be OK. Keep fighting me and you'll end up paying. Love hurts. Get used to it. I've had to."

"I thought if I played fair that you'd eventually see reason. I don't have anything else to add."

"Fine. I will go to the police. I'll say that you forced me. The whole under-age thing will be more of an issue then too."

"What a ridiculous notion! Why would you marry me if I'd assaulted you?"

"Because you said you were sorry and you wanted to make it up to me. Because, despite your faults—and, believe me, there are many—I love you."

"I give up, Juliette," he says. "You're stooping even lower. Plain and simple requests don't work. Threats don't work. Reasoning doesn't work."

The mere fact that he is calling me Juliette alerts me to the fact that he is trying to lull me into a false sense of security.

I remain patient, however. "And nothing ever will," I say calmly.

He suddenly seems to break. Like he's given up. He sighs loudly and turns to walk away. And there is something about him turning his back towards me, something about the whole finality of our marriage hurtling towards a brutal and cold end unless I stop it, and stop it now, that makes something in me ignite. I look around, release a fire extinguisher from its brackets, ready to whack him with it. He must sense something, because he swings round and grabs it from me. He yanks it from me so violently, I fall down. The pain to my right arm is momentarily shocking. Cold air blasts me from the chillers and I focus on the debris below the trolleys—a teaspoon, an olive and a cork—before I look up and see Tara's horrified expression looking down.

There is also another passenger; an elderly man, who looks utterly confused. Nate tries to help me up but I ignore his offer and stand up myself, rubbing my arm.

"Are you all right?" the man asks.

I nod. "I think so."

"I'll go and get one of your colleagues," he says.

"It's fine," I say. "But thanks, I'll speak to someone if I think it's necessary."

Despite looking unsure, the passenger heads for the magazine rack and takes his time browsing the selection, making a deliberate show of glancing back at us every few moments. I look at Tara. "We need some privacy, please."

She looks torn, but Nate gives her a slight nod. She gives us both a look of bewilderment before she walks slowly back to the sanctuary of her seat.

"Finish with her," I say as I re-stow the extinguisher. "I'm putting my foot down, which is something I should've done a long time ago. If there's one thing I regret it's that I didn't fight hard enough for you. I caved in too quickly to the pressure you and James put me under. Well, no more. Tell her it's over. Tell her to get the next flight back to London. Tell your family I'm joining you in Whistler on some kind of getting-to-know-the-family type of honeymoon mini-break."

"Absolutely not."

"Fine." I list my weapons, one per finger. "Under-age sex, forced or not—your own sister will be able to bear witness—plus adultery, assault, just witnessed by your own girlfriend and another independent person. And don't forget that I can show everyone *recent* photos of us *happily* getting married. I can make such a good story out of this, trust me." I pull a sad face and put on a pathetic voice. "I forgave him for the past, because he was so remorseful. But I shouldn't have allowed him to talk me into a quickie marriage, because it meant he thought he could continue his game-playing with my feelings. I never knew where I stood. It's been dreadful." I switch back to my normal voice. "Who do you think they're going to believe?"

"I don't love you."

"Well, try harder."

I'm actually getting quite sick of begging and pleading and being so bloody pathetically patient. He has no choice. I just want all this resolved so that we can get on with our lives.

"Go and talk to her," I say calmly. "You're running out of time."

"It's not fair to throw this on her mid-air. I'll talk to her when we're alone and explain the situation properly. It's also not fair on my family."

"All that I've asked of you is non-negotiable. End of. Don't push me any more than you already have."

"I need time to think." He pauses, before adding, "Please," as an obvious afterthought. "Look, I get it. I understand. But you're not coming to Whistler with us. I want time to talk to my family. Alone. At least give me that." He pauses again. "Your night-stop is only—what?—thirty hours or so at most, anyway. So it's not like it would be that great for you."

On second thoughts, perhaps it is best right now if Nate doesn't know of my immediate plans. I'll reveal things on a need-to-know basis. Because, come to think of it, there's no glamour in being formally introduced to his parents beside a baggage carousel or in an overcrowded arrivals hall. From now on, things are going to be done properly and in style. I intend to make a grand entrance in Whistler and turn it into a truly memorable occasion.

"Just get rid of Tara," I say. "And I'll keep you up to date with our future plans."

Nate walks slowly over to Tara's seat, looks back at me, sees me watching him and sits in the guest seat opposite her. He leans forward. I return to the galley but watch from the other side. Nate looks as though he is trying very hard to placate her.

Things are looking good.

Martin and Nicky return from their break, but there's no way I'm going on mine. There's too much to keep an eye on. I pretend to read a paper, every now and then checking the cabin. There is much exchanging of seats, like musical chairs, and seemingly intense chat between them all.

I ask Nicky to deliver Miles a folded-up note discreetly, "...because he's asked for some advice on a gift for his wife." Really, it's more of a *See Me* note.

Moments after she's delivered it, Miles meets me in the business-class galley.

"Can you keep a secret?" I say. "Well, yes, as we both know, of course you can. Silly me."

"I haven't got much time," he says. "Bella will come looking."

"I'm joining all of you in Whistler. But I don't want anyone else to know in advance. All you have to do is make an effort to help me blend in. Be a friendly face. The harder you try to fight my corner, the less likely I am to drop you in it."

"Please, don't…" he starts to say.

"I took photos. Inside your house. And of you, asleep in Tokyo. So, I'm going to assume we have a deal?"

"I can't. Please. I appreciate that things were tough for you in the past, but Bella's sorry. She doesn't deserve this."

God, he's spineless. I shrug and walk back up the aisle towards the front.

"Wait!" he calls out.

Several passengers look over at us.

"OK," he says. "I don't like the sound of it, but OK."

The smell of fresh coffee hits as I approach the galley. Martin and Nicky are already busy with the service. Everyone orders hot food and there are last-minute duty-free requests.

I peek into the cabin several times, but all six are now glued to their screens—as if, by concentrating on another world, they can ignore their current one.

When, as I know only too well, reality always finds a way to seep back in.

At the top of descent Bella seeks me out.

"Can I have a word?"

"You should have your seat belt on." I point upwards to the illuminated sign.

"So," she says, ignoring my command. "Things all seem a little complicated. And it appears that I've inadvertently played my part. I'm sorry about school...you know, with re-gards to Nathan. I think we can all agree that we were young and immature."

I don't reply.

She seems emboldened by my lack of reaction, so she takes a deep breath and continues. "The thing is, Tara is a nice per-son. She and I are very good friends. Why don't you leave them to get on with their lives? You can't want Nathan after his behaviour, surely? You deserve better."

"That's not what you said at school."

"Well, like I've just said, I'm sorry. It all got a bit silly."

Martin interrupts us. "Madam, you need to go and strap yourself in."

Bella gives me a look—as though "we're all sorted now"—and obeys him.

On the approach to Vancouver, I feel hot and cold. But I reassure myself, over and over, that Nate's got it. He finally understands. However, the flaw is that I can never fully trust him, given his propensity for changing his mind. This is his final test; if he fails I will have to resort to strong measures.

And as for Bella's pathetic attempt at an apology—she acted as though she was clearing up a mere nothing of a mis-understanding. I feel angrier than ever towards her.

I look out the window but can't see anything apart from scattered lights in the darkness. I know from previous day-light trips that we are flying over a vast expanse of water; and beyond, majestic snow-tipped mountains are visible in the distance.

As the wheels touch down and the aircraft loses speed, I am almost consumed by excitement and longing.

Not long now. Not long at all.

I think I've finally got Nate right where I want him. My tenacity and ingenuity are about to pay off.

The aircraft comes to its final stop. I stand at the disembarkation door, a genuine smile on my face.

Tara strides off first. She doesn't look back.

Nate's parents leave next, followed by Miles and Bella.

And finally, Nate.

I grab his arm. "So, everything's sorted, is it?"

"Yes."

"And I'll see you back home in a week? No more Tara?"

"I've got to go."

He leaves. I watch him disappear round the corner of the air bridge.

It takes an age until the final person disembarks. I am not far behind.

Following the signs written in French, English and Chinese, I clear Immigration with the rest of the crew before I approach baggage reclaim, then hesitate because I see Tara reach up and give Nate a kiss on the lips. I hold my breath and watch what happens next. I exhale as she turns away and exits through Customs. I look at the remaining five, huddled around baggage trolleys, as Nate and Miles lift their luggage off, case by case, as it filters around the circular loop.

Ignoring them, I aim for the neat row of crew suitcases and select mine. I look over. Miles catches my eye. I give him a cheery wave before walking away in the direction of Customs. "Good afternoon," I smile at the official.

"Welcome to Canada. Enjoy your stay."

"I intend to, thank you very much."

I exit, my head held high. The automatic doors close behind me.

I spot Tara immediately, sitting on a seat, pretending to

read a book. She looks up, but quickly glances down again. She could do with some acting lessons. I head for the crew bus, but as the driver loads my luggage, I act as though I've dropped something. Ignoring my colleagues' moans—"Don't be long," "I'm exhausted"—I cross back over the road towards Arrivals.

And sure enough, one by one, they are all stepping into a people carrier. The parents first—how nice and respectful—followed by the other four, of course, including Tara.

They must think that I'm stupid. Which, maybe, I am. Because I dared to hope that, this time, Nate would understand.

I shake my head. He should know me better by now. I stand and watch their car pull away from the kerb.

They all think that they're fine. They should think again, because Nate has just failed his test.

And enough is enough. It really is.

CHAPTER THIRTY-ONE

Red digits illuminate the pitch-blackness. It is 1:38 a.m.

I am stuck here, trapped in a small hotel suite in the down-town area of Vancouver, because the first bus to Whistler is not until the early hours. I lie, surrounded by darkness, re-living the past. The way that I now see it is that I've spent ten years of my life leading up to this. Say I live to be seventy, it means that I will have wasted about a seventh of my life. And for what? To try to meet an inferior man? Accept a mediocre life? As if.

Unable to settle, I switch on the side light, load a coffee capsule into the machine and sit cross-legged on my bed, going through all my plans, revisions and photos. I double-check that I have the key to the Whistler holiday home—one of the many items I took or had copied whilst I was at Nate's, because experience has taught me to prepare for any eventuality. Taking occasional sips of my coffee, I count my stash of local currency before I get up, shower and order a club sandwich from room service.

I repack and keep busy until it's finally time to leave. The last thing I do is place my laptop, phone, passport and ID card inside the safe. I need to travel light.

The door to the room clicks shut behind me. I'm perfectly dressed for the bitter temperature: a woolly hat, gloves and a large neck-warmer. Between my rucksack and duffel bag I have all my ski-wear—ski pants in a discreet grey with thin stripes of navy, a jacket in a matching colour, reflective goggles and ski boots.

The bus is on time.

I settle near the back, behind a young Australian couple who don't show any interest in me. I keep my face as covered as possible, without drawing unnecessary attention, and pretend to doze—which is fine, as other passengers are also taking a nap.

It is dark and the windows are misted up, so I rub a small section clear to see outside. Beams highlight the snow and ice surrounding Sea to Sky Highway. Intermittently, the driver calls out unseen landmarks: parks, waterfalls, forests.

By the time we approach the outskirts of the resort, nearly two hours later, early daylight reveals postcard-perfect snowy mountains, dotted with trees and patches of rectangular ski runs.

I feel a twinge of nervous anticipation as I disembark. I stand still as others crowd around to retrieve their ski gear from the trailer. Taking a few icy breaths before I cross the road and head for a pavement, I walk in the direction of the holiday home which I memorized as best I could from Google Maps. I could get a bus, but it's only a ten-minute walk. I'm taking a small risk in assuming that everyone will have been up early—given the time difference—ready for the lifts to open. I need time to orientate myself without bumping into anyone.

To start off with, it's easy enough. The pavement has been gritted and cleared; dirty snow piles up along the edges. I cross over a bridge, beneath which is a gentle-running river.

But the images I studied were taken in summer, so the route isn't quite as I pictured. After walking up the wrong street, I backtrack until I recognize a bend in the road. When I spot the chalet-style villa, I am certain it's the right one, and the number confirms it. It is set back from the road, along a short drive, which has been gritted too.

I walk past the side of the property and round to the back, following a track which leads up a slope and into a wooded area, treading carefully because of the frozen ground. Half-way up, I stop, put my bag down at my feet, lean against a fir tree, take out a bottle of water and sip. The place is even more magnificent than it appeared in the pictures. Wooden walls help the building blend into the surroundings. I can see directly through the high windows into the spacious living and dining area. Icicles hang from the edges of the wooden shutters. High above these rooms, two large balconies face me, one of which houses a hot tub. Below, there is a covered area with benches, a pile of logs and racks supporting ski equipment: a mixture of skis, poles and spare boots. Looking around, over to my left, I can see one of the nearby ski lifts and snow-tipped mountains in the distance. To my right, there are more houses of similar design.

There is no sign of anyone.

Despite my thick gloves, my feet and hands feel frozen, yet I wait for a while longer, listening to the gentle rustle of a faint breeze among the trees, before deciding that it's safe to head back down. As I hide my bag behind the pile of logs, I spot a rear entrance. I dare to hope that Nate's key will work, but it is completely the wrong type for the lock. I'm going to have to brazen it out and walk round the villa to climb the stairs leading to the front door.

I knock, prepared to make a run for it, but no one comes.

I experience a sliver of fear as I push the key into the lock; it's a bit awkward with my gloves on, but thank God it works. I'm in.

Silence. Light pours through the large windows.

I look around, taking in the space: the high-up wooden-beamed ceiling, the gleaming marble and glass surfaces, the cosy sitting room with its rich red-and-orange sofas and large cushions.

A rush of anger hits, because I can picture myself fitting in nicely here.

Buoyed with fresh indignation, I risk exploring further by going upstairs, opening and closing each bedroom door until I find Nate's. I can't bring myself to think of it as Nate and Tara's. I feel room-spinningly sick. Even though I thought I was mentally prepared, it's still a punch in the stomach to see the physical evidence. She hasn't even bothered to completely unpack; some of her clothes remain in a suitcase, whilst Nate's hang neatly.

I have such an overwhelming desire to destroy all her belongings. So, as a distraction, I slide open the door to the balcony and inhale deep breaths of cold air. I navigate past the covered-up hot tub and lean against the wooden railing. Scanning the stunning wooded area, I seek out the exact spot where I recently stood. The area's still deserted. I glance down. It's much higher up than it looks from the outside, making it impossible to use as an escape route if they suddenly return. The thought jolts me into action, so I return inside to the warmth.

I search through Tara's bag until I find something of use: a receipt for pre-booked ski lessons. That's useful information, because I'm going to find her and tell her why she needs to leave. She needs to know why it can never work between them. I can't resist having a quick rummage through Nate's belongings too, before I leave. I've so missed having access to his world. It's intoxicating, like being reintroduced to a drug. Downstairs, I exit through the back door, leaving it unlocked. I retrieve my bag from its hiding place and slide my ski-wear on over my clothes. There are plenty of spare skis and poles, which will save me having to hire any. I select a pair that look like they'll do and push my feet into my ski boots, adjusting the tightness.

I retrace my steps in the direction of Whistler village, and join a long queue.

"Where are the ski schools based?" I ask the woman behind the booth as I hand over cash for a one-day lift pass. "Are there learner slopes?"

She hands over a map and points to the Olympic station on Whistler Mountain.

I wait in a different queue, in the singles line—story of my life—before joining a group in one of the gondolas, alighting at the first station. It is hectic. Bright ski colours crowd the area. It is tricky finding Tara. But I intend to persevere, because that is my plan, and I need to approach her alone. I scan the different groups, but the sun reflecting off the snowy whiteness means that everyone is wearing goggles, as well as hats and helmets.

At midday, I give up. My cheeks sting and my lips are dry. At the top of the slope, I have a moment's hesitation before I push away with my ski poles. I'd forgotten the initial fear, the jolt of nervous anticipation before I let myself go. However, exhilaration takes over and I fall into the rhythm.

I watch my shadow, dark against the white, almost unaware of other skiers.

It feels surreal, that I am here, now. Yet tonight, I will be flying back to London.

And Tara will be disillusioned and heartbroken.

After a sandwich and a coffee, I retrace my steps to the house.

Several more pairs of skis are leaning against a wall at the back, so it doesn't feel wise to climb up the slope and look in; it feels too exposing. Slowly, quietly, I try the back door. It opens. I ease it open wide enough for me to step in. There is an array of boots on shoe racks and a messy pile of gloves, helmets and goggles. My heart thuds as I stand at the bottom of the stairs, listening. They're all up there, including Tara. Snippets of conversation drift among the sounds of clinking cutlery and china.

"Splendid morning."

"Anyone up for the other mountain this afternoon?"

"Couldn't ask for better weather."

I silently pray that Tara will announce that she's tired, that she's going to stay behind and take a nap, but no such luck. When they make noises about leaving, I slip out and conceal myself in the woods, behind a large tree trunk, slightly to the left of the property. I've worked out that they will ski off in the other direction. Bella and Miles leave first, followed by her parents. Nate and Tara remain inside. As I struggle to contain my rage and jealousy, I force myself to go to the safe place in my mind, because I can feel myself slipping out of control. I know that if I don't get a grip, I will storm in there. And if I see them together, I will crack.

It takes half an hour before they emerge. And every painful minute strengthens my hatred of Tara.

I follow them, which is easy, because they walk close together. She is wearing an orange jacket and a matching hat. Nate, being all gentlemanly, is carrying her skis as well as his own. They queue up for the gondola. I follow, one behind, and alight at the same place as before. Nate accompanies his soon-to-be-ex to her lesson. She is late. As soon as she's joined in with the mismatched group of old and young, male and female, Nate pulls down his goggles, adjusts his skis and, after giving her a wave by raising a ski pole, he leaves.

I watch her. An instructor demonstrates positions. I see her trying so pathetically hard to fit in with Nate and his family. Trying so hard to please. I want to ski over and tell her not to bother; to point out that she is wasting her time. Ten hardworking years it's taken me. A few days on the nursery slopes will do bugger-all for her. And she's rubbish: too full of fear. Too cautious.

I approach a skier dressed in the same blue ski clothes as Tara's instructor. "Excuse me. Do you know what time the lessons finish?" I point out Tara's group.

"Usually an hour before the slopes shut."

"Thank you," I say, checking my watch.

She has an hour and a half left. The bus to Vancouver leaves in under three hours. If I don't make it, I will miss the flight, which wouldn't be good.

To keep warm, I ski down the nearest slope twice whilst I mentally prepare what I'm going to say to her. When the group breaks up, I board a gondola ahead of her, so that I am ready for her at the bottom.

She disembarks, removes her skis from the side holder, and carries them awkwardly. I follow. I'll speak to her when it's less crowded. She walks slowly, as though she's in pain, towards the outskirts of the village. She stands in the bus queue, which throws me for a moment. I hesitate, before deciding to walk, so I can catch her by surprise as she approaches the house.

Less than a couple of minutes after I set off, I see the bus drive past. *Damn.* I speed up as much as I can, ignoring the rubbing of my boots against my ankles. But there is no sign of her on the road to the chalet. I approach the house from the back. I feel a sense of rising dread, because she needs to be there and I am running out of time to speak to her. Nate and the others will be back soon after the slopes close, if not before.

As I remove my skis, I see a blob of snow run down another ski and plop on to the ground. One pair. They have to be Tara's. I change my boots and take off my ski gloves, swapping them for thinner ones. I climb the slope to double-check that it's her and that she's definitely alone. I peer over. The living area is empty, but then…elation! She is alone. On the balcony. I watch her. She shrugs off a robe and climbs into the hot tub. I see her lie back. Fearful of losing my chance, I almost break into a run back down.

The back door is locked; clearly, she's the cautious type. So I'm forced to enter through the front again.

Inside, it's quiet. I make my way upstairs and open the door to Nate's room. I can see the back of her head through the glass. On the side rests a glass of white wine, her phone and two small speakers. I slide back the glass door. The sound of a local radio station blares above the noise of the water bubbling in the hot tub. I move closer. She looks completely chilled, her eyes are closed. I could push her head down and hold it there, but I won't. I stand still. Her cerise swimsuit shimmers with white bubbles. I pick up her phone. When I switch off the music, her eyes fly open and she twists her head round.

I sit on the edge of the pale blue tub, out of her reach.

"Hello, Tara."

She stares at me. "What are you doing here?"

I give her a friendly wave. "How's it going? I don't blame you for being in there, I bet you're aching all over. I remember what it was like when I learned to ski. But it's all a waste, you know. All this hard work and effort." She looks for her phone.

I hold it up. "How about I look after this?"

She clambers out and reaches for a nearby towel. "Give it back!"

"Not just yet. We need to talk about Nate. He doesn't have the guts to tell you himself, so it's down to me. We're still together. You're just the other woman."

She rubs herself semi-dry. "That's not what he says."

"I'm his *wife*. You know that. And you also know another thing, you saw him attack me on board. He was furious, because he wants me to keep quiet about us, to keep you in the dark. Nate, you see, as always, wants everything his own way, on his own terms. That's what the real Nate is like. And you're letting him get away with it."

Tara fumbles with the sleeves as she tries to slide on a white robe. Once it's on, she appears more confident. "You're lying. And the reason I know is because he's going to take out a restraining order."

I don't give her the satisfaction of a reaction, even though it's hurtful news. Still clutching her phone, I shrug off my rucksack and take out a Vegas picture. I hold it up so that she can see how relaxed and normal he looked.

She gives it a quick glance before looking me in the eye.

"That doesn't mean anything. He says that you twist everything. Why can't you go on a spa weekend or join a dating site like a normal person? Now, give me back my phone. Everyone will be back here any minute. So if I were you, I'd leave."

Shoving the picture away, I hold her phone above the water.

"No! My photos aren't backed up."

She comes towards me, so I stand up and take a step back towards the railing.

"Look, Juliette…" She pauses. "This isn't achieving anything."

I ignore her. "I need you to pack your things now and come with me."

"What for?"

"It's the only way. You can write Nate a Dear John note, and then we'll leave together. I'll return your phone once we're on board the flight home. You don't belong here."

She looks behind her, towards the room, then turns back and glances below, as though she is desperately willing Nate to appear like her shining knight.

It reminds me that I'm losing precious time.

I give it a final shot. "You can't be with Nate, because he's not yours. It's that simple."

"Give me my phone. We'll call Nate and then we can sit down, the three of us, and have a proper talk."

I smile. "No."

Neither of us speaks for a moment, until I'm forced to break the silence.

"No one will ever love him the way that I do."

She stares. I think she realizes that I mean business, that I'm not going anywhere. And realization dawns for me too, because I know now that Tara will never see reason. She'll tell Nate that I was here.

As she approaches me, drops of water drip down her face from her soaking hair. She tries to grab my right wrist to get her phone, but I am taller than her, so I can hold it up high. I lean back over the wooden railing. She reaches for it. And...

I do it. I do the only thing left that I can. I lean across and push her.

I think, somehow, I've known all along that it would come to something like this.

She's momentarily stunned; her eyes widen. She grabs my arm but I prise her off. She screams as she kicks me and tries to grab me again. But two great, big shoves and she's gone.

There's an almighty thud, like ice cracking.

I look down, taking deep, heavy breaths.

She is still. Serene. Snow White.

Her wet hair is semi-fanned over the white frozen ground, her left leg is bent back awkwardly. Her head is twisted towards me, her nose looks bloodied. Her eyes I can't quite make out; they seem half-open. I lean over—not as far as possible, but as far as I think she could—and take several photos of the snowy view beyond her. Layers of snow cap the trees and branches, it is peaceful and calm. I drop the phone. It lands near her.

Maybe now, when Nate realizes that he's destined to be

unlucky in love, he will appreciate what he is always so quick to throw away. I'm reliable and consistent. I'll always be there, unlike all the others.

My eyes dart around. I leave everything as it is and run down to the back door.

I move fast. I pick up my bag and walk further up the track, so that I can look down and see her. Dusk is imminent, I wonder how soon they will spot her.

I look at my watch; the return bus to Vancouver isn't for another forty-two minutes. Darkness falls and, soon after, I see flashes of head-torches gleam as the others return and gather en masse around the back, faffing around with skis and boots, oblivious to Tara, mere metres away. I watch.

Inside, lights come on. After several minutes, they are all seated around the breakfast-bar area drinking wine. Nate picks up his phone. I hear Tara's come to life and see it shining in the darkness, until it dims again. I remain, transfixed, watching Nate and his family like a reality show. There is a spare seat. I stare and imagine it's saved especially for me.

I yearn to be able to join in. I want so desperately to alter the scene in front of me so that I merge in and it ends with: *And they all lived happily ever after.*

Instead, I leave and join the main road, hood up, scarf wrapped tight.

Waiting for the bus, I feel as though I've been away ages. It starts to snow.

After twenty minutes, just as I start feeling a bit panicky, I see the bus headlights. I don't have time for any delays.

Safely on board, I close my eyes and think of Tara's lifeless form and remind myself that she had it coming. Another thought takes hold: Nate. He's solely mine again. He will be upset, of course he will, but he'll get over it. She was hardly the love of his life. And maybe it will make him think. Because if he had dumped Tara—like he agreed to—she'd still be alive. Had she got on a flight straight back to London then she wouldn't have met her end in a freak photo-taking accident.

It's his fault, not mine.

The bus pulls into Vancouver leaving me with less than an hour to spare.

I catch a cab and keep the conversation to a minimum. I get the driver to drop me off a block away. I dump my boots into two separate bins and walk back into the hotel lobby.

I make my way to my suite, praying that I don't bump into anyone. I retrieve my belongings from the safe, shower, pack and reply to a text message from Babs asking about my trip.

Rubbish. Spent the whole time in bed with a terrible cold. Have felt awful. xxx

Operating on pure adrenalin, I take the lift down and join the rest of the crew in the lobby.

Moments before we push back, the captain announces a delay whilst we wait for the plane to be de-iced. But after an hour, as we lift into the air, I feel relief—sheer, blessed relief—at having had the guts to take firm action. The future, by its very nature, is intangible. However, when you wrestle back some control, then anything is possible. I've just proved this.

At 35,000 feet, cocooned in the clouds and separated from the real world, the growing distance helps me to stay focused on what I need to do next.

As the aircraft doors open, I half-expect to see the police waiting for me.

But nothing happens.

And by the time I take out my keys and step into my home, I feel certain nothing will.

I keep busy on my three days off.

I phone Babs and tell her that I'm back with my one true love. When Nate returns, he'll be worn out through shock. But we'll work through it. I fire off an email to James Harrington, explaining that Nate and I are going to make a go of our relationship when he returns from skiing.

I also think about Will a lot. But somehow, seeing how peaceful Tara was, I also feel a little comforted.

Covering all bases, I message Nate saying that I look forward to seeing him on Wednesday.

He doesn't reply.

I avoid the internet, so that I can't give in to temptation and google news of Tara.

The day before Nate is due home, assuming they're able to fly back as arranged—I wonder if Tara's body will be in the hold?—I travel to the Report Centre and check the obituary board.

Tara's death is announced as a tragic holiday accident. Which is kind of true. There will be a memorial—anyone who knew her is welcome to attend and celebrate her life.

I won't go, but I will send flowers. Lilies, of course.

Nate doesn't fly home on the Wednesday.

I call in sick for my next trip and wait in all day. Restless, I wander around, plumping up the cushions. I rearrange apples in the fruit bowl, ditto with the food in the fully stocked fridge and cupboards. The mini chocolate muffins rest neatly on the side. I brush down every item in the wardrobe, especially my favourite dress. I drink coffee from the mugs Nate bought me and run my fingers along the fridge magnets stuck back to their original home. A huge, framed wedding photo takes pride of place, alongside the ornaments and vases. It's all in the details.

On Thursday, after watching Rainbow swim along his tank for hours, I hear voices—Nate's and the caretaker's—before a key twists in the lock. I stand up, smooth down my dress and have a smile on my face, ready to be his shoulder to cry on. His rock. His lifetime companion.

"Hello, darling," I say. "Why didn't you reply to my message? I've been worried about you." He drops his bag. His face is white.

"Sorry to hear about Tara. I heard about it at work—but you should've told me. You look exhausted. Come in properly. I've made a few changes, by the way, moved a few things around, but I'm sure you'll agree it's for the best."

"My keys?" he says.

I hold his gaze. "I took them from your jacket pocket on the flight. It made sense."

He'll never be able to prove that I took them from Whistler. Because I wasn't there. He ordered me not to come.

He stares. He can't quite put the pieces together. Which is fine, because from now on we're going to do things the hard way. Or the simple way. His choice. And it's so much better if he's uncertain. People are more compliant when they are fearful. Like Miles will be, when I invite him and Bella over for dinner. He's going to have to persuade her to come, to tolerate me. Maybe she'll even be nice; compliment my cooking, that type of thing.

"No way. This cannot be happening."

"This is what we agreed," I say, calmly but firmly.

And it is. Because, like I told Nate in the video diary, the girl gave her heart to the boy and their fate was sealed. Seriously, he should have listened, because no one can fight fate.

No one.

Nate became my blueprint from the moment I saw his picture on Bella's bedside table at school. And the fact that he subconsciously sought me out by the river proves it. He saved me from myself, from some of the darkness and guilt trapped inside. And yet, the shadows from that night still linger; invisible swirls of grey and black continuously cloak me.

Nate owed me love and respect all those years ago, and he still owes me that. He'll always owe me that.

Nate doesn't move, so I walk over and close the door. We're alone. Just the two of us.

The dream is real. I've fixed everything and put us back together again.

I was right to persevere, to not accept anything less. We now have a fresh start; a whole new understanding. The only way it can ever be.

★ ★ ★ ★ ★

ACKNOWLEDGEMENTS

Writing this was difficult because there really are so many people to thank that it was hard to even begin. After much deliberation (I wrote a lot of lists, concerned about unintentionally leaving someone out), I decided to just go for it, to try to express as much heartfelt appreciation as best I can.

A huge thank you to Sophie Lambert, my incredible agent, who is wise, kind and one of the most dedicated, hardworking people I have ever met. Thanks for your fantastic insight, patience, brilliant guidance, and for making my dream come true. Much gratitude also goes to Alexander Cochran, Emma Finn, Alexandra McNicoll, Jake Smith-Bosanquet and, of course, the wider team at C+W Agency.

Another very big thank you to the wonderful Wildfire trio and brilliant editors, Kate Stephenson, Alex Clarke and Ella Gordon—an amazing team with endless energy and enthusiasm, who are also incredibly insightful. They are a real pleasure to work with and I feel so grateful to be a part of the family. Again, these thanks are also extended to the wider team at Headline—Viviane Basset, Becky Hunter, Frances Doyle, Ellie Wood, Becky Bader, Siobhan Hooper and Sarah Badhan, and to Shan Morley Jones and Rhian McKay for their expertise and keen eyes.

In North America, huge thanks to Hillary Jacobson and Brittany Lavery for believing in *The Perfect Girlfriend*. I am overjoyed and full of gratitude that they have done so. A very big thank you also to Lisa Wray, Pamela Osti, Ana Luxton, Sean Kapitain and the rest of the team at Graydon House.

I've learned a lot over the past year or so (I'm sure I will continue to do so) and I've realised how much time, careful thought and effort so many readers put into blogging and reviewing in order to share their love of books. I am hugely grateful to everyone who writes these.

My decision, and journey, to "become a writer" took a number of years. I slowly began to immerse myself into the writing world. I attended literary festivals, courses, meet-the-author events, and this feels like a good point to give a special mention to Jenny Ashcroft, who has been an immense source of loyal support and generous help, and a fantastic listening ear. Thank you too to Emily Barr and Craig Green for their very kind encouragement. All very much appreciated.

Mention and thanks also goes to my local creative writing tutor, Nicky Morris, who encouraged me to broaden my writing skills and who first gave me the confidence to read my work out loud. I have fond memories of swapping stories on Tuesday evenings. And to all my other local talented writer friends and the dedicated group who run the fantastic Hampshire Writers' Society; their events are varied and well worth attending.

In 2014, having given up my flying career, I joined the "Writing a Novel" course at the Faber Academy. There, under the skilful guidance of course director Richard Skinner (thank you so much for encouraging me to *"keep going"* and for giving me the confidence to trust my instinct with this book), not only did I learn so much of great value, I was very fortunate to join an incredible group. They are a bunch of talented, supportive, generous writers. We still meet regularly to share successes and buoy each other up during the inevitable hard times—wine is often involved too! *Thank you* and thank you again, Laura, Fiona, Mia, Joe, Rose, Rohan, Antonia, Jess, Roger, Maggie, Phil and Helen. For everything.

Much gratitude to my early readers, Geraldine (who read the entire book several times), all my Faber group once again, and, for their help and advice, many thanks also go to Amanda, Ian, Lindsay, Roy and Walter. Thank you all for being so generous with your time and your wise, valuable feedback.

My husband never once questioned my desire to become a published author. Ever. And he must've been tempted many, many times. Thank you for your unwavering belief, support and love. And for my three sons who make me realise how time really does fly, and the need to fill it with the people and things that matter.

To the rest of my family: my mum, dad and sister, with lots of love. For always making me believe that I can achieve anything. And to my in-laws for their unquestioning support too. Much appreciation and gratitude for all the childcare offered by both sides of the family, because without the teamwork, I would not have been able to attend the courses and events which have led up to this. I'm so relieved that your collective faith in me has led to this.

Almost last, but of course, never least, thanks to my many wonderful, supportive, kind, funny, loyal, generous friends, some of whom are scattered around the world, but who are always in my heart. Without you, life would not be as much fun—you force me out of my shell. I wrote a list (another one!) but it was far too long, so all I can do is write a huge, all-encompassing *thank you* for everything, for the shared experiences, for being there. Always. You definitely know who you are. Also, for believing that I could write a book. And to all my flying friends, past and present, there will always be a big part of me that misses the airline world: the camaraderie, the team spirit.

Because this is not an exhaustive thank-you list, I could go on and on. And on. But, as I clearly must end somewhere, my final thank you has to go to readers; an enormous *thank you* for choosing to read this book.

BIOGRAPHY

Karen Hamilton spent her childhood in Angola, Zimbabwe, Belgium and Italy and worked as a flight attendant for many years. Karen is a recent graduate of the Faber Academy and, having now put down roots in Hampshire to raise her young family with her husband, she satisfies her wanderlust by exploring the world through her writing. *The Perfect Girlfriend* is her first novel.

THE
PERFECT
GIRLFRIEND

KAREN HAMILTON

Reader's Guide

GRAYDON
HOUSE

A Q&A with national bestselling writer Kimberly Belle, author of The Marriage Lie *and* Three Days Missing

Kimberly: *The Perfect Girlfriend* is your first novel. Tell us what it's like to be a debut novelist! What have you learned and is there anything you wish you'd known going into the process?

Karen: Thank you. It may sound clichéd, but the words dream come true do describe it best. I'd been trying to become a published writer for many years. The Perfect Girlfriend is the third book I wrote. The first (quite rightly) will never see the light of day, and the second, I'd like to revisit at some point in the future. I feel as though I'm still learning all the time. I'm in awe of how wonderful a team there is working behind the scenes of a book and how much time readers put into reviewing or blogging about books. Other authors are very supportive, too, and I wish I'd felt more confident about approaching those I met at events to ask for their advice or helpful hints earlier on.

Kimberly: How did your background in the airline industry inform your writing?

Karen: I liked the idea of a thriller set in this potentially claustrophobic, unique world. While writing, I considered all the questions I was asked as crew and tried to include scenarios that would hopefully make for a rich and interesting environment.

Kimberly: When you worked for the airline industry, did you ever have to handle an emergency like Juliette does in the novel?

Karen: I didn't have to handle anything too potentially serious. However, I did experience a very frightening landing during high winds when we were diverted to another airport. Most emergencies involved medical situations. I recall a time when once, during a long night flight, our aircraft had to make a diversion for a serious medical situation. We landed at a fairly quiet-seeming airport. While the paramedics boarded and treated the patient, I noticed a male passenger who would barely make eye contact and seemed to be acting strangely, which was odd as he'd been quite chatty before. We kept an eye on him, as we were concerned about his change of character. He didn't seem to like the crew trying to engage with him. When we took off again, he confessed (after seeking us out in the galley and asking for an alcoholic drink) that he'd fallen asleep, obviously hadn't heard any announcements, and when he'd woken up, he'd assumed that we were in a hijack situation and he hadn't wanted to draw attention to himself!

Kimberly: What books are on your nightstand right now?

Karen: Like most readers, I have lots, but some of the next few I'm looking forward to reading are:

Bitter Orange *by Claire Fuller*
The Dry *by Jane Harper*
I'll Take You There *by Wally Lamb*

Kimberly: Juliette's narrative is chilling. Was it hard for you to spend so much time in her head? Was it easier or harder to write Juliette in the first person? Does she have any redeeming qualities?

Karen: She is a very chilling person. I'm not sure I'd wish to encounter her in real life! It was hard at times as her voice is intense. I found it easier to write her in the first person because that way I was able to reveal how she justified her own twisted actions. I attended a six-month Write a Novel course at London's Faber Academy, and on the first evening, our tutor suggested that we experiment. I'd begun writing Juliette in the third person, but I decided to switch to first. When I submitted a sample to the group for feedback, everyone agreed that she came alive in the first person.

When it comes to redeeming qualities...this is a very hard one! She can be sympathetic when she feels that someone is suffering through no fault of their own, so she is kind to children (this is shown early on in the book when she takes an unaccompanied minor under her wing) and she empathizes with people who become homeless as she understands how easy it is to lose everything. (There is a minor reference to this much later in the book.)

Kimberly: What or who are some of your influences as a writer?

Karen: I attended an international school in Rome when I lived in Italy. A teacher there was incredibly passionate about Egyptian, Greek and Roman mythology, and this inspired me, too. Naturally, I read a lot as a child, and one of my all-time favorite authors is Agatha Christie. I also really enjoy The No. 1 Ladies' Detective Agency series by Alexander McCall Smith as he writes so beautifully about

Botswana. I tend to enjoy most types of travel writing, in both fiction and nonfiction.

Kimberly: You had a very peripatetic childhood. Do you have any interesting stories from that period in your life, and did traveling so much play a role in your decision to become a storyteller?

Karen: One of my first memories is of traveling by plane. I lived in Zimbabwe and flying was very glamorous—people would get dressed up to fly. I recall standing at the balcony at Harare Airport waving off planes. I always knew that I wanted to be a flight attendant and a writer, but it wasn't until after the birth of my middle son that I decided to take the dream of being a writer seriously. I'm still fascinated by travel and love airports, especially looking up at the departure boards. It amazes me how people can be scattered across the world in such a relatively short space of time. I believe there are so many stories you subconsciously collect as a traveler and I always tear up in the arrivals hall when I see friends and family so obviously delighted at being reunited.

Kimberly: What made you decide to make the Juliette character a woman? Did she arrive in your mind fully formed, or was it a conscious decision to make her female? Obviously, a male version of Juliette would make for a very different story, and—unfortunately—one that we see play out often in real life.

Karen: Juliette's character is female because I first "sensed" her when I was changing out of uniform one day. I experienced a sense of returning to anonymity instead of being the public face of an airline and I thought, what if a damaged woman really was "changing" her identity, removing "her mask" before and after work? I believe it was around then that her character began to form in my mind. I also had an image of her (this isn't in the book) walking in heels down a quiet residential street, listening to the lonely echo of her footsteps on an early winter's evening. As she walked, she glimpsed inside people's houses where the curtains or blinds hadn't been drawn yet, while experiencing an overwhelming ache to belong, to have a "happy family" of her own.

Kimberly: How does Juliette's bond with Barbara inform her character?

Karen: Barbara is the only relative in Juliette's life with whom she has a "normal" relationship. Her scenes with Barbara show that Juliette is capable of spending time with someone who knew her from childhood and perhaps show brief snapshots of how Juliette may have turned out differently had she received more love as a young girl.

Kimberly: What's next for you? Any clues you can give us about the next novel?

Karen: I'm working on my next book, which is a psychological thriller with another troubled woman at its heart.

Dear Reader,

One of my first memories is looking out of a plane window at the clouds. We travelled a lot during my childhood and lived in Angola, Zimbabwe, Malawi, Belgium, Italy and the UK. Flying was considered really glamorous in those days and people would dress up to go on a flight. I remember standing on the balcony at Harare International Airport, waving off planes. Some passengers would choose a brightly coloured piece of clothing, such as a jumper, to wave at the window so that their friends or relatives could identify them once on board.

Flying fascinates me. I love looking at departure boards, especially the older-style ones with the white numbers that would twist around as they listed the arrivals and departures. I still find it hard to believe how quickly people can be scattered around the world in such a short space of time.

From a young age I yearned to be a writer and to travel as much as possible. I loved reading and libraries, bookshops, the smell of books, the different worlds.

I recall always having a book in my hand and feeling disappointed whenever I had to engage in real life.

I was fortunate to spend some time at a wonderful international school in Rome where I was introduced to Greek, Roman and Egyptian mythology by a wonderful, passionate teacher. We were given a lot of freedom to be as creative as we liked.

Upon leaving school, I obtained secretarial skills and became a secretary in a travel agency, supplementing this with part-time evening jobs in the catering and hotel industry before becoming airline crew. I wish I'd kept a diary of my travels, as it would be such a rich source of information for me now.

About ten years ago, I decided to "become a writer." I had no idea what to do, other than to write. And so I did. I set myself a daily word count that I stuck to (as much as possible). I gradually immersed myself into the writing world: local creative writing classes, literary festivals, meet-the-author events. I wrote a couple of books but didn't get anywhere with them.

The idea for the protagonist in *The Perfect Girlfriend*, Juliette, came to me when I was changing out of my airline uniform one day in the airport toilets before travelling on public transport. I felt a sense of returning to "anonymity" and it made me think about the real personas behind public faces. I wondered what it would be like if a damaged or sociopathic character actually was deliberately hiding behind the illusion of the safety of a work uniform.

After giving up my flying career, I took a writing course in London. There, encouraged to experiment by our tutor, I wrote the first draft of what was to become *The Perfect Girlfriend*. I undertook research into sociopaths and nature versus nurture, and I also read a lot of self-help books as some of them use incredibly powerful language, wondering what it would be like if a character like Juliette twisted the words in her mind to justify her actions.

I wrote a thriller, as it's one of my favourite genres and I found the idea of being "trapped" with a character such as Juliette at thirty-five thousand feet very frightening and claustrophobic. I really enjoyed working as a flight attendant, and the airline world that I loved so much is there in my book; it is the world of my characters.

1. Juliette has an assured, if unsettling, voice. Did you sympathize with her at all? Why or why not?

2. Juliette's experience at the dance, when she was a teenager, is a difficult scene. What did you think when you read it? How does this scene fit into the #MeToo movement?

3. One of the things Juliette struggles with is forming solid female friendships. Why do you think this is? But still, when she thinks about Amy, Juliette says "Every girl needs a best friend." Can you reflect on that statement and how it relates to Juliette's behavior?

4. How do you think the incident with Juliette's brother impacted her as a person?

5. What did you think of Nate? Do you think he is a sympathetic character? Why or why not?

6. Nate and Juliette took very different paths as they grew into adults. How much of that has to do with the differing ways our society treats men and women?

7. What do you think leads some people to become overly possessive of their partners and other people in their lives?

8. Do you think Barbara has any idea about Juliette's true self?

9. Juliette says, "I will never trust anyone again. Trust is a luxury." What do you think of this statement?

10. Can you reflect on the airline and international settings in this novel? How does it tie into the story and allow for character development?